JANEK'S WAY

Cecil Friedlander

ATHENA PRESS
LONDON

JANEK'S WAY
Copyright © Cecil Friedlander 2004

All Rights Reserved

No part of this book may be reproduced in any form
by photocopying or by any electronic or mechanical means,
including information storage or retrieval systems,
without permission in writing from both the copyright
owner and the publisher of this book.

ISBN 1 84401 243 3

First Published 2004 by
ATHENA PRESS
Queen's House, 2 Holly Road
Twickenham TW1 4EG
United Kingdom

Printed for Athena Press

JANEK'S WAY

To my wife

Acknowledgements

Many thanks to my wife, Maria, and to our dear friend Richard Baker for encouragement and for converting a hand-written manuscript by a computer illiterate into a presentable 'manuscript'. Also to my publisher for sensitive and constructive editing.

Contents

Prelude   9

Book I

1   Warsaw   15
2   England   28
3   The Todds   43
4   Early Days   52
5   Discovery   78
6   Colloquy   93
7   Action   101
8   Progress   111
9   Despair   125
10 Understanding   142
11 Coming to Terms   151
12 Friendly Advice   171
13 Some Soul Searching   179
14 Plans and More Plans   186

Book II

15 Six Years Later   193
16 A Visitor from the East   197
17 Brothers   200

18	Crisis	205
19	The Birth of Two Ideas	210
20	Ideas Grow	219
21	Madeleine and Molly Go Trawling	225
22	Katarzyna Calls In a Debt	233
23	Ruth's Seventieth	237
24	Honour	242
25	Some Practical Philosophy	244
26	Sanctuary	246
27	Joy	248
28	Disasters	252

Book III

29	Betrayal	261
30	New Growth	273
31	Kismet	278
32	Peace	282

Prelude

Under the burden of his weight the massive gate shifted on its hinges. A small encrustation of lichen fell to the ground rubbed off by his sleeve. The hard wood of the gate was comforting, reassuring, fortifying. It had stood, and served its purpose, since long before his birth. James leaned on it, and contemplated the gentle dip of the Gloucestershire hillside, the hedgerows frozen in the pattern that had been fixed longer than men could remember, the three church towers and the distant wooded hilltops.

He took from his pocket the wooden cigarette holder that was one of the two material objects left to remind him of his father. It was mellow, smooth to the touch and, in its own way, like the roughness of the gate, satisfying; satisfying but not comforting. He returned it to his pocket. Ghosts surrounded him; for the most part friendly, remote, beckoning from afar, unapproachable but distantly loving.

Along the track from the village a party of boys scampered past him.

'Morning, Mr Todd.'

He nodded at them, and smiled. These boys were at home, secure in the countryside – their forefathers' countryside. They bore names that appeared on generations of tombstones in the village graveyard and on the war memorial in the parish church. They had roots, even if they were unconscious of them; indeed, the very absence of conscious relationship to their environment was the certificate of their security. One does not think particularly about home while one is there.

A flight of fighters from the squadron at Chardon streaked overhead. The boys looked up, and dived for imaginary cover. '*Dum, dum, dum!*' one of them shouted, and they hid their heads from the imaginary bullets.

James's mind was too far away to share their enthusiasm. No cover for him – real or imaginary.

Prelude

A moment later the boys were away, laughing, knocking the tops off dandelions with their sticks.

James was no prude, but he was not amused. What do these boys know of war? he said to himself. It is a game for them. A game...

He did not pause to consider that boys have always played at war, and gone home to tea afterwards. At any rate English boys did, for whom war was a romantic luxury to be enjoyed far away, with few embarrassing permanent reminders on their doorsteps. He did not dwell on the theory that a certain amount of ritualised violence might be preferable to its release in society at large. Instead the ghosts pressed in on him again, the crumbling streets, the flame-shot eyes of the blazing buildings, the stink of fear and death, hope raised and shattered, the Nazi tank with its commander's face, parents, brothers and sister... all rushed past.

He was conscious of his irrationality in resenting the boys' playing at war, but resent it he did.

The English made a game of everything: they never grew up.

The warmth of the summer morning enveloped and distracted him in spite of his resentment. Thoughts continued to thrust into him. So much achieved already, so much lost, so much retained. Uncertainty hammered through his mind like a drill in a coal seam and his whole body ached in response. Uncertainty and imbalance, as though he were outside the assured rightness of his physical surroundings. He envied the sturdy gate, the settled fields and even, in spite of himself, the unthinking enthusiasm of the boys. They formed part of a system; they made sense and enshrined a unity denied to him, something to which he was a stranger, notwithstanding his outward appearance.

James would have struck a casual observer as fitting in completely with his environment; patched sports jacket, wellington boots, pipe, a tie not too scrupulously tied but not scruffy, a neatly trimmed ginger moustache. His head was square, eyes somewhat deep-set and cheekbones perhaps a trifle higher than most Englishmen's: he would have passed, unnoticed, at a gathering of moderately prosperous farmers.

'Call yourself a farmer?' He remembered Madeleine's mocking voice. 'You're only a farmer by mistake!'

Prelude

There was truth in the bitter jest. He did not really belong, and yet many of today's farmers were not of long standing. They had bought farms all over the country since the war, worked them well and become accepted. Not he, though. He was different. Success had won a certain amount of local respect. He was not disliked in the community and was even looked to in times of need, but he did not belong.

He felt very much alone. It was not a new sensation but none the easier to bear for that, and he often wondered whether his isolation stemmed from deep within himself or was merely the consequence of his troubled life.

For a few minutes he came dangerously close to immersing himself in a sea of self-pity, but he quickly dragged himself out. A procession of people and places drifted through his mind: the desperate journey out, the English school, old Mrs Todd, whom he had loved as one might worship a remote but benign goddess; the company, Madeleine, the farm, all the experiences he had either enjoyed or survived. And here he was, neither one thing nor another, with a wealth of experience and only a handful of close friends, leaning on an English gate, wholly uncertain of what he should attempt or where he should aim, and now in 1955 still near the threshold of adult life.

James Todd, originally Janek Zagorski, born in Warsaw, was exactly twenty-five years old.

'Why must you always be so introspective?' Madeleine used to ask. 'It's unhealthy.'

That was characteristic of her. She had such a simple and direct way of looking at life, treating it as a job to be got on with and taken seriously when the occasion demanded but not thought about for its own sake; the problems of the day, and not the problem of life, exercised her. And yet she was shrewd and full of vitality and... he sought the right word... *intelligent*. Yes, that was it, she was intelligent, but had not loved thought as a process in its own right.

'You're not the practical sort,' she would say, irrespective of his achievements in business and farming, as if there were an inconsistency in combining effective 'practical' thinking with a philosophical attitude of mind. 'You live in a different world.'

Prelude

He supposed he did. It was a world of memory and imagination from which he made forays, or extensive expeditions, into the 'real' world whenever necessary and, having achieved his purpose, retired to and resumed his inward life.

Their marriage had, on balance he reflected, been a mistake. He could now see that they had drifted into it, drawn like pieces of timber on an incoming tide, floating side by side, often impinging and finally, inevitably, becoming locked. Not that affection as well as passion had been entirely missing: they had liked and respected each other, but in different circumstances might not have selected each other as partners. Indeed, James had committed the cardinal error of marrying her to please Mrs Todd, perhaps too in the hope that the mother whom he worshipped would be perpetuated in her daughter. Of neither motive had he, of course, been conscious at the time.

There, he thought, unrepentantly, I'm being introspective again, just as she said.

The sweetly flowing summer day swamped him and pressed him gently into the depths of his recollection. How quickly we are able to travel in our minds through years of experience, calling up vividly whole episodes, often in great detail, in a way that would be impossible were we trying to write them down or even to speak them to a friend or a recording machine. In such a frame of mind did James now survey his life.

Book I

1: Warsaw

His memories of early childhood were indistinct. It was not that he lacked recollections, but their details had been swamped, thrust aside, by circumstances so vast, so momentous both nationally and personally, that they now seemed dim and in a sense unimportant across the chasm of changed life and culture.

The home into which he was born in 1930 was happy: happiness was one recollection that shone through the intervening events. What had been wholly good could be destroyed – indeed had been, by external events – but it had actually existed, it was an historical fact, he had been part of its imperfectly remembered daily progress, and quietly he gave thanks for it. But its details were obscure.

His father was a doctor in general practice, his mother taught philosophy part-time at the university. There were always visitors to the flat, and from his earliest days he experienced adults whose conversation bubbled and bore little resemblance to that of most of the middle-class families he was later to meet in England.

His parents were indulgent in the matter of bedtime and he mastered the art of lingering in the drawing room listening, not understanding but savouring the strange sounding words that differed so greatly from those that adults outside his parents' circle used in trivial speech. In that way language grew up with him and regularly he experienced the exultation of discovering the meaning of some treasured word. Great indeed was his joy if it happened to mean what he had come to imagine it did.

Stefan Zagorski was a good doctor, took his vocation seriously and charged modest fees, but his work and patients were only part of his life. In his spare time, which he insisted upon even if it had to be enjoyed late at night, he pursued his interests among the arts and the sciences. He did so widely and in a quite un-nationalistic manner, in which he differed from many of his contemporaries, who tended to regard certain other cultures – especially the

15

Anglo-Saxon – with a resigned toleration, rather as a patriarch might view the undisciplined behaviour of juveniles. James, in spite of his adopted Englishness, was not entirely free of that attitude.

Stefan was a pious Catholic. His devotion to his religion went deep, far beyond external observance or passive acceptance. In his total emancipation from racial prejudice, including anti-Semitism, he was at variance with many of his contemporaries, even members of his own circle. His wife could not have claimed quite his degree of enlightenment because, ebullient and sophisticated as she was, she had inherited the attitudes of her very traditional family. Stefan's love had largely cured her, after philosophy had been rather less successful. Anna's teaching was on a fairly casual basis: she delivered occasional courses of lectures on her special topic, and often held gatherings of her students at home, which left her sufficiently free to attend to her own children's education. James's elder sister, Katarzyna, hoped to become a nurse, and he had twin brothers, Kazimierz and Antoni, three years younger than himself.

Antoni had shown a feeling for music and dancing from his earliest days and was one of the few boys at the ballet classes to which Anna took him each week.

Life was spent essentially in the city. Apart from playing in the public parks, the children did not see much of nature, rural life was to be learned about from books rather than experienced, and what they did not know they did not miss. The city was paramount in the lives of all the family and its circle, and in long walks on his own James came to know it so well that its museums, galleries and churches became virtually extensions of home. Museum attendants became familiar with the slight figure of the small boy moving confidently among the exhibits, outwardly in reverie, inwardly intent. They did not worry that he seemed too young to be out by himself, for he was obviously not up to any mischief and conveyed a sense of belonging, as if by walking slowly through the galleries he was mentally checking their contents. In a sense, he was. Throughout his exploration of the museum he was being reminded of the conversations he heard at home. His parents opened the treasures of the museums

Warsaw

and galleries to him and his sister, and the appetite thus whetted he slaked in visits of his own.

He played games against himself. He would stand in front of a painting, avoiding the label, give himself credit if at least he placed it in the right school, and glow inwardly if he identified the painter. The Museum of Natural History was one of his favourites. He repeatedly visited the section on human evolution: the strange-sounding names fascinated him; *Sinanthropus, Pithecanthropus*, characters in a mysterious drama which he caught glimpses of during conversations at home. He would savour the difficult words, turning them over in his mind, nursing them with his tongue and matching them with the often fanciful physical reconstructions of early man that the museum supplied.

He was an unusual little boy, seeming to strangers solemn and reserved, but full of life in his own surroundings. Teachers who enquired whether he was unhappy annoyed him. Although he was too young then to analyse his situation, it was one of total bliss. Secure in his family, his imagination nourished by its stimulating energy, religion and patriotism part of the air he breathed, always present, never oppressive, he was growing up free of care. He thought in a remote sort of way that he might become a doctor, but his parents were too wise to pester him with the dreaded question beloved of so many adults: 'And what will you be when you grow up?' Other, boring, parents asked him the question, but not his: not by the wildest flight of imagination could he see his parents as being boring.

The world was very, very good.

It was not to last.

He became conscious that conversation at home was changing. His parents' guests were introducing unfamiliar words that had nothing to do with philosophy, art or science. They began to speak of frontiers, allies and air raids. Uncomfortable silences would punctuate the conversation.

The change became increasingly noticeable as 1939 wore on.

The German invasion changed everything, suddenly, savagely and apparently irreversibly. Poland was no stranger to occupation, but anticipation had not dimmed the shock. The speed and ferocity of the blitzkrieg, the deliberate brutality towards civilians,

Warsaw

the Russian stab in the back and twenty years of independent nationhood extinguished in less than a month, left the population with a sense, initially, of numbness and then of fury mixed with despair.

Children shared the feeling of total perplexity at what had happened to them, and why. Gone overnight were his parents' jolly gatherings, the animated conversation, the walks by himself and the visits to places of interest. There was less to eat, and his mother spent much of the day queuing for it. Most of all he was struck by the change in his father. Stefan had been one of those men who, understanding things at their true value, thought and spoke of serious matters seriously but without a trace of solemnity: he was able to stand outside his subject, view it dispassionately, objectively, lighting it with an outside light, engrossed in, but not consumed by it. James now saw only an unaccustomed solemnity and to his surprise felt unable to tax his father with it. Instead he spoke to his sister.

'Why doesn't Daddy ever laugh with us now?'

'Because the Germans are here, I suppose.'

'But they're not *here*, at home…'

'It feels as though they are.'

Yes, that was true. Everything had become soiled, nothing was sacred, not even – dare one think it? – home. If one's homeland was occupied, the mere fact of being within one's own walls was no remedy: they were not really one's own any longer, and one knew it. The shabbiness lay in having to try to pretend to oneself that things were not quite as bad as they were.

One day Father Kowalski visited them. He was a close friend, James's usual confessor.

'Father, I hate the Germans.'

'Yes, Janek, go on.'

James wanted Father Kowalski to assure him it was permissible to hate the Germans.

'They're not human. If I could I'd kill one.'

'Well, that would be murder, wouldn't it?'

'Would it have been murder to kill them while the war was on? Suppose I'd been a soldier?'

'No, then you would have been defending your country. But

now it wouldn't help Poland at all if you were to kill one German. It would only make things worse for people. You know that.'

James saw the point, if only dimly.

'But I can hate them all the same.'

'I understand how you feel, but you know as well as I do that it can never be right to hate. I feel the hatred myself, of course, but I know I must try to resist it. If we meet hatred with hatred we only lower ourselves to the Germans' level.'

'Then what can anyone do to get rid of them?'

'For the moment, nothing, I fear, except praying. And have you ever thought that none of Poland's disasters could happen if God were unwilling to allow it?'

'You don't mean that God *wants* us to be like this!'

'Of course not. God wants us to lead good lives and get to heaven. He lets men act according to their free will and unfortunately we are suffering the effects of it, but you can't blame God for that.'

James half accepted the explanation, less out of conviction than out of his inability to provide an alternative. He felt, though, that Father Kowalski had to speak as he did because he was a priest, and had given him a textbook answer.

Thoughts that he could barely articulate, about justice and punishment, lurked in his mind. He brooded.

The darkness of life contributed to the blackness of his thoughts. The official closure of the schools had not stopped his education because a certain amount of clandestine schooling was carried on, and his parents and friends supplemented it, but the restrictions on movement meant that he saw less of friends of his own age: there was too much time for introspection.

Even important events in family life were reduced to shadows by the misery of the occupation. Birthdays and saints' days continued to be celebrated at home, but very quietly, without much relish and not only because of the absence of material goods.

One day during the winter of 1943, James was at home looking after his brothers while his mother and Katarzyna had gone separately to queue for food. Weakened by cold and deprivation, Anna had collapsed in the queue and been taken to hospital, where she died. Stefan had been informed but arrived too late. For the children it was as though their mother had simply vanished from the domestic scene, almost casually, swallowed up in the encompassing gloom. Katarzyna slipped quietly into her mother's role, and life of a kind continued.

James grieved silently, for in the almost perpetual absence of joy, grief itself was muted. His mother's death was absorbed into the general misery: just another event to be blamed on the Germans. His hatred for them grew. It burned steadily within him and he fostered it assiduously in the course of long conversations with himself, his boy's mind formulating exquisite tortures, which he expressed with all the power of his sophisticated command of words. He yearned for action.

His opportunity came unexpectedly, in the summer of 1944.

One Sunday, when the family was at lunch, came a knock at the door. After the immediate involuntary shiver of apprehension, Katarzyna rose from the table saying that it must be old Mrs Sikorska from the flat above, since no one else would call at such a time. Stefan and his sons remained, making desultory conversation until she should return. She came to announce that an unknown man wanted to see the doctor, and Stefan went to speak with him in the hall. He was away for only a few minutes, and on resuming his place at the table exchanged an earnest glance with Katarzyna, spoke little and seemed lost in thought. At the end of the meal he told Kazimierz and Antoni to go and play in their room.

'Has the time come?' asked Katarzyna.

James had not realised the extent to which Katarzyna was in their father's confidence.

Now Stefan explained to him that with the Russians at the gates of Warsaw the Polish Home Army would go into action so that Poland might play its part in liberating the city. It would be a hazardous venture; the Germans would fight with the greatest brutality but, on account of the Russians' strength, would inevitably be defeated. Tomorrow he would be leaving to join a unit as its medical officer and Katarzyna would look after the family 'until I return'.

He finished with a grin that left both brother and sister unconvinced.

Warsaw

'Let me come too!' begged James.

He could never think back without remorse on his selfishness and Katarzyna's spontaneous generosity. He had not paused to consider whether his sister needed his support: he saw only glory and revenge ahead.

'Yes, Daddy, let him. I can look after the little ones on my own, and I can always ask Mrs Sikorska for help if necessary.'

'All right. I'll tell the colonel you're my first-aid expert,' said Stefan, with a mischievous little smile. And so it was settled. Even today he could scarcely believe the prosaic way in which matters of such gravity had been decided, rather as if they were the subject of a Sunday outing, and his father's almost casual attitude in the face of the imminent disintegration of the family they all held so dear.

Later that day, Katarzyna packed a few essential articles for her father and brother. At evening prayers Stefan told the twins that he and James would be going away for some days, and James noticed that afterwards Stefan and Katarzyna spent an hour together in the study.

Early the following morning an unremarkable couple – a middle-aged man, soberly dressed and carrying a medical bag, with a fourteen-year-old boy – walked quietly out of the building on their way to glory.

The colonel had raised no objection to the presence of a boy in the unit, beyond telling him not to get in the way. James's recollection of the next few days was clouded. He remembered the fighting beginning the day after they left home, the barricades across the street, the field 'hospital' improvised underground.

Stefan's medical post was in the vaults of a bank where, under improvised lighting, he performed operations assisted by two nuns, nursing sisters, who had turned up and somehow become part of the unit. The incongruity of their religious dress went unnoticed in the general atmosphere of unreality. James assisted the sisters by fetching and carrying. As far as possible they tried to keep him out of the operating theatre during the most painful operations, but they need not have worried for, after the initial revulsion, buoyed up by the prevailing spirit, James found he was able to assist stoically even with the most gruesome cases. He realised later that he was unconsciously imitating his father, whom he now saw in yet another light. James had known him first as the lively intellectual, jovial and serious at the same time, always full of fun. Then, during the war, withdrawn and somewhat shrunken; now, finally, an altogether larger figure, working day and night as the casualties came in, first a trickle, then a steady stream.

The rising had begun simultaneously all over the city, taking the Germans completely by surprise. As they recovered and struck back in huge strength, the Home Army men barricaded themselves within a large number of fortified areas that the Germans tried to reduce. Hopes were high that most of the positions would be held and that when the Russians arrived they would find much of the city already in Polish hands. National pride demanded that an attempt at self-liberation be made. It was a gallant and bold idea with a fair chance of succeeding but, with artillery and tanks pitted against men and buildings, everything depended on a swift outcome. Once the German defence had been sapped by the rising, the Russians would soon overcome them. Such had been the expectation...

James recalled vividly the day when the Russian guns fell silent, their aircraft ceased to fly over the city and the men of the Home Army grasped the dreadful truth, that they had been abandoned. The full political significance of the Russians' cynical policy of allowing the Germans to destroy the non-communist resistance was not generally understood by the men at the time, but the fact that they were left to their own resources stared them in the face.

Towards the end of the third week, James's fortress had shrunk, German tanks had thrust through some barricades only to find fresh ones built behind them, and the casualties were increasing fast. The hospital's supplies were virtually exhausted and it became necessary to replenish them from a large pharmacy at the boundary of the fortress. The two sisters had volunteered, and set off from the hospital carrying large bags. James had obtained permission to accompany them in order, as he put it to his father, to help them over the rubble with their loads, but he could recall his mixed motives to this day. Dissatisfied with his humble, though genuinely useful part as a hospital porter, he longed for an opportunity of fighting, which he hoped, as he stuffed bottles filled with petrol into his jacket pockets, that the expedition would supply. He got more than he had bargained for. The little party's outward journey was easy enough, in spite of occasional shell bursts and streets partially obstructed by fallen masonry. A squad of Home Army men raised a cheer for the sisters who, despite their dishevelled appearance, were still recognisable as nuns.

James knew that on their route was a small museum of antiquities that he had greatly enjoyed visiting in happier days. It was not a particularly important institution, and the bizarre array of exhibits was somewhat haphazardly displayed, but the very confusion held an attraction for him, together with the comforting solid mahogany of the showcases and the stuffy atmosphere redolent of an old church rather than a scientific institution. Old Janek, the head attendant, had always found time for a chat with his young namesake. Was the museum still standing? James wondered.

The group kept close to the walls and moved as fast as they could. As they drew closer to their destination, and the edge of the fortress, the noise grew louder and the destruction more evident. They were all afraid because here they were more exposed to fire than they had been in the hospital.

James was both buoyed up with excitement and sickened with apprehension. They were close to the pharmacy when he saw his museum. It had not survived. The front had collapsed into the street. Shattered exhibits could be seen within on the ground floor, and sticking out over the street from the first floor, like an absurd crane, was the skeleton of a dinosaur, perched perilously, its long neck swinging gently as if it were surveying the scene: the uncomprehending observing the incomprehensible.

The sisters hardly noticed it, but to James the affront was gross: his dinosaur, preserved for sixty million years, destroyed by the Germans in a second. Desecrated. He remembered the label on the dinosaur, *Presented by Doktor C Schlumper*, written in the curator's elegant script. Would the good Doktor Schlumper have been a Nazi were he alive today?

Warsaw

James hoped not. The damage to the dinosaur affected him even more than the human suffering he had witnessed in the hospital, more than national disaster, more even than his mother's death, which he had known but not seen. An irrational response? Perhaps, but he shook with fury.

They entered the pharmacy without difficulty. Its walls were breached and it had become almost part of the barricade. Home Army men occupied it. There was firing very close by. The men warned them to be quick. The sisters made their way to the stock room and hurriedly filled their bags. On their way out the sound of firing deafened them.

'That wasn't rifle fire,' said Sister Krystyna as they emerged, and James shouted, 'Get down!' and pulled them back into the building as the grey bulk of a German tank came slowly to rest in the debris outside, with dust from the powdered rubble rising in contrast with the tank's temporary immobility. There was no evident sign of life nearby.

For a moment James saw the tank as a beached prehistoric monster, an evil dinosaur awaiting its next act of destruction. He rose gingerly, and simultaneously his eyes met those of the commander erect in the turret – cold, evil, saurian eyes, all sight and no soul. Their look of detached contempt turned away up the street: the voice began issuing orders to the driver. James thought, He can't even be bothered to turn the machine gun towards me, I'll show the bastards!

He recalled the drill for tossing a Molotov cocktail that he had heard the Home Army men describe. The sisters were scarcely aware of what he was doing: the entire incident occupied no more then five seconds. The tank was beginning to crunch forwards again when James's bomb exploded. The commander's head disintegrated, the tank stopped and from nowhere two Home Army men appeared and placed an explosive charge against its tracks. James grabbed the sisters and shouted, 'Run!' and it was over.

For the moment the street was blocked. The barricade would be rebuilt around the tank, the fortress had shrunk a little more, resistance went on.

Elation kept him going while he and the sisters ran back to the hospital with their supplies. On arrival, he was sick and the sisters tended him before returning to his father and their work.

Was that the day on which he had grown up? He had fought for his country in the presence of the enemy and had killed his man, killed deliberately, with satisfaction and without regret. Even now he could feel no remorse. Would it, he wondered, have been the same if he had killed a man whom he scarcely saw as an individual but just as a map reference on an artillery plan? An anonymous killing like that might, perhaps, be accompanied by regret for the individual and his family, however inevitable the action was at the time; a kind of cruel necessity. But there had been something in the commander's utterly remote aloofness that placed him in a class apart, not truly human. What would poor Father Kowalski, if he were still alive, say to that? And again, suppose the commander's remoteness had been merely the product of his training. Perhaps beneath the external frigidity lay, well concealed, as much fear as James himself had felt. Possible, but unlikely. After eleven years James could feel no regret: it had been not so much a killing as an execution.

And yet, the shadow of a doubt lingered. James was conscious that his split-second decision to kill the tank commander had been triggered by the man's arrogant aloofness which, at that very moment, had seemed even more offensive than the fact that he was the brutal enemy. Indeed, James had consciously and deliberately killed a *man*, not the anonymous enemy.

He had once made the mistake of mentioning his scruples to Madeleine, who had been quite unable to understand. 'Jolly good!' had been her reaction to his description of the event. To Madeleine, as to the local boys, war was a great game in which you played to win and, as in most games, what escaped the referee's eye did not matter. But, he wondered, did they know the referee?

Two weeks later when he reported as usual to his father in the hospital he sensed a change in the general mood. An atmosphere of dejection, of hopelessness, had replaced the high spirits that used to prevail in spite of physical danger. It was clear that something had happened or some firm news had been received but, much as he wanted to, he could not bring himself to ask. He continued fetching and carrying, helping the sisters.

In the evening his father called him to a corner of the hospital, and the chaplain who had been moving among the wounded joined them. James saw in his father's eyes an expression he had never seen before; not physical terror, not panic, but a weary sadness indescribable in words. He spoke fast, and calmly.

'Janek, listen. We must be quick because we all have our work to do. We cannot hold out much longer, perhaps a week, and we must simply stay here and do our duty. Your duty is to try and get away, and live. In a moment or two Father will give you Holy Communion, and as soon as it is dark I want you to get out and make your way to the West. I can't tell you how to do it; use your intelligence and leave the rest to God. Sooner or later you will meet the English or the Americans. Never forget Poland.'

James could not find a word to utter in protest. He knelt and received Holy Communion from Father Tadeuz, and his father's blessing. Then Stefan took off the silver cross that he wore around his neck and put it on James, and groping in his pocket he found the cigarette holder that James had always seen him use and thrust it into his hand.

'Here, these things will help you to remember me. God bless you, my boy.'

He held him tightly in his arms, kissed him, and returned to the operating table.

Not once did it occur to James to ask what would happen to his father, or how he was to get to the West. Sister Krystyna gave him a small bag of food, and soon afterwards he set off, torn between despair and excitement at doing his father's bidding. As he walked gingerly towards the barricade, from time to time he put his hand over his chest to press the cross against his skin, and felt in his pocket for the cigarette holder. Even in his desperate situation he could not suppress a small smile at the incongruity of the mixture of the sacred and profane that were the only material reminders of his family. He approached the barricade, which was now much closer than when he had met the German tank, crept into a ruined building and waited for an opportunity to get out.

*

Six months of terror and lonely anguish were to follow.

James reflected that this had been the most wretched period of his life, the only one in which he had been utterly alone with no obvious successful outcome in sight. The thought of it chilled him even now. Indeed, the details had become blurred in his mind: waiting, hiding, and scavenging for essentials, constant fear. None of it did he wish to recall. Ah well, however isolated he might feel today, it was unlikely that he would have to endure anything like that again...

He stood back from the gate, took another long look at the amber landscape, and strode back along the hedgerow to his house.

2: England

Briar Cottage was no humble dwelling. Three adjoining cottages had been altered and extended to form a fine farmhouse, which served James as home, farm office, study, library and sanctuary. If in its furnishing it lacked a woman's hand, it was certainly not wanting in taste and even a certain sombre elegance that contrasted with its bland outer appearance and rustic setting.

Mrs Brand came to the door when she heard James.

'Oh, Mr Todd, I wasn't expecting you back quite so soon. Father Ryan rang, and I told him you'd be back for lunch.'

'Do you know what he wanted?'

'He said something about sanctisties and worms. I didn't really understand.'

She spoke with the air of baffled resignation not uncommon among those who are unversed in the more arcane aspects of an exotic church.

'Thank you, I'll go and see him,' James replied without great enthusiasm.

Father Patrick Ryan presided over his small scattered flock, from his presbytery in Great Walling, with a genuine simplicity and fervour matched only by his complete absence of imagination. The sleepy country parish suited him: he nursed it with a mixture of autocracy and humility, confident in the certainty that he knew what was best for it. Since his pronouncements were never challenged, neither was his equanimity. His parents had emigrated when he was a young boy and his entire education had been in England. He spoke softly with a trace of his native accent which his congregation adored. As old Mrs Wickett used to say, ad nauseam, 'Don't he sound just like John McCormack?'

James drove to the presbytery after lunch.

'Why, Mr Todd, it's very kind of you to come so soon. You'll join me in a glass?'

'No thanks, Father, it's too early in the day for me.'

'Ah well, never mind, I hope you've been keeping well. This is a lovely summer we are having.'

'Fine, thanks, but I don't suppose you rang me up just to enquire after my health.'

'Well now, as a matter of fact there is something on my mind at the moment, and I was hoping you might give me the benefit of your business acumen.'

'The best I can do is give you the benefit of my mistakes, I fear. What's the problem?'

'In a word, woodworm... the sacristy floor is riddled with it. The ladies who do the cleaning discovered it when they lifted the carpet yesterday and I'm sure it will spread everywhere. What do you think I should do? Will it not cost a great deal to have it put right professionally?'

It was clear to James that Father Ryan was not after his advice but his money. Why did he not simply ask him for it?

'You should be prepared to spend up to five hundred pounds if you want to protect the building as a whole from a bad infestation.'

'And how will I be raising that kind of money in a poor country parish? It's almost as much as my annual income.'

'I suppose you'll need second collections, fêtes and all the usual money raisers...' said James, knowing perfectly well that such methods could not possibly produce the necessary sum, 'or else ask the Bishop for help. After all, it's no fault of yours if the church has been attacked by woodworm.'

'I'll not take that sort of problem to His Lordship. I deal with problems in my parish myself.'

James permitted himself a little ghost of a smile.

'Well, thank you for telling me about it. I'll try and come up with some ideas.'

He went home, sat in his study and filled his pipe. The study was his refuge now that he had little social life, and it contained mementoes of his splintered past; an ink drawing of Our Lady of Czestochowa looking sadly out of place in the English countryside, a group photograph of some English schoolboys, a portrait of a grey-haired lady whose business-like manner was softened by a

England

wistful smile, and a few good Victorian watercolours. Our Lady hung improbably between views of the Lake District in mellow gilt frames. James had no talent as an artist but his fortunate business activities had allowed him to indulge his natural good taste by purchasing pictures which he selected partly for their artistic quality and partly out of respect for his adopted country. Had he adopted England, or had she adopted him?

With undemonstrative warmth a foreign country had welcomed him, and allowed him to grow to manhood. Its citizens had treated him with a mixture of incurious attention and occasional positive help. He returned loyalty and gratitude, but deep inside the emptiness remained. 'Never forget Poland' rang in his heart: he neither could, nor tried.

Lucky England: no bombs, burning or brute savagery for her country parish churches, just woodworm.

He went to his desk for a sheet of notepaper and his chequebook.

Dear Fr Ryan, recent business ventures having turned out favourably for me I hope you will allow me to do something about the problem...

He settled into the armchair, lit his pipe, looked out through the French window on to his garden and withdrew into himself. Why was he here? How had he come?

Armed with little more than a pocketknife and a simple compass James had trudged westwards, keeping out of the way of the Germans as far as possible. His main aim had been to keep ahead of the Russian advance but he was in no hurry to leave Poland until it became absolutely necessary. He believed, correctly, that while he was in his own country he would usually find shelter with few questions being asked, but he knew that sooner or later he would have to enter Germany, and the prospect terrified him. He knew a little of the language, but could never pass for a native: as soon as he was in Germany he would have to live the life of a hunted animal. His recollection was of weeks spent hiding by day, walking stealthily by night, wholly ignorant of the geography, feeding on leaves and grass. And, in the spring when Allied aircraft swept constantly overhead, James took refuge in a wood and waited for deliverance. It came one evening in the form of an English voice from the turret of a tank as the squadron entered the wood to bivouac for the night. He ran out into the clearing, waving his arms and shouting, 'Polish boy! Polish boy!'

A quarter of an hour later he was squatting near a mess tin of boiling water with a blanket wrapped around him, about to be initiated to the ritual of a mug of British Army tea. In his very few words of English, and his schoolboy German, helped out by the squadron commander's own sketchy German, he told the essentials of his story.

The commander said to his second-in-command, 'Good heavens, Jack, do you realise this boy's come from the Polish Home Army?'

'Well, that's what he claims.'

The soldier who was pouring out the tea said, 'Here you are, mate. Never seen a skeleton drinking tea before. Bangers and mash coming up soon.'

The strong tea, thick with condensed milk and sugar, almost made James vomit.

He had not understood the word 'skeleton' but the expression on the man's face was enough. James ran his hands over his limbs. He felt himself to be a shrivelled thing next to these beefy kindly men who, for their part, observed him with amazement and curiosity. They had seen hungry townsfolk and peasants in their journey across Europe, but nothing like this. Only later did James realise how close he had come to death: determination and fear of detection had nourished him and blinded him to his physical condition. The warmth of the tea surged through his body, and before the sausages were ready he was asleep.

'What are we going to do with him, sir?' asked the squadron sergeant-major who had a son of fourteen at school. 'We can't just leave the poor little bugger here in the morning.'

'Of course not, I don't suppose he can give us much useful information, but we'll send him on to Intelligence and they'll have to pass him back to the Poles – if only to understand what he's saying. Then he'll be home and dry, poor little devil.'

So it was that James found himself in the company of a Polish

England

officer, speaking in his native tongue for the first time in several months. It soon became obvious that he could supply no information of military value, and he was sent to the Medical Officer.

Captain Kuczynski took a long look at him and shook his head.

'Well, Janek, how do you feel now?'

'A lot better, thank you.' And indeed he was. A few days of rest, food and being with friends had begun to take effect. He was still skin and bones but his mind was clear and he knew what he wanted.

'How is the war going, and what happened in Warsaw?'

The captain averted his eyes. 'The war is going very well. It'll be over in a matter of weeks.'

'And Warsaw? What happened to the Home Army?'

Captain Kuczynski realised that it was futile to deny the truth to the earnest boy who had come on a man's errand, but perhaps he might spare him a little.

'In the end it had to surrender. They had nothing left to fight with. The Russians didn't help at all.'

After a lengthy pause James asked,

'What do you mean? What happened afterwards?'

'You know the Germans as well as I do, Janek.'

'Do you mean...' James's voice trailed away.

'I'm afraid so, the swine.'

'So, I'm probably an orphan?'

Captain Kuczynski stared hard at the floor.

'What is going to happen to me now? Can I stay here and help in the hospital?'

'We're going to send you to England where you'll be looked after by a Polish organisation. You'll have to go to school and finish your education. Life is going to be difficult for us Poles, even if we are able to go home, and I am sure it would be your father's wish that you prepare yourself for the future.'

James knew he was right, and at the same time saw with grief that his future was not to be in Poland: Captain Kuczynski's 'even if' had not been lost on him. It was at about this time that he began to be aware of the deep change that had taken place in him, although he could not then have put it into words; a hardening of spirit, an external crust of assumed indifference to his surroundings put on to conceal a pit of longing within. He had not wept since leaving his father and he would not do so now, but the trauma of the last few months worked on his emerging puberty and thrust him inwards. It made for the introspection that Madeleine had mocked and caused him to exist on separate levels; to act at one level, to dream at another. His spirit was of iron, his heart of lead.

The transition from street fighter and backwoodsman to hospital patient and schoolboy had not been easy. Adaptation, he remembered Stefan saying, was essential. The dinosaurs had perished because they had failed to adapt. Well, he would not make that mistake, but there was much to unlearn and a price to pay. It seemed at times that adaptation meant forgetting about Poland, putting his personal and ancestral past behind him if he were to survive in an alien environment. To erect compartments in his mind was the answer, to exist on different planes.

A short period in a country hospital, long walks in the grounds and his sound constitution restored his physical health. His native wit quickly enabled him to learn enough English from the other children to conduct a simple conversation. On the day of the German surrender cries of 'We've won!' and 'Now Daddy can come home!' needed no interpreter. James tried hard to join in the joy of the ward, but saw little joy for himself. To these English children it seemed as though there had been no war or, if there had, the game was over and everything would soon be back to normal. The faces of visiting mothers showed joy and relish, and he could hardly blame them if they took little notice of the quiet boy in the corner with his head buried in a book; but it hurt.

By the time he was taken to see the Polish Resettlement Committee in London he was alert and outwardly confident. He instinctively liked old Count Rózycki, who received him with great courtesy and absence of condescension. In his civilised presence James felt at home. Indeed he was highly conscious of the sympathy and respect that were so evident in the Count's manner, and was rather surprised at being treated as an adult. It was not to be the first time that he would find respect given to

England

him as a survivor of the Warsaw Rising: in bestowing it, Count Różycki was giving vent to an unspoken desire to have been present during that heroic sacrificial act.

'Janek, I am glad to see you looking so well. You really do feel quite recovered, do you not?'

'Yes, sir, there is nothing wrong with my health now, thank you.'

'I know what you mean. Health is one thing but hope is something quite different, is that it?'

'Exactly, sir. Please, what's to happen now?'

'Well, none of us can see into the future, but we have given a lot of thought to what is best for you. You have been lucky, a lady in London has offered to have you live in her home and treat you as her son, at any rate for the time being. You will be able to go to school, and of course we shall keep in touch with you, so you will not be cut off from us. I am sure you want to keep in touch with a Polish atmosphere.'

'You mean the lady is not Polish?'

'No, Mrs Todd is English, but I understand she has had some business with us which is why she has offered to help.'

'It is very kind of her, sir, but I'd rather be with a Polish family.'

'I'm sure you would, Janek, but there are not many here and very few of them would be in a position to do what Mrs Todd can. It really is a wonderful opportunity for you: we very much want you to give it a try.'

'But what about my own sister and brothers?' murmured James desperately.

'Oh, Janek, we simply cannot find out. We may be able to discover something but it will take a very long time. In the meantime you must prepare yourself for life, which means finishing your education and getting used to living in England.'

It was with a heavy heart that James gave in.

'But you will come and see me, won't you?'

'Yes, of course.'

James could never forget his emotions as Count Różycki drove him through London. It was comforting to find himself once more in the bustle and warmth of a city, but inevitably the

England

phantom of Warsaw pursued him and he barely heard as the Count pointed out the Houses of Parliament, Buckingham Palace and the parks. Hardly any signs of war remained in their original starkness. There were empty spaces in the rows of buildings, some blackened walls and many holes in the ground, but in many places trees in leaf and flowers in the parks, and even on bombed sites, softened the grimness. Even the men in uniform bore human faces. Across the Thames the big buildings gradually changed into long streets of small houses, with many telltale gaps among them, where children played, men and women walked, stood, talked, unafraid, untortured: it seemed unreal.

James kept on talking to the Count, inventing conversation, making the most of the opportunity to speak his native tongue. On, past a broad expanse of open parkland to a leafy suburb of wide streets whose handsome houses rested discreetly back in expansive gardens. From their large gates gravelled drives curved towards elegant porches. At one of those they stopped.

'Not here, surely?' asked James in wonder.

'Here we are. Now, remember there is no need to be nervous. Just behave as you have been brought up to do: you know you are welcome here.'

The door was opened by a girl of about his age, simply dressed in a sweater and tartan skirt. She shook hands with him and, with easy confidence, led him in, saying, Hello, I'm Madeleine... Mummy is in the drawing room.'

James had been a stranger to drawing rooms for a year. He had become familiar with barricades, soggy corners of fields, deserted farm buildings, improvised shelters in deep woods and, more recently, offices and hospital wards. And now, he was in an elegant room presided over by a mother. Half of James's self leaped at the prospect of being at home with a family: the other half felt a growing sense of disloyalty to his own parents. Why had he been offered this chance of a home?

Mrs Todd was small and spruce. Her intense blue eyes and greying hair neatly drawn back produced an impression of calm energy while the twinkle in her eyes softened the feeling of severity that her appearance, for she was dressed entirely in black, might otherwise have conveyed. She rose from her desk and,

England

advancing pleasantly towards James extended her hand. He accepted it and, completely naturally, raised it to his lips. He thought he heard a suppressed chuckle from Madeleine, but if Mrs Todd was surprised at his greeting she showed no sign of it.

After the usual courtesies had been observed, and Count Różycki had left, Mrs Todd said, 'Now, Janek, I should like you to go around the house on your own for half an hour. Explore wherever you like, make yourself really at home, and then come back to the drawing room and we'll talk. You'll know which is your room: I put your name on the door.'

He was taken aback at the directness of her manner, but over the years he was to become familiar with her brisk way of conducting business which reflected her straightforward personality. He had been touched at the complete trust which she seemed to place in a stranger, for he doubted whether he would have invited a totally unknown person to wander freely through his home; but at the same time he was embarrassed as to how literally he should interpret her invitation. Was he to go into her own room, and her daughter's? In fact, Mrs Todd had already solved the problem for him by making sure that both rooms were left with doors ajar and had neatly written labels: 'Mother's room' and 'Madeleine's room,' stuck on them. James was thereby able to match her sensitivity by taking a quick peep inside each without actually going in. He realised that this was the first time he had been in a family house; all the friends whom he had visited in Warsaw lived in flats.

From the first floor landing a narrow staircase led to a small door which he pushed gently open. The attic was spacious, with exposed rafters, and the two sides sloped at the angle of the roof so that it seemed as though he were stepping into a large ridge-tent. A comforting male odour of rough timber pervaded the room. On one wall were pinned small pennants and other Scouting emblems. Much of the other side was covered by a big poster illustrating the ships of the Royal Navy in silhouette, and two *Daily Telegraph* maps, one of the world and the other of Europe. Flags on small pins had been inserted on the map of Europe, and his eyes immediately sought out Poland. All the pins related to the German invasion. He looked at the Western front.

England

Again all the references were to 1940, and the maps had clearly not been used for several years. On a small table lay waterline models of British fighting ships: a few pots of paint and brushes revealed that some of the models were home-made.

At the far end of the small room a small window looked out far to the south, across the outskirts of London, to the Surrey hills. A small telescope and planisphere hung near the window. Most of the floor space was occupied by a model railway system lovingly set out, on which dust lay evenly. In various parts of the attic lay items of camping equipment: a rucksack, a set of billycans, and a couple of hand-axes. It was an Aladdin's cave, and James was entranced. For all that his experiences of the past year had given him an awareness and a defensive coat inappropriate to his age, the atmosphere of the room had seduced him back to boyhood. But whose treasures were they? He returned to Mrs Todd in a state of subdued excitement.

She was still at her desk, wholly absorbed in her work, and did not hear his approach. The desk had the cluttered but organised look of a busy and efficient person's, and when she became aware of James's presence she asked him to sit down and, in a few quick moves, tided her papers before joining him. On the desk he noted a mixture of letters, big books like ledgers, and some family photographs, including one of a young man in naval uniform. He remembered every detail of their conversation. He was thankful that she did not dwell on banalities to try and make him feel at home. Characteristically she went straight to the point and, without his asking it, answered the question which most of all exercised him.

'I dare say you have wondered how you come to be here...'

*

James was still in reverie when Mrs Brand came in with his tea. He thanked her politely but appeared scarcely to notice her. She remarked to a friend that she could not understand how Mr Todd managed to make so much money when he seemed to spend so much of his time dreaming. James knew his reputation for absent-mindedness and, insofar as he dwelt on it, it rather amused him. Mrs Brand was not alone in confusing thought with idleness and stillness with inactivity. Belief in the merit of visible activity, irrespective of its nature, was an error made by many, even those who had the advantage of a more privileged upbringing than hers. The delusion was harmless enough as long as they kept it to themselves, but the believers were usually propagandists for the supposed virtues of the ant and the bee. Madeleine had been like that, paying lip service to the intellect but suspicious of its manifestations, working hard to acquire knowledge because the effort was intrinsically meritorious, reading books but not loving them. The illusion seemed to be that real work should involve an element of discomfort, or at least of inconvenience: one ought not to enjoy it too much. Games, of course, were different. They were meant to be enjoyed, and the fact that most of them involved manifest physical activity rendered them doubly acceptable, even though it had to be admitted that they were not, strictly speaking, work. A games player was obviously doing something.

Of course, the favouring of the active and the feeling of guilt at the reflective attitudes to life were to be found everywhere, but they were magnified in England. He remembered Madeleine's schoolgirl enthusiasm for hockey, and subsequently for racquet games: a tennis engagement was considered sacred, and letting a partner down was regarded as a solecism of the first order; while failing to return a library book was a mere peccadillo.

*

On first exploring Mrs Todd's house, his discovery of the intriguing world of the attic had left little room for other sensations. It was not long, however, before he was making comparisons between his home in the London suburb and the one from which he had been driven. Leaving aside the inevitable differences in style between a house and a flat, there were more fundamental signs of the profoundly different culture into which he was being welcomed. There could be no doubt about the warmth of the welcome: Mrs Todd's offer to receive him as a member of the family had come from her heart, and she expressed it in simple direct terms that flew straight to his, but the house as a whole struck him as being unexciting and empty.

For so large a house there were few books, and for the most

England

part they were of an uncritical and unadventurous nature. In fact they were fairly representative of the range of reading that would have been found in many middle-class homes of the period whose owners did not happen to be of a literary or philosophical bent: a good proportion of the English classics, whose merit and interest James needed many more years to appreciate; plenty of humorous books and books obviously intended for children; works of travel and exploration; some anthologies of verse; and the collected works of Shakespeare and Dickens. There was scarcely anything by foreign authors, except for the Bible; no science, philosophy or art at all, and very little religion apart from a few battered bibles, obviously former school books which had been misused, and a few presentation anthologies of religious verse – Confirmation presents, perhaps – that had remained entirely unused.

The pictures on display struck James as no more exciting than the books. Mrs Todd owned not a single original of note, although her means would have enabled her to purchase freely. Most of her pictures were prints of sailing vessels, hunting scenes or flowers. Had James been familiar with English homes he might have half expected to find a neglected print of 'The Monarch of the Glen' in some dark corner. He would have searched in vain, for although the family had possessed a copy, Mrs Todd had shunted it off to an elderly uncle before they came to this house. Madeleine did have a couple of Impressionist prints in her room, but the house contained nothing more recent. It seemed quaintly staid to James, whose parental circle was often visited by friends who spoke enthusiastically of modern art and the school of Paris. One of them actually possessed a Picasso sketch.

The greatest difference that James felt was the total absence of any visible symbols of religion; no crucifix, holy pictures or statue of Our Lady. Nothing. In Poland there had been little talk of Protestantism, but James had gathered from the occasional allusion that Christianity abroad could take forms very different from those in which his country was steeped: he had not grasped the extent of the gulf until he saw the inside of an English home. It struck him as cold and soulless, and only the passage of time revealed to him the deeply private nature of much English

England

spirituality, so unspoken and personal that it rarely surfaced, and then often in a disguised form, as if the people were embarrassed to put their convictions into words. Later, indeed, he was to call the conviction itself into question, but at the time he felt a barely conscious unease at the absence of the familiar symbols of his culture.

Father Ryan's old style of piety reminded him of some of the external forms to which he had been accustomed. So did the reverence that the parishioners gave their priest: they deferred to him not only in matters of religion, which would have been reasonable enough, but in all kinds of little ways; adjusting their opinions and spoken comment to suit his. It had not been quite the same in the London parish, where the clergy met with different responses from their socially humble parishioners, many of Irish extraction, and the middle-class professional people who made up half the congregation.

James wanted to feel affection for Father Ryan, and respected him for an honest man, but was repelled by the rigid adherence to custom and tradition for which he stood. He recalled an occasion in Warsaw when Katarzyna had broached the question of becoming a nun. Their father had replied, 'Learn to think clearly for yourself first, my dear. Don't be swept along on a tide of enthusiasm and sentiment.'

The manner of the reply was characteristic of Stefan who always addressed his children in real language. He had then gone on to explain the splendour of dedicating one's life to God by sacrificing many of the pleasures that most people take for granted, but pointed out that any state in life might be a vocation through which God could be served.

'So if I become a nurse and also marry, I shall have two vocations?'

'Yes, of course. One can have several vocations. Look at your mother. She had one vocation as a wife and mother, another in the influence she exerted on her students, and another in the way she stimulated thought in the circle of friends who used to gather here. She helped people to fulfil themselves in all sorts of ways: that's a vocation, or several vocations. I don't think it matters how you look at it.'

England

'I think I want to give God everything, and give up the chance of marrying and having children, but I'm not sure.'

'Well, as things are now we can be sure of hardly anything, but in any case the essential thing is to learn to think – war or no war.'

Even as a boy in Warsaw he was aware that many of their neighbours went in awe of the clergy and deferred excessively to them, and he had not liked it. Stefan and Anna had many friends among priests and members of religious orders, and James was often an attentive listener when points of philosophy and theology, which the priests would have hesitated to voice in different surroundings as being too 'advanced', were discussed without embarrassment and often with humour. After one such soirée he remembered Anna, who still bore traces of her straight-laced family's attitudes, asking Stefan if he did not think that conversation had been just a little too free, perhaps disrespectful or even disloyal. Stefan had replied, 'You don't do God a favour by not speaking your mind with Him.'

That, James now realised, was the point. His father's faith was so strong that he not only could, but needed to, explore and even to speak of sacred things in terms that shocked some people by their familiarity and apparent irreverence: he had no use for humbug. James had noticed a similar phenomenon in some of his English friends, staunch royalists, who among their own kind would refer to the Queen as 'Liz', not out of disrespect but of affection that made them members of a charmed circle, a family or club, where nicknames were normal currency and a healthy spirit of debunking reigned.

That, James knew, was what he really lacked. He was a member of no close circle, even though many people considered him as a friend in the overworked sense of the word. In all probability, a little more warmth on his part, a greater willingness to reveal himself, would evoke more genuine affection on the part of many people. He blamed no one. The cure lay within him, but he could not give himself as he would have wished: he had been hurt too often and a deep-seated reserve kept him from sharing. But in spite of the hurts there was much cause for gratitude, and none greater than what Mrs Todd had opened up to him.

His mind returned to their first meeting.

England

'I dare say you have wondered how you come to be here.'

James remembered the conversation well in spite of the passage of years. At the time his English was not up to grasping fully all that she said, and she was not sufficiently familiar with the needs of foreigners to exclude nuances from her speech, but there was no doubt about the general trend. She neither could nor would have given him an account of the family history, but from his memory of the conversation, enriched with details that he had subsequently gleaned from her and Madeleine, he had been able to piece together a history of a family so utterly unlike his in every respect that it had called for a European cataclysm and personal tragedy to bring them together.

3: The Todds

Peter Todd's father had owned a small engineering works south of the Thames in which he did skilled work for a wide range of customers, especially the increasing number of small motor manufacturers who were unable to produce all their parts themselves. When Peter was born, in 1890, the factory was little more than a very well run workshop employing three men, but then his father's active mind began to develop ideas which he patented. Some patents he sold to his customers, but others he retained and developed himself, so that by the time Peter was twenty, Humphrey Todd and Son was a thriving company with its head office in the City. Foreign companies, too, bought their patents, Humphrey travelled widely, exported, became very rich and a Freeman of the City. By 1912 they were sub-contracted to do specialised work for the aircraft industry, and Peter became a weekend aviator. Father and son were close, and Humphrey, who became a widower early, lived with his son to the end of his life.

Peter soon showed himself to be an imaginative and practical engineer, and ran the factory while his father spent more time in the City. When the Great War broke out Peter wanted to volunteer, but his father pulled strings and caused him to be exempt. At first this distressed him, but as the firm's reputation as a war-winner soared so did his spirits, only periodically dampened when the death in action of yet another of his flying club friends was reported.

The end of the war left him less than fulfilled as a man. His father had been knighted, his contemporaries had been decorated or were revered memories, while he was a successful engineer and businessman and heir to a considerable fortune: when he took stock, which was not often for he was not of an introspective nature, a certain dissatisfaction lurked beneath the prosperous surface. When Sir Humphrey appointed Guy Rowlands DFC, who was both able and pleasant and not merely a famous name, to

The Todds

the board of directors, Peter had to make an effort at concealing his envy. He found refuge in work and marriage.

He was not a man of great imagination or inquiring spirit outside his engineering, and did not look far for a wife. Constance Sharp was the daughter of the firm's chief accountant. She was quick-witted, full of fun, a couple of years older and far better educated than Peter. They married in 1922. Nigel was born the following year and, after an interval of six years, Madeleine. James was only two months older than she.

From the beginning Constance displayed an interest in the business side of the firm, taking little part in the empty social life of so many of her age and social position in the aftermath of the war. Peter had the sense not to discourage his wife's interest, and the marriage was successful: they were a happy family. While most comparable families employed nannies to enable the mistress to engage in the social round, those whom Constance employed while her children were young were intended to enable her to spend at least a part of each day either at the works or in London. In each place her presence was at first viewed with a mixture of surprise and suspicion. Some women had been employed at the works during the war, but never in positions of responsibility, while in the City a woman beyond the level of typist or junior secretary was still a rarity. When Peter and his father had agreed, in her own words, to let Constance 'see what goes on' in the firm, they assumed that after the initial enthusiasm her interest in the male worlds of factory and business would wane, because women were not renowned for consistency.

They could not have been more mistaken. Soon her earnest little face and trim round form, simply dressed, were to be found turning up in all sorts of places. At first she would ask the man at the lathe, 'What exactly is the difference between mild steel and high speed steel?' or the toolmaker, 'What is a template?' Then with a winning smile she would add that she wanted something to speak to her husband about over breakfast. Situations that could have given rise to resentment were saved by her unpatronising manner: she was never seen as the boss's spy. Once her presence in the factory no longer gave rise to comment, she began to speak with the men about other things than their work; bit by bit she delved into their personal and financial difficulties; she encouraged the apprentices, visited families at times of trouble and became an unofficial welfare officer. There was little union resentment of her activities because the firm, large though it had become, was essentially still a family business, and paid more than the going rate: labour relations were good.

Strangely, perhaps, she was less well received in the City office, and in the staff section at the works. She did not endear herself on her first visit to the works office by enquiring of the office manager why work began there at nine whereas the factory opened at eight. To Mr Allsop's astonished reply, 'Well. They're works. Staff have always started at nine,' she returned, 'But we're all one business, aren't we?'

The 'we' was not lost on him. Constance felt more in tune with the men and the junior engineers in the factory who, in keeping with the firm's tradition of pride in workmanship and technical innovation, were committed to their work and were usually prepared to try and explain why and how things were done, than with the office staff, many of whom often – on the basis of fewer qualifications – exuded an air of self-satisfaction.

Constance was a realist and soon saw that her contribution to the firm could not be on the engineering side on account of her lack of technical education, and the resistance that a woman would encounter as an engineer even if she were able to qualify. The business side, though, might be a different matter, and so might the bridging of 'they' and 'we'. From her father she obtained books on the principles of accountancy. She began to study the business pages of the national newspapers and would corner old Sir Humphrey to have him explain what she could not understand. To her surprise, she often found that shrewd though he was in the practicalities of business, there was much he did not understand about the underlying causes of the situations with which he dealt pragmatically, and although she was unable to understand them herself she felt that a greater grasp of principles would lead to better decision making.

In her endeavours she found an ally in Guy Rowlands. Sir Humphrey had recruited him to the board for cosmetic reasons; a distinguished airman who was still remembered as a minor ace and blessed with excellent connections at the Air Ministry, and social graces with which Humphrey and Peter were more frugally provided. He had expected to land an elegant, docile and semi-sleeping partner; but behind Guy's conventional 'service' exterior and country-house manner lay a keen mind that had not met many like his in the course of his service and social life.

At first he was amused at the sight of the incisive, bustling young woman buzzing hornet-like on the outside of a male world, but soon his judgement told him that she was no ordinary wife trying to seem interested in her husband's business; she meant to become involved, and her interest fired his. But for her he might have remained the kind of director that Sir Humphrey had intended. A platonic relationship evolved, almost unconsciously. At no stage did they sit at a table with papers before them and decide to reform the company; their plans grew as he became a kind of unofficial coach in her search for knowledge – not that he possessed it himself, but his self-confidence and contacts enabled him to help her acquire it.

Peter did not exactly resent the relationship, which always remained sexually innocent, but felt somehow excluded when Constance expounded her views on economics to Guy who, though ignorant of technicalities, was interested in causes and effects and served as a stone on which to whet her arguments. She was never sure, but strongly suspected, that the family's move from a substantial but modest house not far from the works to the splendid suburban mansion was an attempt on the part of father and son to deflect her attention from the firm to the task of home-building.

If so, it failed, because she treated the task of fitting out the house as though she were equipping an office, ordering this, that and the other, tolerating no feeble excuses and chasing suppliers on the telephone with her steely precise voice so that within six months The Aspens was transformed into a residence worthy of any magnate. Sir Humphrey used the stately house for business entertainment. Directors and senior members of the firm were often guests at dinner, and Constance found a resistance, perhaps not unreasonable, to her searching questions: she had a devastating 'Why?' which did not find favour with men who had been used to having their opinions heard with deference and their decisions treated like the word of God. Once, when she asked Peter whether her interventions embarrassed him, his gentle disclaimer could not conceal his feelings.

She had to tread warily between her reluctance to hurt her husband and her father-in-law, for whom she felt real affection, and the conviction that the firm could not prosper indefinitely on its pre-war methods, irrespective of the quality of its products. There was great pride and spirit within the firm, verging on self-satisfaction, which was not unjustified in view of its success during the war; but she felt that in its very success lay the root of what would surely become its dilemma. The vision that Sir Humphrey had shown in earlier days, seeking business abroad, had inevitably been curbed by the needs of wartime production, and now he was old, less resilient and inclined to trust in the firm's sheer technical excellence to see it into the post-war world. The same attitude of 'that's the way we do it' was shared by most of the senior managers, and even by Peter who, while he continued to display an innovative mind in technical matters, contributed little to general policy.

Constance saw the future only dimly, and was not able to point with confidence and authority at weaknesses: she lacked the language for translating her intuition into compelling argument.

In her direct way she saw that the obvious solution was to acquire the language. She could never forget the day when she told Peter that she intended to take a degree in commerce and economics. He was not so much antagonistic as baffled: how could she do it as well as running the house and looking after Nigel? Did she know what she was letting herself in for? Indeed, was there any way in which she could do it without danger to her health? He was, by nature, suspicious of 'paper qualifications': his father had none, he himself had taken a few examinations at draughtsman level, and there were a few graduate engineers on the staff. They, and a few accounting qualifications in the office, were the sum total of 'paper'. The firm had prospered on inspired amateurism, which he called good practical engineering. He would not raise any serious objections to her studies, but claimed, quite truthfully, that he had no idea how she could set about them. He need not have worried. She solved the problem through Guy who, though no academic himself, had a brother who was; and she enrolled for an external degree at the University of London.

It took her five years to graduate, but after the first two came the opportunity of making her mark. She had submitted occasional articles to *The Financial Times* on commercial and economic aspects of contemporary trade, and one was eventually published over the pen-name of 'Mercator'. It was short and pithy, deliberately not highly controversial, but made some telling points on the relationship between the growth of business and company organisation. The ideas had been in her mind before she embarked on her studies, but now she was able to use technical language and illustrations from foreign – especially American – practice. With Guy's help she used a little subterfuge.

At a board meeting he drew attention to the article, in his urbane manner not pressing its conclusions too strongly but in such a way as to give the directors food for thought. Heads nodded wisely. It was admitted to be a well thought-out contribution which they might usefully bear in mind for subsequent consideration…

That was all she wanted. After dinner a few days later, when some directors were present and Guy steered conversation to the Mercator article, she offered some comment from which it was evident that she was familiar with its contents. One of the directors said, 'I didn't know you read *The Financial Times*, Mrs Todd.'

'Well, actually I wrote the article. I've got a copy of the typescript next door,' she said, and produced it from her morning room.

'In that case, Sir Humphrey, I suggest that Mercator be invited to our next meeting to expand on her ideas. I think the board, as a whole would be interested, don't you?'

That was how Constance came to be at first co-opted to attend board meetings, and was subsequently elected a director. She was shrewd enough to play a cautious game to begin with, urging no dramatic changes but impressing the directors generally with the relevance of her comments. In that way, by the time she

The Todds

graduated in 1935, no voices were raised to complain about the new graduate teaching her grandfathers to suck eggs. Sir Humphrey having died in the previous year, and the economy showing signs of recovery, she felt no sentimental inhibitions about urging changes throughout the firm. With Guy's support, factory and management were tuned up to meet the needs of the war she felt certain must come. Once again the firm geared itself for the production of aircraft parts and special equipment. Peter, whose technical creativity had flagged in middle age, became infected with the prevailing enthusiasm: the Todd pilot escape mechanism, the Todd airfield fire tender and many others went into mass production. It was a time of high endeavour and professionalism.

It was about this time that Doktor Silvermann, the émigré German engineer, joined the firm.

Throughout the years Constance had not allowed her interest in the business to distract her from attending to her children's upbringing. Nigel was doing well as a day boy at his public school and, since he showed an aptitude for science, his father hoped that a third generation of Todds would join the firm. Peter asked Guy to find out which was the right college at Cambridge, and Nigel was taken round the works from time to time. He confided to his mother more than once his reluctance to be seen as 'father's boy' in the firm. He did not actively resist the gentle pressure, but displayed no more than the usual enthusiasm of most boys of his age for cars and aircraft: if anything he was keener on ships. Peter had bought a cabin cruiser, which they kept on the Thames, and many weekends were spent cruising. They lived the comfortable life of rich people.

When war seemed inevitable, Peter began to worry about Nigel, and did something that came close to causing an estrangement between them: it was at the beginning of 1939, the year in which Nigel was to take his General School Certificate. Peter had discovered that some of his business connections who had never before spoken of the countryside and agriculture were buying farms far away from London. At first he assumed they were merely making long-term investments, benefiting from the low price of agricultural land. Then he realised that they had sons, and

49

The Todds

that in the event of war, farming would be a reserved occupation...

Constance had her doubts about the wisdom of the plan from the moment he told her: she knew her son better. But Peter was adamant, unusually for him, and Tithe Barn Farm near Great Walling became part of the family property. Gloucestershire, he felt, was suitably remote from the likely bombing. Nigel for his part was furious when his father, switching direction, urged him to begin an agricultural college course as soon as his General Schools examination was over. In the event he complied, with a heavy heart, but as soon as he could after war broke out he volunteered for the Navy.

The war was disastrous for the family. Madeleine's school was destroyed in the Blitz and moved to Worcestershire. Constance, relieved of any need to be a mother, threw herself into voluntary work and drove an ambulance. She became associated with organisations for the relief of refugees, originally, through speaking with Dr Silvermann, German Jews, and subsequently Poles. Peter worked all hours at the factory, which survived the early raids. One night in 1942 when he had stayed there to untangle a production difficulty the factory was bombed. He was killed. Some months later Nigel was lost at sea.

*

Constance Todd's first conversation with Janek, much briefer and less detailed than his subsequent reconstruction of the family's history, evidently put a strain on her emotions. Their eyes converged on the photograph of the sailor on her desk.

'Yes, Janek, you are quite right. I do want a son. I can't replace your mother, but I shall try to be a friend. I do hope you will stay with us.'

Janek, who had not wept since he left Warsaw, cried unashamedly and clasped her in his arms.

When they had both recovered their composure, he asked, 'But why me? Why not an English boy?'

'That is a long story. You see, I'm a bit of a fighter too, and so was Nigel, and in the course of working with refugees I came to know Count Rózycki quite well. He told me about you and your

The Todds

family and what you'd done. And shall we just say that I thought we might have something in common.'

James remembered the little woman with the strong face only just cleared of her tears. Indeed, across the difference in age and tradition they were destined to be great sharers.

'I see,' he had said, not really understanding.

'And now, I think it's about time we had a cup of tea. Let's go and make it together.'

Strange people, these English, thought Janek. Tea seems to be the inevitable accompaniment of everything.

4: Early Days

Mrs Brand came in to remove the tea tray. She wore the tidy apron and grey expression that cloaked her for most of the day, softened up to a point by a watery smile on her infrequent visits to the Barn Owl. It was as though she were challenging life to prove that it held any joy for her. When first he employed her James had tried once or twice to coax a laugh, but her reluctance to be amused was so evident that he soon desisted and settled for efficient service in place of cheerfulness.

'I've got Mr Stonor's usual rooms ready. He's arriving some time this morning, isn't he?'

'Yes. Thank you. If I'm not in when he comes perhaps you'd just make him feel at home. Some coffee, and show him to the library.'

'Will he be staying long?'

'A couple of days, I suppose, but we won't need any special arrangements. Just the normal routine.'

Indeed, no special arrangements were needed for John Stonor's visit. Their friendship had begun soon after Mrs Todd had sent him to Nigel's old school. He recalled the lesson with Mr Asp.

'And so you see, gentlemen, that in the arousing of national spirit among the peoples of Europe, which contributed so strongly to Napoleon's downfall, lay the seeds of subsequent disasters which, at the time, few could foresee. And by the way, Mr Stonor, on the subject of arousing the spirit may I suggest that your chances of passing the examination will be materially improved if you rouse yourself from contemplating the infinite?'

'Indeed, sir, I shall, and thereby no doubt avoid subsequent disaster.'

Mr Asp, to his credit, took no offence at a witty, if cheeky, reply, and Stonor had made his mark. His many gifts included that of simulating a lounging indolence while his mind was fully

Early Days

alert. This immediately fascinated Janek, who both felt and showed greater respect for education and authority than did most of his English schoolfellows.

Janek loved the school. Luckily for him he had come to Mrs Todd during the summer holidays and she had been able to enter him in time for the start of the academic year. The school had been considerate and imaginative: in view of Janek's general culture and obvious enthusiasm he was placed in the fifth form and given the opportunity of gaining the Certificate in a year. Not only did a genuine desire to learn spur him to prove himself, but also he felt he owed it to Mrs Todd and, as the only Pole at the school, to his country. He did so not aggressively, for that would have been against his nature, but with grim determination.

His first experience of organised games and of the gymnasium had come as a shock, not because he disliked them and certainly not from a reluctance to take what Mr Hackforth, the games master, used to call 'hard knocks', but in astonishment at the seriousness with which physical activities were taken in England, and the way in which competitive games were raised to the level of a religion by the school authorities. He was not rebellious by nature, and accepted the system painlessly enough, especially since the rugby game in which he found himself consisted of the weaker and less dedicated players and 'old Hack', in spite of his talk of hard knocks, conducted it in a fairly relaxed way. He had been short of a lung since he was gassed in the First World War, smoked like a power station and would exhort the laggards with colourful imprecations which supplemented the English that Janek learned in class.

At the end of a game in which Stonor had been urged to go for the ball in a manner 'not entirely suggestive of an emasculated hippopotamus', Janek had asked John what the long word meant. The reply was not only enlightening but was couched in terms that introduced him to an alternative vocabulary. It was not always obvious which words were all right and which were not suitable for use in the drawing room. Once or twice when he had, in all innocence, uttered the unutterable at the dinner table, Madeleine had ostentatiously choked and Mrs Todd had quickly changed the direction of the conversation. Afterwards, when they were alone she would explain, 'We usually say...'

Early Days

Indeed, he reflected, in the early days Madeleine had displayed a good deal of hilarity at his expense.

Hack was a willing conspirator at creating what he called 'natural breaks' during the game. Half-time was often extended to permit him to finish an anecdote and, after a try had been scored, much rubbing of 'bruised' limbs would produce some more breathing time. John Stonor, who could easily, had he wished, have got himself promoted to a higher game, was an expert at those tactics. In the very cold weather after Christmas, old Hack fell ill and the game was taken by a keen young master who thought it would be a good idea to show those idle boys what rugby was really about. Half-time became an occasion for criticising tactics; there was even a hint of special practice sessions in the lunch break. Stonor, whose parents were very High Church, produced some incense which was ceremonially ignited in the cloakroom to hasten Hack's recovery. It, and antibiotics, worked.

It was rumoured that in his spare time Hack wrote lyric poetry, but he was always coy in the matter. Only much later did James discover that it was true.

Janek did not, at first, find it easy to undress in front of the other boys. The cause was not prudery but a relic of his earlier upbringing in which frankness about the facts of life was accompanied by a certain unfussy modesty. The rest of the class would cram into the changing room and fling off their clothes in a completely natural way. Few foreign boys attended the school and even they – mostly German Jews, like Isaac Silvermann – had been there for some years and become accustomed to English ways.

He was good at gymnastics, which he enjoyed more than rugby, but whereas he felt real affection for Mr Hackforth he crossed swords early with Mr O'Neill, the assistant physical training master. O'Neill was an Ulsterman, deeply and irrationally anti-Catholic and anti-Semitic. He would try and ingratiate himself with the majority of the class, making sideways allusions to 'our friends from Eastern Europe', usually being careful not to appear to aim his remark at any one boy but succeeding in annoying or distressing the Jewish boys as a whole.

Early Days

By no means all the class were amused, but he won a few sycophantic grins. Before a game or a gym lesson it was customary for the boys to remove their watches and give them to the master for safe keeping. After a few lessons Janek decided it would be prudent not to wear his cross in the gym, so he took it off and handed it to Mr O'Neill who examined it with feigned surprise.

'What's this, boys wearing jewellery nowadays?'

'It isn't jewellery, sir, it's my father's cross.'

'I can see it's a cross. I suppose you're RC like most of the Poles. Do you carry a rosary as well?'

At that a small titter came from some of the surrounding boys.

'No, sir.'

'Anyhow,' O'Neill went on, with incredible lack of sensitivity 'why are you wearing it if it's your father's?'

'Because my father is dead, sir. He was killed fighting for his country, and yours.'

The boys who had sniggered looked away: the remainder relished the strong reply. The situation was too much for O'Neill, who felt himself threatened, lost his head and told Janek to report to his form master for insolence. Naturally no action followed. On the contrary, the incident served to help Oliver Rudge to come to know Janek better and sooner than he might otherwise have done. Rudge was a scholar, humanist and a wise man, not given to instant verdicts and the feeling that something must always be done about every infringement of the rules. He was the right man to be in charge of the fifth form, which often became fragile and needed urbane handling as the Certificate year progressed.

Mr Rudge dwelt little on the incident.

'Tell me about yourself,' he suggested, and Janek did.

'So you really were involved in the Rising. The Headmaster did tell me you had walked from Warsaw, but there wasn't much detail. Did any of the actual fighting come your way?'

Janek had warmed to Mr Rudge, and trusted him. He told him about the barricade and the tank.

'Hmm. School must seem a bit dull by comparison...'

'No, sir,' said Janek from the heart, 'I love it.'

Rudge was not used to such demonstrative approval of school. This chap was different, he thought.

Early Days

'I dare say you felt that Mr O'Neill was making fun of your religion. I don't suppose he meant any harm, you know. Of course you'll have to be careful how you get on with him.'

That was the end of the incident as far as Janek was concerned. For a man of peace Rudge knew how, in a good cause, to thrust home the knife. Later, in the Common Room, he said gently to O'Neill,

'Bad luck finding yourself out on a bit of a limb with Zagorski this morning. Of course you weren't to know the exceptional sentimental importance of that cross, and how he came to have it. I don't think you'll find he gives you any more trouble. Just one of the hazards of having a war hero in your class, I suppose.'

'Oh, it was nothing really.' O'Neill's instinct for survival told him to leave the matter well alone.

The outline of Janek's history soon became known in the Common Room, although little was said to him. In retrospect he realised that many small acts of consideration could be attributed to it.

His friendship with John Stonor prospered. They formed a good pair. Both were intelligent: James hard working, idealistic, loving knowledge for its own sake; John relaxed, professing cynicism, fond of short cuts. It was he who persuaded Janek to become known as James, but Janek had some misgivings which he aired one evening when Dr Silvermann and his wife had come to dinner.

'John Stonor says it would make it easier for people, but I'm not sure I like the idea of changing my name.'

'It's a serious decision,' said Dr Silvermann.

'Well,' said Mrs Todd, practical as ever, 'what's in a name? I dare say that over the years it may save quite a bit of embarrassment, particularly when you are introduced to people who find foreign names difficult. We're not exactly a nation of linguists.'

'While you're about it,' said Madeleine, 'you might as well go the whole hog and change your surname as well. People can, can't they?'

James hesitated, partly because his familiarity with English did not yet rise to 'going the whole hog', and partly because there seemed to be something indecent about changing one's parental name.

Early Days

'Yes,' said Mrs Todd, 'it's done by deed poll. I think you might have to be twenty-one, but I'm not sure. But it's not difficult.'

'"Zagorski" is pretty hard for most people to say. It doesn't exactly roll off the tongue,' said Madeleine.

James was thinking furiously. Would it not be a sort of a betrayal: how did it square with 'Never forget Poland?'

'I know several Poles who have taken English names,' said Mrs Silvermann, 'probably for that very reason. And a lot of people with foreign-sounding Jewish names did so too.'

James plucked up his courage. 'Is that why you never changed your name? Because it sounds just like an English one?'

'No, Janek... or James,' replied Dr Silvermann with a distant twinkle in his eye that belied the solemnity of his words, 'not at all. My relatives have been persecuted in that name for generations, and died in camps all over Europe with it, and I propose to die with it myself.'

A hush settled on the company. Not even Madeleine could turn that statement into a joke.

'But', continued Dr Silvermann, 'not all my fellow Jews have felt the same. One has to live, and it might be best for one's children not to inflict a very foreign-sounding name on them. I don't blame them for changing: it's a personal decision.'

That lightened the atmosphere. In the event Janek became James quite quickly at school, and remained James at home until Madeleine renamed him Jim. For a long time there was no more talk of changing his surname.

James remembered his first year at The Aspens with a mixture of guilt and delight. Guilt because, being young and resilient, and with life before him, the narrowing memories of his recent past became blanketed by the richness of present experience and the delight of being accepted by strangers at home (for that was how he came to refer to The Aspens) and most of his schoolfellows. Even more beguiling was the knowledge of being appreciated by the masters for his intellect. The staff had its share of hearty games players but there were also plenty of scholarly inquiring men whom James thought of as intellectuals, although most of them would not have claimed the description. The natural and wholesome result was that thoughts of what he had left behind in

Early Days

Poland began to recede, and many a time when he said his prayers at night he realised that he had not thought of his family all day. Scruples of neglect and betrayal assailed him sufficiently to make him mention it to his confessor, a level-headed man who reassured him.

'I am sure', Father Bickerstaff had said, 'that when your father made you get away from Warsaw he wanted you to live. That means living now, not in the past.'

'But he told me never to forget my country.'

'That means not being disloyal to it, never being ashamed of your origins. It doesn't involve living in the past. That's unhealthy.'

James had been told what he wanted to hear. Occasional self-reproach was gradually swamped in the excitement of each day.

The aftermath of the O'Neill affair was that James's history became common knowledge among his contemporaries as well as among the staff. He was granted a distant respect, although his reticent nature did not make him outstandingly popular. He had few enemies and a small group of friends. He was closest to Stonor, but Isaac Silvermann and William Sturton too were frequent visitors to The Aspens. They all lived within easy bicycling distance. All three were ambitious, and so were their parents although parental and filial aspirations did not necessarily match. Their conversation naturally centred on their studies for the Certificate, in which all were, for different reasons, keen to excel, but then it would digress into discussion of their hopes and ambitions.

In Silvermann, James found strands of a common European culture. Izzy's father was a perfect example of the folly of the Nazi regime, which drove out many of its best brains for no other reason than that they happened to be Jewish. Jacob Silvermann could have enjoyed a brilliant career as a university teacher or in industry, and even in his reduced émigré circumstances made enough money from his publications to supplement the salary he originally drew from Humphrey Todd & Son. By the time James knew him he had been on the board for several years. Any money that he had to spare was devoted to buying works of art, chiefly modern painting and sculpture. When James used to call at the

Early Days

Silvermann house he almost felt that he was going abroad, to his parents' flat. In Jacob Silvermann's company conversation would switch from technology to politics, to the arts, even to literature, because his command of English had been complete before he left Germany. Then it would turn, ultimately and inevitably, to philosophy. Jacob was a large man, and when he made his points, moving slowly about the room in a cloud of cigar smoke, he looked like an amiable performing bear. James loved the whole atmosphere, material and intellectual. On his return, with the smoke clinging to his jacket, Madeleine would sniff at him archly, crinkling the sides of her nose as she twitched it in a way that he found increasingly attractive.

'I know where you've been! You've been living it up with old Silvermann.'

James did not resent being teased, but did not like her way of referring to Dr Silvermann, partly because he knew that she would not have referred to one of her mother's non-Jewish friends by his surname alone and partly because he did not think the 'old' was meant as a term of affection but to indicate stuffy, or boring. He could hardly imagine anyone less stuffy then Jacob Silvermann, but made no comment about it to her.

Stonor's parents, on the other hand, were archetypal bores. There was no reason why they should have been, their parents were not, and they had both enjoyed the benefits of an education that should have gone some way to prevent it, but their minds were irreparably pedestrian in spite of professional success.

Mr Stonor was an eminent surgeon, his wife the daughter of a judge. They lived in some opulence and were pillars of the parish church of St Michael and All Angels, which was traditionally 'High' but regarded by the Stonors as tottering on the edge of being evangelical. They did all the right things; Mr Stonor served as a churchwarden, she supported fêtes and embroidered church hangings. They were indeed very decent and accomplished people who had, unfortunately, left behind in the nursery any originality with which they were endowed. When they had travelled abroad before the war, which they did because it was the thing to do, their continental breakfast consisted of ham and eggs. Strangely enough John had considerable affection for his parents in spite of

Early Days

sharing hardly any of their beliefs and attitudes. They had ambitions for him, but felt they were being very broad-minded in not expecting him necessarily to enter either medicine or the law: 'Some other profession, perhaps,' they would say, but the unspoken assumption was that he would go in for something highly traditional and respectable. John had his own ideas.

William Sturton's parents were tradespeople who had prospered and been able to give him an education that had been denied to them. From grandfather's corner shop they had built up a small chain of butchers' shops in South London and were probably as rich as the Stonors, although they lived more modestly. Mr Sturton made no secret of his hope that his son would join the firm and carry on the tradition, but William had very different ideas, for he was by nature an artist. The school did little to develop his considerable talent for drawing and painting but it did fire his romantic imagination in literature: by the age of sixteen he was well read and eloquent at expressing enthusiasms that both impressed and baffled his parents, who lived so close to their business that they failed to bridge the gulf that was growing between them and their son. William lived in terror of the day when he would have to convince them that he had no intention of being a butcher.

James recalled one glorious sunny day in the Easter holidays before the Certificate. They were all at The Aspens and after tea they retired to the garden.

'Very decent of Mrs Todd to ask us all to tea,' said John, 'my mother says even tea parties are difficult with rationing.'

'Yes, she's been frightfully good to me, from the beginning. I've been lucky to come here.'

'You jolly well have,' said William, 'and we're all very glad you did. Not just because of tea.'

'Thanks.'

They had reached a small hollow where a rockery had existed, now neglected. They squatted on the rocks. William hesitated and then said, 'I've often wondered what it must feel like to be stuck far from home.'

'I try not to think like that. After all, I'm not the only refugee in the world. By home, do you mean Poland? Well, I don't know much of it: we didn't often go outside Warsaw. As for my actual home, I just don't know whether it still exists, or how much of the Warsaw that I knew exists. It sometimes feels as if I'm living in one place and my body is in another. Does that sound silly?'

'No,' replied William.

'What happens to your nationality?' asked Isaac. 'Are you stateless?'

'I really don't know. Poland still exists, so I suppose I'm still Polish but it may not be safe for me to return and I'm not sure I want to. You see, I may have no relatives left at all!'

'How can you find out?'

'There's a Polish organisation here that gradually gets hold of news. As a matter of fact there's another problem... Strictly speaking, I can't even prove that I'm me! I came away without any means of identification except my father's cross, which you all know about, and that's engraved with his name. But I can't prove that he gave it to me, can I? So here I am, *homo incognito*. Didn't your parents have the same difficulty, Izzy?'

'No. Dad was shrewd enough to get out well before the war, and plenty of technical people here could vouch for him, so there was no problem about identity. Anyhow, he had a job to move to. And then he became naturalised, so we had no nonsense about internment during the war. There must be some way you can prove who you are.'

'Actually there is, in a roundabout sort of way. The Polish authorities here have a register of doctors, so by asking lots of people lots of questions they will be able to satisfy themselves. Unofficially they already have. Perhaps I can become British too, but I'm not sure I want to give up my nationality.'

John was serious for once.

'I suppose it does make my problems look rather pale by comparison.'

'What problems?'

'Well, one really. My people.'

'Don't you get on with them?'

'Oh yes, I'm very fond of them as people, but they're such crashing snobs. If I weren't so fond of them I'd say sanctimonious snobs. We talk about bishops at breakfast and deans at dinner, and

Early Days

who's to be next for such and such a diocese, and liturgical niceties and all that sort of stuff. It quite turns me off religion... and actually, you know, I'm not really "anti", not deep down.'

It had been a sacrifice for John to admit to even the distant rumblings of enthusiasm. For the last two years he had worked hard at affecting an exterior of elegant boredom and cynicism.

'You're horrible about your parents,' said James, 'it's just that their enthusiasms are not the same as yours.'

'I'll say they're not! I think if by some miracle my pater were to go out and buy fish and chips he'd still insist on having it wrapped in the *Church Times*!'

They all laughed. John had adopted the custom of referring to his parents as 'pater' and 'mater' out of mischief, and they, happy in the illusion that he was showing devotion to traditional forms, had not deterred him. He now used the terms quite naturally, without affectation.

To James, any parents, however boring, seemed preferable to none.

'As a matter of fact, I quite like my parents, too,' said William.

'But?' suggested John, wickedly.

'But we have nothing in common. If they weren't my parents I doubt if we'd even talk: their conversation is so...'

'Pedestrian?' suggested John.

'I move that it is definite, incontrovertible and established', said Isaac, 'that John is horrible. Those in favour please indicate.'

All raised a hand, John higher than the others.

'At the risk of sounding a prosaic note,' continued Isaac, 'let me say that I don't find home boring. It's not that Dad and I have the same ideas, any more than he and Mother do, but we find plenty in common.'

'That's because there are a great many subjects of conversation *chez toi*,' said James.

'Exactly. Family conversation is not stuck in a groove. I actually like being at home. So does my little sister.'

Isaac used to refer to Rebecca as his little sister, although she was only eighteen months his junior. She was dark, exotic and vivacious, and moved with an ease which William thought worthy of a painting by Delacroix; a thought that he kept well to himself.

Early Days

'Mind you,' Isaac continued, 'there hasn't been all that much time for long family discussions this year; the work's been getting pretty hectic. I hope we'll be able to take it a bit easier in the Lower Sixth.'

The conversation returned to the subject of school and the impending examination.

In the event none of them need have worried about the result; they all did excellently; James slightly less well than the others which, in view of his English, surprised no one. Fortunately, Madeleine had also done well, which averted embarrassment at home. Mrs Todd was delighted. She brought Madeleine and James into the drawing room.

'This is where we began a year ago,' she said, 'I suppose we should look seriously at the future.'

James already had. Mrs Todd said, with mock solemnity, 'First of all, James, I ought to ask you how you feel about staying on with us. We mustn't take your feelings for granted.'

'My feelings... You know I love being here. There's nothing I want more than to stay with you, if you'll let me.'

She smiled. 'So that's settled. Now the next part is a bit delicate, James, and you should know that Madeleine and I have already spoken about it.'

Madeleine nodded, and James looked blank. Mrs Todd continued.

'You have been a joy to us. I have found a son, and your occasional squabbles with Madeleine are just what I would expect between brother and sister. I had seriously thought of asking you to let us make the situation official.'

'You mean...'

'Yes, I wanted to ask you to let me adopt you legally. I have spoken recently with Count Rózycki. There is no reason to believe that your father is alive, but just in case, since there is no positive proof either way, it seems wiser to wait longer!'

'Yes, I understand that. But if I knew for certain that Father was dead, I should be proud to be your son.'

He put his arm round her, and she wiped away a tear.

'Let us wait, then. But in the meantime I want you to feel that you are my son in every way.'

Early Days

James paused, overwhelmed, yet wanting to go further.

'In that case... I've been wondering how to ask you for some time... Now, can I call you "Mother", Mummy?'

She laid her hand on his arm. 'I hoped you would, but I didn't like to suggest it. I didn't know how you would feel about your... real mother.'

'I know, I've thought about it too, but I believe she approves.'

Madeleine attributed his use of the present tense to the imperfection of his English, and assumed that he meant 'she would approve': she was not familiar with the doctrine of the Communion of Saints.

They had discussed what Madeleine and he should do next.

'All right, Madeleine, you can do your secretarial course, and James can continue at school. But let this be clear, you are both to do what's right for you. I don't think business or engineering are really what most appeal to you, James, and you mustn't pin your life to the firm; but of course there'll always be room in it for you.'

James marvelled at her generosity and compared her attitude with that of some of his friends' parents. Indeed, business did not attract him: he had thought tentatively of becoming a philosopher. It seemed that, in spite of the cultural difference between his original home and his new one, what The Aspens lacked in intellectual warmth it compensated for by its open-hearted generosity.

Count Rózycki had come to see him soon afterwards.

'I am very pleased that things have worked out so well for you here. You have completely won Mrs Todd's affection: how did you do it, Janek?'

'I have simply behaved towards her as far as possible as I would have to my own mother.'

'It cannot have been easy.'

'Not entirely easy, because there are some big areas where we have no contact. For example, Mrs Todd does not talk much about books, and neither do most of her friends, but I am introduced to a lot of people, which has helped my English, and they have all been very pleasant to me and asked a lot of questions about life in Poland. They seem to treat me as though I were a lot older than I am.'

'That is partly because your reputation came ahead of you, partly because events have made you mature. Tell me, what other areas of no contact have you found?'

'Only one that matters: religion. The Catholic Church is only a short way off, as you know, and I have a good confessor with whom I quite often speak, but as soon as I come home I have to keep my religion to myself. It can't be a part of family life, not because Mrs Todd is hostile to it – of course she isn't – but it's just never mentioned.'

'You're doing well to keep going to Mass. I dare say in time you will make friends in the parish. How about Madeleine?'

'What about her?'

'Well, how do you get on with her?'

'Fine. We argue a bit from time to time.'

'She's a good-looking girl.'

'Yes, I suppose she's not too bad.'

James had found himself adopting a laconic English way of speaking which was useful when one was disinclined to pursue a subject.

Count Rózycki left it at that.

★

Mrs Brand looked in.

'I'm going home now, Mr Todd. Supper's in the oven.'

That ritual took place each evening. Mrs Brand was not resident. She lived only a short distance down the lane from Briar Cottage and came in daily. Except when he entertained, James led a somewhat spartan bachelor existence, to a great extent looking after himself with help from Mrs Brand.

'I've got a good lunch for you and Mr Stonor tomorrow,' she said, managing to announce good news in a tone more suggestive of condolence. 'It's special.'

'I'll look forward to it, then. Goodnight.'

Thinking back to the conversation with Count Rózycki he reflected that he had remained unaware of Madeleine's femininity for a remarkably long time. He had never experienced embarrassment at sharing a home with a girl because his sister had always been with him in Warsaw. In spite of occasional irritations,

Early Days

Madeleine had, he was obliged to admit, behaved kindly towards him, the stranger in the midst. Perhaps she had been prompted by a wish to please her mother who yearned to fill her big bereaved house; and, if so, all credit to her. Not every girl would have welcomed a stranger: jealousy might have been a natural reaction but, to be fair, meanness was never one of Madeleine's characteristics.

Of course, she had exacted a price. She probably had not realised how much her teasing hurt. It was mainly about James's frequent misuse of English idiom. Had he arrived at The Aspens knowing no English at all, and had she taught him, his lot might have been easier; but as it was he had learned the basics of the language quickly, and people, tending to assume he knew more than he did, were surprised when he failed to grasp a meaning. Mrs Todd had been so good at correcting him, never making him look a fool in company. In her methodical way she used to keep a record of his mistakes each day, and on the next would check that he had understood. Madeleine had been less charitable, but then she had been only fifteen at the time. She could have made life far more awkward for him had she wanted to; in fact she must have liked him from the beginning. And then there was his accent. Before the end of his first year at school his speech was virtually native. The occasional slightly unusual intonation did not seem particularly foreign, merely an individual peculiarity, but at the start Madeleine had not tried to conceal her amusement. She was always natural and found fun everywhere, and at the time he was fair game. Or rather, as he saw it, unfair game.

She had few friends. The war had not been conducive to parties and much travelling, and life in the large withdrawn house had been spent quite happily within the family. Since her father's and brother's death she had grown close to her mother. Apart from two or three school friends who came infrequently, her circle was almost as limited as James's, and far less stimulating. During James's last year at school, when his friends became increasingly frequent visitors, she often joined them. She liked all three and, although she was not very interested in the substance of their deeper discussions, she enjoyed their wit and would take sides at random in order to provoke it. John's sophisticated

Early Days

manner particularly appealed to her. He was the only one of them who smoked, a habit of which his parents disapproved, and she introduced him to the newsagent and tobacconist in the small group of shops a few roads away where he could obtain his supplies without risk of recognition. Kevin, the boy who delivered their newspapers, was sometimes to be found helping in the shop; a strange unkempt youth, whom John described as a latter-day Caliban. James tried out his father's holder on one of John's cigarettes but found little pleasure in it; he smoked rarely, and then only out of sentimental association.

The last two years at school had indeed been memorable, and he now realised they had brought him close to Madeleine by unobtrusive but ineluctable stages. He found the school work far easier than in the first year when the language was still an obstacle. His teachers were beginning to allude to the Oxford examination, and Mrs Todd was enthusiastic about it: she always urged him, 'Do what's right for you.'

He received the respect of his fellow pupils and of his teachers; more often than not his essays were returned marked alpha. He spoke in the debating society, and with Mr Asp he founded a group that met regularly to discuss philosophy. It was a heady atmosphere and he rejoiced in it. Naturally and inevitably, thoughts of Poland receded. Madeleine was attending a celebrated secretarial college in London where she was taught much more than mere clerical skills: it was also a training in the elements of commerce and, as business was often discussed at home, conversation flowed readily in the evening. Economics was one of the subjects that James was studying, and he found it stimulating to see how Mrs Todd's practical experience illuminated his academic learning. Madeleine was able to join in with her remarks on organisation and office procedure; suddenly the three of them felt very close, not only as a family but also as if they were in some way colleagues. The interests were not the same as those he used to hear discussed in Warsaw, but the very fact of their being common interests was important. Madeleine used also to type up his notes for him, and they would find themselves discussing them.

Guy Rowlands was Madeleine's godfather. The religious

Early Days

connection had never counted for much, but the association had meant that he was a frequent visitor – socially as well as on business matters. James liked him. At first he had admired and respected him simply as a hero of the First World War who had killed a lot of Germans; but subsequently he came to appreciate his wisdom and consideration: Guy was one of the few adults who did not ask him many questions about the war. He took James to visit the factory and the London office on several occasions, and sometimes Madeleine, who was very fond of her Uncle Guy, accompanied them. The office was spacious, comfortable and well planned: Mrs Todd had seen to that. On a large display stand were photographs of the types of aircraft in which Todd patents had been fitted, and the devices themselves were to be seen with parts cut away so as to reveal the mechanisms.

James remarked that there had been little in the way of new ideas since 1942.

'You spotted that quickly,' said Guy. 'I wish others would: that's part of the trouble.'

'I didn't realise there was trouble.'

'You're not alone in that. Unfortunately, many people whose job it is to read the signs haven't grasped it either.'

Guy explained that Peter Todd had been the brain behind the technological innovations and that since his death the firm had been able to run on heedless of the need for new ideas because the emphasis had been on mass production for the war.

'I dare say that if Peter hadn't died he would have seen the need for looking ahead to peacetime requirements. As it is, the firm is living off its innovative fat.'

'What about the design department?'

'Oh, it updates the existing ideas. There is no dire immediate danger, but the firm's weary. You see, people have been here too long – me, for instance – and design and production managers have grown old together. We did splendidly during the war, and for some years before it, and now we're shagged... Sorry, I used a word that perhaps I shouldn't.'

'Don't worry. I've been at school in England for a year and a half, you know.'

'True. Well, business is dropping even now, and it will go on doing so. It might not matter if we were still a family business, but shareholders will be asking questions before too long.'

James was greatly disturbed. 'But surely Mother knows about this?'

'Yes, but there isn't much she can do to turn it round. She's against sacking staff because there's still the feel of a family business in the air – but we try not to replace people as they retire. I'd say your friend Dr Silvermann is one of the few people who see things clearly, but he's a production man rather than an inventor: he knows what we need but he can't supply it himself. And even on the production side he has a job trying to get certain people out of their comfortable ruts. It's not good at all.'

'So what happens next?'

'We plod on. But what I'm afraid of is that we may be faced with an offer of a merger sooner or later, and shareholders outside the family will be offered very tempting terms.'

'But why should another firm want to buy us out if we're doing badly?'

'The point is that the firm's name alone carries a lot of weight in the public eye. Reputations last a long time, you know, and the sites and equipment are first class. It only needs some fresh blood to bring the whole thing to life again.'

Guy had then taken him to lunch at his club.

'There's something else that worries me. Are you sure that your mother is in the best of health?'

James was taken aback. He reproached himself for not having enquired more often after her health. There had been little need, for she always seemed energetic and very much alive. He said so to Guy. He was surprised, too, at the directness of Guy's question, almost as though he were treating him as the head of the family.

'I think it's something that you and Madeleine should take seriously. It isn't in Mother's character to give in easily, and I hope I am mistaken, but I thought I could detect some loss of thrust lately. Be very kind to her, James. She needs you.'

He did speak with Madeleine who, like him, had noticed nothing untoward, so they agreed on a little subterfuge. When James asked her how she felt she looked a little startled and

Early Days

wanted to know what prompted the unusual question.

Madeleine said, 'Well, Mummy, it's just that you haven't been quite your usual self lately.'

To their surprise she admitted to not having felt very well. That was the beginning of a dreary sequence of visits to the doctor, tests, and short spells in hospital for observation and, eventually, operations.

The revelations of his meeting with Guy gave James much food for thought. Characteristically he made his own mind up.

'Mummy, I've decided not to try for the Oxford exam. You don't mind, do you?'

'Of course not, but what's behind this?'

'I've been thinking a lot lately. Business could be good fun and I can always read philosophy for myself. So I thought of going to the LSE and taking an economics degree instead. There shouldn't be any problem about getting in.'

'I expect not. Do what you want, but I'm still puzzled about the reason why. It seems a rather sudden change to me.'

He was pleased that the conversation needed to go no further for the moment. He could not tell her that he felt he could be more useful to the firm, and give her some relief, if he were able to associate himself with it sooner rather than later. He could save a year by not taking the Oxford exam, and above all he could look after her better if he were living at home instead of in Oxford. He did not regard giving up Oxford as a huge sacrifice. The LSE would be an intellectual challenge, and London would provide plenty of opportunity for philosophical debate. He did have some regrets at not reading philosophy formally, but had no time for those intellectuals who derided commerce whilst enjoying its fruits.

A few days later Mrs Todd spoke to them again.

'I've been thinking. Now that it looks as though James is going to take economics and business seriously, he'd better start gaining some practical knowledge about finance. So, I'm going to give you both some money and I want you to use it for learning how to invest wisely. You won't learn that sort of thing from an academic course: you've got to get the feel of it by doing it.'

In that way Constance achieved two ends; the one that she had

Early Days

stated; and also solving the problem that had been exercising her for some time. She had been giving James the same amount of pocket money as Madeleine received, a very modest allowance, but she felt that in view of his anomalous situation he should have some money of his own. The problem had been how to give it to him without embarrassment.

To his surprise, he discovered a flair for handling money. With the help of the family stockbroker, and by speaking with Constance and Guy, he quickly acquired more than a basic grasp of the world of finance, and began to make small amounts of money. Great was his joy when he was able to mark his first profit by presenting Constance with a potted azalea. She was delighted.

'You'll never become rich if you spend your money on your girlfriends!'

Making money so easily stirred his scruples. It was not that he objected to money or its making. The experience of his short life had been enough to make him disenchanted with political attitudes at either extreme, but he felt that reward ought to bear some relation to effort. Presumably it could be argued that profit on the Stock Exchange was a reward for clear thinking, bold action and taking calculated risks, and was therefore justified. Even so the rewards seemed disproportionate.

On the other hand, he could not deny a feeling of sheer pleasure at making a profitable judgement. In some measure it was the same satisfaction as he could derive from making a telling point in a philosophical debate; in each case a matter of getting it right. The parallel, though, was valid only up to a point because whereas the intellectual process was wholly rational, speculation on the market was, in the end, a gamble. The degree of risk could be reduced by the use of intelligence and judgement, but ultimately the most rational decisions could be upset by unforeseeable forces. He resolved the dilemma by accepting that as a potentially profitable game gambling on the Stock Exchange was justifiable, but he could not see himself devoting much of his life to it. That, he considered, was in Madeleine's mind when she blamed him for not being practical. She lacked his flair for finance but told him plainly that she would make the most of what gifts she had instead of wasting time on philosophy. The one's hobby

Early Days

was the other's main interest.

He was now learning more and more from Guy and from Jacob Silvermann, both of whom treated him as a friend and without a trace of condescension. Each, in his own way, established an almost paternal relationship with him. He was highly conscious of their influence and became a willing if not uncritical disciple, gaining an entrance to two different worlds each with its own magic and wisdom. Jacob's was the more familiar magic, an extension and broadening of the one in which he had been brought up. It was a broadening process, because whereas in his father's house the world had been viewed and enjoyed from the security of a strong national tradition enriched with external influences, just as a gardener might embellish his local garden with exotic importations, at the Silvermanns the environment was more akin to a sea of ideas and stimuli in which one bathed. Occasionally the Silvermanns seemed to set foot briefly on the solid ground of a middle-European Jewish culture, only to immerse themselves quickly once more in an international flood. James had once asked Jacob whether he did not regret the absence of a national tradition, and whether the fact of being Jewish was an adequate substitute.

'One does not miss what one has not had. I know that many Jews expect the creation of the state of Israel to put everything right, but I shall wait on events. You see, there has been no Jewish nation since AD70 until now, and there is a lot of cant talked about the homeland. We don't know how it will develop. We shall have to re-learn how to be a nation.'

'Surely the fact of being able to go back physically to one's origins must be a great comfort?'

'I expect we shall visit Israel and absorb atmosphere, but you see we have been away so long that the actual ground is not as sacred as you might think – not to me, at any rate. It's different for you. Poland has had a chequered history, but its people have suffered on the spot, so the tradition is a national one. For us the tradition is cultural, and we can live it anywhere. Isaac and Rebecca regard themselves as being British; in fact he regrets having been too young to have fought in the war.'

'You don't consider yourself British?'

Early Days

'Certainly I do, and by deliberate choice. I could have emigrated to America, or France, but I chose to come here and now I would not willingly be anywhere else. This country has been good to me and my family, and I give it my loyalty. Yes, in that sense I'm British.'

'And in other senses...?'

'Oh, simply that I am not of the country. My children can feel British; in fact they usually call themselves English, because they were brought up here. Rebecca was born in London. I can't feel British in the same way. You'll probably be able to if you stay.'

'I wonder. There certainly are a lot of boys with foreign names at school, but their families have lived here for generations, and they're as English as Guy Rowlands.'

He regarded Guy as the epitome of Englishness.

'And what do you consider to be the hallmark of being English?'

'An impossible question to answer. Suppose I were to ask you what it felt like to be German?'

'I couldn't tell you. I was a German Jew; it couldn't be the same as being a German. One was always apart.'

'Do you think it is the same for British Jews?'

'I'm not sure. I believe many do feel themselves to be really part of the fabric of British society, and not only the bankers. That is what seems so strange to all of us foreigners, that while the British regard all foreigners with a mixture of pity, contempt and amusement, on the whole they do not single out any one group for special derision. It is partly attributable to the English Channel: immigrants are seen as being odd, not as threats, because their numbers are small – so why should they persecute them? I expect that in pre-war England it was as unpleasant to be a poor Jew as to be any other kind of poor person, and conversely.'

'I have heard my history teachers say more than once that Britain is much the better for its immigrants from "horrid continental persecution".'

'I've heard it said too, and they mean it, in a detached kind of sense, and of course it makes them feel broad-minded, but in practice you'll find that retrospective historical appreciation does

Early Days

not necessarily go hand in hand with being welcomed into their drawing rooms.'

James became conscious that he had not met any Jews in his parents' drawing room either, in spite of frequent allusions to Jewish writers and scientists, not because of any anti-Semitism on his father's part but because the family simply did not know any. The Silvermanns were the first and, so far, the only Jews that he had met in the flesh. He said so to Jacob.

'I'm not surprised. I would not have mentioned it but for your raising the matter, but the regrettable fact is that there was a lot of anti-Jewish feeling in Poland. If we had been Polish it is highly unlikely that you and Isaac would ever have become close friends: the air of a truly free country was necessary to bring that about.'

Jacob Silvermann opened James's eyes to wider and more general issues, but it was from Guy Rowlands that he learned the ways of the world. Guy was to a great extent a stereotype of his class. His intellectual education had ended with his school days. The books on his shelves consisted largely of the English classics that he had read as a boy and rarely re-read. As a boy he had learned to play the piano and was not devoid of natural talent. But he had allowed his skill to rust so that the instrument now served mainly as a topic of conversation, or was used by guests for playing an occasional popular song of the Twenties or Thirties. His pictures were wholly predictable: sporting prints, some Victorian landscapes, a couple of family portraits and a few prints of First World War aircraft in action, signed by a well-known war artist. He attended an occasional concert, and quite often went to the theatre, chiefly as a social occasion and because it was the kind of thing that his kind of person did. If he visited an art exhibition his comments were predictably at the level of 'What on earth is it meant to be?' or 'That reminds me of...' In matters of art and literature he knew what he liked. He took his holidays on the French Riviera in the company of similar Englishmen, read the right newspapers, deplored 'Trade Union mentality', contributed generously to charities and served his God formally as a member of his church choir – except when practices clashed with his social commitments.

It was easy to see him as a caricature, as though the umbilical cord of his intellectual development had been prematurely cut. In matters of the imagination and in all aspects of aesthetic appreciation he had remained at the level of a sixth former, and not a very sophisticated one at that. His intelligence, though, remained: he put it to a different use. What he lacked in wit and imagination he compensated for by wisdom and shrewd judgement of men and affairs. He was above all a very kind man, a respecter of persons and, in spite of his patrician manner and appearance, no snob.

He and Constance were James's guides to adult English society. He gently and often humorously corrected James's schoolboy English, and his literal translation from Polish, into language that would not cause amusement in adult company. James unconsciously imitated his diction, turns of phrase and use of understatement, so that by the time he went to university his English was not only grammatically, but also idiomatically, perfect. Constance wisely left much of the task to Guy, preferring to reserve for herself the role of mother. When she went to hospital for her first operation it was Guy who arranged visits, drove James to town and generally acted as friend of the family and practical philosopher. One evening they were driving together to London on their way to visit Constance: Madeleine, whose secretarial college was in town, would meet them at the hospital.

'Do you know just how ill Mother is?' asked James.

'It is hard to tell just yet. These growths are easy enough to remove, but the doctor suspects more may keep on appearing, so I'm afraid we must get used to seeing quite a lot of hospital from now on.'

'Is it deadly?'

'Fatal? Possibly. Well, we all have to die of something or other and in her case the cancer will probably be the cause of her death, but unless things get much worse very suddenly I think she'll be with us for many years yet. And feeling quite well for long stretches of time, too.'

There was a pause. Guy continued, 'How are you managing at home?'

'Oh, there's no problem about that. Madeleine and I both have a decent lunch, and she knocks us up a bit of supper. Not that I

Early Days

couldn't do it myself at a pinch.'

Guy smiled at the 'knocks up' and 'at a pinch,' further instances of James's adoption of his own slang.

'I think we'll have something to eat in town after we've seen Mother. Only if you can spare the time from your work, of course...'

'Thanks very much. I'm up to date.'

'Good. By the way I'd meant to ask you... you don't mind staying at home for the time being, do you?'

James was bewildered.

'Sorry, I'm not sure what you mean.'

'Well, because Mother had to go to hospital in a bit of a rush she didn't have time to mention anything... but Madeleine's a pretty girl, isn't she?'

It still took James a moment or two to grasp the point.

'Oh, you mean...'

'I mean you should be aware that it's a slightly delicate situation for you. You just have to be careful. I say, I do hope you don't mind my telling you this.'

'Of course not. Quite honestly, the thought hadn't occurred to me.'

Quite honestly, it had not. James was aware that he liked Madeleine. He had made a point of being pleasant to her from the beginning exactly as he had to her mother, out of natural courtesy and sheer gratitude for the welcome he had received. When she had teased him over his English he had taken care not to rise to the bait: instead he laughed with her and no resentment had been sown. Sometimes on Sundays, taking care that Constance was not present, she would poke fun at his going to Mass: that did irritate, and hurt. As his confidence grew he spoke more to her. He looked forward to evenings at home when they would tell Constance about their day at school and she spoke a little about the business. They squabbled occasionally, usually over some triviality, and she would storm out, banging doors. He liked the way she tossed her head when she was angry, he enjoyed arousing her high-pitched laugh. Yes, there was much that he enjoyed about having her near him; she was fun to have as a friend as well as a sister, especially as she got on well with his three main friends at school. He regretted that she did not share his more deeply felt interests, and yet that shortcoming did not make her uninteresting. He had, however, been totally unconscious of any stronger feeling than companionship until an unforeseeable circumstance, after he had left school, had jolted him into awareness.

5: Discovery

On the following morning James was busy. He left Briar Cottage in buoyant mood at the prospect of John Stonor's visit, and drove to Brocklechurch where he briefly attended an auction of farm animals and spent time at Mr Honeyman's bookshop. Mr Honeyman ran a small but discerning business. The little market town could sustain one good bookseller because it was the only one for miles around. His stock was modest, but he knew and loved the book business and what he did not have he knew how to obtain. James had made more acquaintances through visiting the shop than he had in his immediate vicinity, chiefly people much older than he, retired teachers and country parsons, with whom he browsed and then joined for coffee. He could just as well have ordered his needs through one of the big London booksellers, but his weekly visits to old Honeyman were the closest he could come to an exchange of ideas, and he treasured them. On this occasion he met Ivor Rudge, the Vicar of Folding, a rural parish not far from Brocklechurch.

Rudge, unlike most of Mr Honeyman's habitués, was a young man. James was intrigued to know how one so energetic as he could find fulfilment in a small country parish, and was keen to know him better.

'Well, Mr Rudge, what is your quarry today?'

'Nothing very profound this time. I'm looking for a present for my niece. Are you good at selecting books for eight-year-old girls?'

'Not really my forte. Is she a thoughtful girl?'

'Yes, I should say so.'

'Then how about a book of suitable poetry?'

'Perhaps, but it might not be what she'd most enjoy. I'm thinking about one of the Laura Ingalls Wilder's books, like *The Little House on the Prairie*, but I don't know which ones she already has. You're not an uncle are you?'

Discovery

'Alas, no. Or to be precise, I don't know.'

Rudge looked puzzled. James continued, 'You must find that strange. It's a complicated story but I'll tell you about it on a suitable occasion.'

'Do you fancy dropping in at Benn's for some coffee?'

'I'd like to, but an old school friend is coming to lunch so I ought not to dally.'

On his way back he stopped in Great Walling to deliver his envelope at Father Ryan's, and arrived home to find John Stonor in the drawing room.

'Greetings, oh most worthy son of the soil!'

'I'm glad Mrs Brand has made you comfortable. Did you have a good journey down?'

'Indeed, my magnificent chariot bore me like the wind.'

'Ready as ever with the flowing phrase, I see. I take it you refer to the geriatric barouche without.'

'Nay, sir – not geriatric, but venerable.'

When they met John usually began by affecting the extravagant language that he had practised at school, and James played up.

'Oh, come and have some lunch.'

John, intent on supporting his friend in his grief, was making his third visit in the eight months since Madeleine had gone away.

'Are your parents any happier about you now?'

'A slow and painful progress, I fear. They still feel that being a probation officer in Birmingham is a poor return for an Oxford education, but to their credit they strive valiantly to come to terms with my humble status. In fact I gather that in public, at least, they claim to be proud of what I'm doing. My pater is a model of loyalty, you know.'

'It is strange how unevenly society rewards different functions. One hears of eminent surgeons and lawyers, artists and footballers, successful businessmen and distinguished soldiers, but however well they may perform their task the most useful probation officers or nurses are unlikely to be described as eminent or distinguished.'

'Actually they might call them "devoted", like teachers, but there is a kind of condescension in calling someone devoted as opposed to distinguished; a kind of pat on the head for a worthy but distinctly lesser mortal.'

'But,' said James archly, 'think of the merit you are accumulating, your feet set firmly on the path to sanctity.'

'You jest, *mon cher ami*, but as a matter of fact I have been doing some serious thinking lately. About God, and suchlike.'

'Really? I thought your parents had put you off religion pretty effectively.'

'They did, although I went along with the externals for a long time because I didn't want to hurt them. They put me off the frills and the sherry and sandwiches aspect of church, but deep down I was never entirely serious when I used to scoff at faith.'

'I'm glad. Of course it's difficult for people like me, who have never seriously doubted, to get inside the thoughts of those who cannot believe.'

'I suppose that's true, but what surprises me is that doubts have never troubled you. I can understand a simple faith on the lines of "I believe it because that's what we were taught". That's all right for a peasant population, but your faith has never been at that level and yet it sticks.'

'I think it's unwise to decry what we call "simple faith", if only because who can tell what really goes on inside anyone else's mind? I suspect that much of the apparent "simplicity" arises from the use of simple figurative language to try, quite inadequately, to express complex abstract concepts. No doubt there was a time when most people actually thought of heaven as a place "up there". It seems silly to us today, and I doubt whether the "peasant" actually believes in the literal truth of that, but it is convenient to go on using the language. I don't suppose you help most people by knocking out the props unless you replace them by carefully thought-out reasoning, which most people are just not going to devote enough time and effort to understanding. But, look here, I'm giving you a lecture.'

'Perhaps you've missed your vocation. But seriously, did you never have a moment's doubt about a caring God during the war, or even... more recently?'

'During the war, no; possibly because so many of us were in the same boat, and our religion was part of the fabric of the nation. Besides, our country has been through so many vicissitudes over the centuries that we have come to see God as an ally in misfortune rather than as a handy solution to the practical problems.' He paused.

'Yes, I see that.'

'But as to more recent and personal history, I must admit that there have been times when in sheer despair I have been tempted to blame God for my own shortcomings. But that's not the same as doubting the wisdom of His basic plan.'

'You and Madeleine? I've never said this to you before, but I always did wonder just how suited you were to each other. I felt that you bore the burden of generosity; you were the giver and she the taker. I know that sounds a little hard, but do you know what I mean?'

James knew.

He had been in his first year at the LSE, enjoying a full and active student life, clouded only by Constance's ill health. She was back in hospital for an operation which, it was hoped, would at last stem the progress of her disease. He and Madeleine stayed at The Aspens; meeting briefly in the evenings, taking turns at visiting Constance. One day he told Madeleine he would go from college to visit Mother, and afterwards attend a meeting of the university Catholic Society.

'I'll have something to eat after the meeting. Don't bother to wait for me, I shan't be back much before midnight.'

The evening had not turned out as planned, and by eight o'clock, as he was walking up the drive, he noticed that the house was unlit. Inside was silent. He was not easily frightened but his heart quickened and he felt a prickling of the hairs on his neck. Making hardly any noise, he switched on a small table lamp in the hall, instinctively armed himself with a stick from the hallstand, and cautiously inspected the ground floor rooms. He found nothing sinister. He went softly upstairs and peered right and left on the landing. A thin slit of light glowed under Madeleine's door. He stood at the door and asked gently.

'Are you all right, Madeleine?'

He sensed a presence, but heard no reply, and boldly thrust the door open.

Discovery

Madeleine lay on her bed, dressed in her underwear. Also on the bed crouched the long-haired boy from the newsagent's, similarly attired. Both stared at him in terror and disbelief.

Misinterpreting the situation James leapt at the boy, grabbed him by the hair and round the neck, and forced him to the floor.

'Ring the police!' he shouted.

But Madeleine stayed, frozen where she lay, and covered her face with her hands.

'No,' she whispered. 'It's not like that.'

In blind rage James dragged the gibbering boy to the top of the staircase, thrust him down, pursued him, grabbed him again and flung him out of the front door. Then he came in and leaned against the wall, heart pounding and mind in anguish. Madeleine's sobs were clearly audible.

When he had recovered his composure a little he went back upstairs, each step feeling like an eternity, wondering what he should say to her.

She was still on the bed, sobbing uncontrollably into her hands, looking both pitiful and absurd.

He sat on the bed beside her.

He was pitiless. 'Would you like to know how Mummy is?'

She looked up at him in shame and anger, and fell to sobbing again.

He went below and returned with a large bag and the fire tongs. With the tongs he picked up the various items of the boy's clothing and dropped each, with an expression of cold contempt, into the bag.

'What are you going to do with them?' she whimpered.

'I'm going to put them in the dustbin.'

She looked desperate.

'How's he going to get home? It's freezing.'

'That's his problem,' James replied coldly. 'I think he is unlikely to return to claim them.' With that, he left to perform the task.

He returned to Madeleine bearing a glass of sherry. He drew a blanket up over her. Violence, and the passage of a little time, had abated his fury, leaving only sadness. Gently he said, 'Madeleine, why?'

Discovery

She just gazed at him, limply.

'Why did you let him see you?'

'He wanted to. He asked me.'

'What's that got to do with it? What about you? Why did you let him?'

'He asked me,' she murmured in a tormented whisper.

'Why him, for goodness' sake? What right has that creature got to ask?'

She rallied a little, and replied with returning spirit, 'As much as anyone else, I suppose.' Then her budding courage failed her and she added, 'But nothing... happened – really it didn't. Kevin said he wanted to see me, and that's all there was to it.'

James would not speak the boy's name.

'So he got his cheap little harem scene because you felt sorry for him. Is that it?'

'You can call it that if you like, but, Jim–' and there was desperation in her eyes, 'nothing happened. You must believe me!'

In spite of the cruelty and despair in his heart he did believe her. He felt a great weariness.

'How was Mummy?'

'Fine. The operation took place this morning and they seem to think she's come through it well. She was still a bit drowsy so we didn't speak much. She sends you her love.'

The obligation of conveying her mother's message to Madeleine, notwithstanding the fact that in the circumstances it would embarrass rather than cheer her, gave him a certain savage satisfaction. He did not find his reaction edifying.

'Well, I'm off to bed. Would you like me to make you a pot of tea?

'No thanks, Jim. Goodnight.'

The next day was Saturday. When they met at breakfast time, he was surprised at the extent to which she had recovered her composure and even her spirits. He had expected to find her more subdued.

'We'll go to see Mummy together today, shall we? he asked.

'Yes. That would be nice.'

'And afterwards I'll take you somewhere for dinner.'

Discovery

'Good. Jim, about last night. I know it was silly, and what bothers me most about it is having caused you so much distress, unnecessarily.'

She saw his face grow stern, and went on quickly,

'Will you be saying anything to Mummy about it?'

'Certainly not. As far as I'm concerned it's over and done with. In any case it's not really any of my business.'

'It didn't seem like that last night,' she said archly, with just enough twinkle in her eye not to appear facetious, and wondering how far to push her luck. 'You reacted more like a jealous husband than a brother.'

It was a measure of James's ingenuousness that her words had been necessary to make him conscious of his feelings, to awaken him to the nature of sentiments that had lain hidden in the mundane exchange of everyday life at home. For a man of his intelligence, James was as naive in matters of emotion as he was sophisticated in those of the intellect. Madeleine's words had jolted him, but he did not immediately leap out of his reserve. Half of his mind tingled to the question 'Is this an invitation?' while the other half commanded, 'Don't lower your defences.'

★

As he sat opposite John in the study, reflecting on his friend's penetrating judgement – 'you were the giver and she the taker' – he could not entirely blame Madeleine. She was essentially honest and had never promised more than she had given. Perhaps he had expected more than she had ever intended. He had never told John about the incident with Kevin, and even now would not lower her reputation gratuitously in the eyes of his best friend.

'Do you know what Madeleine is doing now?'

'Yes. She's working hard at making a success of her secretarial agency. I believe it's going very well.'

'Do you actually meet, or speak?'

'We haven't met since she settled in London, if only because I don't often go up, but we have spoken on the telephone. It really is an absurd situation.'

'How is it going to end?'

'You'd have to ask her. There's been no talk of divorce and as far as I'm concerned there is no dispute, no acrimony. It is still as she said at the time: life with me is unexciting, and she doesn't think much of being stuck in the countryside. I don't believe she hates me, and as for my feeling...'

'Yes?'

'I'm very fond of her. Don't ask me about love; I've come to the conclusion that I've a lot to learn,' he said ruefully. 'Obviously, for me divorce is out of the question. I mean that even if a legal divorce took place I'd still consider myself married. Madeleine hasn't even mentioned it. I think business is consuming all her interest for the time being.'

'If you are still fond of her, in spite of some of the pretty unkind things she said at the time, I should think you still want her as a wife.'

'It's very strange. In a sense I was wrong to have married so soon; I still had some adapting to do, and I think I was swayed partly by a semi-conscious wish to make Mother happy. Mind you it's all very well to be analytical about it now. At the time I was convinced I wanted to marry, just like anyone else. Always assuming that people do get married for the same reason... Why *do* people marry?'

'You are not talking to an expert. At Oxford I had the customary round of girlfriends, but since I've been doing my present work my life has been positively monastic. You see, much of my visiting has to be done in the evenings, or even at the weekends, whenever my clients are free, and in the daytime I have to attend courts and write up my reports. It amazes me that probation officers ever get round to marrying, although some do. You should ask Bill Sturton.'

Bill had married Rebecca Silvermann eighteen months previously, to the delight of Jacob who gained a son-in-law after his own heart and to the distress and confusion of the Sturtons at being joined to a family that was not only Jewish, albeit non-practising, but foreign. They survived the experience because Jacob's urbanity and sheer kindness broke through their defences, but for some time they existed in a state of cultural shock.

'I must ask them down before the autumn. Guinevere is six months old by now I suppose?'

Discovery

'Yes. I saw them a couple of months ago when I attended a conference in town. Bill is quite a doting father and, although babies aren't really in my line, I must admit that Guinevere is delightful. Trust Bill to chose an Arthurian name; he's an incurable old romantic.'

'I fancy it was romantic attraction, in the artistic sense of the word, that drew him to Rebecca in the first place.'

'Definitely. He fell in love with her particular sort of beauty about the time you came to school, and nursed a secret passion for years. Do you know that all the time he was at the Slade he used to write to her twice a week? He had to keep his feelings away from his parents because he had already given them one shock in deciding not to go into the business, and knew how they would react to his wanting to marry Rebecca! I had a similar problem over my choice of career. Parents take a lot of managing, particularly if you happen to be fond of them.'

'I've sometimes wondered how my relationship with mine would have developed had circumstances been different. I can't believe we would have quarrelled.'

'One never knows, although from what you've told me your relationship seems to have been pretty exceptional.'

'They still seem very close to me, but I can't be sure to what extent I remember them in an idealised way. I suppose I see my parents in the same light as parents remember a child who died very young; all joy and no scowls. Anyhow, so Bill and Rebecca are making a success of marriage?'

'They are a perpetual mutual adoration society. He paints a portrait of her every few weeks, and she sketches Guinevere almost daily between nappy changes. They will be one of the most highly illustrated families in history.'

'So he is concentrating on portraiture, is he?'

'Yes. He's gone a long way since he painted that,' said John, looking towards Constance Todd's portrait. 'Mind you he was able to manage a decent likeness even then.'

'It was his first commission, although I bet he'd made several portraits of Rebecca from stealthy observation before that. I remember Mother had a hard job persuading him to accept a fee. It wasn't that he actually needed the money, but she thought it would encourage him, which it did.'

Discovery

The rest of the day passed in friendly reminiscence. James felt his world widening whenever he met one of his old friends, thrusting open the gates that enclosed him in his self-imposed seclusion, and admitting life from a wider, more exciting, but also hurtful world into which he had ventured and from which he had retired wounded.

On the following day James took John round the estate, of which he was rightly proud because its present efficient condition was entirely the result of his energy. It had remained in the family, having been bought in vain for Nigel, largely idle and ineffectively run by a local manager. Not long after he and Madeleine were married, the problems in Humphrey Todd & Co. that had so greatly exercised Guy Rowlands came to a head, and the foreseeable merger took place in 1953. The Todd family relinquished all interest in the new company, and most of the board, including Guy, resigned. The terms were generous. Constance became very rich and so, on her death the following year, did her children.

They sold The Aspens, bought a flat in London and went to live at Briar Cottage. Madeleine immediately set to turning it into a home while James became an instant farmer. It was ironical that the business for which he had elected to read economics instead of philosophy should haven been shot from under him almost as soon as he had qualified, but, nothing daunted, he threw himself into estate management with as much vigour as he had into business.

James drew up at a gate that led into a large copse.

'This was a wilderness when I took over, total chaos, everything competing. We cleared the floor, took out the feeble saplings and then trimmed the good trees. Eventually it will yield a reasonably sound crop of ash, but obviously a plantation started properly from scratch would be more productive: I'm hoping to do that on the next slope in a year or two. Let's walk through.'

They walked through the copse, James enthusing about its features which showed every sign of careful management. On reaching the far side they looked out on a large meadow that sloped down to a stream. A herd of beef cattle grazed peacefully. The meadow was well hedged; the gates were strong and easy to

Discovery

operate, the willows along the stream were neatly pollarded. Everything that John saw bore the mark of a plan, the result of thought and of considerable energy.

'Seeing all this, I can understand the kind of driving force that saw you through the war.'

'How do you mean?'

'Well, you are really two different people. I can see you more clearly now. Half of you is a dreamer, wanting nothing more than to read and dream in seclusion, the popular imagination's image of the absent-minded scholar in his book-lined study. The other half is pragmatic, energetic, determined to succeed. I saw it in action at school when you bashed your way through to a marvellous Certificate. Now, what did you know about estate management when you came here? Nothing, I imagine, but you have turned a run-down estate into a model of efficiency.'

'I have a lot more to show you, and it isn't all in good order yet. It hasn't really been difficult because luckily I had money to start with and it enabled me to begin by putting things right while I am learning on the job.'

'How did you decide where to start?'

'By a simple process of reasoning. I knew nothing of estate management or agriculture, so there was no point in embarking on anything very sophisticated. I decided first to stick to beef cattle and tidying up generally. I sacked the idle manager and advertised for a competent cowman, and employed local men to lay hedges, restore fences and do some very elementary forestry. The cattle give me an immediate return, which covers most of the current expenses, and in the meantime I am learning. I got in touch with a university department of agriculture, which put me on to publications and courses. I read a lot and visit plenty of places. My aim is to make an estate that will leave me enough time to spend on the things that really interest me – there's your absent-minded scholar coming through – so I shall probably concentrate on forestry. I'm full of ideas.'

'You've got it all worked out, I see. It's a pity that Madeleine couldn't make it a part of herself.'

'It began well. The house is almost entirely her creation; in fact she planned everything apart from the study. She talked about

Discovery

starting a boarding kennel, and then about running some kind of employment agency, and various other plans but she found it difficult to settle down to any one idea. Quite apart from any of my shortcomings I think she missed London, not that she led a particularly social life when she was there, but I suppose she liked to feel she was living in the midst of a lot of people.'

'You know, James, that sounds so unconvincing to me that I find it hard to think you really believe it yourself.'

'Touché. The fact is I am baffled. Our marriage seemed just to evaporate, without drama, except at the end when she announced her decision to return to town.'

'Any chance of a change of heart?'

'Who knows? Perhaps. I should like to think so, but don't know what to do about it. You now observe me in my ineffectual role.'

'From the depths of my vast bachelor experience I should say that the remedy may require a little time... but that the start should not be too long delayed. The man who set out to learn agriculture from scratch should not be daunted by this challenge.'

'It's not the same problem at all. One can learn by going to the right authorities: are there any professors of wife retrieval?'

'Well, different authorities. What you need now is wisdom, not knowledge. Who are the wisest men you know?'

'Jacob Silvermann and Guy Rowlands, of course.'

'I prescribe an urgent appointment with the good Doctor. In the circumstances a married man may have more to offer.'

'You may well be right.'

They continued on their tour of the estate and the rest of the day passed in pleasant conviviality. Late in the evening when he was on his own, James's mind turned to what John had said.

It was evident that, for all his refusal to play the amateur psychologist, John's intuition had sped to the heart of the matter and brought James to grasp that he wanted Madeleine back. The shock of her departure had numbed him to such an extent that he had passively accepted the situation. Now he felt angry at his acquiescence, whereas previously he had blamed himself for inadequacy. He had stumbled into marriage, floundered in it, and now he must thrust himself back into it. John was right; every day

Discovery

that passed without action on his part made the road back more arduous. What had gone wrong? How had each of them failed? Each, for now he refused to accept all the blame.

Madeleine had fallen in love with him before he knew his own feelings, at a stage when he merely noticed that she was a pretty girl, was amused at some of her mannerisms and liked her company. He was too immersed in other demanding pursuits, chiefly of the mind, to notice the signals that she vainly gave, but her nature was growing unconsciously on him. He now saw more clearly what lay behind the pathetically grotesque incident with Kevin in her bedroom: he recalled her words – 'He asked me' and 'He wanted to see me' – the implication being that his own apparent lack of interest in her as a woman had led her to acquiesce to Kevin's bizarre request. It had taken James, who was not endowed with an English sense of humour, several years to see the comic side of that incident, and even he and Madeleine had not alluded to it. A mistake, he now thought; it would have been wiser to have laughed about it together and exorcised the ghost.

Things had moved fast after the incident. The fire it kindled in him roared. He hardly recognised himself in his role as ardent lover. His friends observed the phenomenon in amazement. Constance, who had returned from hospital feeling much better, watched it with delight mingled only with concern lest it should burn itself out. James ceased being an excessively serious young man and revealed a lost boyishness, which did not prevent him from devoting himself to his studies; his energy was boundless. They married a fortnight after his final examination, which gained him a first class degree, and immediately set themselves to learning the workings of the firm at first hand.

They had been joyous days, looking to the future before it became clear that the merger was inevitable, but when the family interest in the firm came to an end and, with it, their common task, the spirit changed. Constance's terminal illness kept them together, but after her death and their coming to live on the estate they had simply drifted apart, Madeleine's disenchantment with country life turning first to moroseness and then to desperation.

James had not been excessively distressed at the loss of the

Discovery

business because he had confidence enough in his financial acumen to believe he could make his own way in the world, even though at the time he had no idea of the wealth that he would inherit. Constance's death, however, although long expected, dealt him a cruel blow. It left him feeling more isolated than his own mother's death, when he had had the protection of his father and sister. Instead he was Madeleine's support.

Constance's final decline had been gentle and only intermittently painful, and she had been fully conscious of it. As the time for parting came manifestly closer, James could not but contrast the negative, secular, attitude to death displayed by Constance herself as well as by Madeleine and Guy, who was a constant visitor, with the sacramental and positive attitude that he remembered from his original home. Constance, ever practical, spoke about the likely consequences of her death in the material sphere. She was concerned about its effects on Madeleine. Her attitude was full of kindness and consideration; all the paperwork was set in order because she did not want to be a nuisance to anyone; but of any sense of the ultimate purpose of life and death there was no visible sign.

Guy's and Madeleine's concern was all about the alleviation of pain, just as they would have worried about the dying of an old and much loved family pet. How James longed to be able to pray with Constance instead of only for her! He admired her strength in the absence of any apparent sense of resurrection, and wondered what was going on in her mind: did she really regard herself merely as a machine running out of power? Was her sense of immortality so private that it could not be discussed, even with those who were closest to her? Did it exist at all? He could not share his thoughts with Madeleine, but he did mention them to Guy who, unusually for him, displayed embarrassment and confusion and confined himself to saying that these matters were too personal to be discussed, locked in too many mysteries. It seemed to James that dying in post-Christian England was a very lonely business, to be swept as far as possible under the carpet, almost as though it were rather bad manners to cause so much trouble to one's friends and relatives.

Eighteen months had now elapsed since Constance's death,

Discovery

and nine since Madeleine had left. James remained emotionally drained, numb and perplexed, while he carried on his daily work energetically and externally unaffected. He could not believe that Madeleine hated him, but did he love her sufficiently to do whatever was necessary to reunite them? What was necessary? A wise man's counsel was needed, as John had prescribed. Or should he speak with Bill Sturton as being of his own generation? Better not, perhaps. Before going to bed he wrote to 'My dear Jacob', and felt the better for having done so.

The next morning, over breakfast before John's departure James told him he had taken his advice.

'I'm glad,' said his friend. 'You'll do better asking Jacob than Bill and Rebecca. They're such a pair of lovebirds that they wouldn't begin to understand your problem.'

6: Colloquy

The days between the despatch of the letter to Jacob and his reply were a period of turmoil for James. He had embarked on his working life earlier than his friends because after their university days they had done their National Service, from which he had been exempt. Now, while they were feeling their way in the world, he had already come to grief. He felt not only sadness but also a sense of the ridiculous, the embarrassment of an intelligent man contemplating failure in marriage – the sphere in which, as a Christian, he most wanted to succeed. It was an insult that this should have happened to him.

Another matter exercised his mind too, a mere administrative detail but yet another aspect of his ridiculous situation. Where should he stay during his visit to Jacob? At the club to which Guy had introduced him, or at Madeleine's flat? His flat, after all, for were they not married? What if she were no longer alone? He did not believe she had a lover, but suppose she did? His intrusion might destroy any chance of reconciliation. Or would a bold approach be best, just to let her know he was coming and take her out to dinner, as though he were courting her? 'Well, make your mind up,' he could imagine her saying, 'be practical.'

In the event Jacob solved the problem for him. He telephoned. As James heard with joy the deep confident guttural voice he imagined the cloud of cigar smoke that swathed it, and waited for comfort.

'So you're going to bring us a breath of country air? I think I can just about stand it.'

'It's wonderful to be talking to you again, Jacob. I'll come up tomorrow if it suits you, and as soon as I've settled in at the club I'll ring you.'

'Don't be silly. Ruth insists you stay here, for as long as you like. Rebecca is here too, with little Guinevere, while William's away at a conference; she's longing to see you.'

Colloquy

The Silvermanns still lived in the house that James had known. Jacob had retired from the firm at the time of the merger, and now he and Ruth devoted themselves to their artistic pursuits and to following their granddaughter's progress with undisguised pleasure. They had been delighted to watch the growing attachment between Rebecca and William, had understood his intentions even sooner than her, but had feigned complete surprise when, having put on his best suit, he had asked for an audience with Jacob and formally requested his daughter's hand. Jacob and Ruth then worked hard at reconciling William's parents to the unconventional match.

Jacob was out when James arrived. Ruth and Rebecca welcomed him effusively, and he was duly taken to worship at the shrine of Guinevere.

'What's Bill doing?' asked James.

'He's been ever so lucky. He's been asked to design murals for the conference hall at Rushford University, so he's gone there for a week to have a look at the site. It could be a big opportunity: I think it was offered to him because the Vice-Chancellor saw some of his work when he visited the Slade.'

'That's very good news. And what about his everyday work?'

'Well, he was lucky there too. He gets plenty of commissions for portraits of sweet young things, in debutante-type dresses and hairstyles, for which their proud papas are prepared to fork out appropriate sums. It keeps the wolf from the door, with a little help from both sets of mummies and daddies. Here she gave Ruth one of her large-eyed smiles, which had originally entranced Bill. Ruth purred in silent appreciation.

'Does Bill actually enjoy painting these glamorous creatures?'

'No, of course not. He says they either have no character at all or else are stuck-up little so-and-sos, but one must live. Obviously he'll drop that kind of work as soon as we can manage without it.'

'Where is Izzy at the moment, Ruth? Still in Germany? Do you miss him terribly?'

Izzy had surprised, though not disappointed, his family by becoming a soldier. He had taken a first class degree in civil engineering at Imperial College before doing his National

Service. He enjoyed the Army, was commissioned just in time to see service in Korea and won the Military Cross. At the end of his service he took a regular commission in the Royal Engineers.

'I miss him, obviously, but he's very happy with what he's doing, even though he doesn't think much of being in Germany. He's a good letter-writer.'

When Jacob arrived they talked again about Izzy.

'I must admit I was surprised,' said Jacob, 'because he had talked about doing research, and in view of his degree he would have been welcome in any institution in the country, or in the States for that matter. I had rather assumed he would go in for an academic career: we hadn't discussed it in any detail but that seemed the likely outcome.'

'What caused the change?'

'Well, strange as it may seem he really enjoyed being in the Army. He turned out to be a lot tougher physically than we had imagined. You remember how you all disliked games at school... I don't think he had any interest in the team games for their own sake, but the strenuous exercise and camaraderie he found in the Army did appeal to him, perhaps by contrast with the academic concentration at Imperial. A different aspect of his personality showed itself.'

'He didn't write to me very much, I fancy he was too busy. But from what he said I gathered he'd discovered an unexpected satisfaction in service life, and reading between the lines I detected something else too; a wish to prove something not just about himself, but about himself as a Jew.'

'Ah, you spotted that, did you? One might go further and say as a Jew of German extraction. See it through his eyes. He was brought up in a country that lived heroically through a war; in fact one of his best friends is a Pole who took part heroically in it. But he was born in Germany and his parents still speak with a foreign accent. His people have been murdered en masse, virtually without resistance, which may be the acme of martyrdom, but it is a rather passive form of glory in the eyes of someone of his age.'

'And in addition,' said Ruth, 'he has come from a country where it was very difficult for a Jew to make his way in public life. Even here at school he came up against some prejudice, as you know. So when he found he got on well in the Army he began to think hard about his future.'

'I think it goes back further than that, Mummy,' said Rebecca, 'because even before he went in he said something about the need to have Jews represented in the armed forces.'

'I never heard him say that.'

'Now we are hearing secrets from little sister,' said James. 'What else did he say?'

'He felt it would be a kind of exorcism if he were to get to the top, because during the war lots of German Jews who wanted to fight were either interned as aliens or only allowed to join something rather unexciting like the Pioneer Corps.'

'That's exactly the impression I formed from his letter, although he didn't say so in as many words.'

'That accounts', said James, 'for his mixed feelings about serving in Germany. On one hand a kind of poetic justice, on the other a terrible, empty sadness.'

'Didn't he have difficulties regarding nationality for getting his commission?'

'Immense difficulties, but in the end "they" agreed. Our own anti-Nazi credentials were very positive and documented, and Guy Rowlands used some influence to move the bureaucracy along, but it took time... Ought you not get your own nationality position cleared up?'

James was still officially stateless and travelled on a British document that was not a normal passport.

Owing to worries about Constance Todd's health, they had never completed the procedure for his adoption, although for several years he had come to use the name Todd-Zagorski out of courtesy to her. In practice he was known as Todd, but he was loath to part with his family name. He replied, 'You're right of course. There comes a time when one must face facts, and the fact is that my Poland doesn't exist and England has become my home. But it isn't easy, even so. You once explained that a German Jew found it hard to feel a sense of nationality, but for me the present regime in Poland is merely a phase, however long it may last, and the country is still my country.'

'I rather envy you,' said Jacob.

Later in the evening, while Ruth and Rebecca were attending to Guinevere, Jacob said, 'Well?'

'I'm not sure where to start.'

'You start by asking yourself what is the one biggest problem on your mind. The rest will follow.'

'Fair enough. The one biggest problem is my injured pride – a very Polish disease, I suppose,' he said wryly. 'How do I know how much of my dismay to blame on injured pride and how much on rejected love?'

Jacob smiled. 'You know, my dear James, for an intelligent man you can be singularly obtuse.'

'Now you're sounding just like Madeleine.'

'Let me explain. I don't see how you can fail to feel some injury to your pride on being rejected, whether you love Madeleine or not. It is always hurtful to be set aside, and even a saint would feel it. So the real question is whether you do love her. It would be impertinent of me to answer that for you, but there are ways in which you can answer it yourself. If you conclude that you still do, then act.'

'I miss her, but can't honestly claim to feel miserable without her. That's what worries me when I compare our situation with Bill's and Rebecca's. I should think that if Rebecca were to walk out on Bill – which heaven forbid – he would feel desperate.'

'True, but the situations are not strictly comparable. Quite apart from physical compatibility, William and Rebecca are linked by many common interests. They share the same world, and Guinevere.'

'You mean children are the answer?'

'Not necessarily, but they can help. In any case, you don't have to love your wife in the same way as William loves his, or I mine. You say you miss her. In what way?'

'Physically, up to a point...'

'Do you mean sexually?'

James realised that he had never before spoken with an older man about such personal matters. He was familiar with the Church's teaching on marriage and sexual ethics, but in a dispassionate, detached way, and the circumstances of his own boyhood had deprived him of the homespun wisdom which would certainly have come from his father; while Guy Rowlands had been as coy in those matters as he had been forthcoming about business and the practicalities of living.

'Yes, but that's my main worry. Our life was so troubled to begin with, Mother's sickness and the business worries, that sex never became the dominant feature in our married life. The time somehow never seemed to be right. Is that bad?'

Jacob's eye twinkled with merriment.

'Many people would regard it as disastrous. I don't think it has to be, although nature usually finds a way of creating opportunities in newly married couples. It may be simply that the physical side of love matters less to both of you than it does to most people and, if so, there's nothing to worry about as long as you have other things to share. How else do you miss her?'

'It's mainly that I enjoyed her physical presence, just having her around the place. It doesn't sound very dramatic, but it meant a lot to me.'

'An excellent sign, although it's an aspect of marriage that usually comes later. Quiet affection is a much better basis for lasting happiness than ardent passion. Perhaps you have a more mature attitude to marriage than your age would suggest. My difficulty is to see the problem, whatever it is, through Madeleine's eyes, and why she should have felt so strongly about it as to go away. How do you suppose she sees it all?'

'Put bluntly, she came to find me boring. I ask myself why she discovered it only after we were married, considering that we had lived in the same house for several years before.'

'Forgive my asking, but do you mean that she ought to have formed an opinion of you as a sexual partner before you married?'

'No, of course not. As far as I know we both remained chaste. I meant she found me boring as a person, in a general way.'

'You know, this is a more intimate conversation than I ever had with either of my own children. I think it is time you stopped denigrating yourself, stop blaming yourself for everything. Be positive, and...'

'There again, that's just what she used to say.'

'Look, she had a point. I'm no psychologist but it seems to me you are a complex character. By nature you are reflective, what

Colloquy

people who don't understand thought call vague, but when you are engaged in business you can set that aside and become direct and incisive. The dreamer's side of your nature invades your private life, which appeals to your philosophically minded friends, myself included, but may grate in the everyday business of marriage. I know one must beware of generalisations, but in my experience most women like things to be cut and dried, one thing or another, and are less interested than men in "ifs and buts". I think that applies very much to Madeleine.'

'Absolutely right, but surely she should have known what I was like long before we married?'

'She may have half known it, but she was very young; and don't forget that before you married and for a short time afterwards you had a common interest in the firm, where she may have experienced the more compatible side of your personality.'

'Are you saying that if we are to get together again and make a success of it I shall have to do some changing, to fit in more with her original picture of me?'

'In a word, yes. It's not a case of changing your personality by some deliberate manoeuvre. That would be absurd, if not impossible. You are yourself, and she must accept that, but little adjustments to your responses, meeting her halfway or even further at times, taking an interest in things that matter to her, even though you may regard them as unexciting – all that kind of thing oils the wheels – and eventually, almost without knowing it, you will find that your marriage runs smoothly. Always assuming that love is really present.'

'Isn't there a touch of acting about that? I wouldn't go so far as to call it hypocrisy, but you know what I mean. Isn't there a danger that in moving towards each other we'll lose our individuality?'

'Not so much a loss of individuality as a willing surrender of it as occasion demands. To others, except perhaps to very close friends, you and she would appear no different from what you were before. The sinking of individuality is something between the two of you: without it marriage fails, and if it is one-sided the marriage is warped and becomes a matter of mere convenience for one party and servitude for the other.'

Colloquy

'The time has come for being positive, hasn't it?'

'I think so, if you want to retrieve your marriage. And, as a thought on which to leave this Socratic dialogue for the moment, my dear, dear James, don't take yourself too seriously.'

He winked at James, through the smoke, and James felt, deep down, stirrings that he had not known for two years, which filled him with a mixture of excitement and apprehension. Should he, or should he not? He was greatly inclined to try.

7: *Action*

Sleep largely eluded James after his conversation with Jacob. As he had hoped, his wise old friend had opened his eyes to the reality of the situation, giving him the desire and strength to deal with it but not telling him how to proceed. In Jacob's comments there had been none of the 'If I were you' and 'Why don't you?' beloved of intrusive, pushing, advisers who are more concerned to make their friends the prey of their own self-esteem rather than to serve them.

He sat up in bed for a long time after he had finished saying his prayers, unable to sleep and deriving no help from reading. He prayed again, in his own words, with long pauses, uncertain what he was praying for, scarcely conscious at times even of what he said, at first earnestly, then desperately and finally with quiet confidence. What would he say to Madeleine? Phrases came with difficulty and were quickly rejected: one was trite, another too contrived and the next would merely make her laugh derisively. He flung reason and calculation aside, would plan no more but let himself be led by the Spirit when the time came. If it were God's will that they be reunited, reunited they would be. At two o'clock in the morning, sleep finally overcame him.

He woke late, missed breakfast, and came upon Jacob in his study. James was surprised at the absence of the customary smokescreen and then realised that Jacob was not alone: he was cradling Guinevere in his arms.

'Good morning, my dear boy. You observe me in an unfamiliar situation. Most of my womenfolk have gone shopping and given me an opportunity to be useful. I haven't been able to do this for a quarter of a century.'

'You don't seem to have lost the touch.'

'One doesn't.'

'What would you be doing if you weren't doing this?'

'Scribbling something or other for a technical journal, or

Action

reading *The Times*, or roughing out some ideas for a book on art history on which William has been kind enough to ask me to collaborate – all of them eminently deferrable in favour of this task.' He paused briefly. 'For a while, at any rate.' He fondled Guinevere, and continued,

'Do you know what proportion of Jewish parents in Europe in 1939 are now able to do what I am doing?'

'Regrettably few, I imagine, but I've no idea.'

'I can't quote a statistic either, but I look back at the people I knew. Of the seven Jews I worked with closely in the firm that I left in '36, one other saw the way things were going and is now in America. One somehow survived the war and is now in Israel. The rest perished, with their families. So you see that what I am holding here is not just another baby. She is what I suppose you would call a miracle, just like your own presence here.'

During the many years he had known Jacob, James had not often heard him allude to the Holocaust. Indeed, he had rarely known him to be solemn, though often serious in a humorous kind of way, a trait that greatly reminded him of his father and had helped endear Jacob to him. James said, stroking Guinevere's hair, 'Certainly I regard this as no less a miracle than my survival. You are a happy man.'

Jacob, with his customary tact, did not ask James whether he had come to any decision about his dilemma. Instead, James asked to be allowed to use the telephone. He rang the Galaxy Secretarial Agency, and was about to ask for Mrs Todd when he realised that Madeleine had answered the call herself.

'Madeleine, I didn't expect to find you on the end of the line. Isn't this taking democracy too far?'

'My receptionist has gone sick suddenly and my secretary's on holiday, so we're a bit pushed today.'

'Well, if you can't solve a secretarial problem, what hope is there for the rest of us? When can you get a replacement for your receptionist?'

'I expect we'll have one tomorrow. Where are you?'

'I'm in town. How about a highly qualified male receptionist for today? And what are you doing this evening?'

'You're rushing me, Jim.'

Action

'That's a fair comment. I'll be with you by midday.'

Within minutes he had rung for a taxi, packed toothbrush, shaving gear and pyjamas in his briefcase, and was on his way to the West End. Jacob had permitted himself the observation, 'A promising start, as the school reports used to say. *Finis coronat opus.*'

Madeleine's premises were small but exuded an air of efficiency, which immediately commended them to James who recognised the result of Constance's methodical mind in her daughter's well-run establishment. It looked businesslike, the systems worked, and the atmosphere was softened by a feminine touch in the decoration and layout. Madeleine had prudently begun on a modest scale, putting her money into a good address and a first-class secretary, but had kept her staff small until the business grew. This was James's first visit, and he was impressed.

Their meeting had been accomplished with less embarrassment than he had feared, if only because Madeleine was single-handed, except for a temporary typist, and the business of the day had to be done. He kissed her gently, not passionately, immediately he saw her. She responded awkwardly, cautiously, as though she wondered whether a precedent was being set.

'You're looking splendid,' he said. She was wearing a simple black dress with just enough jewellery for unostentatious elegance.

'You're very smart. No gumboots?'

'No. I left my felling axe behind too. Now show me that reception desk.'

Then the telephone rang and there was no more time for pleasantries. At one o'clock Madeleine sent the typist out for her lunch and asked James what he proposed to do about his.

'I'll stay here. It won't hurt me to do without for a change. Besides, I'm looking forward to a good dinner. You go and have a bite.'

'You're going to share my sandwiches. I knew I wouldn't be able to get out today so I brought some.'

They munched her sandwiches in the office. She produced a flask of coffee.

'There's only one cup,' she said.

Action

'You have some first, and pass it on to me. Like a loving cup.'
She raised her eyebrows.
'A loving cup?'
'Yes, a loving cup'
'Oh Jim, what went wrong?'
'Speaking for myself, I was selfish.'
'I'm not sure that's true. But I was. I still am.'
'Tell me, darling, is there anyone else?'
'No, absolutely not. It's not like that.'

His mind returned to the night of the absurd incident of Kevin in the bedroom. She had used more or less the same phrase then. Why did she always tell him 'what it isn't' instead of 'what it is'?

'Please, I'd rather know now. It would hurt less than hearing later.'

'Jim, I promise you, there is no one else. You may find it hard to believe, but when I finish here I go back to the flat, make myself a bit of supper and go to bed early, worn out. Apart from an occasional semi-business engagement I have hardly any social life. No time, and not much inclination.'

'Wedded to your work, as it were…'
'You might call it that.'
'Have you made many changes in the flat?'
'Hardly any apart from redecoration. What do you mean?'
'So the double bed is still there. Good.'
'You are rushing me. I don't know. Give me time to think.'

'In view of the present pressing state of business I suggest dinner earlier rather than later, and early to bed to ensure a good night's sleep. I'll make the arrangements.'

'There's a hungry look about you, Jim.'
'Well, I didn't have any breakfast…'
'That's not what I meant.'

Then the telephone rang and their lunch break was over. In the course of the afternoon James booked a table for the evening, told the Silvermanns not to expect him until the next day, and arranged for a temporary receptionist to start work the following morning. There were many calls, from firms and organisations wanting secretaries, and secretaries seeking employment. James was kept busy. Madeleine was running a general office staff agency but dealt only with highly qualified secretaries, many of them multilingual, because she had foreseen the expansion of business at home and on the Continent. Although she was not a skilled linguist she had detected a growing market and had advertised accordingly. She was, without a doubt, highly intelligent.

James saw little of Madeleine during the afternoon. He spoke to her several times on the internal telephone when he needed to check details, and he showed a couple of callers in to her, but all the time his mind was in turmoil. She had not greatly resisted his invitation to dinner, nor his intention of spending the night with her: a token resistance, perhaps. Thus far his plan, if he could call his atypical, unconsidered actions a plan, had succeeded beyond all expectation. Could he sustain it through dinner, and after?

He felt almost certain that Madeleine had told him the truth when she asserted that there was no rival claim on her affections. He was buoyed up on the flood he felt he had released, now he must let it take him where it willed, but at some crucial moment he must guide it where he wanted. Where, he was not yet quite certain, but he would trust to... what? Would he call it instinct, or trust in God? Matrimony was a sacrament after all, so it was not unreasonable to expect guidance if sought in good faith. There, he thought, I'm off again, theorising. For some time there had been a lull in the office, the telephone was not ringing. Idly, he looked at the calendar, the fifteenth of August. 'Good heavens, the Feast of the Assumption,' he said out loud.

So engrossed had he been in his private worries that he had, for the first time, clean forgotten a holy day of obligation. It disturbed him. Even during the Warsaw Rising the Assumption had been remembered in his father's enclave. The chaplain had celebrated Mass for those who could attend, and had gone on his rounds distributing Holy Communion as best he could through the fire and the shells.

No terrible circumstances justified his forgetting today, and yet although he experienced regret he felt no discouragement: in trying to save his marriage he was substituting one good for another, and, in any case it was now too late to repair the

Action

omission. He would have liked at least to visit a church this evening and pray in the Lady Chapel, but to do so now might complicate matters. Madeleine was not hostile to his religion; she thought it rather odd and un-English. They had been married in church, although since it was a 'mixed marriage' he had had to forego the joy of the nuptial Mass. Why now run the risk of provoking a situation that might militate against the evening whose outcome lay in the recesses of his mind, which he scarcely dared articulate but from which he hoped for so much? He would make a point of praying to Our Lady privately.

When the office closed James changed roles. The receptionist metamorphosed into... the husband? The suitor? He was still unsure which part to take: he would let events decide.

They went first to the flat and James deliberately kept out of Madeleine's way while she changed. He remained in the drawing room, reading and looking. He was almost a stranger to the flat, although in fact he had a key, because when they sold The Aspens he had devoted himself to the farm and they had left the flat almost in the state in which they had bought it. It contained a lot of furniture from The Aspens, but the redecoration had been undertaken by Madeleine after the separation. She had done it well, the flat was elegant, and his only criticism was that he had to look hard to find a bookshelf, for Madeleine's reading was confined largely to coffee-table books.

She did not keep him waiting long, and when she appeared he was surprised but not disappointed. The young wife whom he had known only a few months ago had blossomed, transformed into a handsome woman, confident on her own ground, demanding attention, commanding respect.

'You're looking lovely,' he said with genuine appreciation.

She smiled. She knew he would be impressed, and was pleased. 'Where are you taking me?'

'Wait and see. Now give me five minutes in the bathroom while you get on with the sherry I've poured for you.'

That little husbandly action touched her much more than a lot of words would have done. She curled up on the settee and waited. Like James, she seemed calm and composed, but inwardly she was in as great a turmoil as he. The business day had allowed

Action

her little time for serious thought, but continually at the back of her mind lay the awareness of the absurdity of her situation. Here she was in her office, running a business that she was building up with energy and efficiency, and enjoying it, while out there in the reception area was the man whom she had left. No that description would not do, she was too honest to deny it: the husband whom she had let down. He had turned up out of the blue, and almost without asking or ceremony had taken command first of her problem and now of her evening. His motive, although not much had been spoken about it, was plain enough – but how ought she to respond? What did she want? Certainly not to give up her venture and bury herself in the country again; and yet she did feel a warm affection for Jim in spite of his silly ways. The flat felt the better for company, and it was a long time since anyone had brought her a glass out of love rather than just out of social courtesy. What, *what* should she do? His decisive action had commended itself to her, just as had his quixotic action on the occasion of the Kevin incident, although she had been careful not to let him know it at the time. Now, one half of her felt the urge to restore their relationship while the other shied away lest, once re-established, she should be ensnared rather than fulfilled by it.

James took her to an excellent restaurant. Wheeler's was always reliable for fish, and with the Dover sole he ordered a rather exotic-sounding wine from Alsace. It was delicious.

They were at no loss for conversation. He spoke of the estate, vividly but not at great length, preferring to hear her describe the business of which his day in the office had given him a clear impression. As they spoke, ideas were exchanged, and Madeleine began to feel that she was talking with a partner. After some time she brought the conversation back to the estate.

In spite of herself she was drawn along on the flood of his enthusiasm, and she asked questions, made suggestions. All of a sudden she paused. The unaccustomed interest alarmed her. Was it but the influence of the occasion? Or the wine? It made no difference; she could not switch off now even though she knew she was opening the gate to a road along which she did not want to travel. They spoke of mutual friends. He told her about John Stonor's visit, which pleased her because John had always been

Action

one of her favourites; about Guinevere, which alarmed her; and about Izzy making a career of the Army. While they drank their coffee James said, 'Well, I suppose you'll be wanting an early night.'

'It wouldn't be a bad idea,' she replied non-committally, 'there's a lot to do tomorrow.' Then she found her voice adding, despite herself, 'But I must admit I haven't enjoyed myself so much for ages.'

'I'm glad. Neither have I.'

Back in the flat they soon retired to bed, each trying to conceal from the other a sense of excitement, mixed in his case with hope, and in hers with both desire and alarm.

'Jim,' she murmured, 'I'm right in the middle of the month.'

He held her very tight, and said nothing.

Madeleine's alarm clock woke them. James, who was by nature an early riser, brought her a cup of tea, and they took breakfast together in a close and earnest silence.

'I'll see you to the office, and if your new receptionist fails to turn up I'll stay – if you want me to.'

'Of course, but I expect she will. It's a very reliable agency.'

In that case I'll take the opportunity of looking in on my stockbroker before going back. Mind you, there's a lot we haven't spoken about yet.'

'Yes, I suppose there is.'

'I'll come again soon, and in any case, I'll write.'

'I'd like that. Funny isn't it, how less than a day can change things? Almost like an accident.'

'I don't believe important things just happen accidentally, even when they appear to.'

'*Now you're being profound again!*' they said simultaneously, and laughed. He kissed her.

'Do you know that's almost the first time we've laughed together?' she said.

'I think you may have just made a very profound remark...' he replied.

The temporary receptionist did arrive, and James set off.

Action

Madeleine saw him to his taxi. They kissed warmly and she said, 'Thanks for coming, Jim. Thank you very much indeed – and for, you know...'

'God bless you, darling.'

He drove first to Westminster Cathedral, where he spent a few minutes in thankful prayer, and then went to see the Silvermanns, who were all at home. Their discretion was perfect, although the attention with which they greeted his every remark betrayed their hope that he would broach the subject of his mission.

Eventually, having described Madeleine's business, the state of her health and what she had worn to dinner he said, 'Of course I don't want to burden you with mere personal details.'

'Of course not,' purred Rebecca, 'but we're dying to know.'

'I think the visit was not in vain. Perhaps the moment was right. I felt closer to her than we had been for months before she left, and I believe she shared my feelings.'

'Some bridge-building was achieved?' Jacob asked.

'At least a beginning – what Izzy would call a pontoon bridge. Something more permanent will have to be built now, and that's what I'll be praying for.'

James's relationship with the Silvermanns was such that he often found himself making Christian allusions in their presence, quite naturally and without embarrassment, even though Jacob could only be described as a humanist and Ruth at best a nominal adherent to her faith. Rebecca, as far as he knew, never mentioned religion at all. In spite of being remote from him in the confessional sense, they had become his surrogate family so much that, although they could not follow the terms of his religious language, he found more solace in opening his heart to them than to any of the few Catholics whom he knew. Jacob, especially, had an intuitive grasp of the direction of people's thoughts, so that James would have found it difficult to mislead him even if he had wished.

'I think you will be seeing rather more of me from now on. Madeleine wants me to come.'

'That's wonderful news,' said Ruth.

When James took his leave Jacob accompanied him to the door.

Action

'So it would seem that the end did indeed crown your endeavour.'

'So far, yes. As to the future, I devoutly hope.'

It was night by the time he returned to Briar Cottage, and he was not long in falling asleep in spite of the sudden summer storm that broke over the countryside.

8: Progress

Mrs Brand arrived punctually, as usual, wet but undaunted by the rain.

'It's very good of you to have come.'

'I'm not easy to put off, Mr Todd. My work's my work. Did you have a good holiday?'

Mrs Brand could not conceive of any reason for going away, except for the holidays that she knew town people took.

'Not quite a holiday, but it certainly was a useful journey. Is there any news?'

'Father Ryan rang yesterday. He didn't say what he wanted.'

'Never mind, I'll ring him. I'll be staying in this morning, but I'll keep out of your way in the study.'

He looked at the mail of the last three days; an unexciting set of envelopes which he did not trouble to open for the moment. Instead he stood at the study window, enjoying the storm. A few days earlier the majesty of nature in turmoil would have evoked in him sombre reflections on the lot of man and the chaos of life, but today he saw instead only the unrestrained excitement and thrill of nature, and his heart sang in response. He paced the room from one side of the big window to the other, pausing intermittently to revel in the storm's reckless energy, and in the midst of its passion he experienced a calm, expectant, peace. Thank God for his friends, for John and Jacob who had dragged him and guided him out of his fruitless inactivity, and for the words and manner with which he had addressed Madeleine. He prayed, not in spoken word or even in ordered thought, but blissfully, from the depths of his being and with peace in his heart.

For a long time he remained in that state of quiet contemplation, and emerged from it to analyse his new situation. What had he achieved by his journey? Was the achievement real, or was he building a dream on the strength of one lucky day?

Progress

There could be no doubt about the warmth of Madeleine's welcome; it went far beyond mere gratitude at being helped out of a temporary business problem. She had let him make himself at home in the office, their dinner had been a complete success and their night a joy. What if her apprehension was to be realised... suppose she should conceive? The possibility had not deterred her on the night, but how would she respond: with delight, horror, dismay? Would she then give up her business and hate him for it? Or she might seek to get rid of the baby: no religious scruples stood in her way.

His whole being revolted and he felt sick at the very thought. Was his horror at the possibility of what she might do, or at his sneaking inability fully to trust her? And in the absence of trust what point was there in going any further? Of one thing he could be sure, that although she might not act in accordance with his conscience she would not act deceitfully. She would tell him what she intended to do, for her honesty was a virtue he could not deny.

He realised that his sombre thoughts had robbed him of the final minutes of the storm's beauty. It was no good to raise hypotheses about the course of events; once again he was allowing thoughts to run away with him. He must be positive. The need was clear, he had to fan the flame that he had relit, and he would no longer be a tragic husband but a lover. Before beginning his day's work he would write Madeleine a letter.

It was his first love letter. Having lived as a member of the family ever since he entered The Aspens, he had never had cause to write to Madeleine. Circumstances had deprived him of all the fun, excitement and anxiety of courtship; no meetings, no waiting for the postman or the telephone call, no need to devise elaborate stratagems. Now, instead of merely writing he would send her flowers and telephone her frequently. At first she was to be overwhelmed and perplexed at the onrush of his enthusiasm. Then, swept along by it she would enter into the spirit of the game.

As he sat down to start his first letter he could have foreseen none of the happy outcome. He wrote at length, telling her of his joy at their reunion. Without pretending to be anything but a

Progress

fervent suitor he laid his heart bare and wrote freely, passionately, not caring whether he made a fool of himself for at least he was a happy one. A shaft of darkness intruded: what if all this were to be in vain, suppose she were to laugh at his earnestness? He cast off the unworthy thought. After all, had she not taken him at face value on his visit? Perhaps the months of separation had been necessary to make them appreciate each other. He returned to his writing, filling the pages quickly, concentrating on feeling rather than art. It did not take him long to finish. He leaned back, feeling both spent and elated.

I hope she enjoys reading it as much as I did writing it, he said to himself. Oh Madeleine, reply quickly.

He lit his pipe and dressed against the weather. A walk to the post office was exactly what he needed. Might it not be more prudent to post the letter in Brocklechurch? At a village post office there was always a danger of something going wrong, a letter carelessly allowed to slip out of the box or, who knows, perhaps the postman might fail to collect. The fact that he had always posted letters, however important, in Great Walling without accident did not weigh with him. He went to the garage, drove quickly to Brocklechurch in order to catch the midday collection, and posted his letter before going to old Honeyman's bookshop. He did not merely push the letter into the box, but listened to hear it strike the bottom, and checked carefully to ensure that it had not become stuck. Then he checked again.

James realised he had come to Honeyman's out of habit; exceptionally he had neither a specific purchase in mind nor the intention of browsing on any particular shelves. Old Honeyman, who was finely tuned to his regular customers' behaviour as well as to their tastes, noted James's indecision and trundled amiably towards him. With his wrinkled face, bald head and pouchy cheeks, he reminded James of a patriarchal chimpanzee.

'Good morning, Mr Todd. You seem a trifle adrift today. Can I help?'

'I was somewhat preoccupied, but happy.'

Old Honeyman was mildly surprised at James's assurance of happiness, out of keeping with his customary reserve. He always treated his customers with friendly courtesy but addressed them

Progress

without any trace of a shopkeeper's deference. He continued to be a bookseller from choice, not necessity, and could easily have retired many years earlier; but he preferred to exchange both banter and ideas with his customers, whom he regarded as visitors: his shop was his 'salon', the customers his guests whom it was his duty to entertain.

'It is good to be happy. I have always made a point of it. Of course, joy cometh from within.'

'Who said that?'

'To the best of my recollection, I did.' He stretched his broad ape-like grin. 'Mind you, by the time you get to my age you'll find you've read so much that you can't remember whether you are speaking in quotations or not.'

'Is it a good thing to speak in quotations?'

'For some people it would be quite the best thing.'

'I suppose it might. Has anything of special interest come in?'

'Not a great deal. A new edition of your illustrious fellow countryman, but I expect you've read all of him.'

James looked puzzled.

'Conrad. Wonderful stuff, great writing. I've loved him ever since I was a boy, but he is one of those writers who speak to you differently at different times in your life. I fell in love with the sea through reading him as a boy, but when I read the same books now I realise that the sea is only the vehicle for what he really wants to tell me, magnificent vehicle though it is.'

'I must confess that I have not read all that much of him. I always thought of him as a writer of sea stories.'

'It used to annoy him to be thought of like that. He would say that he wrote stories about men and women, which is what novels are about.'

'In that case I ought perhaps to have read more novels,' James said with feeling.

It was old Honeyman's turn to be puzzled.

'Do I detect more than a literary interest?'

'Oh, it was just an aside, really. At the back of my mind was the thought that anything which enhances an understanding of life is worth studying.'

'Are you sure that you are expecting the right things from your

114

reading? Novels are about life, but they're not meant to be sources of information. They're like extra windows on the world, but to get into it there's no alternative to opening the door oneself and travelling on the path using one's own feet.'

James was seeing old Honeyman in a new light. They had often passed the time of day and even discussed philosophy, but never had he revealed enthusiasm like this. The furrowed old face, simultaneously loveable and absurd, grew more agitated as he warmed to his argument.

'You see, the characters in a novel are particular people, set in particular conditions. The working out of their individual stories reveals something about human nature. In a way one does move from the particular to the universal, but everyone has to make his own journey towards understanding the universal, so you can't expect novels to shed much light on your own particular journey. What they may do is sketch out some characteristic human situations, in which you may recognise your own. Even so, they can't give you the answers: it's not what they're designed to do.'

Their conversation was interrupted by the arrival of another customer who claimed Honeyman's attention – to James's regret, because he was fast forming the impression that in the old man he had found a local extension of Jacob Silvermann, a man with whom he found an affinity, with whom he could speak instead of merely exchanging words.

He nodded goodbye to Honeyman and went across the market place to Benn's coffee shop, thinking he might find one of Honeyman's habitués there. He saw no one he knew, but decided to stay for some coffee and a pipe before going home. It was strange how a few minutes' conversation with Honeyman had exchanged the world of Madeleine and emotions, in which he had been immersed but an hour ago, for the world of the intellect and the imagination. Both worlds were good, and he could easily switch from the one to the other, but he regretted that there was so much he could not share with Madeleine. It was not that she was antagonistic to abstract thought, but rather that she allowed it to pass her by. Did it really matter that there existed areas which they could not tread together? He had to admit that it did. Of course it did, but was the lack of common interests so great as to ruin their chances of happiness in marriage? His visit to Madeleine suggested that love and affection could overcome differences, but how much did that recent experience owe to the drama of the occasion, and would it stand up to daily wear?

'There, you're being introspective again,' he heard her say, and he was sufficiently on the road to recovery to laugh at himself.

For the next few weeks he devoted himself to the estate, working long hours at walking over it, measuring and preparing in great detail for the winter planting of trees. He chose to map the area himself, which amused the labourers whom he hired from the village and whom he turned into surveyors' assistants. He could well have afforded to have the land professionally surveyed, but it gave him aesthetic pleasure to do it himself and produce his own large-scale map over which he placed tracing paper for working out his use of the land. He was full of ideas, as he had told John, and only needed time to work them out. Although he did not draw or paint he had a highly developed aesthetic sense, which his parents had sown in him, and he wished to make his estate an object of beauty as well as of profit. Trees were grown mainly in order to be felled, but that was no reason for unimaginative planting. He made good his ignorance of nature by reading and seeking advice, which he often took.

He intended to plant in great variety, which the experts told him was economically unsound, he wanted to build some model cottages in order to house his workers and, above all, he wanted to start a nursery for rare and exotic trees. The idea of the nursery appealed to his aesthetic imagination and also to his business sense because he believed there would be a demand in Britain for things to enrich the country as it enlarged its post-war pleasures. His business schemes had developed over the last two years, but now he looked at every idea to see how and where Madeleine could fit in: would she be interested in designing the cottages, or in the business side of the nursery? Probably not, but that did not prevent the possibility of her participation forcing itself into his thoughts. After all, most husbands and wives didn't work together, but now she might at least take a comradely interest and not scoff at his enterprise. He refused to be discouraged.

A few weeks later, Count Rózycki's sudden death brought James back to London. During the ten years he had known the gentle old man they had met only occasionally and corresponded infrequently. James had remembered him particularly at Christmas and Easter, when they exchanged greetings, but since his move to Gloucestershire he had not seen him. Now he reproached himself for not having called on him a few weeks ago. Various Polish groups had kept in touch with James, especially in the first years of his settling down in England, and he read their publications, but Count Rózycki was the only individual whom James knew well and who had been personally involved in his introduction to the country. Although they had never been very close, he felt gratitude and affection, and now a deep sense of the loss of yet another link with his native land. He felt the pinch of conscience too: 'Never forget Poland.' Up to a point he had forgotten, and he was displeased with himself.

He had telephoned Madeleine immediately, although he had done so only the day before. She pretended to be put out.

'Jim, you're killing my work! I got your umpteenth letter this morning. I can't keep up with all this attention.'

He told her about Count Rózycki.

'Oh. I am sorry... he was a nice old man. We hadn't met since he came to Mummy's funeral. Yes, of course I'll come to the funeral.' She paused. 'In a way I suppose you could say he started it all, didn't he?'

Emotion surged within James.

'I feel I owe him a great deal.'

'Yes, darling. Me too.'

After the funeral they dined with the Silvermanns. James had kept Jacob informed of his bridge-building, as they called it, and when he let it be known that he and Madeleine would be attending Count Rózycki's funeral together, Ruth wasted no time in inviting them.

The entire family was present, Isaac having returned from Germany on a week's leave, intent on doing his duty as an uncle. They wandered around the garden, enjoying the beautiful Indian summer's evening before going in to dinner, Isaac making a fuss of his little sister, who walked with one arm in his and the other

Progress

in her husband's. Jacob was talking earnestly with Madeleine on the subject of gardening, about which neither of them knew anything, because he wanted to engage her attention and break ice before dinner so that subsequent conversation might flow freely. They had scarcely spoken to each other since Constance's death. James and Ruth walked together. She had produced a splendid garden, and he was genuinely interested in what she had to say because not only had he taken to gardening out of a wish to improve the appearance of Briar Cottage, but also his fertile mind had sensed business opportunity in garden plants as well as in trees.

'Now tell me, Ruth, you have a huge variety of plants here. Where do you get them from, and where does the average suburban gardener go?'

'All over the place.' She named several specialist suppliers. 'Depending on how fussy one is. But I suppose your average suburban gardener just goes to the shop in the high street.'

'And finds what he needs there?'

'Yes, but not much variety.'

'So that a place which supplied everything the gardener wants, from seeds and plants to gardening equipment and composts, and even things like cold frames or small greenhouses, would fulfil a need? The gardener's equivalent of a good grocer or ironmonger.'

'Yes, as long as it was big enough to carry a large stock. You know, somehow I feel that your interest in this is not just horticultural: I think your mind is on to something. But we'd better go in now.'

She called the family together.

'I'll just go and see that Guinevere's all right,' said Rebecca. 'Want to come and have a look?'

She took James and Madeleine upstairs. Bill joined them.

'Only a quick peep,' said Rebecca, 'because Mummy's got dinner ready.'

A quick peep was quite enough for Madeleine, in whom babies aroused little response, although her manners concealed her indifference. Rebecca adjusted Guinevere's little blanket, which needed no adjustment, because mothers always do. Bill gloated. They looked briefly at Rebecca's small easel set up on a table, on which was her latest sketch of Guinevere. James sensed Madeleine's lack of enthusiasm and his heart sank a little at the thought of yet another potential hazard to the success of their union, but he set the thought aside and as the four of them stepped gingerly out of the room he put his arm gently round her shoulder.

He again felt the absurdity of his situation. They were still separated, were they not? Nothing had been said by either of them about the formal resumption of their married life, although he thought of little else, and fancied that the idea was in the forefront of her mind too. Indeed, his continuous correspondence made it impossible for it not to be, but while his letters declared his love he had held back from suggesting formal reunion for fear of frightening her off. They would sleep together tonight, and in all probability... Now with his arm round her, and in the absence of resistance on her part, he felt more like a lover than a husband; their meeting had the flavour of a tryst. Perhaps Jacob would describe that as an excellent sign. Actually, it was rather fun.

Conversation at dinner was animated. James was seated opposite Isaac, observing the extent to which he had changed. Earlier in the evening, Rebecca, whose generous nature always made her live in other people, had proudly shown James the photograph of Isaac in uniform. She pointed out the ribbon of the Military Cross and the Korean Medal, more pleased at his achievement than if it had been her own. The photograph revealed a scholarly soldier, for even as a young officer Isaac had made no attempt to ape the military image; no carefully trimmed moustache, no dashing figure. On the other hand, looking at him now in civilian clothes, sitting between his mother and Madeleine and paying lively attention to both, he saw no longer the quiet self-effacing Izzy of their schooldays. He had changed; very confident in his bearing, more positive in his movements, occupying the large powerful body in which he had formerly seemed rather lost.

'What's it like being an intellectual soldier?' asked James.

'I know what you mean. In practice one learns to distinguish between the job and one's self. There is time for reading and thinking, and one has to make sure one uses it, but the job itself can be stimulating, particularly if one looks beyond the day-to-day

Progress

work and asks oneself what will be needed in ten years' time, and how will it be done?'

'But what of the brutal and licentious soldiery?' asked William, whose National Service in the Navy had left him with mixed feelings. 'Don't you often feel rather lonely? Can you find kindred spirits?'

'The soldiery, or for that matter my fellow officers, are probably no more licentious than any other group of men in a factory, or on a farm, or even in an office, which means that they are pretty licentious. That's the nature of the beast. When men are away from their families they don't behave in quite the same way as in their semi-detached suburban homes, but I've come to accept people as I find them.'

'So you've become all things to all men,' said James.

'That's rather well put,' said Jacob.

'I can't claim authorship,' replied James with a broad smile, 'it's a quotation from a part of the Bible that you may not be familiar with.'

'Well, now that I have more time, perhaps I should put it on my reading list.'

'I'll make a good Christian of you yet!'

'But what about Bill's kindred spirits,' asked Rebecca. 'Have you found any?'

'I'm not too sure what a kindred spirit is, but I think one can be good friends with people in the absence of a close intellectual affinity. And anyway, how often can one hope to find really deep friendship apart from one's partner in marriage? We four have been lucky in having come together at school – if John were here we'd be complete – but I can't say I have found a really close friend since then. Has either of you?'

'No,' said James positively, 'not among my contemporaries.'

'I'm not so sure,' said William. 'I think one or two of the people I met at the Slade may turn out to be close friends.'

He turned towards his father-in-law whom, like James, he regarded as a fountain of wisdom.

'What constitutes friendship? Do you think it can be analysed?'

Jacob thought long.

'I would distinguish between friends and kindred spirits. I am ignoring the popular use of the word "friend" to mean acquaintance. I should call a friend someone whom I like, although I might not find it easy to explain exactly why, and who shows me affection in return. It may help if we have some common interests to begin with, but there need not be a great many. I'm not at all sure what causes the initial attraction. It may be things of which we are only partially conscious at the time, like facial expression, or tone of voice, or sense of humour.'

'And kindred spirits?'

'Oh, that has a much less elevated status than friendship. I presume that Hitler and Mussolini were kindred spirits in the sense of being fired by many of the same ideas, but their association was merely one of convenience, whereas the essence of friendship is that it holds firm even when it becomes inconvenient.'

'Then surely', said William, 'Izzy must have come across kindred spirits in the Army, since he is with people who have chosen to follow a rather special sort of life.'

Isaac agreed. 'Yes, but people join the Army for all sorts of reasons, not all idealistic ones, so it doesn't follow that my brother officers are necessarily kindred spirits – although some of them are.'

'Taking Father's point about suffering together,' said Rebecca, 'didn't you find Korea helped?'

'Yes, of course, men become very close in the presence of danger, especially if it is prolonged, and it makes them glad to see each other occasionally at reunions, but that's not the same thing as friendship. Being at school together is different because the friendship can grow over a period of years.'

'And', said Ruth, 'it happens at a formative time of one's life.'

'And', added James, 'it is an environment in which one not only laughs and suffers together but also loves and hates people together. Incidentally, has anyone heard how old Hack is getting on? Has he published again?'

The ladies exchanged the slightly desperate expression that they often do when their menfolk start reminiscing about their schooldays, which is the same look trapped husbands wear when their wives launch into a dress discussion.

'Very much so,' said William. 'He's having a fruitful retirement. When I met him recently at an "arty" gathering he was declaiming some very unschoolmasterish verses. It seemed a far cry from the scrag-end rugger team, except that he was still smoking himself to death. A remarkable old chap, and quite a poet too.'

'Do you remember how we used to speculate on where he kept his muse? I wonder whether he ever had one.'

'She would have had to have worn a gas mask.'

'Poor woman, if she ever existed,' said Ruth, who for twenty-six years had protested unavailingly at Jacob's cigars.

'Sorry, Daddy, I raised the forbidden subject,' said Isaac with a laugh, looking at his father's mock-alarmed face. 'I'm sure cigars don't count.'

'I'm sure they do,' replied his father.

Madeleine was taking little part in the conversation but felt, and looked, involved in it. She watched and listened as this extended group of relatives and friends joked, reminisced and discussed serious matters. The sight of these happy and successful individuals, obviously not cast in a uniform pattern but evidently united in kinship and friendship, stirred her, and reminded her that here was something of which she had long been deprived owing to the family bereavement when she was still a young girl. Apart from Guy Rowlands, who had windows on a wider world, all her parents' circle had been tied up in engineering and business. She had done well at school, had received a good education and passed all the required examinations, but here, in the company of a soldier, engineers, artists and philosophers who all felt at home in each other's world, she felt completely inadequate, ignorant and uneducated.

Ideas, apart from technical ones, had hardly ever entered into her parents' conversation. She realised, with a touch of pain, that almost the only occasions on which really live conversation had taken place had been when Jim's friends had visited, and she had sat on the edge, not deliberately excluded but unable to mesh in: she simply lacked the equipment. Did it matter? Now she was launched in business, was proving herself to herself, and was probably as shrewd as any of the present company. She certainly had Jim's respect as well as his love, and they could share interest in each other's material activities even if they did not share the activities themselves, but was that enough for life together when the world of ideas, which was so important to him, was foreign territory to her? Could she invade that territory? Did she really want to? Was it too late to start, and would she feel a fraud? She had to admit that the friends' discussion had held her attention, and it felt as though her eyes were being opened.

William interrupted her reverie with, 'How's business, Madeleine?'

Any inadequacy she felt vanished as she warmed to her subject. Urged on by the family's perceptive questions, her reserve dropped away and she described the problems of breaking into an established area of business, how she had identified a specific need for highly trained multilingual secretaries, how she selected them, and advertised. She thought, These people are interested in everything, they're not just being polite because I'm their guest, or Jim's wife... Then she suddenly realised she was monopolising the conversation and declared, 'I'm talking too much. Sorry!'

'On the contrary,' said Jacob, 'I find it fascinating to see your dear mother's energy and enthusiasm coming out in you. It makes one wonder how much you would have contributed to the old firm if history had been different...'

'Another woman at its head in ten years' time, perhaps?' said Ruth.

'Who knows', said Jacob, 'to what extent these talents and inclinations are inherited. Now James, for instance, has shown a facility for making money on the stock market and a talent for agriculture, neither of which as far as I know are areas in which his original family were particularly interested.'

'That's quite true,' said James. 'In fact money was hardly ever spoken of at home. That sounds smug, doesn't it, suggesting either a simple life or lots of money. In fact it was neither; our parents' circle was highly sophisticated, but the pleasures we enjoyed didn't depend on having a great deal of money. There was enough, and that was that. I suppose my talents – as you call them – for making it arose out of necessity. No one led me into them.'

Progress

There followed a discussion about the relative importance of inheritance as against environment, a field in which none was an expert, but Jacob and James had some knowledge through their reading.

It was very late when James and Madeleine returned to the flat.

After they had left, Jacob said to his family, 'I think Madeleine felt at ease, don't you? It may have done something to help them.'

'You're a crafty old bird, Daddy,' said Rebecca.

'What, me? Crafty? – I just let nature take its course.'

'But of course,' she laughed.

When James and Madeleine returned to the flat well after midnight they wasted no time in going to bed.

'Don't forget that I'm a working girl. I need my sleep.'

He put his arm round her, and drew her close.

'It's not the right time, darling. But I am glad you came with me today. It meant a lot to me.'

She squeezed him in reply. They said no more, and fell asleep in each other's arms.

9: Despair

It was late October, and the rapprochement between James and Madeleine had grown apace when she discovered that she was two months pregnant.

All her self-possession deserted her. How could she reconcile the life of a busy and successful businesswoman with dull domesticity? She knew virtually nothing about babies, but a vision of nappies and little clinging arms and sleepless nights tormented and appalled her. Her mother, splendid in so many ways, had not prepared her for this, this ghastly fate. Would she have to employ a nanny, never be able to go away for a weekend, fill the flat with a mess of toys? On top of all that what about the birth itself, the pain, the sheer inconvenience? Most worrying of all, she could imagine Jim's response, and dreaded the thought of her indifference jarring on his delight and corroding it. It was so unfair that this disaster should strike her now, just when she was launched in business. The only answer was to get rid of it quickly, before Jim realised... But how to go about it?

She must speak with someone, but she lacked friends. There were no women to whom she could go, not even one really close school friend. It would have to be Guy Rowlands. He was her godfather and she had confided in him before, and he was a man of the world: he would know what to do, and even though he was a bachelor he would know where to ask.

She asked him to dinner at the flat.

'I'm so glad you were able to come so soon, Uncle Guy–' she still used the girlish 'Uncle' –'because I'm in rather a mess. I'll tell you all about it later.'

Guy knew her well enough, having watched her over the years, to realise that much lay behind her attempt at putting up a calm exterior.

'By all means, my dear, but if you were thinking of offering your parched godfather some pre-prandial solace, we might make a start on the problem sooner rather than later.'

Despair

She was relieved that he invited immediate discussion because she held him in some awe as well as affection and, treating him with more deference than most women of her age would extend to their godfathers, had been reluctant to press him.

They sat by the fire with their drinks. He smiled at her, his strong boyish smile encouraging her to begin.

'I'm going to have a baby.'

'Oh, well done. What's the problem?'

She stared, uncomprehendingly.

'After all, my dear, it often happens to married people.'

As she remained frozen in silence he added, 'You mean the baby isn't...'

'Oh yes, it's Jim's, but I can't have it. I'm not ready to be a mother yet. I couldn't possibly manage.'

'But my dear, I'm sure Jim will help to make things work out. He's a pretty resourceful chap, you know, and I bet he's absolutely delighted.'

'The point is, Uncle, he doesn't know, and I don't want to tell him. I can't. You must help me.'

'Help you not to tell him?' he murmured disingenuously, playing for time.

'I must get rid of it!' she blurted out vehemently.

Guy was, as Constance had often described him, a man of the world, and wasn't embarrassed at speaking about intimate matters with a young woman, but his debonair manner concealed a deep respect for the old proprieties, including a reverence for human life. He was profoundly shocked at Madeleine's brutal attitude towards her child, but too wise to let her see it lest he should lose her trust. He continued to play for time.

'I suppose you could have the baby adopted immediately it's born, but how on earth would you be able to conceal things from Jim?'

'No, no that's no use at all. I must have an abortion.'

She felt the better for having uttered the word. Her confidence returned and she smiled archly as she cajoled her godfather.

'Surely, Uncle, in your long life you must have heard of girls in the same trouble. You must tell me where to go.'

Despair

She watched him, at first expectantly and then, observing the pain and displeasure on the handsome old face, with alarm turning to panic as she realised how badly she had misjudged him. She had gone to the wrong place for help, and her plan was in ruins even before it had been properly formulated.

'I see,' he said slowly. 'You do realise what you would be doing to Jim, don't you, quite apart from to the baby? Even if you were able to conceal it from him now he might discover it later as a result of some other medical trouble, and in any case you would know that you'd deliberately deceived him. Could you really look him in the face again? You don't know this, but soon after you decided to come away from the farm and live here, Jim and I happened to meet, and he said that whatever differences might exist between you, you had the great quality of honesty. He trusts you. Can you really contemplate killing his child? Quite apart from the fact that it's also a criminal offence, and can be very risky.'

'I know it's supposed to be a crime, but people have it done, don't they? You must have heard of it happening.'

'Oh yes, I've heard of instances but I've no knowledge of ways and means – and – quite frankly I don't want to. I'm not a professional moralist and I haven't always been a terribly good boy, but there are some things at which I draw the line, and this is one of them. In any case, my dear, I think you're running away from what you see as a difficulty, and that's never a sound solution.'

'What is a sound solution?'

'What would you do if your dear mother were still alive?'

'I suppose sooner or later I'd talk to her about it. Probably.'

'And instead you're talking to me. I can't tell you how much I appreciate it. I'm greatly touched and I hope you'll always feel you can come to me, but really you should be having this conversation with Jim. You're not afraid of him, are you?'

'A bit. I don't want to hurt him, and anyhow I don't suppose he'd give me the answer I want, any more than you have.'

'Honesty again. However, you're in too distressed a state at the moment for making serious decisions. I think you underrate Jim. If you were to put your "problem" to him I believe you'd find him much more understanding than you seem to fear.'

Despair

They remained by the fire, saying little, and Madeleine was surprised to discover that she drew some strength from Guy's gentle firmness even though he was not telling her what she wanted to hear. She had prepared a light dinner and Guy's savoir vivre helped them over the embarrassment that filled both their minds. He guided conversation to her business, a subject in which her interest never flagged, and by pretending great ignorance about it encouraged her to talk freely and at length. He in his turn was surprised to discover how much it meant to her, that it was serving as a substitute for a child and consumed most of her waking thoughts. It helped him to understand what lay behind her self-defensive and seemingly brutal response to the discovery of her unborn child and, if *tout comprendre* was not quite *tout pardonner*, at least he felt a warm sympathy for her, and something akin to pity for a young woman who in spite of material wealth was so ill equipped for life.

They retired to the fireside for coffee. She said, 'You remember I was telling you about the last time I saw Jim and we dined at the Silvermanns'? Well, the atmosphere in that house was almost too much for me. I don't mean that I didn't like them, they're dears, but the sense of family was so strong, and Jim fitted in so naturally that I should have felt quite out of it if they hadn't drawn me in, very tactfully, and made me feel a part of them. Well, one thing worrying me, quite apart from how I could cope with a baby and business, is that that is the kind of family life Jim was used to and would want to have, and I just can't see myself being a sort of warm protective mother figure like Ruth Silvermann, presiding over the generations. I'm scared.'

'I don't think I've ever heard you express yourself with such vehemence and at such length, my dear, except about business. That's good, you're getting it out of your system. I forget who said that all Englishmen are born two whiskies under par: you see the beneficial effect of a little festive dining.'

'I know I'm a bit of a cold fish but I can't help it, and the thought of getting all tied up in domestic life frightens me. It's not that I was unhappy at home, but after Daddy and Nigel died Mummy was so wrapped up in the business that life was never the same again. Even before that the family was the business, if

Despair

you know what I mean. I didn't realise it at the time because I felt part of it, even as a little girl. I was probably wrong ever to have got married. I should have been a grim-faced spinster in business and made pots of money.'

Madeleine finished her remarks with a broad grin. Guy smiled appreciatively in reply, and waited. She then added, 'Not that marriage doesn't have some rewards too...'

'I wouldn't know, but I can imagine,' he said with mock solemnity, and they both laughed. He went on, 'Of one thing I'm sure you're mistaken. I assure you that by no stretch of the imagination could you be mistaken for a grim-faced battleaxe. You are a very handsome and attractive woman, Madeleine, and when you try you can use those assets. You know, I believe that you and Jim drifted towards each other because in different ways you were both isolated and lonely people and perhaps in the ordinary course of events you would not have come together – different interests, and so on. But you did, and I think it is going to be a case of mutual love coming in maturity. You're both intelligent and honourable people and you owe it to each other to talk about your difficulties and face them together.'

'I'm afraid I don't feel the least bit honourable at the moment.'

'You know, my dear, there are times when this kind of honesty, seeing things clearly as black and white, can be a vice rather than a virtue. I used to think as you do, but time has taught me when to compromise. Don't judge yourself too harshly; nothing's easy, but difficulties really do look less alarming when one discusses them. In this case, with Jim.'

Guy's compliments were not lost on her, and he was gratified to observe her pleasure when he used words like intelligent, attractive and honourable. She only half believed him but, by the time he said, 'Well, my dear, it's high time an old gentleman was safely tucked up in bed,' she felt more composed. 'Won't you have a nightcap before you leave?' she asked.

'No thanks, I'll do that when I get back. And don't forget to have one yourself.'

She walked him down the stairs. At the front door he kissed her gently and said, 'Thank you for asking me, my dear. Be strong, God bless. And let me know how you get on.'

Despair

'I shall. Thanks, Uncle.'

She stood in the doorway, saw him hail a taxi, and retired to the flat in a state of confusion mixed with elation. She realised that her wicked, worldly-wise old Uncle had caused her to drink far more than was her custom, and when she had followed his injunction to take a nightcap, sleep overcame her in spite of her worries.

Guy for his part did not retire as soon as he got home. He sat at his desk and wrote a letter to catch the first post.

My dear James,

A brief note. I happened to speak with Madeleine today, and formed the impression that a visit from you would not come amiss. She is as beautiful and interesting as ever, and seems to be making a great success of her business.

Yours,
Guy

P.S. This letter, of course, has never existed.

When Madeleine woke, early, she did not immediately succumb to alarming thoughts, so soundly had she slept, but within minutes the pattern of her worries was playing across her mind. Last night she had received the impression of comfort, and although it had been but an illusion it had helped her to a more rational frame of mind. She worked through her options... There was what Guy would call running away, having the abortion. But how? She dared not approach a doctor and could not begin to think where to look for some underhand source. Did drinking vast quantities of gin really work, or was that just an old wives' tale? In any case the very thought sickened her. Adoption was too complicated: she could not keep Jim out of it and, anyhow, he was bound to notice. Was Guy right in saying she should confide in Jim? Could they work out a happy solution together? And, if the solution meant keeping the baby, would she have done the right thing for the wrong reason, keeping it not out of joy but from sheer unavoidability?

She lay still, staring across the bed to her dressing table on which stood a photograph of her and Jim taken on their honey-

Despair

moon. When she had moved into the flat the photograph had been placed on the window ledge, never banished right out of sight but rather remote, and since the resumption of their relationship it had been promoted to its present central position. She moved in a flash from one frame of mind to another, back and forth. To have the baby was unthinkable, but on the other hand how could she deprive Jim of his child? Slowly, conscience stretched out its grasp towards her. Whereas once she would have thought, But Jim need never know, the facile response no longer satisfied her. Jim might never know, but she would, and would go on knowing it forever, and quailed at the prospect of having to live behind the duplicity.

She looked at the clock. It was getting late, and the businesswoman in her asserted herself. The time for decisions had come. Jim would have to know, but how to tell him? Meanwhile it was time to get ready for the business day, and her personal problem would have to wait until the evening for further thought.

James was blissfully unaware of her distress.

He had taken much counsel with himself since their last meeting and, mingling caution with desire, had contented himself with spirited letter-writing, joyful anticipation and hard work. He threw himself more vigorously than ever into running the estate, using the late autumn months for maintenance and tidying-up on a large scale. He was about to embark on a project long dear to him, an indulgence which, thanks to the money that he had made on the Stock Exchange, he was now able to satisfy: he would plant a small park and forest, and landscape them. So close to his heart was the project that he had not mentioned it even to John Stonor on his visits, and in the past it would have been futile to try and engage Madeleine's interest: even now he could not imagine her being enthusiastic about it for its own sake, though perhaps if she knew how much it meant to him...

With characteristic romanticism he dreamed his forest as he walked his land, and with equally characteristic thoroughness he spent his evenings designing it, making a detailed plan of the ground and studying nurserymen's catalogues. From his wide reading, and consultation with many authorities on forestry, he knew that he was young enough to expect to see the reward of his imagination well within the likely span of his life. Sometimes he paused to ask himself why he had the urge to create a forest; certainly not for profit, because this one was to be for posterity rather than as an investment in timber. Nor was it out of botanical interest as such, and although it would be a lasting contribution to the country which had welcomed him, it would have been hypocrisy to claim that his motive was one of gratitude to England. In Warsaw the countryside, and nature in general, had been the stuff of books and museums; forests were what stories were made of and he would have been hard put to identify a dozen real trees.

He had fallen in love with forests on his journey to the West: during long periods when their huge expanse and deep gloom were his protection, when days spent lurking within them gave him time to savour the hot resin and the smell of the damp undergrowth. Lying on the fringe of the woods he used to press his body tightly against the vegetation while he kept watch on the surrounding countryside, gingerly parting the stems, stung by nettles and torn by brambles. His physical contact with the ground and the rugged bases of the great trees had brought him comfort, serving him as anchorages in a perilous existence. In the absence of family and friends, the forest's silent, anonymous but pervading presence acted as a living being that answered his need for security. As his body became emaciated his bones literally came closer to the wood and the soil; he would cover himself with the undergrowth and relish its roughness against his skin. He spoke to the trees, at first mentally and then, as he grew weaker, out loud. The deep forest had a pulse of its own, and not all his hunger and fear could blind him to its mystery and romance.

It would be difficult, he thought, to find a way of conveying these feelings to Madeleine; in fact it might be better not to try, but rather to capture her imagination with the organisational aspect of his project, if not to play a part at least to take an interest in it.

He walked his estate before breakfast on the morning after Madeleine's dinner with Guy; thoughts of romance and profit jockeyed for position in his mind. The stimulating chill of late October hastened his step, and as he exerted himself his breath congealed slightly on his moustache. The first touch of frosty weather always stirred him, evoking memories of childhood, mufflered walks in the Warsaw parks hand in hand with Katarzyna, pushing his young brothers on their toboggan, and then the terrible yet inspiring winter of 1944 when he had clung stubbornly to life in the teeth of all the suffering that man and nature had thrust on him. He enjoyed all the seasons, adapting his mood to their changes, and rarely shared the jokes about the English climate because its very variety was both a delight and a challenge. The prospect of November gave him pleasure. He looked forward to its quiet severity, sombre trees and its astringency, heralding winter.

The thought of November turned his mind to the forthcoming Remembrance Day which, he foresaw, was going to present him with a situation in which he would have to make a choice that was bound to cause offence. His friends in the British Legion had invited him to the local service at the war memorial in Great Walling, for although he was not a member they claimed that he had been a soldier too, and he was loath to decline. Since it was not yet customary in those days for Catholics to participate in others' religious services, James had mentioned it to Father Ryan as a matter of courtesy, and had been surprised at the vehemence of his reaction.

'Oh, I couldn't give permission for that. It would give grave scandal. I doubt very much whether I could even ask the Bishop to agree because it is not as though your position in the Legion required your attendance.'

'To avoid misunderstanding, Father, I should make it clear that I was not so much making a request for a dispensation as simply letting you know what I propose to do.'

Father Ryan's expression assumed a mixture of perplexity and annoyance, and his face clouded over. He was not used to being addressed in such terms by members of his congregation, and, like many an amiable autocrat, turned swiftly to anger when his will was resisted. But he was no fool, and recalled James's recent help in the matter of the sacristy roof. Perhaps with an eye to future benefactions, he said with a disarming smile, 'Well, if your mind is made up! And I dare say your local standing puts you in a difficult position when they ask you to participate. Anyhow, thank you for telling me!'

James was half inclined to leave it at that; to let his attendance at the service be passed off as a regrettable public duty, and settle for peace and sweetness and smiles. Father Ryan's automatic assumption of authority, however, and his equally ready compromise, had raised his hackles, and looking straight at him he found himself saying in an unaccustomed glacial tone, 'I am bound to say, Father, that I am not going to this service out of a sense of social obligation, but in response to a warm-hearted invitation from men with whom I have something in common. You see, in 1944 we did not enquire into our comrades' state of soul, or even their belief: it was enough that we were on the same side of the barricade.'

Even as he was saying this James reflected how strange it was that insensitivity in one man should evoke pomposity in another. All the same, feeling the better for having said it, he continued, somewhat irrelevantly, 'And I might add that in my experience the utmost kindness has been extended to me by people outside the household of the Faith.'

'I would not deny that there is goodness to be found in all men.'

Father Ryan's soft answer had extricated them from a potentially explosive situation, and soon afterwards James had taken his leave, an awkward peace prevailing.

As he continued on his rounds he pondered on the situation of his Church in England. Long conversations with John Stonor had given him an understanding of the historical causes for the embattled attitudes of the Catholic Church and the proliferation of Nonconformism, but he still found it strange that religion should be so splintered and that doctrinal and historical factors should have so fierce and persisting a legacy. In Poland he had been faintly conscious that various small sects existed, but he had not known of anyone who was not either a Catholic or a Jew and, on arrival in England had been surprised to find that Catholics, if they did not exactly live in a ghetto, at least had to contend with a

Despair

certain amount of verbal teasing, and seemed to find it necessary to defend their beliefs. He remembered an occasion when Constance was entertaining guests, one of whom referred to a Mrs Miller, and added, 'But did you know she's a *Catholic*?' Madeleine had rather slyly said, 'So is James,' and the guest had replied, 'But you're Polish aren't you, James?' He clearly remembered how Constance had then deftly and without condescension spoken well of Mrs Miller. It seemed that there had to be an explanation for the oddity of being Catholic, and of course being a foreigner would account for anything.

At school he had attended the annual Remembrance Day services, even though he was vaguely aware that he was not supposed to, and some of the other Catholic boys opted out; he felt it right to attend and even before his English became perfect he responded to the beauty of the words and the simple solemnity of the proceedings. He felt that these services displayed a reverence that compared favourably with the way in which the occasion was marked in his parish church where the special prayer for the fallen was the only way in which the Mass appeared to differ from that of any usual Sunday. He discovered that in some parishes the priest did go further, placing a wreath of poppies on the altar and making suitable allusions in the sermon, but that was by no means always the practice.

Last year when he had tackled Father Ryan on the matter he had replied, 'I offer the entire Mass for the souls of the dead; surely there is no better way of commemorating them? The Mass itself is the commemoration.'

While James would not disagree it seemed, all the same, that Father Ryan's attitude revealed a reluctance to allow British Catholics to be seen to participate fully in the life of the country.

He received Guy's letter at breakfast on the following day. He knew Guy's style, and immediately drew the right inference from his elegant understatement. In Guy's code 'a visit from you would not come amiss' meant 'come at once', and the problem was how to engineer a sudden return without arousing Madeleine's suspicion.

It was a measure of James's detachment that the reason for Guy's warning never occurred to him. He wondered whether it

Despair

might be about some business problems, in which case it must presumably be a serious one, and yet Guy had written that Madeleine was making a great success of her business. Perhaps he was worried about her health: was she working too hard, not getting enough sleep? Surely Guy would have taken it on himself to help her over that kind of problem. It must be something both more serious and compelling. Even so, James's mind did not turn to the obvious explanation.

He decided not to go straight to the flat, as if his visit had been intended specifically for her, but instead rang her at the office.

'You're back very soon. Is anything wrong?'

'Nothing at all, but I found I had to consult some people at Kew about my planting. Are you doing anything this evening?'

'Not particularly.' The conversation seemed unreal to her. 'What planting?'

'I'll tell you about it tonight. I'll be waiting for you at home.'

James's 'at home' was not lost on her. He usually referred to 'the flat', and she welcomed his use of the familiar term which, a few months ago would have seemed out of place. Now it carried implications of protection, refuge, solace and lowered defences, a place of intimacy and, oh God, children. She would have to rely on James's inexperience, and trust that he would not attribute her anguish of mind, which she would be unable to conceal, to its true cause. She felt sorely inclined to use his unexpected visit to tell him frankly what had happened and let events lead them on, come what may. Suppose that were to produce a final break with him? The prospect, which a few months ago she might have regretted but accepted as an unavoidable necessity, was now unbearable. She couldn't win. Either she told him and agreed to bear their child, or she tried to deceive him for a little longer. And what then? She felt consumed by a mixture of fear, shame and indecision.

He was waiting for her by the fireside, with a tray of drinks set out, giving every indication of steady confidence. He rose to greet her. The little courtesies that came naturally to him, and were the product of an upbringing in a more formal society than hers, had from the beginning amused, attracted and occasionally irritated her. When Guy, whose mores James partly shared and partly

Despair

copied, treated her with his old-fashioned courtesy, she felt no surprise, but the same behaviour coming from a young man in post-war Britain struck her as quaint. Had Madeleine been of a reflective turn of mind she might have considered that youth was a relative quality, owing more to disposition and experience than to chronology, but she was not given to analysis except when driven to it, and her reaction to his quaintness was to think of him affectionately as 'funny old Jim'.

She put on a brave face and, in self-defence, greeted him jokingly, unconsciously trying to postpone serious discussion.

'How's Planter Jim tonight?'

'Full of ideas, but only one thought.' She shuddered. Luckily, he went on, 'And how's the queen of commerce?'

'Shattered! It's been a very full day. Business is thriving. I'd better have a bath before doing anything else.'

He drew her down into the settee.

'There's time for a drink first, and your bath is half-run already. I'll just top it up for you.'

She drew a mixture of pleasure and concern from his confidence and solicitude; pleasure at being looked after, concern because with her defences dropping the difficulty of protecting her dreaded secret increased.

James continued, 'Would it suit you if we dined quietly here? I've started making some soup.'

She thought, He's so organised, he's got everything planned. Her heart half leaped and half sank; it was easiest just to let the evening take its course, but what it would bring she dared not imagine...

They dined quietly, as James had planned, by the fireside. She endeavoured to make him talk as much as possible about himself, putting off the moment of truth.

'Now tell me all about this planting, and what's Kew got to do with it?'

In the warmth of the setting James talked freely and fervently about his plans for the exotic forest, and such was his enthusiasm that in spite of herself Madeleine felt borne along with it. He explained that he wished to check some details with authorities at Kew and to see standing specimens of the proposed trees, which

Despair

was not strictly true, because he already possessed the necessary information, but he had no qualms about the slight deception.

'Won't it be rather expensive?'

'Yes, but we can well afford it' (she noted the 'we') 'and if it succeeds it will be a lasting monument.'

'A lasting monument! How English you've become, Jim,' she said archly. 'But a monument to what?'

'Well, darling, at the risk of sounding introspective–' now it was his turn to be arch –'I suppose you could say it would be a monument to my conceit, or a throwback to the dark forests of my Eastern European past, or even an expression of a sense of eternity...'

'Or maybe just fun?'

'Yes, let's settle for that.'

'Well. I think it's a marvellous idea. I hope it works.'

It was the first time for two years that she had shown enthusiasm for any of his plans. His face clearly revealed his delight.

'Look, I've been hogging the conversation. Tell me about your business.'

'Much less exciting than yours, but it's bringing money in. I've got plans too. I want to expand the agency to cover many more languages. Actually I'm being almost pushed into it because of pressure from potential customers.'

'The penalty of success, I suppose.'

'Yes. I've had a lot of recommendations, which I must say is gratifying. As a matter of fact only yesterday I had an inquiry from some people who are to organise a Polish cultural event and want bilingual secretaries. I'll tell you more about it when I know more. There can't be many attractive young ladies who are fluent, can there? How is your Polish nowadays?'

'I don't think of myself as an attractive young lady. But seriously, I have kept it up pretty well except for the latest slang expressions, I suppose. Let me know if I can help.'

'Thanks. Of course.'

'I'll make us some more coffee,' said James.

'I'll do it,' she replied. Perhaps because it was getting late, the room was warm and she felt tired, when Madeleine suddenly

Despair

stood up she felt a momentary dizziness and sat down abruptly.

At first James noted only the slightly comic movement and thought she had just slipped.

He joked, 'Steady on, old girl, you're not supposed to swoon unless you're either drunk or pregnant!'

She put her hand to her head, and James, noticing her pallor, stared long and hard at her.

'Oh, it's nothing,' she said, and burst into tears.

Where a few moments before a confident-looking woman had sat next to him he now saw a crumpled figure choking with emotion, gripping his hand, inarticulate, quaking. So that was what Guy had been trying to tell him... James's education had not trained him to cope with the situation, not even fully to comprehend it. Even now he wondered whether her hysteria was the result of sickness or pregnancy.

For a long second images flashed before him. If sickness then it must be something serious. Pregnancy was more likely... He had vague notions about morning sickness and irrational behaviour, no firm knowledge but merely bits and pieces of information that even a reticent bachelor picks up through hearing people speak. He had considered the possibility of becoming a father, contemplated it dispassionately, from afar, without wild enthusiasm and without displeasure. He had married in order to have a wife rather than for children; if they came, they came, and would no doubt fit into the scheme of things, optional extras submerged in a sea of obviously interesting and important things like philosophy, and the arts and religion, and the whole world of ideas. And now... now children's arms reached up towards him like the great fronds of seaweed from the deep, clutching at his light. He would be a member of a family again, would give them names, impart his enthusiasms to them, and teach them the Faith.

There must be both girls and boys, it would be a wonderful experience to share their upbringing with Madeleine, it would give point to everything, including his forest; especially the forest, no doubt now as to its purpose or to what it would be a monument. He saw himself in the role of patriarch... 'unto the fourth generation'. But why had Madeleine said nothing to him?

Despair

He did not apply his reason to his actions. Instinctively he acted in the most useful way, drawing her to him, holding her not too tightly and saying nothing. He let her cry, stroked her neck gently and gradually she drew her sobbing under control. The furious thought bored through his mind, corroding his spirit. Why had she said nothing to him? What should he say to her?

'Tell me, darling.'

She raised her head, looked at him for a moment and burst into tears again. He tightened his arm round her a little, and waited, feeling in their unspoken communion closer to her than ever before. Almost for the first time she seemed to need him, literally clinging to him. The only other occasion on which he had been in a position to comfort her had been at Constance's death, but then his distress had equalled hers and they had comforted each other: now she needed him. He tried, not entirely successfully, to quell a certain feeling of satisfaction at the situation, felt ashamed at the unworthy thought but savoured it none the less, and continued waiting.

Madeleine, for her part was thinking furiously through her tears. As she slowly regained her composure her thoughts became more concrete, practical. In James's close presence she felt the uncleanness of deception shaming her into telling him the truth, laying her fears before him, cost her what it might, and engaging his help in solving what she still regarded as a problem rather than a blessing. Honest by nature as she was, she felt a great load lifting as soon as she decided to unburden herself.

She gripped his hand, looked him in the face and said in as steady a voice as she could summon, 'Jim, we're going to have a baby.'

Why had she said 'we'? Until this moment she had thought of the baby as hers, her problem.

James reacted as she had expected and feared. He expressed surprise, delight and then concern for her health and how she would manage at the office. The conversation seemed unreal to her, as though the flat voice of the woman answering James's concern had no connection with her fearful self. How long must she wait for the inevitable question, the one she must meet head-on and on whose answer her self-respect and their future must

Despair

depend? She watched him closely as the conversation flagged a little and she became acutely aware that his external silence indicated a change in his line of thought. She could not bear to watch the question being asked and, turning away, studied the fireside table with blank intensity.

'But darling, why didn't you tell me sooner?'

Like a fish on the end of a line her mind darted frantically from one last possible lie to another, all palpably incredible: 'I wanted to be absolutely sure,' or 'I meant to tell you in bed,' or 'I wasn't sure you'd be pleased' – all utterly, pathetically, futile. Her tears were spent, her mind made up.

'You'll hate me for this, Jim. I wasn't sure that I really wanted a baby.'

No, that would not suffice. Nothing but the truth now, whatever the outcome.

'I – I even wondered whether there was any way of stopping it.'

James just stared, knowing but not grasping. Was he waiting for her to utter the word? In a whisper she said, 'I considered having an abortion.'

There, she had said it.

James felt very old, his spirit shrivelled, and yet he rejoiced that she had at last faced him with her fears.

'Well, darling, we don't think very clearly when we're frightened, do we? But now, you want the baby?'

Even in her distress her honesty asserted itself.

'I'm not sure I'd want it just for myself, but it's ours, and I wouldn't dream of doing anything to hurt it.'

James's expression of joy was her reward and guarantee of forgiveness. The problems remained but they would face them together: her ordeal was over.

10: Understanding

The breeze in Kew Gardens was gentle for the onset of winter, and the casual observer of the well wrapped-up couple strolling slowly through the parkland might have been excused for thinking they were courting. The earnestness of their grasp was broken only intermittently as they stopped by a tree and the young man reached in his pocket, not for a knife with which to carve initials, but for a notebook in which he wrote briefly before they linked arms once more and moved on.

On the morning after her confession James had, without much difficulty, persuaded Madeleine to telephone her secretary and explain that she would not be attending the office. Indeed, the mental and spiritual catharsis of the night had left her drained of energy and in no condition for business. She was glad to have James look after her, without fussing, and after a leisurely breakfast they had set off for Kew. The orderliness and evident professionalism with which the grounds were kept pleased her and held her interest, even though she knew little about horticulture and did not naturally warm to it; for she, like James, appreciated anything that was well run and, furthermore, she felt a great yearning to try and share his enthusiasm.

James had spent the night in turmoil. After Madeleine, exhausted, had gone to sleep, he had remained in a state of mixed delight and confusion. Although he did not doubt the sincerity of her decision to bear their child, he wondered whether her resolution would survive the experience. Most of all he could not bury the nagging worry that she had even considered destroying their baby. How could she have nursed the idea? His love made him hope that she had given but a passing thought to the abortion, a mere flash through the mind in a moment of folly, but his reason told him that she had entertained it seriously, deliberately, consciously. By what devious paths had she justified it to herself? The English were good at rationalising their

Understanding

emotions: when they wanted to do something very much they had to convince themselves that it was intrinsically desirable in order to lift the action out of the realm of self-interest or expedience, because they wanted very much to feel virtuous. They were, in fact, greatly guided by their emotions, however much they might like to think of themselves as being less emotional than other races.

Kindness was often used as a measure of the rightness of a course of action. James, who thought his way through life on principles rather than living it pragmatically, was suspicious of kindness, with its overtones of emotion and subjectivity, when it was elevated to the level of a virtue such as justice. Had Madeleine managed to convince herself that it would be *kinder* not to have the baby? If so, kinder to whom? To the baby presumably, on the grounds that a child would not be happy with a reluctant mother who lacked maternal instincts... Surely that would require too great an act of self-delusion even for a desperate woman, and would be out of keeping with the honesty that he had always attributed to her, which left only the revolting probability that she had acted with full and conscious intention, full knowledge of the gravity of what she was proposing, and giving it her consent. A mortal sin. Thank God she had not acted, had turned away from action, but surely even to have played with the idea was terrible enough.

What if he had not unexpectedly visited her: might she not have decided to commit the act? And yet, after all, who was he to judge her? He did not know how much she had anguished over the possibility; all he knew was that she had finally confided in him. Had Guy and he not been instruments of God's will, and if so should not his feelings now be of gratitude rather than misgiving? Watching her in deep sleep he imagined her saying, 'You're being introspective, you're taking yourself too seriously.' Perhaps he should take things as they were and simply be thankful for what had been saved from potential wreck. Perhaps he should be pragmatic, stop striving to understand and control events, and leave something to God.

These thoughts piled up on him, jostling for position, pounding each other like close-set branches in a gale until, as sleep

Understanding

overcame him, he was repeating to himself, 'We must make it work.'

Thanks to his youth and health he had risen little the worse for the disturbed night and now, walking across the grass with his arm round Madeleine, and feeling her relaxed and appreciative of his support, he chatted easily and in so light-hearted a mood that he felt surprised at himself.

'It's almost as though we were stealing a day off school, isn't it, darling?' he said.

'Not that you'd ever have done so. You were far too saintly.'

'Not really. There was no virtue in not cutting what I liked. Don't forget that I loved school.'

'It seems such a long time ago, and yet it's only a few years.'

'They've been huge years for us; Mother dying, the firm closing, and leaving The Aspens. Your world has been turned upside down, and mine for the second time. It's no wonder we've got ourselves a bit confused.'

He did not, in fact, consider himself in the least confused, although he was, but thought it prudent to attribute the condition to both of them. The present moment required that everything be shared, even confusions, and if one did not actually experience them it was probably wise to assume that one ought to. In this devious way did James confound confusion not out of any deliberate hypocrisy but from a genuine desire not to set himself apart.

Madeleine squeezed his arm and said, 'It's getting better. It's all becoming clearer, I think.'

'I know what you mean. There's a great deal to sort out, but just for the moment I'm still skiving off school and the first thing I'm going to do is fill you up with cakes and tea. There's a nice little place outside the gates. Come on.'

'Don't you need to do any more work here? What about seeing your experts?'

'The experts can wait. I didn't have any firm appointments, and in any case I'm going to be in town a lot more, aren't I?'

'I suppose you will...'

'And there aren't many things in forestry that can't be done tomorrow instead of today.'

Understanding

He was relieved that Madeleine did not suspect that his visit to London had been directed entirely at her. They went to the coffee shop and sat near the window through which they watched the last few leaves fleeing the trees, and the occasional passer-by. The café was peopled mainly by ladies of indeterminate age and rampant respectability, some with elderly gentlemen in tow, unmistakable survivors of a bygone England.

'That old couple over there… do you suppose we'll be like them in forty years' time?'

She laughed. 'You're not being serious, are you?'

'Why not?'

'Well, he's obviously a bore and I'm sure you won't be. And I hope to goodness I don't end up looking like her!'

James was delighted at her compliment.

'But how can you be sure he's a bore? He may be great fun beneath his old-fashioned exterior.'

'Oh, I know that just looking old-fashioned doesn't necessarily make one a bore, but most of the people here are of a type; they're almost wearing a uniform. It can't be a coincidence that they gather in one place. I'd say they'd mostly behave predictably in a given situation.'

He watched them more closely. The ladies sat very straight and their conversation, in level positive voices, was just loud enough to be heard, but not understood, two tables away. A few sported regimental brooches on their tweeds, and most wore just a little lipstick. He imagined them, differently dressed but instantly recognisable, on the verandas of their bungalows in Kenya, or dining politely in Rhodesia. These women were of Constance's and his mother's generation, but almost a different species from the busy businesswoman and the lively academic whom he had loved. Had their children, in their boarding schools and Service academies, loved them? Had she lived, would Constance have drifted into this little subculture; backward-looking, deploring the absence of servants, fussing over their dogs and pursing their lips when they referred to the trade unions? He doubted it. And yet, for all their banality, these women were part of the country's backbone, Churchill's people. In their own unimaginative way, perhaps because of it, they had contributed to the victory whose fruits the country was now enjoying.

Understanding

'Mind you,' he said, 'it's easy to caricature people in one's mind. In fact I've been doing it myself, but I expect when we do so we are really trying to reinforce our own assumptions and prejudices, perhaps building up other people's caricatures of ourselves.'

'Are you saying that only insecure people put others into categories?'

'You know, my dear, you're becoming distinctly profound. In fact, you are in danger of getting involved in talking about ideas.'

She smiled. 'Just put it down to having known you for some years. You see, all that time listening to you and your learned friends has had its effect on my tiny brain. I may have sat on the edge of the conversations and even appeared to scoff or be bored – in fact I often was bored at the time – but some of it rubbed off. I actually do think. I may not know very much, and I suppose I'm too lazy intellectually to read the books and get right inside the concepts, but I won't deny I find ideas more interesting than I used to. One can't live with genius and come through untouched.'

James just stared. This was extraordinary. Had he heard correctly? She was not only implying a bond that he had not known, but even expressed herself in real words instead of the schoolgirl language to which he was used, and which, in its simplicity, he rather liked.

'Tell me, darling, has this peculiar state grown on you very gradually, or has the curve risen sharply recently?'

'As I said, the foundations were getting laid for many years without my knowing it at the time, and without any conscious cooperation on my part – by osmosis, as you might say.' She looked hard at him to see how he reacted to her use of the word. 'But strangely enough I have become more aware of it since we've been apart.'

James had the common sense not to reply, but to wait for more revelations.

'I don't think it would be right to say I've missed the environment, but I've been aware there was something I ought to be missing. I suppose that sounds silly.'

'Not at all. I'm only sorry I didn't spot your broadening interest sooner.'

Understanding

'It wouldn't have been easy. I kept it pretty well hidden, almost concealed from myself. As a matter of fact my business has helped to broaden my interests because I've met so many and different kinds of people. Foreigners, too. I've really had windows opened by some of the overseas firms who've asked for staff. You know, I never used to be comfortable with foreigners, didn't know what to say to them even if their English was good. I still find some difficulty, but now I know the problem lies with me, not them.'

'My dear girl, you have travelled far, and I had no idea... So while I've become the perfect Englishman, you're fast growing into a good European. Well, well!'

'I'm not so sure about growing fast, but I've got to a stage where I resent the feeble little innuendoes people make about foreigners. You know the sort of thing – "He's not a bad chap, for an Italian." I expect foreigners have the same silly attitudes towards us and make the same silly jibes, but that doesn't make it right.'

'Indeed we – I mean *they* – do. Sorry, Freudian slip there.' They both laughed.

'I've never quite dared ask you before, Jim. How English do you feel? Is it a constant effort?'

'No effort at all to feel at home in England, thanks to the kindness of a certain family and its friends. And going to school was quite the best introduction. It's not that I ever made a conscious effort to turn myself into an Englishman, in fact if anything I was always highly conscious of remaining loyal to my Polish roots, but yes, I did set about deliberately trying to fit into the externals of English society, in dozens of little matters that you probably can't imagine, from which words to use when and where, to table manners – huge scope for misunderstanding there – and relationships with adults, and the little courtesies and the taboo subjects. To a great extent I was anxious to get these things right so as not to embarrass Mother in front of visitors. Of course she was amazingly free of prejudice for a woman of her generation. But as for becoming English deep down, developing thought processes so that one reacts to situations and ideas in an English way, assuming it exists, I simply can't tell. I suspect that psychologically I have become a crossbreed.'

Understanding

'I had no idea of what was going on inside you, or that you were trying so hard. If I thought about it at all I suppose I just imagined you learned quickly because you were horribly bright, but I never resented you because you were so good with Mother and I didn't think of you as a rival. I was pretty bitchy, though, when you did drop a few bricks, wasn't I?'

'Yes darling, but in such an attractive way. I know you didn't resent me, and believe me I was thankful for that. I'm sure Mother had prepared the ground before my arrival and had discussed it with you, but I did wonder whether you might see me as a threat to Nigel's memory.'

'That was never a problem, because Nigel and I weren't frightfully close, though I was fond of him. And the fact that you'd also had a hard time in the war somehow made you all right in my estimation.'

They continued exchanging confidences, each aware that they were getting to know each other after seven years of acquaintance and three of marriage. Each felt that they were only scratching at the upper layer of personalities hidden by reserve, and that time would yield further delightful revelations. Each felt a desire to dig deeper now, and yet held back not from fear but from a wish to save some of the delight of discovery for later. Madeleine suddenly realised that in her new-found security with James she had spent an entire morning without dwelling on what had not been out of her mind during the last fortnight. In spite of her present happiness, none of the underlying problems was actually solved: there would have to be some hard thinking and discussion later in the day. She paused, and went quiet momentarily.

'You're tired, darling. Shall we go home so you can have a rest? Later on we can talk again. There's quite a lot of arranging to be discussed, isn't there?'

She smiled assent.

'So we'll just steer ourselves out through these groups of earnest Anglo-Saxons.'

They walked between the tables of tweedy ladies and sports-jacketed gentlemen. James whispered in Madeleine's ear, 'Just how predictable do you suppose their reactions are? Let's try a little shock experiment.'

'What are you up to now?' replied Madeleine.

At a small table near the door sat a rather severe-looking old lady on her own. Her grey hair was drawn back into a bun and she looked quietly into the middle distance. James stood politely in front of her and, making a small bow, addressed her in Polish.

'How do you do, madam?'

The old lady's face glowed with undisguised pleasure as she emerged from her reverie and replied in Polish, 'How good it is to hear the language spoken. Please forgive me, I am very old and my memory is not as good as it used to be, but I fear I cannot recall where we met.'

James felt well and truly hoist with his own petard, delighted at hearing Polish and embarrassed at the frivolous manner in which he had provoked it. He thought fast.

'I am younger than you, madam, but I must make the same admission. I am sure we met at some Polish function... in London, perhaps. In any case, I hope that you are very well.'

'My health is excellent and I have met many good people here. What more can one want? And I see that you too are happy.'

The old lady's cryptic words intrigued James. He introduced Madeleine, who endeared herself to her by using the few words of Polish that she possessed by way of greeting, and began to excuse himself on the grounds that they had business to attend to. And yet, not wishing to leave her with so little ceremony, he produced his card while the old lady probed finely in her bag for her own. She spoke in English now, for Madeleine's benefit, a quaintly distorted English but fluent enough.

'Todd-Zagorski... I knew several Zagorskis in Warsaw.'

'It is hardly an uncommon name, Mrs Sikorska.'

'Neither is mine. My husband had a great friend called Zagorski, a doctor, but we left Poland in 1938 and lost touch, of course.'

James wanted very much to pursue the conversation, but not wishing to keep Madeleine from her rest, excused himself again, and very softly said a few words in Polish.

The old lady got up with surprising alacrity, kissed Madeleine and said, 'Oh, that is so good, so good.'

Madeleine's new-found affinity with foreigners was not quite

Understanding

up to the occasion, and all she could respond with was a very Anglo-Saxon, 'Thank you very much.'

'I shall write to you,' said James as they went out.

'What was all that about?' asked Madeleine.

'I told her you were pregnant, so that she shouldn't think us rude to leave so soon.'

'How sweet of her! I was rather taken aback, I'm afraid. But didn't you want to stay on and talk with her?'

'Yes, but the important thing was to get you some rest. So much for our typical Englishwoman.'

11: Coming to Terms

At Briar Cottage James settled into his study and telephoned Madeleine.

'Hello darling. How are you feeling?'

'Fine. How was your journey?'

'Very easy. Did you get a chance to speak with Mrs Bilton?'

'Yes, she's going to do everything that's needed; there's nothing to worry about. What are you going to do now?'

'I'm going to listen to some music, wallow in contented thoughts and look forward to seeing you soon.'

'Me too. Goodnight, darling.'

He lit his pipe, and reviewed the situation. Disaster had clutched at them and been thrust away in the nick of time. Thank God that Guy had written. Had it been done out of certainty, or merely an intuition that something was wrong? The point was of no practical importance, but it intrigued him.

When they had returned to the flat, after meeting Mrs Sikorska, James had prepared supper while Madeleine rested. By unspoken consent they had refrained from talking about the future until they should be able to do so in the calmness and intimacy of the evening. It had been a wise decision. By the fireside, clear thought and practical measures grew out of a mutual desire for understanding, and blossomed into a clarity that would have seemed impossible to Madeleine but a couple of days earlier.

James had, from the start, urged that there should be no question of Madeleine giving up the business that had become a part of her. As her pregnancy progressed he would spend an increasing amount of time in London, and once the baby was born they would employ help – a nanny, or whatever was appropriate. James was far from clear about such matters but knew that professional women who could afford help somehow managed to combine their work with having babies. The details could wait, what mattered was to make Madeleine comfortable in the knowledge that her 'problem' was solvable. Much the greatest problem that lurked in James's mind was that he could not convince himself that Madeleine really wanted the baby for its own sake. He hoped and prayed that with pregnancy maternal instincts would well up within her and overcome the misgivings that now beset her. He did not yet know her well enough to understand that her misgivings were born not merely of a dislike of the general messiness of having children about the flat and interfering with her business life, as he rightly assumed, but, deeper down, of a fear that she would be unable to behave as a mother should towards her children and that it was therefore unfair to raise a family. Madeleine hardly ever expressed that fear to herself, and James, who never doubted her adequacy, never suspected it.

They had discussed the need for James to spend much more time in London once the baby was born. He did not mind. Any regret he felt at the prospect of spending less time in the country was redeemed by the knowledge that he was winning Madeleine back and casting off into a fullness of life for which he had barely dared to hope. To what extent, he wondered, should he attribute his joy and relief to the tangible, fleshly, reality of his love for Madeleine, and how much to the consolation of knowing that he had saved the ideal of marriage, the concept rather than the experience? His apparent inadequacy as a husband had certainly weighed on him, and even more the fact that he was failing to make a success of a union to which he had taken God as witness.

His belief that he was not to blame was irrelevant; failure was failure, and his pride was hurt. Had he made the error of trying to conduct his life according to principles, precepts and idealised images, confusing concept with substance? Introspective again. Did it matter? he imagined the practical Madeleine saying; surely the fact that they had come to understand each other again, or perhaps even for the first time, was all that mattered. Of course; and yet the habit of analysing one's motives died hard. Madeleine had always failed to distinguish between constructive self-criticism and looking inwards out of mere curiosity or worse, and used to ascribe all forms of self-examination to introspection.

Here he was, being introspective about introspection. Enough!

His practical nature reasserted itself and he began to list the measures he would have to take to ensure that the farm and estate would run properly in spite of his frequent absences. It did not take him long to formulate his plans, and then his mind turned again to the near future. Madeleine had agreed to spend a few days at Briar Cottage in order to attend the Remembrance Day service with him and to be shown round the estate. He thrilled in anticipation.

Before going to bed he wrote,

My dear Guy,

A brief note in return. I am just back from a most fruitful short stay with Madeleine and am deeply grateful to you. Her business, and everything else, is making steady progress.

Yours,
James

P.S. This letter has never existed, either.

On the following morning he felt a sense of unreality as he opened the mail. Thoughts of paternity jostled with the contents of boring brown envelopes; bills and horticultural catalogues intruded into images of Madeleine as mother and were quickly set aside, even Honeyman's latest list failed to evoke quite the usual thrill, although he lingered over it for a while. Not until he saw an envelope addressed in Jacob Silvermann's strong, elegant, hand was his mind fully committed.

Dear James,

May I export my wife to you for a few days? Ruth has been feeling a bit low lately. It is nothing particularly serious; probably the effect of excessive excitement over Guinevere, and the doctor has recommended a rest and a change. So may I take up the standing invitation you so kindly gave us? I could drive Ruth down whenever it suits you, and summoning up great courage I might even remain with you myself for a while although, as you know, fresh air is not good for me. Perhaps you will not mind too much if I produce my own microclimate.

Yours ever,
Jacob

James smiled with delight at the thought of Jacob weaving his trail of blue smoke through the house, a delight clouded only by misgivings as to the prudence of having Madeleine and Ruth under the same roof for a few days. Ruth's conversation, heavily laden with baby love, might not commend itself to a young woman who was only tentatively coming to terms with the prospect of motherhood. Besides, he wanted Madeleine to himself. He decided to ask Jacob and Ruth to come after Madeleine's return to London from her forthcoming visit.

The mail also contained information about a conference on forestry, which he had applied to attend, to be held in London in the New Year. Reading its details brought his mind back to business and, telling Mrs Brand that he would be out for lunch, he set off to walk the estate. A cold wind was blowing and he walked fast, making for the place where he intended to plant the exotic forest. He deliberately tried to put Madeleine out of his mind, without much success, and to concentrate on the task in hand.

He tried to visualise the forest as his child would see it fifty years ahead. From his notebook he checked the proposed positions of groups of trees and isolated specimens, made amendments, walked to and fro assessing the view from different aspects, grouping blocks of colour and estimating treetop levels. He had performed all these delightful tasks many times, but repetition brought no lessening of delight. While he worked he became engrossed, but after a couple of hours he selected a hollow in the ground protected from the wind, spread a groundsheet and settled down to lunch, keeping close to the earth for warmth.

He reflected that his fellow farmers who also ate out of doors had their ploughman's lunch lovingly prepared by their wives, whereas he was making do with some bread, a bar of chocolate and a flask of coffee. Not that he minded; he enjoyed what he had and was to some extent even amused at the irony of his situation. Had Madeleine felt it in her to share his love of nature his pleasure would have been the greater, but not for the first time did he know how to accept a good second best in exchange for perfection. His mind drifted away from the careful calculations and practical planning of half an hour ago to the realm of dreams. The rasping smell of the rotting vegetation had an almost intoxicating quality. He passed the leaf-mould through his fingers and held it to his face, savouring it blended with the smoke of his pipe. Some of the leaf-mould fell on the groundsheet: a small spider scuttled out of it, a woodlouse trotted away; London and business could have been on another planet. James thrust himself more strongly into the ground and turned up his collar against the breeze. Here the intellect gave way to the senses, possibilities to reality. Would his children share his appreciation? In twenty years' time, would he and his son be contemplating the view, smoking their pipes? Or his daughter, would she as a little girl be coming out with him, wanting to know about the plants and the birds, or would she instead be interested only in polishing fingernails and listening to records?

He was enough of a realist not to expect his children to see the world through his eyes, but perhaps he might be allowed to hope for some mingling of joys... What would Madeleine expect from her children, and what traditions would she hope to transmit? Of course, their children would be thrust in on them more than most people's; they would have no grandparents or, as far as he knew, any uncles or aunts: no relations at all. A sense of shame gripped him. His sister and brothers had slipped away from his thoughts. Gradually and imperceptibly he had, appallingly, forgotten them, and it was some time since he had sought information through Polish connections in London. Katarzyna and the boys might be alive; he could not tell. She would be twenty-seven, the twins twenty-two. Had they thought of him? Even if they had survived they had every reason to assume that he was dead; the onus of trying to find each other lay entirely on him. He reproached himself bitterly, and unfairly, for his lack of diligence, and resolved to try again, the advent of their child lending urgency to the task.

His time with Madeleine had been so brief, and some of it so tense, that they had not enjoyed the customary conversations of prospective parents. They had not asked themselves whether to expect a boy or a girl, and the matter of names had not been mentioned. The child's sex was unimportant to James, for it appeared to him that the valuable and interesting things in life were available to either, but names did matter, and he spent some time compiling a list for boys and for girls: his favourite saints, some Old Testament names that he relished for their sound, and some that had obvious Polish equivalents in case one day the children should be able or wish to return to their roots. He wondered whether Madeleine was doing so too, but feared that probably she was not. Perhaps a name would be suggested by the date of the child's birth, or even of its conception – although it might be difficult to be sure of the latter. But of course there could be no doubt in the present case: if Madeleine was two months pregnant the baby must have been conceived in August, and it had to be on the Feast of the Assumption. He remembered it very well because in his mental turmoil at the time he had forgotten the date and had missed Mass. If it should be a girl let her be called Assunta. Would Madeleine think it too foreign or, worse, not particularly care?

His mind turned to more immediate matters. Madeleine would be with him within a week, but in the meantime he would telephone her daily and, without betraying his anxiety, give his continuous support to her newly found resolution. He wanted the birth of their child to be heralded with confidence and joy, on the crest of a wave, and free of misgivings.

The days passed quickly until he stood on the platform at Brocklechurch station, experiencing the strange delight of preparing to receive his bride for a second time. He made the most of the occasion, with much tugging at his moustache, consulting his pocket watch every few minutes, and anxiously inspecting his bunch of chrysanthemums for the slightest sign of deterioration since the last examination.

To his repeated relief none occurred. He knew perfectly well he was playing a part, and enjoyed the action as being part of the magic of the cautious unravelling of a mystery; on one plane dealing with the practicalities of his new-found life, and on another letting himself be drawn along in a current whose general direction he knew, but about whose incidental twists he could only guess and whose final destination lay in the realm of hope.

Madeleine was leaning out of the carriage window as the train approached. She waved, and as James returned the greeting he kept his flowers concealed, making the most of his role as expectant father. His embrace crushed the chrysanthemums against Madeleine's back and the petals tickled her neck.

'Oh, you are a silly romantic old thing!' she laughed. 'It's been a long journey. Get me home quickly, Jim.'

He noted with pleasure that she had said 'home' instead of 'the cottage'. A trifle, but perhaps a straw in the wind.

The journey had tired her, and James was careful to confine himself to small talk, which had never come easily to him, about her health and the progress of her pregnancy until they had ensconced themselves in front of the fire with buns and tea before them. The pleasure that they took in each other's company was mingled with a sense of the absurdity of the situation: James welcoming his wife back to their home, one of their homes. Was he to some extent a host, or was she here by right? Of course she was, but Madeleine felt some embarrassment at claiming the house as her own, and felt herself playing a split role as lady of the house and returned prodigal. No, she thought, prodigal was hardly the right term because, slender though her knowledge of scripture was, she associated the prodigal son with a wasting of material goods, and she had certainly not done that. Wayward, perhaps, or simply neglectful. Madeleine's introspective mood did not last long. She seized James's hand.

'You haven't made many changes to the house,' she said, and immediately regretted it.

'Hardly any. Why should I?'

Indeed, why? It was she who had changed, and he had preserved the arrangements that she had made.

'You knew I'd come back, didn't you?'

'I couldn't be sure. You know I don't take anything for granted, you least of all. I hoped and prayed, naturally, and did many new things on the estate. But what you had created in the house I would not have dreamed of dismantling. It would have been a kind of sacrilege.'

She went very quiet, and tightened her grip on his hand.

'Be patient with me, darling. I've come a long way.'

'I know. The rest of the journey can take as long as you need.'

'Don't let's be solemn. Tell me about the estate. I'm longing to see it tomorrow.'

He described his plans at some length and, even though he had referred to them during his visits to London, she was not bored; for now that she was physically present on the estate James's words gained significance, the diagrams he showed her conveyed a sense of reality and she felt herself responding effortlessly to his enthusiasm. His methodical way of implementing his dream had made him, if not an expert, at least highly informed about all aspects of estate planning and management and his enthusiasm communicated itself to her. They wallowed in contemplation of the future.

Mrs Brand came in to announce that she had prepared dinner and was about to go home.

'So you've had a lovely long talk over your tea. There is ever so much to talk about when a baby's on its way!'

'Indeed there is, Mrs Brand,' replied James. 'We can think of nothing else.'

'Well, I'll be off now.'

James gave Madeleine a shadowy smile, which she returned with a schoolgirlish grin. The conspiratorial action brought them even closer; conscious that their child was no longer the only experience that they could share. Indeed, for the last two hours the pregnancy, far from having dominated their conversation, had been but briefly mentioned.

Over dinner James turned the conversation to Madeleine's business.

'Have you added any more exotic languages to your secretarial list?'

'Not yet. I mustn't overstretch myself, and the major European ones are giving me enough scope at the moment. Would you call Polish exotic?'

'Well, not to me, but I don't suppose there are many non-Poles in the country who speak it. Why do you ask?'

'I think I told you last time... There may be a Polish cultural visit, goodness knows when, and a delegation of arts people is coming next year. I believe the idea is to get some Polish performers over here, and the delegation is coming to discuss the

Coming to Terms

possibilities. For the time being it's only a matter of translations. As a matter of fact I was thinking of offering Mrs Sikorska some work. She didn't look very well off. You must give me her address.'

James concealed his surprise. Madeleine was becoming a constant source of unexpected remarks, and he rejoiced at hearing her express such consideration for someone whom she hardly knew, and revealing a strand of tenderness that contrasted with her businesslike manner and her reluctance to display emotion.

He said, 'That's a kind idea. I'll look up the address tomorrow,' and reproached himself for not having thought of the old lady since the day they had met, whereas Madeleine had done so in spite of her anxiety about their child.

His lack of excitement at the prospect of some cultural contact between Poland and Britain demonstrated the extent of his acquired Englishness. Yes, he loved the land of his birth, and carried within himself a little parcel of ideas about its culture and history, ideas that had been sown in the animated environment of his early childhood. The war had deprived him of knowledge of his country beyond the circle of family and friends in Warsaw; he realised that he was in love with an idea of Poland rather then with its present reality. Had he been brought up in the countryside it might have been different. Geography is not easily changed, and the landmarks of his early youth would be there for him to see; but the world of his childhood had perished, literally buried in the ruins and another had been substituted. He had to admit, not without a sense of guilt, that the countryside of Gloucestershire, alien though it was in many ways, and however remote he might feel from most of its inhabitants, was more like home to him than was Warsaw. Were his plans for his forest partly a desire to create something that would truly be home? The feeling of guilt prompted him to add, 'I must say that this cultural visit is an exciting idea. Do you really think it'll happen, and even if it does, won't it be just a propaganda exercise?'

'I don't know anything about the ins and outs,' she replied with her customary disarming frankness. 'I'm only involved in it as a business proposition. But for your sake I hope something comes of it. I'm sure you must miss having contact with Poland, so if Poland comes to you that'll be marvellous, won't it? And I remember how your eyes lit up when we met old Mrs Sikorska.'

James felt thoroughly confused. He who had long thought of himself, not without reason, as the giver of meagrely requited love now found himself in the presence of consideration and affection which, if not necessarily allied with passionate love, had a power of its own; penetrating, fruitful and compelling. What had wrought the change in Madeleine, bringing forth care and concern where formerly he had experienced coldness and a reluctance to become involved? Had this other facet of her personality always existed, and he been blind to it? Or was it something new, burgeoning in response to the warmth he had shown? Whatever the cause he rejoiced at its manifestation.

'It's about time I had another shot at trying to trace my brothers and sister, though it's a pretty hopeless task.'

'Yes, you should. It would be good for the baby to have some relatives apart from us, even if they hardly ever meet. You've never actually told me much about your family.'

Constance had induced James to speak about his relatives on many occasions in the early days when she had been trying to make him feel at home, but Madeleine had rarely been present and he had not felt that she was sufficiently interested to broach the matter with her directly, and in this he was probably right.

'I expect we were too busy growing up, and in any case the memories were too painful to begin with. And afterwards life was so full for both of us, wasn't it? It may seem strange to you, but even though it's not much more than ten years ago my recollections are already a bit hazy, and if I were to meet my brothers I probably wouldn't recognise them, though I might know my sister. You see, I haven't even a photograph to remind me of what they looked like then, let alone now – always assuming they're alive.'

She coaxed him on, and as he described his family, rummaging through his memories to illustrate its members, he recalled more and more episodes and little details which had drifted to the edge of his consciousness and were now summoned back through the interest of someone who loved him. They continued talking until late in the evening, and when they rose to go to bed, Madeleine parted the curtains and looked out into the night.

James asked, 'Are you thinking it'll be a cold wet day for our voyage of discovery tomorrow?'

'Yes, that's exactly what I was thinking, but I've brought warm clothes so don't worry. Only... I wonder whether my gumboots are still watertight.'

'No, the ones that you left behind aren't. But you'll find a new pair waiting for you by the back door, and some long woolly stockings to go with them. Size five, if I remember correctly.'

'You think of everything, don't you?' she said laughing lightly, but inwardly marvelling at her strange husband who combined the soul of a romantic with a meticulous attention to detail.

On the following morning Madeleine felt no sickness and they set out early to view the estate. James had wisely planned a comparatively brief expedition, in order not to tire Madeleine or to place excessive strain on her newly discovered interest in the countryside. For their tour of the farm they used the Land-Rover as far as possible, but when they approached the area of the proposed forest he drew up and said, 'I think this bit has to be done on foot, if you feel up to it, like all the best pilgrimages.'

It was almost the first time that he had used a religious allusion when speaking with Madeleine. Such allusions came naturally to him but he had consciously avoided uttering them for fear of placing a barrier between himself and one who, in spite of the love that he felt for her, he could not fail to see as a cherished pagan. That he was now able to use a little of his own language with her was a measure of how much closer they had grown. For James the visit was symbolic, and what mattered was that they should be on the site together rather than that they should spend very long examining it. He was conscious of the need not to expose her to excessive fatigue, but she insisted on stopping repeatedly to look at vistas and refer to the planting scheme that he had brought. She had understood, intuitively rather than through any words of his, what the forest meant to him, and was willing herself into his dream. In the end he had to urge her to come away lest she overtire herself.

'I'm not as fragile as all that,' she said, and tightened her grip on his arm. In spite of her disclaimer she felt weary and the prospect of being cosseted was not unattractive. She added, 'So what's next?'

'We go back and restore ourselves, and later on, if you like, we'll look at the financial side of the estate.'

'Yes, I'd like that.'

It felt strange to be protected and to have one's needs and desires taken into consideration. Since her departure from Briar Cottage the only occasions on which she had experienced such tenderness had been provided by James's visits, and her independent nature and commitment to business had prevented her from feeling any deprivation. Had James tried to cajole her into giving up her business and woo her into the condition of submissive housewife and mother, she would have rejected his protection with spirit, but now she found that it was possible to enjoy the best of both worlds. She let herself be borne along on the firm current of his devotion, uncertain of its destination, trustfully, and to her increasing surprise, joyfully. Her personality became linked with his, not compromised by it.

They spent the afternoon discussing James's plans for the estate's financial well-being, and he was repeatedly surprised at her quick grasp of details and the relevance of her observations.

'You're your mother's daughter, right enough.'

It was intended to be a great compliment and, knowing his esteem for Constance, she took it as such.

'As a matter of fact, Mummy didn't use to talk much about business with me, at any rate not in great detail, but I suppose I couldn't help growing up with a feel for it. What surprises me is that you should have discovered such a flair for finance, because I don't suppose business was talked about much in your home.'

'Scarcely ever.'

'So how was it you took so readily to making money on the Stock Exchange?'

'Didn't you realise?' he replied with genuine astonishment. Then, seeing her pained expression, he immediately regretted his words. 'I dare say I managed to keep my motives concealed. You see, when Mummy and you welcomed me into your home I was overwhelmed. I doubt whether you can imagine yourself in my situation, however hard you try, one moment a displaced person, the next an honoured guest. I know that term may sound a bit high pitched for a boy of fifteen, but that's how it felt. Not once was Mummy's attitude condescending, never was any allusion made to how lucky I was. I was given to feel that I was conferring a benefit on the family. All that made me want to repay the kindness by doing the kinds of things that Mummy would appreciate. Doing well at school wasn't particularly difficult because I enjoyed it and I was ambitious; I suppose I wanted to prove myself as good as the English boys. But even before Mummy gave each of us money to invest I was trying to cultivate an interest in business. Quite simply, I wanted to join in the things that seemed to matter to the family. I wanted really to become a part of it through my own efforts as well as being accepted out of kindness. Does all this seem very odd?'

'No, but somehow it had never occurred to me. I suppose I wasn't a particularly sensitive kind of person.'

'I wouldn't know about that. Anyhow, having made a start in business I found I was getting some satisfaction out of making right decisions, as well as winning Mummy's approval, and gradually I found myself becoming what Guy called a financial wizard, particularly on the Stock Exchange. It was quite intoxicating for a while.'

'And then?'

'Before long the utter futility of the exercise became apparent, and so did its danger and hypocrisy. Dangerous, because making money might have become a goal in itself, and hypocritical because of the aura of respectability that surrounds it. Speculation on the Exchange is simply gambling and no more honourable than Joe Bloggs putting his money on the dogs or horses. In either case a certain amount of background knowledge and study is necessary for success. The money game is more sophisticated and white-collar, but the aims are the same as Joe Bloggs's: to make predictions, to have a flutter and to come away the richer without having produced anything of real value. I've come to despise it, even though I still occasionally indulge as a means of making money for something useful.'

'I'd no idea you were a socialist.'

'Am I? Anyway, this is serious stuff, and it's getting late. Are you sure you'll be up to attending the service tomorrow? It's going to be cold and damp.'

'I'm feeling fine. We Todds are a tough lot.'

'Indeed. Incidentally I almost forgot to tell you that old Father Ryan will be looking in tomorrow afternoon. I don't think he wants to see me about anything in particular, he probably wants to renew your acquaintance and say nice things about the baby.'

'Then perhaps it's just as well he doesn't know how I felt about it a few weeks ago,' she said grimly. 'He wouldn't understand.'

James shot her an enquiring glance. Was she carrying a load of guilt that she still kept from him?

'God doesn't judge us by what we think or do when we're frightened, darling, and we're not to judge ourselves.'

As they prepared to go to bed they reflected separately that each occasion on which they met brought them fresh insights into each other's natures, and Madeleine could not repress a twinge of apprehension at the prospect of meeting Father Ryan. She remembered him as a rather formal, alien figure with whom she had little in common, and whose attitudes towards many things would, she feared, be incomprehensible.

The war memorial at Great Walling faced the parish church across the village green. It was an unostentatious monument consisting of a figure of a First World War infantryman with head bowed, leaning on his rifle. The statue was black, the plinth of grey granite. Its sober and solemn appearance matched the weather. Low cloud enveloped the group of about two hundred people watching the Vicar, Mr Brothers, walking down the steps of the church towards them. A thin little breeze briefly lifted the edges of the British Legion's banners and stirred the Vicar's vestments. A portable radio carried by Mrs Brothers relayed the national service from the Cenotaph, the imperfect transmission failing to detract from the simple solemnity of the occasion.

Madeleine always enjoyed the Remembrance Day service, but this was the first time she had attended one in a country village, and although she was not a religious person she felt seized by the atmosphere which here was emphasised by the encompassing cloud that wrapped the participants and isolated them from the rest of the world. Conscious of her position as a leading, albeit absentee, member of the community, and anxious to support James, she had dressed simply but warmly, taking care not to appear like a smart visitor from London. She wore the Royal Navy brooch that Nigel had given their mother.

Remembrance Day was one of the few occasions on which she thought of her brother; her father's memory was closer. Of the group around the memorial she could not have addressed more than half a dozen by name, though most of them knew who she was. She reflected that had she attended a service in London she would have been in the presence of even fewer people whom she knew. Who did she know? A few old school 'friends', to none of whom was she close, some business acquaintances who were even more peripheral, and Guy and the Silvermanns, her mother's friends who could be depended upon but whom she had not originally sought. Even the child growing within her was not deliberately chosen, and the strange loveable man beside her she was coming to know only after three years of marriage. They had stumbled into marriage – succumbed to it might be a fitter description – but now at last she had chosen. Her presence here was no accident for, by being seen at her husband's side, she was proclaiming her state of life to the public and even more importantly, to him.

The little radio crackled as Mrs Brothers turned up the volume for the sounding of the Last Post. Several of the men came to attention and the atmosphere within the little group tightened as the silence began. Madeleine stole a glance at James, who for an instant looked remote from her, indeed from the very place. He stood straight, substantial, inscrutable. The guns rumbled in London. Droplets of mist began to congeal on his moustache; he seemed not to notice. Where was he? On the far side of Europe? She felt as close to him in his reverie, from which she was excluded, as though he were speaking. While the strains of the Reveille died away he looked down and gently grasped her arm.

'I wasn't away for very long, was I, darling?'
'I was there with you.'

He wanted to kiss her there and then. Instead he contented himself with squeezing her arm tightly and they waited until the end of the service before speaking again.

When, as was the custom, the congregation retired to the village hall for hot drinks, Madeleine found herself in the company of James's friends from the British Legion. Her instinctive apprehension at being in the company of people from a very different background to hers was softened by the obvious regard in which they held James and their evident wish to meet his wife. She was an object of friendly curiosity. A short stocky man came up to her.

'I see you're wearing a Royal Navy brooch, Mrs Todd. There aren't many ex-sailors round here, in fact I'm the only one in our branch, apart from the Vicar.'

'I'm afraid I wasn't in the Navy myself. My brother gave this to our mother.'

In response to his inquiring look she added, 'He was lost on an Atlantic convoy.'

'I'm sorry. I was torpedoed twice myself.'

Others clustered around them; small talk was exchanged and after twenty minutes James took advantage of a lull in conversation to whisper, 'Shall we escape now?'

As they drove home she said,

'I won't be sorry to get home after all that standing, but didn't you want to talk a bit longer with your cronies?'

'Not really. I value their friendliness but I've little in common with most of them apart from having had a rough time during the war, and that quickly dries out as a subject of conversation. Well, it does for me, at any rate. You know small talk has never been my forte.'

'Who was the ex-sailor who came to speak with me?'

'Bill Sugden. He runs a garage a few miles out on the road to Frogbury and spends most of his time mending agricultural machinery, but he's one of those chaps who just know how to make things work and quite a lot of people take their cars to him.'

'He seemed very friendly.'

'Once when he was torpedoed, he was picked up by a Polish destroyer, which made for a talking point when we first met. He's

Coming to Terms

the secretary of the branch and has always tried to make me welcome there as a guest, not that I go very often, but I appreciate the gesture. Bill's a live wire.'

'I'm glad you're so popular with the local people.'

'I don't know about being popular. I put in an appearance at some of their functions and contribute to their causes, and I've been able to help some of them find jobs. But I'm not really close to any of them.'

'We're terribly alike in some ways, aren't we?'

'I had noticed,' he replied with a broad smile.

After lunch James went to inspect the farm and before his return Father Ryan arrived.

'I've come a bit earlier than I expected, now isn't that bad planning. Priests and doctors are poor timekeepers, you know.'

'It doesn't matter at all, Father, but I'm afraid my husband isn't back yet. He won't be long, though.'

Why had she said 'my husband' instead of Jim? Was she protecting herself against informality?

'Oh, that's fine. It was really you I was hoping to see. I can meet Mr Todd at any time.'

As she showed him into the drawing room she wondered whether he was commenting on her absence or merely making some small talk. If he had reservations about the quality of her marriage his bluff manner did not betray them. He sat heavily, legs apart, hands folded, composed, observing her through thin-rimmed spectacles with a gaze that, she felt, needed but a twitch of a muscle to shift from the benign to the inquisitorial, from the bluff to the censorious. His craggy chin jutted forward.

'I was so pleased to hear that you are starting a family. Children are a blessing, indeed they are. And a responsibility too.'

'I'm sure they are. I'm very conscious of what my mother gave me.'

'The Fourth Commandment is a lovely thing.'

Madeleine murmured assent while trying to recall which commandment was the fourth. He went on,

'You'll excuse my mentioning it, but if you have any difficulty in the education of your child I shall always be available.'

'Oh... thank you very much, but I can't really see so far ahead

Coming to Terms

at the moment. We have plenty of time to choose the right school for him, or her.'

'I wasn't thinking about schooling. I meant your child's upbringing in the Faith.'

So that was the reason for the visit. Madeleine had given the matter not a moment's thought.

'Don't worry about that, Father. When I married Jim I promised to bring our children up as Catholics and mean to keep my promise.'

He detected an edge to her voice. 'Please don't think I was suggesting you would not, but there's a big step from the honest intention to knowing how to do it. You see, what a young child receives from its mother is so important, and with all the goodwill in the world you may find it difficult to give what perhaps you do not have in this respect. Don't misunderstand me, I am not questioning your sincerity, I just don't know how easy you will find it to instruct your child in the Faith.'

She appreciated his polite but direct approach. 'If you are asking me how I feel about religion...' he nodded imperceptibly... 'I suppose I'd have to say that I've never thought much about it. I call myself C of E because that's what I am officially, but my family weren't church-goers, and although I know religion means a lot to Jim it's an area in which we haven't much in common.' She paused, and added, 'I suppose that's a pity, but I can't pretend to an enthusiasm I haven't got.'

'That's very honest of you, Mrs Todd, but you can see that it must make it difficult for you to perform the task with conviction, and the responsibility will fall on Mr Todd. I hope you and he will feel free to consult me.'

'Don't Church schools help in teaching religion?'

'Of course, but that is formal instruction, the preparation for Holy Communion. I am talking about the daily growing up in the Faith, the general atmosphere in the home and the prayers that a mother teaches her children. It is indeed a pearl without price.'

'Well, I'm sorry, but as you say, I can't give what I haven't got. All I can do is encourage Jim in what he teaches our child as best I can, and naturally I'd welcome support from anyone in doing so.'

'Children learn by imitation. The best way you can help is by being with your child at Mass, going as a family, from the beginning.'

'Surely you don't want babies in church. They'd make a noise and interrupt your sermon.'

'Oh, Mrs Todd, I don't think you understand what the Mass is about. I try to preach as good a sermon as I can, but it's only a small part of the Mass. It's far less important than the people's presence there, and I don't suppose the loss of a few of my words matters very much. You see, the Mass is not like a theatrical performance; it is a celebration of our blessed Lord's sacrifice and His presence in the Eucharist. We try to make it as beautiful as possible with words and music and vestments, not for show but out of reverence for the Eucharist, and the children's innocent noise is not irreverent. I won't deny that their crying can be a distraction, but they've as much right to be present as anyone else.'

'Even though they don't understand what's going on?'

'Of course. Understanding is a matter of degree. Not even the most intelligent man in the world can hope to understand the mystery of the real presence, but it is God giving Himself to us, so it would be a dreadful thing to deprive children of that gift.'

Madeleine felt baffled and lost in his terminology. When they were preparing for marriage James had tried to explain what Catholicism meant to him, but she had been unable to summon up interest in a religion that seemed far more alien than her fiancé.

By unspoken consent the subject had been quietly dropped, and James had not revealed the aridity that its loss brought to his life.

'For Jim's sake I wish I could respond better to his religious feelings, but even though I can't I'll still do anything that's necessary to fulfil the obligation I undertook. I'll take our child to Mass even when Jim's not with me.'

It was Father Ryan's turn to be puzzled.

'But Mr Todd never misses Sunday Mass.'

'I mean on those Sundays when he's down here and I'm in town.'

Fr Ryan was even more perplexed. His expression alternated between confusion and displeasure.

'Will you not be living here permanently, then?'

'I can't. I've got a business to run. Sometimes Jim will come up, and sometimes I'll come here at the weekend.'

'But...' Father Ryan's cheeks whitened with the beginning of the anger that showed in the only word he spoke before his jaw tightened as he checked himself. He was unaccustomed to speaking with women of her class, and his instinct told him he would do no good if he addressed her in the authoritarian style that he would have employed with one of his rural parishioners who showed signs of neglecting her duty. Besides, she was a Protestant, or rather an agnostic, and would not be browbeaten. And yet she was clearly an honest woman, and he believed her assurance that she would do her best to bring up the children of a mixed marriage. He suppressed the urge to comment on a mother's place being in the home. The craggy face relaxed and a vestige of a smile flickered round the tight edges of his mouth. As usual, when he knew he was beaten, he retired gracefully.

'I'm sure there's more than one way of doing things, and I'm confident that yours will be a good Christian home. And remember that I'm always available.'

'Yes, Father, I know, and believe me, in spite of the difference in our outlook I appreciate what you have said.'

The moment of confrontation had passed. Father Ryan made some polite conversation on life in London and Madeleine's business, and soon after James's return he left.

'A dry old stick, but not a bad chap,' said James, 'even if he is a bit set in his opinions.'

Madeleine pondered that, and murmured, 'At least he knows what he stands for.'

12: Friendly Advice

'You know,' said Jacob Silvermann as he thrust his huge shaggy head out of James's study window, 'I dare say I can survive a few days of natural beauty as long as it is accompanied by conversation and certain other essentials of life. You don't mind if I smoke?'

'Of course not,' replied James, bringing out his pipe, 'we can puff away here for all we're worth, and as long as we keep the door closed it won't worry Ruth. How is she, really?'

On their arrival Ruth had retired upstairs to rest after the long journey, leaving James and Jacob together.

'It's hard to tell. The doctor thinks it's just a mixture of excitement and exhaustion brought on by looking after Guinevere – not that she needs to, because Rebecca does all that's necessary, but Ruth can't detach herself and wants to share every minute of Guinevere's day.'

'It's natural enough, I suppose, and shouldn't do any harm provided Rebecca doesn't feel she's being upstaged, or Bill for that matter. Lucky Guinevere.'

Jacob looked hard at James; understanding through the almost parental bond between them all that his friend had left unsaid.

'You know that to the extent you care to use us, your child can have proxy grandparents. I think we're both good for a few more years.'

' I do know, and believe me it's a great comfort.'

'How did Madeleine's visit go?'

'Perfectly, in every respect. Each time we meet we wonder why we were not able to achieve happiness in the first place. In what ways have we changed since she went back to work in London?'

He had not been able to bring himself to say 'since our separation'. Jacob said nothing, inviting him to go on speaking.

'Of course I have prayed for this greater understanding, so perhaps it is unreasonable of me now to be surprised at its coming.'

'You would not expect me, as a practising atheist, to comment on that.' He smiled. 'But it may be that you had each rather taken the other for granted, through long acquaintance, and needed the shock of separation to make you appreciate what you were missing.'

'That's true of me, but I'm not sure that Madeleine was missing me until I went back to see her. She was getting on very well without me.'

'Anyway, all that is history. What matters now is the future. Have you solved the problem of who will live where?'

'Yes, in principle. Madeleine should have no difficulty in finding a suitable nanny. She will try and work slightly shorter hours and come here some weekends, and I'll go to town a great deal more than I've been used to. Not an ideal arrangement, perhaps, but I think our children will be the richer for the experience as they grow up. I hope.'

'I half agree with you, but I'd have had a job selling such an idea to Ruth when ours were young.'

'Of course, and yet presumably when Izzy marries he'll have a similar problem.'

'That is just one of the reasons why Ruth was sorry he decided to become a soldier. Well, sorry is an inadequate description – almost hysterical would be nearer the truth. And, with perfect logic, now that she sees how happy he is, and how well he is doing, she can't remember her initial disapproval. Indeed, there is no more enthusiastic "Army mum".'

'And you didn't mind?'

'It would not have been my personal choice, but I could understand his reasons, and now I'm sure he was right.'

'Is it really true that you never addressed envelopes to him when he was called up? He told me it was always done by Ruth or Rebecca, although you wrote at length.'

'Quite true. I could never bring myself to address my son by his army number. It seemed an affront to his individuality, and historically numbers had a very unpleasant connotation for us, as I'm sure you understand. So I took the coward's way out and let Ruth address the letters because, like most women, she is not beset by philosophical considerations. How's that for a sweeping generalisation? And now tell me all about what you're doing to this place.'

James would rather have discussed the sweeping generalisation, but did as his friend asked and spoke about the estate, which did not prove to be an easy task. Jacob was entirely a man of the town, and ignorant of the most basic aspects of country life. For a man whose walls were lined with original works of art, including many landscapes, he knew as little as a small child about nature itself. He had watched his wife's enthusiasm for their garden with detached amusement, happy that she should have her enjoyment, and was now genuinely surprised that a man like James, whose intellect he admired, should find fulfilment in a world so far removed from pure thought. He found himself asking the most elementary questions, being bewildered at discovering that there was more than one kind of grass, or that trees were not limited to oaks and pines.

After an hour, Ruth joined them and Jacob announced, 'I am now an expert in country matters, and shall be able to advise you on horticulture,' adding sotto voce, 'as long as it is strictly armchair advice.'

'I'm sure that's all it would be.'

'It's all she'd accept,' he told James. 'The garden is second only to Guinevere on Ruth's scale of importance, and she won't let anyone work in it. I am resigned to having to take a passive interest, much as I should like to set to with fork and spade.'

Jacob's reluctance to concern himself with gardening was a standing joke in the family, and he played up to it.

James derived joy from having them under his roof. From early days he had respected Ruth if only because she was his great friend's mother. Affection had come later as he came to know her better when the friendship with Izzy had become closer, and visits to their house had given him a feeling of belonging in a family whose atmosphere, in spite of the difference in race and religion, had much in common with his own. Ruth complemented the more distant, though no lesser, affection that sprang from Constance's stronger and more assertive character. The one provided the uninhibited warmth, the other the driving spirit. Each loved him in her own way and he responded accordingly to

Friendly Advice

each. For Jacob, however, his love went deeper still, because it lay not only in the human touch and at the level of loving devotion but far, far beyond, to the realm of the intellect, where what was savoured was neither gastronomy nor commercial initiative but the wide-ranging exploration of ideas.

He had often felt when, as a schoolboy, he used to order the future of the world with John and Izzy and Bill, that Jacob, in spite of the difference in age, could well have been one of their group. Indeed, when he had occasionally looked in on them the flow of ideas had usually burst into a flood, and in a short time he had enriched the discussion, speaking with the four intelligent young men naturally and as a contemporary. Jacob had not been entirely frivolous in suggesting that philosophy played but a small part in women's conversation. From his limited experience James had come to a similar conclusion, and the existence of some exceptions merely proved the rule. On the other hand, might not the same be said of most men?

He recalled a conversation with John Stonor on that very point, which John had brought to a temporary conclusion by proclaiming, 'But my dear chap, it is a truth universally acknowledged that most men are interested only in beer, money and sex – not necessarily in that order.'

Good old John, never at a loss for a quip, and at heart very serious behind the façade of facetiousness.

James had resolved to make the most of his friends' visit in two different ways. With Jacob he hoped for long periods of discussion while Ruth took the rest for which she had come, but he needed to speak with her too, for she was the only person in the world who could help him in one particular respect. He seized the opportunity by the fireside one evening when Jacob, under the influence of hospitality, had dozed off.

'Ruth, tell me about babies.'

She looked up and stared at him wide-eyed and innocently.

'Well, they come in various shapes and sizes, and some are more cuddly than others. What else would you like to know?'

He was taken aback by her whimsical reply, delivered with a schoolgirlish mischievousness that seemed out of keeping. He attributed it to her feeling comfortable and carefree away from her domestic responsibilities, whereas it was a reaction to his own puzzled solemnity, of which he was wholly unaware.

'No, but seriously, you know what I mean. What is their effect on a couple, particularly on the mother? You see, I know nothing about babies; in fact Guinevere is the only one I've ever held.'

Ruth knew James better than he knew her. She sensed what he wanted to know, and why he had to ask her. She hedged a little.

'It makes everything very different, and fuller. In fact for mothers it's very full indeed, a whole-time occupation for some years. But you must have spoken with Madeleine.' She paused. 'What exactly do you want to know?'

'As you've guessed, it's not always easy to sort these things out with Madeleine. I don't think I'm being disloyal in saying that in her eyes maternity is not the most wonderful state in the world. Not yet at any rate. Is that serious?'

'Oh James, you can be such a solemn boy!' She laughed. 'Jacob has said that more than once. Oh dear, perhaps I've betrayed a confidence. But you do take things terribly seriously, and I think you've been making assumptions about women. Perhaps you imagine that we all rush for babies like – what do you call those little mouse things that run into the sea?'

Very occasionally Ruth still hesitated over an English expression.

'Lemmings?'

'Yes. Well, many do, but quite a lot are prepared to wait, and when babies come they do their best for them and become good mothers. They have to, don't they? The fathers are too busy earning a living to look after the children, even if they want to.'

'You make it seem as though motherhood is often an occupation undertaken out of necessity rather than purposeful delight.'

'Yes, it often is. The delight nearly always comes, but most women marry for husbands, not babies. And don't forget that quite a lot stay single out of choice. You seem to think that all women have the same reactions. Men don't, do they, so why should we?'

'Quite right, my dear.' Jacob sounded more guttural than

Friendly Advice

usual as he cleared his throat and shook his huge body awake.

Ruth and James said simultaneously, '*We thought you were asleep.*'

'You know I never sleep except in bed. Quite right, James has been making unwarrantable assumptions about the genus woman when in fact there is no such thing as "woman" but only individual women. Categorising all women as a group is a piece of convenient card indexing by men. I'm afraid James has been guilty of a sweeping generalisation, unworthy of a philosopher.'

'You old hypocrite!' said James. 'Who was making a sweeping generalisation not so long ago?'

'About what?' asked Ruth.

'Oh nothing of any importance, and even if I did I am to be forgiven because I am not a philosopher but a mere engineer.' And he brushed the matter aside with a majestic sweep of his hand. He continued, 'We're not answering James's question, or rather the one behind the question.'

'Namely?'

'To what extent your way of life will have to change.'

'That's about it. Sounds selfish, doesn't it?'

'Not at all. You're right to think about it now rather than be unpleasantly surprised later.'

'Unpleasantly?'

'Yes,' said Ruth, 'because you've only just got Madeleine back and soon you'll be losing part of her again. Once the baby's born it will be the most important thing in her life for a while, and you'll feel cut off. And your scholarly peace is going to be shattered.'

'I'm prepared for that. What worries me is how to make things work out, especially for Madeleine. You see – and please forgive my burdening you with my personal problems, but who else can I ask? – I know her feelings about becoming a mother are a bit ambivalent and I'm afraid she may see the baby as competing for attention with her business. Can she do justice to both?'

He did not add, 'and to me', and neither could he reveal even to his close friends the initial revulsion that Madeleine had felt at the prospect of motherhood. He did not know how they would have reacted to learning that she had contemplated abortion and

Friendly Advice

did not want to risk lowering their esteem for her. He added, 'Is a nanny ever an adequate solution?'

'I wouldn't have wanted one myself, because I'm an old-fashioned Jewish mama and I wanted my children around me, but the English seem to make it work. Up to a point. It's like their boarding schools. It seems a crazy system to me; why have children and give other people the pleasure of bringing them up? But sometimes it doesn't work out too badly.'

In that summary manner did Ruth dismiss a large part of traditional English education. It was one of her hobbyhorses, but James was keen to return to his immediate problem.

'How can we reconcile working nearly two hundred miles apart with sharing in our child's upbringing? Especially since Madeleine could do with more support than many young mothers? That's my problem.'

'Without underestimating the problem,' murmured Jacob, 'don't underestimate Madeleine either. One of the advantages, I dare say you'd call it the blessing, of the human gestation period is that it gives the parents time to think and plan, and in your case, to come to terms. Obviously, for some weeks around the time your baby is born, Madeleine will be fully committed, but after that it shouldn't be difficult to find a suitable nanny. As long as you and Madeleine don't mind a lot of travelling, it can work.'

'We've already discussed the mechanics of it, and I'm sure at the practical and superficial level it can work. But is it really fair to the child, or to our marriage? I've even wondered whether we ought to give this place up and get a house near London.'

'Don't,' said Ruth emphatically. 'Madeleine would feel the sacrifice was all on your side and it would be a burden for her.'

'Ruth is right,' agreed Jacob. 'Avoid the great quixotic gesture, keep this place which you love and which fulfils part of your nature, but be prepared to spend rather less time here. As you mentioned earlier, your child will be the richer for having this to look forward to. And think of those long journeys... what an opportunity for writing poetry.'

'But I'm not a poet.'

'It's never too late to start,' Jacob murmured as he settled back in his chair and studied the ceiling with rapt attention.

Friendly Advice

Their conversation, inconclusive though it had been, had reassured James. His friends had told him little that he had not already known but in their different ways had reinforced his confidence and given him an often needed reminder not to take life, or himself, too seriously.

The rest of the visit passed uneventfully and when, after a fortnight, Jacob and Ruth returned to London, she claimed to feel much restored and he sang the praises of the living countryside while continuing to maintain that he preferred to experience it through glass rather than through the soles of his feet.

13: *Some Soul Searching*

James's next visitor was John Stonor. They had kept up a frequent correspondence since the visit that had precipitated James's and Madeleine's reconciliation, but John took his work seriously, as a vocation, and could rarely take a weekend off because that was the only time when he was able to find some of his clients at home. On this occasion he had been able to spare a weekend and arrived at Briar Cottage just before lunch on Saturday.

'Greetings, oh mighty lover,' he said. 'I see the table is set for two. Aren't you going to have lunch? It is quite unnecessary for the ardent lover to be wan and under-nourished. In fact a hearty appetite is much to be recommended.'

'There's only the two of us after all. Madeleine had to cry off because of some panic at the office. She's sorry not to see you on this occasion, but I'll go up and spend some time with her myself well before Christmas.'

'Give her my love. I hope that under the beneficent influence of marital bliss she is feeling as well as you look.'

'Everything's going very well.' He described the way they proposed to divide their time between London and Briar Cottage, and how Madeleine would combine motherhood and business. He ended by saying, 'I'm optimistic about the outcome.'

'You seem to have it all wrapped up with your customary efficiency,' remarked John, staring innocently at the ceiling and nursing a long pause.

James knew his friend well enough to realise that some asperity must follow on the heels of John's commendation. He filled his pipe as he awaited the oracular pronouncement, which, in the event, was both gentler and more sphinx-like than he had expected.

'Of course it's all a matter of priorities. I merely wonder whether the right mental balance is being struck between practicalities, important as they are, and the deeper essentials. In response to your figuratively raised eyebrows, let me enlarge on that. I have no doubt that both of you will come to terms with the practical difficulties of geography and being part-time parents, not that you should underestimate them; but won't physical distance between you and your child make for problems in its early education?'

'Elucidation, please.'

'Well, I know how deeply you feel about religion. Unless Madeleine has undergone a sudden change, she won't be in a position to give the sort of maternal teaching that Catholic mothers are supposed to impart, and you will have to make up for it. Physical separation won't help.'

'This is remarkably perceptive from such a sceptic as you.'

'I'm not blind to religious feelings, as I explained last time we met, but only to the stuffiness and hypocrisy that often accompanies their expression. I suppose the labels of cynic and sceptic will stick for a long time owing to the youthful utterances with which I burdened my friends ad nauseam.'

'Never ad nauseam, rather *delectandum*,' said James, grinning. 'But enough of this schoolboy twaddle, what's the answer?'

'You supply the answer, I merely point to the problem.'

'I was rather hoping to establish a custom of saying prayers in the early days, and building on that later on. Doesn't that seem sound to you?'

'Fine, but if you are the only one to say prayers with your child, isn't there a danger that it will associate them exclusively with you, and eventually think either that you are odd for saying them, or that its mother is for not?'

'It might be right, either way. But seriously, I think one must do one's best in this best of all possible worlds, travel hopefully, and leave the outcome to God.'

'I'm touched at the combination of Voltaire and the Gospel.'

'Why not? Do you mean you're surprised that as a Catholic I should quote Voltaire?'

'I should hardly have thought that he would have been approved of in pre-war Poland. In fact his works are almost certainly on the index of books that you chaps aren't supposed to read.'

'I think it's best not to know what's on the list. You're quite right, *Candide* would have been frowned on by many people where I came from, and in other places too, but I remember my father referring to it sometimes, if only to annoy his mother-in-law, who was more Catholic than the Pope. He used to say its irony was a comfort when he was feeling low, but he urged me not to read it. He said I should wait until I was sixteen in order to appreciate it properly.'

'And did you?'

'Yes. Was it in the school library, or did I borrow it from the public library? I can't remember now, but it was while we were in the sixth form, and I think Father was wise to have advised me to wait. I devoured and savoured it. You probably read it about the same time.'

'Yes, but I don't think we discussed it much.'

'We were probably too busy planning the future of the world.'

'Indeed.'

John thought much, and said little, and the two friends sat in the stillness of concentration. After a while James said, 'We'd better avail ourselves of the stew which Mrs Brand has prepared for us.'

'Yes, it would be a culinary disaster of cosmic proportions to keep the stew waiting.'

After their lunch James took John for a brisk walk, during which they discussed the estate until, by unspoken consent, they fell silent, and moth-like steered their way back towards Briar Cottage's lighted windows. James wondered what went on in John's mind, a very different John from the carefree, rather flippant friend of his youth. Who had so far led the happier life? John had suffered no great trauma of war or love, and if he had given up the possibility of a brilliant professional career it had been in order to substitute the labour of his choice. And yet, what would John be looking forward to at the end of this weekend? To a small flat in an uninspiring neighbourhood, equipped admittedly with some of the trappings of civilised living, but which his work left him little time to enjoy, devoting his life to helping total strangers whose troubles were probably largely of their own making. Few of them, if any, were people who could offer a relationship between equals, and John was without any one

Some Soul Searching

person to whom he could dedicate himself in the fullness of his being.

This was the John Stonor whose rooms at Oxford had been a centre of intellectual and social undergraduate life, who enjoyed good food, wine and conversation in the company of sophisticated friends, and had given every indication of not suffering fools gladly. Was this a vocation in action, and if so who, as far as John was concerned, was calling? He had evidently cast off the quasi-atheism of his early days and was groping for... what? For a psychological prop? He was too mature and intellectually honest to deceive himself knowingly, just for comfort's sake, so was he consciously seeking? Was he at the level of philanthropic agnosticism, and aware of its limitations?

James considered his own situation, contrasting it favourably with John's. He had suffered much in his twenty-five years but now looked forward to joy and fulfilment as husband and father as well as in the life of the mind. Was not John's way perhaps the more generous? Whereas he hoped to bring happiness to two or three people, John served a great many, most of whom would bring him little in return. John's celibate life had a sacrificial quality in its single-mindedness and continuous availability to his clients, 'without seeking any reward'. The prayer went on to say, 'save that of knowing that I do Thy will'; but what did that mean to John in his state of doubt and uncertainty?

In its state of social isolation and total dedication, John's life resembled that of a conscientious parish priest who served his congregation unstintingly, available to all, but without real intimacy with any individual except the Christ who seemed beyond John's knowledge. For whom or what was John living? His was too sharp a mind to trade in vague terms like 'the good of humanity'. How would he describe his vocation; what made him stick to his task?

These thoughts possessed him until they entered the house and prepared themselves for an evening by the fireside. Towards the end of the evening James said, 'I'll go to an early Mass. Can you hang on until I'm back for breakfast? If not you'll have to find your way around the kitchen. And which newspapers would you like me to bring?'

'Would you mind terribly if I came with you?'

Some Soul Searching

'Of course not. I can arrange for you to receive instruction if you like, and we'll make a good Catholic of you in no time at all!'

'Perish the thought! But seriously, I'd like to see what goes on. It may even help me to understand the mind of a client of mine.'

'Far be it from me to stand in the way of sociological inquiry.'

They attended Mass together and on the way back spoke about the countryside. Over breakfast they discussed politics. James restrained himself from asking his friend whether he had enjoyed the Mass, and it was not until they had ensconced themselves in the study that John remarked, 'I must admit that the general atmosphere at Mass seemed pretty remote from the world I know, but the Gospel had something to say to a suffering world. I mean about the blind seeing and the lame walking. But it is all rather in the realm of promise, isn't it? The gospel has been preached for a long time and yet there's plenty of work to keep people like me busy. I dare say you'd reply that we should interpret it as meaning spiritually blind and lame, but Jesus cured physical ills too.'

'And so He does today. But to return to the evils of the world. I don't think you should worry about the fact that the world is no better today than two thousand years ago. In some ways it is better, in others worse: every age brings its own problems. What matters as far as each individual is concerned is to strive to leave each day a little better than the previous one, both in himself, that is to say in his inner self, and for his neighbours insofar as he is able to help them. So there will be work for all of us, not only the professional social workers, until the end of time.'

'That's fair enough.'

A long pause ensued. John ventured, 'I would not describe the good Father Ryan as an inspiring personality, would you?'

'No. So, as our American friends would say, what?'

'It might make his ministry more compelling if he were.'

'Probably, but being inspiring is a bonus. Remember that he is preaching to the converted, and what matters is that he should be sound and reliable. In his own down-to-earth way he is kind. He is a country parish priest and serves his congregation well. If you were an old lady dying in a lonely cottage he would be at your bedside even if it meant driving there through the snow, and his congregation appreciates that. The Bishop has to make the best use of his priests just as your superior uses his discretion when he allocates clients to you. As a university chaplain Father Ryan would be a disaster; here he is merely unexciting.'

'But at least he knows where he stands, and so do you.'

James immediately recalled Madeleine's comment couched in similar words. Could it be that his wife and one of his best friends were groping their way towards truth, that they envied him the conviction they were unable to share? He decided to play devil's advocate.

'Knowing where one stands, having convictions, is all very well, and generally leads to action. But conviction is not to be admired for its own sake. Hitler, and Genghis Khan had it. I see no merit in conviction as such. Fools and madmen have it too. It is the quality of the conviction that counts.'

'Whose side are you on now? Don't you believe Father Ryan's convictions are soundly based? After all, their base is presumably the same as yours.'

'I can't assume anything of the sort, although I agree there is a high probability of it, because I don't know what goes on in anyone else's mind. Don't you think there is a danger of confusing conviction based on an intellectual process with an emotionally induced conviction, or prejudice? Seen from the outside they might be indistinguishable. I have come to the conclusion that I know very little about what motivates anyone, not even myself. Or Madeleine.'

'For practical purposes it doesn't matter. When my clients are in court the magistrates can judge only what they did; assessing extenuating circumstances is largely in the realm of guesswork.'

'That is why man cannot dispense justice, however hard he tries.'

'Indeed. But you mentioned Madeleine. Don't you think that after many years of marriage husbands and wives come pretty close to knowing what prompts the other's actions?'

'Ask me again in ten years' time. I dare say that applies to the everyday things, but I am doubtful about the possibility of plumbing the depths of anyone else's motives in important matters. I really don't know.'

They talked about other things until the time came for James to drive John to the station. As they waited, each wrapped in his own thoughts, on the platform John returned out of the blue to the subject.

'Granted that in the mind of a villain or a madman conviction is dangerous, but I must admit it can be impressive when it is linked with kindness.'

'It is the source of energy behind every great thing that man does, for good or evil. You should know, you've got plenty. Otherwise you wouldn't be doing what you're doing.'

The train arrived. John climbed in and opened a window.

'You know, you're an illogical sort of chap. How can you be sure that what I do is motivated by conviction, when only this afternoon you were arguing the impossibility of knowing what motivates people?'

'I don't know what your conviction is, but I'm sure there must be one driving you. Come again soon!'

14: Plans and More Plans

As Madeleine opened the door of the flat a sense of relief overcame her. With Christmas only a fortnight away and James's arrival imminent, the sanctuary of home seemed more desirable than ever, and while business continued to hold her attention, she had to admit that its spell became less compelling as her pregnancy progressed.

A letter from James awaited her; long, loving and lavish with expressions of affectionate expectation, and at the same time, informative. Each had decided, independently, to communicate more by letter than by telephone. The written sheet served as a lasting companion to be savoured at leisure, an enduring tactile presence of the sender, and avoided the abrupt cut-off that followed the lengthy, often inconsequential, process of saying goodbye on the telephone.

While Madeleine prepared her supper she repeatedly returned to the letter, and when she sat down to eat propped it up in front of her and read it again. Her mind was at rest, not only because she had satisfied herself that adequate arrangements could be made for her business to continue in spite of her pregnancy, but also because she had taken the opportunity of Jacob's and Ruth's absence at Briar Cottage to call on Rebecca and speak more frankly with her than she feared she could in what she still felt to be Ruth's swamping presence.

She had called at the weekend when Bill was at home. With characteristic directness she told Rebecca, 'I've come to do some research. Tell me about babies.'

Unknowingly she had asked exactly the same question that James had put to Ruth.

'Mother's the real expert.'

'I dare say, but would you be shocked if I were to tell you that I find her enthusiasm just a little overpowering? That's why I thought I'd ask you.'

Plans and More Plans

'I think I know what you mean, but I let her do plenty of fussing because it gives me a rest and, well, Mummy's health's not good, as you know, and I want Guinevere to enjoy as much of her as she can. And Daddy too, for that matter.' A wave of sadness lapped over Rebecca's beautiful face.

So remote from domesticity had Madeleine grown that until that moment it had not occurred to her that their children would know no grandparents at all. Observing Rebecca's gentle allusion to her parents, she suddenly saw that it mattered.

'But surely your parents are good for quite a few more years?'

'I don't know. It saddens me to see them slowing down, even though there's nothing we can do about it.'

'Our child, or children perhaps, will have not a single grandparent, uncle, aunt or cousin. No one. I suppose it's a bit bleak if you think about it. I wonder whether your mother would care to be a sort of proxy granny?'

'Try and stop her!'

They talked a little about the practical side of raising a baby, and when Madeleine left she felt if not exactly the most enthusiastic of expectant mothers, that at any rate a few of her fears had been dispelled. Rebecca's parting words had been: 'Don't take it all too seriously. Enjoy your baby and see Jim in him, or her.'

As she savoured James's letter, Rebecca's words swam before her. She longed to make Jim happy, and was gradually unravelling some of the differences between their natures. While she found their separated state to be natural and fulfilling, James needed more. He needed to belong, not to the clubs and social activities that people devise to repel loneliness, but to a family, enjoying unspoken bonds which until now she had tended to keep at arm's length lest her privacy be invaded. Well, she meant to satisfy that need, now and even more with the birth of children, but in addition she had been playing with an idea which, if it came to fruition, would bring him a joy all the greater for having been unexpected.

The arrangements for the Polish cultural visit in the following year were slowly taking shape. She remembered James mentioning that one of his younger twin brothers had been interested in music and ballet. If some of James's family had survived, what joy

Plans and More Plans

for him and fulfilment for her if she could be the instrument of their reunion...

Which aspect was uppermost in her mind – his happiness, or hers at being the bearer of good news? A chill thought pierced her. Might the rediscovery of his family deflect, be it ever so slightly, his dedication to her? An unworthy thought, not instantly crushed, and she reproached herself for her weakness. And yet was not the very fact that she found herself living increasingly in the mind and not only in the day's action in itself a sign of the way in which she was growing into James's style? Who was being introspective now? She smiled inadvertently at her inner change, folded the letter and pushed the plate away from her. By the fireside she curled up on the settee, pretended that James was offering her the glass of brandy that, for the baby's sake, she declined, and devoured the letter again.

Would that she were able to reply in language that did justice to his. Closer though they had grown she could not match the warmth, the élan in which he expressed his emotion. She would not attempt an imitation lest it appear ridiculous, certainly to her and probably to James as well, yet she wished that she could bring herself to give as free a rein to her feelings on paper as she now did in his presence. She closed her eyes, tried to imagine him beside her and thrust away the thoughts about business which sought to penetrate her consciousness. That was now the pattern of most of her evenings. She had resolved to make the best of things and, being unable to enjoy James's company every evening, made a virtue of necessity, enjoying the solitude in anticipation of its ending, and indulging in shadow conversation with him – like some old crone reminiscing, she told herself.

A few days earlier she had entertained Guy to dinner at the flat, having declined his invitation to dine out, saying archly, 'I mustn't miss any opportunity of being a good housewife. You're going to be a guinea pig!'

'If it's anything like last time I won't be sorry.'

And it had been an excellent evening.

'For an old bachelor you are remarkably understanding about pregnancy.'

'If one keeps one's eyes and ears open one can learn quite a lot by proxy. Don't forget I have plenty of nephews and nieces, and I've watched their parents...'

'Agonising?'

'I was going to say, coping splendidly.'

'Well, I hope we won't let the side down,' she replied, sliding into his way of speaking.

Their talk was not confined to babies. He reminisced about company days, repeatedly praising her mother's part in its success. That made Madeleine feel guilty, for as he spoke she realised how small a space her mother's memory had occupied in her mind. Constance was remembered more by her son-in-law than by her daughter.

What a selfish bitch I've become, she thought, and simultaneously heard Guy's kind firm voice praising her.

'My dear, I think you must be one of the most unselfish people I've met. I know you've had to make hard decisions lately, and your mother would be proud of you. She was never one to shirk responsibility.'

'You don't think it's selfish to want to carry on with my business instead of living in Gloucestershire all the time?'

'It may seem so to some people, but it's no concern of theirs and it shouldn't worry you. But try not to plan everything in advance. Events may carry you along with them and you may actually come to prefer living down there. Strange though that may seem to you now.'

As usual Madeleine had taken Guy's words seriously, and asked herself whether it might not be possible to combine business life with permanent residence in the country. Of one thing she was certain; she wanted, indeed needed, some responsibility outside the home, some area of her life that was truly her own, shaped by her and through which she could express herself. She would never become – cruellest of labels – 'just a housewife', like Ruth Silvermann. She took great comfort from the knowledge that James understood her need, for she had feared that with his traditionalist background he might have expected a docility and conformity that she could not give.

She toyed with the idea of transferring the Galaxy Secretarial Agency to Gloucestershire but quickly dismissed it. Not even

Plans and More Plans

Gloucester itself was sufficiently galactic for the kind of international business she was creating. Perhaps she might start a more local sort of agency, or possibly something completely different might suggest itself if, as Guy implied, she stopped trying to run the world and gave events a chance to occur.

In the meantime there was Christmas to be arranged. She was determined that nothing should spoil this first family celebration of their restored marriage, and whatever Guy might have to say about the danger of over-planning life as a whole, she knew that successful events did not just happen. She applied herself to the minutiae of festive arrangements with the same energy and precision that had served her well in business. What she did not know about cooking she studied from books and tried out in practice. Although she would gladly have settled for an entirely private Christmas, resting from work, she knew that it meant far more than that to James and had spoken with their friends about visiting. For almost the first time in her life she was putting herself out to give pleasure and was pleasantly surprised to find herself enjoying it.

There was no point in writing James a long letter for he would be with her in a couple of days, and she was tired. Before going to bed she penned a few loving words and caressed his photograph with her eyes.

I suppose this is what being a wife is all about, she thought as she slid between the sheets. I wonder why it took me so long to realise it...

And she slept the sleep of the contented.

Book II

15: Six Years Later

Teddy bears, bunnies and picture books littered the floor. Madeleine had got Assunta ready for school, well mufflered against the December weather of 1962.

'Kiss Daddy goodbye, darling.'

James lifted his daughter and hugged her, and off she went with Madeleine. Assunta had been going to the village school since September, sometimes taken by Madeleine and sometimes by James. Over the years Madeleine had come to feel increasingly at home in the country and, having appointed a manager for the London office, found she could run the Galaxy Secretarial Agency by spending only a part of the week in London. She had kept her promise to participate in her daughter's religious upbringing, joining in saying family prayers and attending Mass on most Sundays. She did so willingly, if without conviction, because she felt no enmity towards James's faith; indeed her attitude towards religion and all matters spiritual remained devoid of commitment and even of interest. If her participation made James happy it gave her pleasure too, and she left it at that. It was the decent thing to do.

Her business had gone from strength to strength. She had come early to the budding market for multilingual secretaries and had quickly achieved an international reputation. Her confidence had grown with success and it had transferred itself to her personal life: she was increasingly at peace with herself. The fact of having succeeded on her own and not having depended on James for it had the effect not of lessening him in her esteem but rather of admiring him for his own success. More and more did they come to share in each other's enthusiasm for their work. She often reproached herself for having thought him lustreless, and accepted his dual nature as dreamer and man of action. They became at last a team.

To her chagrin, the proposed Polish cultural visit which she

Six Years Later

had mentioned to James and in which she had involved him anonymously as translator, had not materialised owing to political complications. However, she continued to nurse its possibilities for she saw it not only as a business opportunity but as yet a further bond between them. It remained latent rather than forgotten.

That day they brought Assunta home together and, after she had gone to bed they settled down for a quiet evening before Madeleine's journey to London the following morning. They were less than delighted when Father Ryan called unannounced.

'I'm sorry to invade your evening unexpectedly but I thought I'd seize the opportunity.'

He had aged since Madeleine had first met him, when they had parted in the spirit of uneasy truce rather than of friendship. The intervening years had mellowed him a little and he felt less uncomfortable in the presence of a Protestant, especially since Madeleine was clearly keeping her side of the understanding: as Protestants went she was a good person.

He contemplated the whisky which had appeared unbidden before him.

The opportunity for what? they wondered.

'We have a problem.'

For some time he had come to use 'we' with James when they discussed parish matters, treating him as an ally on account of his position as local grandee and employer, and almost the only educated man with whom he could exchange thoughts. He had come some distance from his attitude of 'no one tells me how to run this parish' – a huge journey for one of his set frame of mind.

'And what is our problem?'

'Molly Callaghan,' he replied cryptically. 'She's an unmarried mother.'

'Not guilty,' replied James a little wickedly, since he knew that Father Ryan, whose brow clouded slightly, did not share his sense of humour.

'I don't suppose you've met her. She doesn't always come to Mass, and when she does as likely as not she'll arrive late, stay at the back and leave early.'

'I rather think I've noticed her,' said Madeleine, 'long red hair, child about three years old? Where does she live?'

She could not repress a fellow feeling of sympathy for anyone burdened with a child even though she had come to love her own.

'Yes, that's her. She lives in a miserable old caravan on a farm about three miles from the church, which doesn't help her get to Mass. She does her best for the child, but it's a wretched existence.'

'So what's the problem? Money?'

James knew that Father Ryan had little leeway when it came to helping hard cases. The church building itself had been the gift of a rich benefactor, long since dead, and although handsome it had fallen into disrepair and was as much a burden as an asset.

'Well, money never comes amiss – but I wondered whether your charity might come a different way. Molly is a strong capable girl and keeps her wretched home as decent as she can in the circumstances. I don't suppose you could find her any work? I don't think she'd take advantage.'

Madeleine and James exchanged invisible nods.

'Leave it with us, Father,' said James. 'We'll try and come up with something.'

So it was that Molly and little Kate came to live in a very small cottage on the estate. Molly did some housework at Briar Cottage in exchange for rent and a small salary, and later worked on the farm, and Assunta gained a playmate.

After Christmas, John Stonor – 'Uncle John' to Assunta – spent a few days with them. He had lost nothing of his idealism and, being very much a 'hands-on' man, had resisted attempts by his superiors to steer him to a managerial post. 'Time enough for that later on,' he would say, 'I'm happy at the coalface.'

James wished he could have been godfather to Assunta but his agnosticism made that impossible. Instead James had found Tom and Mary Jenkins, a couple still childless after several years of marriage. He was a social worker, she taught at the village school, and good godparents they proved to be.

James and Madeleine savoured the remains of their interrupted evening, and in the morning she set off for London and returned on the Friday evening. She seemed quietly elated.

'I've got some interesting news for you.'
'What, a new and lucrative client?'
'Not exactly new, and I don't yet know how lucrative.'
'Well, spill the beans.'
'You remember the Polish cultural visit that fell through? Well, they've thought again and it seems something will come of it.'
'That's good. I'll be happy to function again if you need me.'
'Thanks. It looks like being on a bigger scale then the original proposal. Quite a range of cultural activities. I do hope it comes off. Now, tell me, have you heard any more from Kew?'

James launched into his favourite subject and once started there was no stopping him. For some time he had been talking seriously with Kew about the possibility of including Far Eastern trees as a special feature of his exotic woodland and, since a survey had suggested that his land might be suitable he enjoyed the active collaboration of the Royal Botanic Gardens. His plans were ambitious and included planting an avenue of gingko in a sheltered valley leading to a marshy area which would be home to some swamp cypresses, and most exciting of all, his plans included a grove of metasequoia near a summer house in the form of an Eastern temple.

'What on earth are metasequoia?'
'Dawn redwoods. Very ancient conifers, which used to be known only as fossils, but in 1941 some were found growing in China. The Gardens have raised several from cuttings and they're willing to let me have some. It might just work.'
'I can see this becoming the Kew of the West.'
'Well, the thought had occurred to me.'

16: A Visitor from the East

In early spring arrangements for the Polish visit began to crystallise and the organisation's administrator was sent to Britain to liaise with relevant bodies. He called on Madeleine's agency.

Roman Chopin was a tall, intelligent-looking man who quickly impressed Madeleine by his engaging manner and ready flow of conversation, which was not limited to the immediate business. She used her maiden name for business, and felt it was prudent in view of the political climate not to allude to her husband's origins. When the main business had been concluded she sent for coffee and invited Chopin to stay and talk for a while 'if you have the time' as she put it.

He grinned. 'You mean perhaps if my political adviser does not object... and perhaps you are surprised that I came by myself. I felt like being on my own today. My colleague is perhaps still asleep because I give him a good time last night, and he does not understand whisky; he is more used to vodka!'

Madeleine warmed to him.

'But you survived the whisky?'

'I do not drink much, I make a little go a long way — how do you say? I spin it out?'

Again a boyish grin. He was pleased at his English idiom.

'I thought Poles were good drinkers.'

'We are, but it is not good for serious dancers. You have to keep fit.'

Her surprise showed.

'I thought you were a professional administrator.'

He looked quite pained.

'Never!' I was dancer until accident a few years ago. My leg was hurt when my car slipped on the ice; how do you say it?'

'Skidded.'

'Thank you, yes, I skid off a country road and was many months in hospital.'

A Visitor from the East

He pointed to his stick.

'No more dancing. So they make me administrator. It is not so interesting but I stay in the atmosphere that I love, and still I travel. Like now.'

'Travel is important to you, then?'

'Of course. When I am abroad *I breathe*.'

Madeleine felt her interest growing by the minute. She found it increasingly difficult to see Chopin as a representative of a communist state, and it would be good to relate this meeting to James in a couple of days' time. She was surprised that a complete stranger from a closed world should speak so openly with her, and could not avoid a lurking suspicion that she was being tested in some way. She did not realise the change that a few years of serenity had wrought in her former diffident and distant self, and only half grasped that she might strike a stranger as being warm and empathic as well as incisive and businesslike.

Was Chopin really being open with her about the current regime in Poland, or did he have some hidden agenda? Much as she enjoyed his account of how he had shaken off his political partner, ought she to swallow it whole?

He looked at his watch. 'I have much enjoyed our conversation, but must not monopolise your time–' he grinned as he said 'monopolise' –'and by now my colleague has recovered from his whisky.'

'I have enjoyed it too,' she replied. 'I don't often have clients with such artistic sounding names.'

'Oh, you mean *Chopin*? That was my stage name, because it sounds romantic. My real name is Antoni Zagorski.'

That afternoon Madeleine, trembling with anticipation, made two telephone calls. First she rang Chopin, or Zagorski, at his hotel.

'I should like to continue our conversation a little, and my husband is very interested in Poland too. Could you possibly meet us at our flat tomorrow evening?'

She sensed a certain hesitation.

'I think so...'

'Flat B, 18 Maybury Gardens, near South Kensington station. About eight?'

Then she rang Jim.

'Darling. I know this is sudden but could you come up tomorrow? I've something interesting to show you at the flat. Get Molly to look after Assunta.'

'You're being mysterious, and it's unlike you.'

Indeed, mystery was out of keeping with her. James was intrigued but enquired no further, entering into the game and preferring to travel hopefully; for it would be totally uncharacteristic of Madeleine to drag him away from his retreat without good reason.

17: Brothers

All next day Madeleine found it hard to keep her mind on business, fervently hoping she had not called James out on a wild goose chase. Neither Antoni nor Zagorski was an uncommon name, and the fact that James's brother had shown artistic inclinations as a small boy might be only a tenuous connection with Chopin's original career, but his age was about right. She could but hope.

James arrived first and she entertained him with small talk. When he pressed her to reveal the reason for her strange summons she said merely, 'Wait a bit longer,' and changed the conversation to estate matters and to the Polish visit in general. She waited on tenterhooks for the bell to ring.

Chopin arrived punctually at eight. In the hall she said quickly, 'I'm glad you were able to shake off your colleague. Whisky again?'

'No. I was able to tempt him to visit a certain "lady" –' he spoke the word with contempt –'in Soho. He is a pig.' He grinned conspiratorially.

She showed him in and he greeted James with a slight bow.

'Mr Chopin, may I introduce my husband? James Todd-Zagorski.'

Chopin looked startled and his deep-set eyes betrayed a certain suspicion.

'Jim, Mr Chopin is the administrator for the Polish cultural visit I told you about. His real name is Antoni Zagorski.'

A great silence seized the room. Both men stood locked in thought, uncertain as to who should begin the process of enquiry, embarrassed at the possibility that coincidence might be playing a trick on them. James broke the silence.

'Do you – we – have any family?'

'I have a twin brother, Kazimierz, and an elder sister.'

He did not reveal her name, waiting on James, only his eyes displaying excitement.

'And how is Kasia?'

Antoni's whole expression and body were transformed. He flung his arms around James.

'Janek!'

'Antek!'

After a while Madeleine's blank expression made them realise that they were speaking Polish, James occasionally groping for the right word through lack of practice. They apologised simultaneously.

'Don't worry about me, it does James good.'

Nevertheless they resumed talking mostly in English. From the day that James and their father left the family home to join the Home Army, Katarzyna had kept her promise to look after the young twin brothers. Since her mother's death she had assumed the role of mistress of the household and her father had given her access to as much of the family's finances as her age permitted. Antoni and Kazimierz were looked after as well as circumstances allowed, and Katarzyna even comforted their old neighbour, Mrs Sikorska, whose confused state of mind brought out her caring instincts.

When all was over and the Russian occupation began, and it was obvious that her father and Janek would not be seen again, she struggled on for a few weeks before deciding to flee to their uncle, who lived on a small farm on the outskirts of the city. With a heavy heart she left old Mrs Sikorska behind, having failed to persuade her to join them. She filled three haversacks with as much food as she could gather, the remainder of her liquid money, clothes, and a few essential family documents and treasures, including the photograph album. She locked the door, saying that everything would be safe until they returned and told the boys, who were young enough to view it all as a great adventure, that at least there would be something to eat on the farm.

They found the farmhouse burned to the ground and their uncle living in a ruined cowshed. Somehow Katarzyna managed to drag order out of chaos, stiffened her uncle's broken spirit and the family survived.

'She is wonderful,' said Antoni, and Madeleine, recollecting her own easy childhood, even in wartime, felt humbled.

Katarzyna had returned to see her parents' home, only to find the building damaged and their flat looted. She never went back. As the country slowly emerged into peace, the boys' education resumed and Katarzyna was able to achieve her ambition of becoming a nurse.

As Antoni talked about their sister his admiration was evident; he clearly hero-worshipped her. She had married Henryk Kuczynski, whose father, Teodor, was active in the Communist Party.

'So she has become a communist too?' asked James.

'Oh no. Kuczynski is a pig, but Henryk is a good man. Naturally Kasia tries to get on with Teodor but she despises him. You see, he is not even a good communist.'

'What do you mean?'

'Many people call themselves communists because it is the way to get jobs, but they are not sincere. If the regime changed they would change too. They have no truth – is that the right word?'

'Integrity would be better.'

'Like the Vicar of Bray,' murmured Madeleine absent-mindedly.

'Who is that?'

'Oh, I'll explain another time,' she smiled.

'Well, Teodor has become an important man even though he is stupid, but his son is quite different. He is an idealist. He dreams and Kasia acts: they go well together. And now, Janek, tell me your story.'

'I shall, but you haven't told us about Kazimierz yet.'

Antoni's face grew stern. 'We don't speak about Kazimierz.'

There was bitterness in his voice. They waited.

'He has given himself completely to the regime. He is a bad Pole. He has lost his soul. He is a member of the Secret Police.'

Antoni spat out the staccato sentences, ashamed of having to own up to his brother's treachery.

'Has he married?'

'No. He thinks of nothing except his "work".'

'Perhaps he could be described as a good communist, unlike Kasia's father-in-law...'

'No. I can have respect for some of the ideals of pure communism but not for the way it develops politically. It is inhuman.'

Antoni spoke fast and fervently, and James warmed to his young brother intellectually as well as sentimentally.

'Perhaps the corruption of ideals is not confined to communism,' he suggested.

'You mean that even the Church is not free from human corruption?'

'Yes, for example, and inevitably since it is composed of fallible human beings.'

They're off, thought Madeleine, and she went to make coffee.

She had long since ceased to be bored at real conversation, although she still preferred to listen rather than to participate because she feared that her contribution would be jejune. In fact the opposite was the case, and when she did join in would often bring a note of perceptive if untrained reality to the discussion. They talked on until Antoni said, 'You have still not told me about yourself.'

Madeleine said, 'We don't mind talking as long as you like, but it is getting very late. Won't your colleague be suspicious? What will you tell him?'

'I don't think so. I will tell him that I spent the night with women, like him. That is the kind of thing he will understand. He is a fool.'

'A pig?' Madeleine suggested archly.

'Of course, a pig!' And they all laughed.

By the time James had related his story it was three in the morning, and when Madeleine had telephoned for a taxi Antoni looked thoughtful and, somewhat hesitantly, asked, 'What I do not understand is why you did not try to discover whether we had survived.'

James's heart sank. 'Well... I didn't know where to begin, and also I was afraid that if you had survived my enquiries might have put you in danger.'

The explanation seemed to satisfy Antoni.

'One other question. How did you get on with the English? Was it not all very strange? They do not think like us.'

'That's true. As I explained, I was shown great kindness and I hardly ever felt that even as a foreigner I was unwanted. A guest rather than a stranger.'

'I see,' said Antoni thoughtfully.

They agreed to meet again in the summer when the Polish cultural visit was to take place.

18: Crisis

James's existence continued on its pleasant path; the estate prospered, Assunta was a delight. He resumed his mixture of the scholarly and the active; his visits to old Honeyman's bookshop and the occasional and nearly always successful forays into the Stock Market.

He hid his introspection from Madeleine as far as possible, and yet Antoni's question haunted him: why had he not sought to discover what had happened to his sister and brothers? The explanation he had given had seemed to satisfy Antoni. It was reasonable enough to suppose that enquiries from an émigré living in the West might have prejudiced their safety, and such thoughts had indeed passed through his mind. Yet, was that really what had held him back? He was uncomfortably aware that the whirlpool of experiences and emotions through which he had passed had, for long periods, dragged his family far from the surface of his mind. He had remembered them in his prayers, in a formal and abstract sort of way, but had he truly missed them as individuals? He recoiled from answering the question even in the secrecy of his heart, fearful and ashamed of the answer. Perhaps, had he set his mind more resolutely to it he might have been able to make discreet enquiries, obliquely and without arousing suspicions. Perhaps; but his daily life had been so full that the latent interest had not blossomed. His father's words 'Never forget Poland' had come to ring faint in his ears. He felt ashamed. Now, thanks to Madeleine's initiative, the possibility of reunion, or at least of communication, however difficult and distant, existed.

In Poland he had always felt closer to Katarzyna than to his brothers and in spite of the joy of meeting he had experienced a sensation of distance between himself and Antoni, having last seen a young boy and finding a man. What was he really like? Judging from his expressed opinions Antoni and he were not

Crisis

dissimilar, by which he meant that their philosophical attitudes were compatible. 'How typical of you,' he imagined Madeleine saying, 'to think more about your brother's opinions than about the fact that he simply is your brother. Surely that's what matters, isn't it?'

He began to see that he had created a world of his own, to his taste and specification, excluding from it what bored or displeased him. He contrasted his tailor-made well-being with what his sister and brothers had been forced to endure. When he examined his conscience he was less than impressed at what he saw.

An opportunity of acting unselfishly presented itself sooner than he expected.

The telephone rang early one morning. John Stonor's usually calm voice was agitated.

'Jim, can you come up for a day or two? I'm in a mess, my parents have died.'

'Where are you?'

'At my parents' house.'

'What happened?'

'I can't talk about it now. Bill and Rebecca are away and I don't know who to turn to.'

'Of course I'll come, but isn't it worth talking to Jacob and Ruth in the meantime?'

'I can't burden them with it, they're not as strong as they were.'

Madeleine was in London, so James arranged for a taxi to take Molly with Assunta to school. He was aware that John's father had been unwell for some time and was having a series of tests, but as far as he knew there was no immediate danger, and why Mrs Stonor should also have died was a complete mystery. It was natural enough that John should be distressed, but he had sounded on the verge of despair: evidently something exceptional had occurred. Murder?

James was familiar with John's parental house although he did not know it well because the three friends had usually met either at the Silvermanns' or at The Aspens. It was a substantial house, comfortably severe with heavy furniture of the first half of the century, and stamped all over with establishment respectability. John used to describe it as boring. He came to the door.

Crisis

'Thank God you're here.'

He took James's hand and held it until they reached the breakfast room where the remains of an ad hoc meal lay on the table. James said nothing. They sat down facing each other. John had difficulty speaking. James waited.

'It was suicide. Both of them.'

James's astonishment showed. That such a solid couple as the Stonors should have even contemplated suicide, let alone carried it out, was beyond belief. It went against not only their religious convictions but also the steadfast conventions of their class and tradition. If they had problems, surely the stiff upper lip was the answer; stand fast and weather the storm. Had there been some financial scandal?

John, steadied by James's presence, explained. Both his parents had left him letters expressing their feelings with uncharacteristic tenderness. His father's cancer was inoperable and his pain unbearable, far greater than he had previously admitted. His mother could not bear the thought of life without him; she preferred that they should die together. They apologised for the inconvenience they were causing him.

'*Inconvenience!*' he blurted out.

Despite the tragedy of the occasion James could not suppress a wry inner smile at the comic absurdity of the word. It reminded him of the sort of people who had been Constance's neighbours in the leafy suburb, of 'Don't make a fuss, dear, people will look round.' Being a nuisance was a crime more heinous than hypocrisy. Even facing the imminence of tragic death, an element of the stiff upper lip, of keeping up appearances, remained. Comic, or pathetic. Under different circumstances he knew that John would have shared his wicked amusement, but now he kept it to himself. The practical side of his nature was what his friend needed now.

'Where are Mother and Father for the moment?'

'In the local morgue. Of course there'll have to be an inquest. I expect it will be a case of "while the balance of their minds was disturbed", but I don't believe that.'

The conversation felt unreal, as though they were watching a film, not discussing John's parents.

'How can we best help?'

'Just by being here. I'm glad you're not shocked.'

John knew enough about the Catholic view of suicide as an act of final despair, the negation of the virtue of hope, to have feared that James might not have been able to come to terms with it.

'How about your job?'

'I've taken a fortnight's leave and a colleague has taken over my caseload.'

'Madeleine and I will be with you as much as you need. We'll help you with the nuts and bolts, like disposing of personal effects and so on, which I suggest should be done as quickly as possible. It's less painful that way.'

It was a measure of the stability of James's marriage that he felt confident about volunteering Madeleine's help. They were indeed a team.

'But you've got Assunta to think about.'

'She can be taken care of for a while. Don't worry about that. How soon do you suppose Bill and Rebecca will be back?'

'In a week or so. In the meantime I'd rather not upset their holiday. I wish I could have been closer to my people, but you know we were so different.'

James knew very well, and saw in his friend's regret at the impossibility of coming closer to his parents a reflection of his own pangs of conscience at not having tried harder to make contact with his family.

The inquest turned out as John had foreseen. It was not a complicated process: his father's sickness was well documented, their parting letters to him were clear and obtaining the poison had been no problem for a medical man. His parents had drifted off side by side in bed like a pair of romantic lovers which, in spite of their suburban respectability, they had been. John's friends saw him through the practicalities, the house was sold and he returned to his work; but he became a more frequent visitor to Briar Cottage.

On one such visit James described the unforeseen circumstances in which he had met his long lost brother.

'You know, I feel I have grown closer to him since he went back to Poland. I really miss him. While he was here our relationship felt unreal; it was so sudden and brief although we talked well into the night. I have been recalling lots of little incidents from our childhood, and my parents have come much closer too, not that I ever felt distant from them as a boy.' He chose his words carefully, trying not to express himself in a way that would renew John's own feelings of inadequacy.

'What baffles me is that you never tried to make contact with your family during all the intervening years.'

Exactly the same question that Antoni had asked, and in almost identical words.

'I suppose I made such very good friends at school and just became wrapped up in my own life and ambitions. I know it sounds absurd, but looking back it's amazing how easy it was to be swallowed up in just living. I realise that's a feeble excuse.'

He used the schoolboy term, like one who had been caught in some minor mischief.

'I don't think you should blame yourself too much. After all, you'd been through a pretty harrowing time and had a life of your own to put together again. Make the most of the opportunity that's been presented to you and look to the future. Are you able to communicate with Antoni?'

'That's a problem. The regime is still fairly suspicious and I don't want to put him in an embarrassing situation. I don't know to what extent private letters get censored.'

'Have you chanced it at all?'

'Not yet, but I'm working round to it. I think I'll start by getting Madeleine to include a few allusions in her business letters to him, and see whether he takes the idea up.'

'That might work. Anyway, he'll be here in the summer, won't he?'

'Yes, the cultural visit is only five months away, but it'll feel a lot longer.'

19: *The Birth of Two Ideas*

Time passed more quickly than James had expected. His life was a constant delight, shared energetically between the routine operations of farming, Madeleine's comings and goings, playing with Assunta – whom he was trying, without conspicuous success, to wean on to poetry; weekends when John stayed, the frequent communications from Kew, occasional visits to the Botanic Gardens, his visits to Mr Honeyman's bookshop and the ever-present anticipation of meeting Antoni again.

On one of John's weekends they went to Brocklechurch on the Saturday morning and James took the opportunity of introducing him to Mr Honeyman. When told of John's profession Mr Honeyman said, 'That is a most worthy calling, though I must admit to not having much about it on my shelves.'

He grinned in his amiable ape-like way.

'I imagine there's no great demand for it. It's hardly the sort of work that arouses wild dinner-table interest either. In fact it can be a conversation stopper, a bit like admitting to being a policeman.'

'Mind you, I do have a small selection on sociology which is presumably part of the theoretical basis for your work. I wouldn't claim to know much about it myself.'

'Neither do I! I think of it as a pseudo-science whereas my interest is in real people, with all their unpredictabilities.'

'I should point out,' interrupted James, 'that my friend takes his work more as a vocation than as a profession and gives himself entirely to it, rather like a priest.'

'A distinctly agnostic priest, then,' insisted John.

Mr Honeyman stood silent for a moment, and said, 'I suppose I should describe myself as a humanist. I've often wondered what makes people act as they do, especially when they make altruistic choices. If I had to declare a faith it would be in humanity.'

'Wouldn't you be putting your faith in a rather fragile and

unreliable instrument?' said James. 'It would be as though when I plant a tree in the wrong environment I trust that it will come to terms with nature and find its own route to survival. The chances are that if it survives at all it will grow stunted.'

Customers then claimed Mr Honeyman's attention so James and John took their leave and retired to Benn's for coffee.

'He's a friendly old chap,' remarked John.

'What he doesn't know about the book trade isn't worth knowing, but he seems more interested in talking about books then selling them. It's hard to see how he makes a living.'

'I wonder what his background is. Where did he study?'

'I fancy he hasn't a degree or anything like that. He's just one of nature's philosophers, interested in most things and presumably self-taught. I've found he's quite a lifeline for me because although I come here only about once a fortnight it gives me an opportunity of exchanging a thought or two. As you well know, with most people all one can exchange are words.'

'Quite true, oh sage. Let us wallow awhile in the pit of our undoubted superiority over the common herd.'

'Ah, I see that you're back on form.'

John was indeed back to his former self. They spent the rest of the weekend happily with Madeleine and Assunta and, later in the week when he was on his own James dwelt on his friend's state of being. John continued living his ascetic life. The sale of his parents' substantial house had made him quite a rich man but, with one exception it induced no extravagance in the way he lived. The exception was the purchase of a fast modern car, an Austin-Healey, which enabled him to reduce the time he spent travelling on his increasingly frequent visits to Briar Cottage. He had few other friends, for most of his contemporaries at Oxford had found their way into politics or business, and their paths had increasingly diverged from his: a provincial probation officer was not an adornment to their parties in the swinging Sixties.

Reflecting on their visit to Mr Honeyman's, James returned to wondering what drove John and evidently brought him fulfilment. If he had to be given a label it would presumably have to be that of humanist, but in his case that begged too many questions. James wished that time had allowed an exploration of Mr

The Birth of Two Ideas

Honeyman's self-description, for he suspected that the wise old man's faith went deeper than a 'faith in humanity', which was too diffuse a definition to be of any use. Did Honeyman believe that mankind was good? The history of the times, as well as daily evidence, surely exploded that idea. Did he mean that in spite of its manifest failings mankind was redeemable? Acts of altruism were abundant, but what of the equally common examples of evil succeeding? And if redeemable, by what? Surely too much was being laid on that vague entity 'humanity'... Honeyman's dedication to 'humanity' seemed to be of a theoretical kind for as far as he knew the comfortable world of books was the limit of his horizon, but John's was practical and involved him in inconvenience, long hours beyond the call of duty and a life of self-sacrifice – although he would not have described it so.

James compared it with his own. Although much misfortune had befallen him, so had many blessings, and the hardships had been thrust on him, uninvited and unwelcome. He had to admit he did little that was not of his own choosing, his life was certainly fulfilling but also extremely comfortable and comforting. For long periods he did not put himself out for anyone, since the little acts of generosity that he performed like any dutiful husband and parent were abundantly rewarded. The term 'selfish', or at least 'self-centred' lurked uncomfortably round the corner. Even his critical examination of conscience came dangerously close to self-indulgence.

He compared his comfortable path with that of his brother trying to live the life of the spirit (in the broadest sense, because they had not discussed religion as such) in an atmosphere of bureaucratic totalitarianism, and of his sister having to cope with another brother and a father-in-law who, in wartime terms, could only be described as collaborators.

As usual he broke his reverie by getting into his Land-Rover and making an inspection of the farm.

The time of the Polish cultural visit arrived, and with it, Antoni. Madeleine met him first, in London, and brought him to Briar Cottage for the weekend. John was there too. He had more than once suggested that it was unfair of him to invade James's and

Madeleine's privacy so often, but she had assured him that he was always welcome, and she meant it.

To her surprise Antoni had used no stratagem to shake off his political colleague – 'the pig' – but simply came when invited. To her query, he merely replied, 'It doesn't matter any more.' This puzzled her but she did not enquire further. His meaning became clear to her at dinner that evening. He had brought a bottle of Polish vodka, and as they discussed it he announced, 'I wish to defect to the West.'

All three were nonplussed. They were aware that occasional defections took place from behind the Iron Curtain, but they were news items, not like real events that concerned them personally. Now history was being made at the table, and they all remained deep in thought.

James said, 'That's wonderful news, and I expect you've thought it through, but there's so much to think about, so many consequences.'

'And so many people, surely,' added Madeleine.

John remained silent, partly because he felt like an intruder in delicate family business and partly because concentration on his profession had somewhat restricted his outlook.

Thoughts and ideas were tossed around. How should Antoni apply? What if he were refused? If accepted, what would he do for a living? What effect would his defection have on Katarzyna and her husband – would the regime vent its spite on them, and would it wreck the cultural visit which was intrinsically a desirable element in building a bridge?

'I think you should behave as normally as possible until something has been arranged,' said James, his practical nature coming to the fore. 'Arouse no suspicion.'

'Yes,' said Madeleine, 'be extra nice to the pig.'

James was thinking hard. 'How long have we got? When does the tour end, and are you supposed to stay with it until it's over?'

'Yes, I stay to the end to – how do you say it? – to pick up the pieces. Until middle of November. I must go to Ministry of Internal Affairs.'

'The Home Office,' corrected James. 'I think we may know someone who can help.'

The Birth of Two Ideas

'Guy?' suggested Madeleine.

'Exactly. Not that he's ever had any direct connection with it, but he knows an awful lot of people.'

Madeleine rang her godfather the next day. She did not beat about the bush.

'Uncle Guy, we've got a problem and you may be able to help. Can I drop in on you tomorrow?'

'Oh dear... not trouble, I hope.'

'No, no, not that sort of trouble. Things are going very well at home, thanks largely to you. It's something quite different.'

'Care to come about twelve? We'll go out for a spot of lunch.'

Guy Rowlands, still spry in manner and alert in spirit, rejoiced at the opportunity of escorting his elegant goddaughter. She described the problem.

'I see. It may not be plain sailing. I'm trying to look at it from the authorities' point of view. They'll feel that they know only what you've been told and won't take Antoni's story at face value. I dare say if he were in possession of information that might be of value to our Intelligence they'd be keener, but that isn't likely to be the case.'

'We thought you might know chaps who know chaps.'

'Most of the chaps I know are pretty long in the tooth, but I dare say I might be able to rake someone up. It'll take a bit of time.'

'At least Antoni doesn't need to declare his intention to his authorities until the end of the tour.'

'I realise that. I'll see what I can do.'

He was as good as his word, and during the following weeks kept them informed about the progress of his enquiries. He had gained the impression that there might not be too many difficulties but, as he put it, there could be many a slip "twixt cup and lip'; and in the meantime, the less they saw of Antoni, except strictly on business, the better.

They waited, tracing the progress of the cultural tour in many provincial cities through the summer and into September. It was the first time since James had become a farmer that the autumn had not seen his mind concentrated on the harvest. In place of the Gloucestershire countryside he saw the Polish plains, or rather

The Birth of Two Ideas

created a mental picture of them, for his family rarely went out of town, and the countryside through which he had made his way to the West was too ravaged, and he too tired and frightened, to be appreciated. Yes, here was the start of his spiritual return to the land of his birth, not that he contemplated ever living in Poland, for he had grown roots in England; but his link with Poland had suddenly changed from mere nostalgia to something physical – a brother, a sister. He felt for his father's cross and pressed it into his skin. Why had he not shown it to Antoni? He must do so next time they met. And the next time might well be at the moment of decision.

He tried to put himself in Antoni's position, to imagine what might be going through his mind. When James had fled his country he had acted at his father's behest, he had in a sense nothing to lose, for all was already lost. Terrible though the circumstances were, it had been a kind of adventure and at the beginning he had been too young to grasp his perilous situation. Antoni, on the other hand, was proposing to give up everything; his friends and family, property, an occupation which carried a certain cachet and kept him in contact with the world of the arts – everything. Why, exactly? He had not asked Antoni the reason, having felt overwhelmed at the sheer delight of the possibility of his coming. Was it just his disgust at the totalitarian regime, the lack of freedom and the absence of any likelihood of change? There had been no suggestion that he was in any physical danger. James had simply taken Antoni's decision at face value, and so had Madeleine and John; 'why' had never entered into the discussion. With the passage of time James occasionally wondered whether there was anything sinister or dishonourable behind Antoni's decision, and thrust the thought to the back of his mind. In any case, that was the kind of thing the authorities would look into.

On a Friday morning in midsummer James received a telephone call from Madeleine.

'I've got a surprise for you. I'm bringing a friend to stay with us for a couple of days.'

'A friend? You can't mean Antoni…'

'No, of course not, but you'll be glad. Wait and see.'

She arrived with Lieutenant-Colonel Silvermann. James, who

The Birth of Two Ideas

had not met Isaac for over a year, rejoiced to see him walking up the drive with Madeleine, his tall massive figure quite dwarfing hers. He hurried out to greet him.

'He's a colonel now,' she said, happy at being the bearer of good news.

'That last promotion was a bit unexpected, wasn't it?' said James. 'Congratulations all the more.'

'I was a bit lucky, quite a lot of chaps had decided to resign,' explained Isaac modestly.

As they made for seats in the garden James considered how little success had changed Isaac. He was still the friendly bear-like figure he had been as a boy, imposing and manly but not quite what people generally expected in a 'military man', being the epitome of that comparative rarity, the intellectual soldier.

'You know, you're looking more like your father each time I see you. How are they both?'

'Dad's all right, getting older but as sharp as ever beneath that misleadingly easy-going exterior. Mama's a lot better than we'd have expected a few years ago. Still gardening, but more slowly.'

'I couldn't resist telling him about Antoni,' said Madeleine, 'I hope you don't mind.'

'Of course not.'

'Look, it may be a bit delicate,' said Isaac, 'especially in view of some of your family's close involvement in the regime.' James detected just a glimmer of professional caution in Isaac's expression. 'But I've often heard Dad remark on Guy Rowlands's amazing network of connections. I do hope he can pull it off.'

'No doubt it would be easier if Antoni were a famous name in the world of the arts, so that his defection would be a coup for the West.'

'Even better if he were a nuclear scientist.' Isaac grinned. 'Now put me in the picture about John's parents. I've heard a bit about what happened, and of course I wrote to him briefly from Germany, but I'm pretty unclear about the details. It's a pity he can't be here this weekend.'

They talked for a while about John, and on the following day took Isaac to explore Gloucester, which he had never visited and where James went rarely. Assunta had heard that Isaac was a soldier.

The Birth of Two Ideas

'Where's your gun, Uncle Isaac?'
'I keep it where it's safe, dear.'
'Is it a big one, like Daddy's?'

James kept a shotgun in a locked cupboard and Assunta had occasionally seen him take it out to go rook shooting.

'Not quite like Daddy's.'
'Do you use it a lot?'
'I haven't for ages. Look at the teddy bear in the window!' he said, and got rid of the awkward subject.

Assunta was growing into a lively, pretty little girl, only slightly spoiled by her father and not at all by her mother. Both had made a point of avoiding baby language, sheep were sheep and not baa-lambs, so that she was articulate for her age and adults enjoyed her company. Recalling his own childhood, James was indulgent about bedtimes and often allowed her to stay up for a while when they had guests to dinner.

Towards the end of their visit to Gloucester, she noticed a man putting cardboard sheets on the pavement and laying some blankets on them.

'Mummy, why is that man making his bed here?'
'I suppose it's because he's a tramp. He hasn't got a house.'
'Can't he go to a hotel?'
'Hush, dear. You see, he probably hasn't got much money. Come along.'

But Assunta was not easily silenced.

'Like the ones who come to our house sometimes?'
'Yes. I suppose so.'
'Why hasn't he got any money?'

Madeleine, though the Anglican faith glimmered but faintly in her, was imbued with the Protestant work ethic, and began to explain that money came with work and that the man probably didn't have any work.

'Why hasn't he got work? Daddy could give him a job on the farm.'

By now they had walked some distance past the man. James, who could remember what it felt like to be cold and hungry paused, turned back and put some money in the man's box. When he came back Madeleine said, 'I hope that money doesn't go where we think it will.'

The Birth of Two Ideas

Assunta could not understand that, but said no more. Later that evening when Madeleine was saying goodnight to her in bed she asked,

'Mummy, has that man in the street done something very bad? Is that why he hasn't got any money?'

'I don't know, dear. Perhaps he'll be lucky soon. Now go to sleep.'

Madeleine told John and Isaac about Assunta's question and both sat deep in thought.

'It's sad to think that such conditions exist in modern Britain,' said James.

They stared at him in amazement.

Madeleine said, 'I hadn't realised how remote you'd become from city life. It's a common enough sight in London today.'

'Sad,' agreed Isaac, 'but sadly true. In her child's eye Assunta spotted a social evil.'

'Out of the mouths of babes and sucklings,' murmured James.

The following day they drove Isaac to the station. As they waited for the train James asked him about the next stage in his career.

'There's talk of sending me to Rome as military attaché. Not the most exciting of postings in a professional sense but it could be fun, and I dare say Mama and Dad would be glad to go out there. You too for that matter.'

'And of course it might make a good Catholic out of you.'

'I'd have to become a good Jew first!' laughed Isaac.

20: Ideas Grow

Towards the end of the Polish cultural tour James went to London for longer than his usual brief visit to Kew, and took the opportunity of calling on old friends.

Guy Rowlands said, 'I think the drums have been beating in favour of your brother. My contacts are a bit cagey, but from the little they've told me I should say the chances are pretty good.'

Jacob said, 'Your brother may not find it as easy as you did to adapt to British society. He will need a lot of support to begin with.'

Ruth said, 'Any increase in family must be a good thing.'

Bill and Rebecca for their part were delighted at the prospect of adding someone associated with the arts to their circle.

James said little, and prayed much. In order to avoid brooding he turned towards a project that had long lain at the back of his mind and which he now saw as an opportunity for combining Madeleine's business acumen with her increasing zest for living in the country. Those thoughts were the germ of what was to become a thriving group of garden centres in the West Country which Madeleine ran, with him as her technical adviser, and which helped to cement their partnership as well as being a financial success.

On his return to Briar Cottage he described his thoughts to her, and so much had their relationship changed since their reunion that far from scoffing at his suggestion she took it seriously from the start. Within a week they had roughed out a basic plan.

Indeed, James reflected, life could be very, very good.

In September the Polish cultural tour came to an end. Antoni attended diligently to the final travel arrangements, concealing his excitement, appearing to behave naturally, and covering his tracks until the day when the members of the administrative team were to leave their hotel for Heathrow. He saw them on to the airport bus, handed their documents to the 'pig', saying he needed to relieve himself, and vanished. He quickly made his way to a nearby pub, where James was waiting for him. Together they then reported to the authorities whom Guy's contacts had indicated and where they were expected.

In the event Guy's intervention had been fruitful. Antoni was accepted without much difficulty and almost immediately found employment in the Polish section of the BBC, which gave him sufficient salary to afford a flat in a district which had attracted a large Polish community. He fitted easily into the London arts milieu, and before the end of the year, and with the encouragement of his family and of other émigré Poles, was beginning to feel at home in Britain.

At Christmas he came to Briar Cottage, where Assunta made much of her Uncle Antek. She was attending ballet classes in Brocklechurch and a bond was quickly established between them. One evening when she had been allowed to stay up later than usual and the family were watching television together, they saw a news item about people sleeping rough in London and attending a soup kitchen. Afterwards she said, 'I wonder if the man we saw with the cardboard bed has got a job now.'

Madeleine did not immediately connect the observation with the incident in Gloucester six months earlier, but James did and his heart went out to the little girl who had stored the memory of the sight that had so disturbed her.

'Perhaps he has, darling. I hope so,' he said.

'Shouldn't we pray for him?'

'Of course.'

And so Assunta's bedtime prayers for Mummy and Daddy, uncles and aunties and her pet rabbit, grew to include the man with the cardboard bed.

Over the remainder of the Christmas period, presents, and playing with Uncle Antek and little Kate Callaghan, were enough distraction for Assunta not to allude again to the man, but the incident lurked at the back of James's mind. His faith as well as his disposition led him to be generous, and in a general sense he knew he was. Good causes did not appeal to him in vain. He was considerate towards his friends. He did not nurse grievances against those who occasionally crossed him in business and he had

Ideas Grow

not even been driven to anger in the early days of Madeleine's separation. It would not have been difficult for him to have come to the wholly satisfying conclusion that he was the most reasonable, fair-minded and generous man imaginable. A good Christian in every sense. Not perfect of course; to believe that would be the grossest form of vanity, but a really good man.

And yet... Was he basking in untried virtue? Had his patience been tested recently? Had he had much to contend with from the stupidity or malevolence of others? How would he have reacted in a situation such as John Stonor had found himself at his parents' suicide: would he have despaired, or wallowed in self-pity? How would he respond to being struck down with a life threatening or disabling disease; would he really be proof against self-pity?

This philosophical stuff is all very well, he thought, but what of the central Christian virtue? Undoubtedly it was love, stemming directly from Christ's injunction. Did he display it in his daily life? How much of his life's work was concentrated on it? Quite a lot, since Madeleine and Assunta were fundamental to his daily life.

And yet again, wasn't there something selfish in that kind of love? In displaying love to those whom he loved quite naturally, was he not simply following his own inclination, his love feeding on theirs, just going round in a circle? Was it not too easy?

The crucial question that he scarcely dared ask himself thrust itself relentlessly, unmercifully, to the front of his mind; when had he last done anything for anybody that caused him any inconvenience, that put him out, that stood in the way of anything he would rather have done? When did he last make a sacrifice? When? When? Probably the only time he had acted truly selflessly was when he had given up the opportunity of reading philosophy at Oxford in order to be of use to Constance Todd. He had done that out of sheer love and gratitude. Subsequently, kindness had been an important rule of life, but it had rarely cost him much. His had been an anodyne sort of goodness, an avoidance of evil rather than an embracing of virtue. He had half listened to God's message.

Madeleine had often criticised his introspection and often she

Ideas Grow

had hit the target, but his current thinking was not a luxury, a self-indulgence. To be of value, introspection had to be positive, an examination of conscience, and must lead to action. He had given the destitute man a trifling amount of money out of fellow feeling for another human being who was down on his luck. It was a minuscule act of generosity and a kind of sop to conscience and in gratitude for his present well-being. Perhaps God had been speaking to him through his daughter.

He realised he must speak with Madeleine, but worried lest she should lack the language to follow his line of thought. To her the word 'charity' had connotations of well-meaning people doing some good during intervals in a life full of business and entertainment; it was not a divine command, a rule of life. Nevertheless he must try, and when he did he was pleasantly surprised at her reaction. His obvious enthusiasm evoked a loving response.

The outcome was a plan to build a group of cottages to which they would bring destitute people to be employed in helping to run the farm, the estate and the garden centres. The plan would take many years to mature, would benefit only a limited number of people and Madeleine and he would be let down time after time; but in retrospect they would judge it to have been the most valuable of all their ventures.

An immediate reward was that they found themselves working towards yet another common goal. When he had helped her in the secretarial agency it was definitely her show, and he merely made useful suggestions. Likewise, when she had taken an interest in the farm and estate it had been as a polite outsider. But the estate village would be different; their project.

On one of John's visits, when the project was in its infancy and not a brick had yet been laid, they sat in the late autumn shade, contemplating the site. Madeleine was in London for a couple of days.

'I suppose this plan must seem a bit airy-fairy to you,' said James, 'the pipe dream of a comfortable do-gooder…'

'Oh come on, I know you better than to think that.'

'Even so, there's an air of unreality about it, isn't there? I freely admit that I've thought less about the nuts and bolts of this scheme than I have about any of my other ventures. Here we are, Madeleine and I, about to embark on a fairly ambitious plan of what you might call social work, a social experiment, without any qualifications and having done virtually no homework on it. The whole thing could simply founder, and we might find ourselves having to rent the cottages out as holiday homes for gin-and-tonic refugees from the world of business. What a cock-up that would be!'

John knew better than to interrupt.

'And yet deep down I feel confident that it will work out. I can't say why, but I know it is something that I simply must try.'

A longish pause ensued before John's reply.

'There are times when one must follow one's instinct. I suppose you might call it following one's star...'

'Now you're teasing me.'

'Only a bit. Seriously though, in my own work I sometimes find myself recommending a course of action that doesn't quite fit the book. Only sometimes, mind you: I don't seek trouble for it's own sake.'

'Surely if it doesn't work out, or even perhaps if it does, mightn't it land you in trouble with your superiors?'

'If so, tough. If they don't like what I do I can resign. As I said there are times when one just knows a certain course is right, a gut feeling.'

'Presumably following one's own bent, or "star" –' James grinned –'is a luxury we can both afford, because we've got some money and you've got no dependants.'

'True, but I did so once or twice even before my parents' death left me financially independent. And you've got the huge advantage of working with Madeleine.'

They strolled back to Briar Cottage and sat in James's study. Molly Callaghan brought them some tea. She often performed small tasks in the house, gradually taking over from Mrs Brand who, in her own words, was 'feeling my age'.

She came in with a tray and as she lowered it onto an occasional table, her long mane of red hair momentarily brushed against James's cheek. He felt a thrill sweep through his body, and all his muscles tightened in an instant of pleasure, shame and

Ideas Grow

embarrassment. He was conscious of having to make an effort to make his voice seem natural.

'Thank you, Molly. I suppose you'll be fetching the girls back from school soon.'

'Yes, sir,' she replied as she went out. She often addressed James as 'sir' although he had never asked her to. She evidently felt more comfortable with that slight formality.

John remarked casually, 'She's certainly a pretty woman.' The words reminded James of the way Guy had once referred to Madeleine at the time of Constance's illness.

'Yes,' he replied simply, wondering how much his perceptive friend had noticed; but the moment of embarrassment passed and he did not follow up John's comment.

21: Madeleine and Molly Go Trawling

Madeleine enjoyed entertaining, producing an elegant meal at a well-set table, and whereas formerly she would have spent much time in the background listening to James guiding a wide-ranging and sophisticated conversation, only cautiously and occasionally contributing, she now engaged wholeheartedly.

They had invited Assunta's godparents to dinner. Tom and Mary were in their late thirties, devoted to their careers and, being childless, had enjoyed more opportunities for wide reading and travel than might otherwise have been the case for people engaged by choice in useful but poorly paid professions. They were excellent company. They expressed interest in the plans for cottages for disadvantaged people, around which conversation at dinner largely revolved.

'Quite apart from the bricks and mortar side,' said Tom, 'which you will resolve easily enough with technical advice, it seems to me you will need a pretty clear idea of just who you mean to get into these cottages; drop outs, people down on their luck, any particular age group?'

Madeleine replied, 'We'd be really grateful for some professional comment, because we realise that it's not fair to act like glorious amateurs when we're dealing with people's lives...' she paused... 'and yet we want it to come from the heart as well as from the head, if you know what I mean. Does that make any sense?'

Jim thought, My goodness what a different person she has become, and glowed inwardly.

'Yes,' replied Tom. 'But I don't think there's any danger of your leaving the heart out of it!'

They discussed what kind of people they should invite, and where to find them. Madeleine continued, 'One could gather any number of people simply by trawling the London pavements and the Underground, but how does one invite those who are likely

Madeleine and Molly Go Trawling

to benefit? I mean that a great opportunity is being offered, but how can we tell in advance which ones will make something of it and which will simply see it as a soft option – spongers, in fact? Quite a lot of the people will have ended up in London after fleeing from the countryside and may not want to return, and others who've been born and bred in cities won't want to bury themselves in what they'd see as the middle of nowhere.'

'I think', said Mary, 'that it's almost impossible to know. You may just have to follow your instinct and hope for the best. Expect plenty of disappointment. You'll be let down at least half the time, but it'll be worth it for the sake of the rest... Try not to be judgmental about whom you select.'

'I wonder,' said James, 'whether we're the right people to do the selecting. We've been so cushioned against life's economic hardships that we're ill equipped to tell.'

'Why not start by consulting the success story that you've already produced,' murmured Tom.

'What do you mean?'

'Well, wouldn't you say that Molly Callaghan was a success story? When she came to you she was in a desperate plight, but you see how confident she has become, given a helping hand. Take her on your trawling expeditions, and go by her reactions.'

'You know, that's a suggestion of genius.'

They talked on and the confused plan began to take shape. Towards the end of the evening Madeleine said, 'I know it's just a detail, but what should we call the village? Hope?'

'Sounds a bit too contrived and holy,' grinned James, 'though it does describe what we mean to offer. Smacks a little of charity...'

'Well,' suggested Madeleine, 'how about Assunta? After all, the idea grew from her concern about the man with the cardboard bed.'

And so Assunta it became, and in a subsequent revision of the Ordnance Survey maps the somewhat incongruous name appeared next to a cluster of buildings in the Gloucestershire countryside. It was something of a talking point at first.

A year later three cottages were ready and a further three under construction.

The first trawling expedition was undertaken by Madeleine and Molly. It was James's suggestion that they should go on their own lest a group of three people going around should look too much like a selection board, and intimidate those whom they wanted to help. There was another reason for his preferring to remain behind. He was still disturbed at his reaction to the brief and slight physical contact on the occasion of John's last visit. Nothing in Molly's subsequent behaviour suggested that she was flirting with him. The incident, which it scarcely was, had almost certainly been unintended and any significance merely a product of his rather puritanical mind. But he was not quite certain yet, even after the passage of more than a year.

Molly was intelligent and shrewd, but her childhood had left her unprepared for life in the world. Abandoned on the church steps by an unknown mother, she was raised in a Catholic institution where she was given a name and from which she got away as soon as she could. Knowing little about the Catholic faith or indeed about anything else, and finding herself pregnant, she had drifted to Great Walling and begged Fr Ryan for help. He found her work with a small local farmer who, without maltreating her, exploited her in return for meagre accommodation and a minute wage. She was merely surviving when Fr Ryan asked James to engage her.

She was on more familiar terms with Madeleine than with James, and addressed her by her Christian name, their motherhood acting as a bond. For Molly the experience of being in London was a revelation. She had never before been outside Gloucestershire. The vastness of the city, the size of the buildings, the rumble of traffic, crossing the busy streets, the shops... all those shops, of such variety that she could never have dreamed of, fascinated and bewildered her. At times she clutched Madeleine's hand like a little girl on an outing with an elder sister.

All those marvels paled into insignificance at her first sight of the Underground. The maze of passages, the myriad arrows and signs – how did Madeleine manage to dart her way through them and always end up where she wanted? She felt real physical terror as the approaching train actually shook the earth. The rush of people in and out of the carriages terrified her – never in any of

Madeleine and Molly Go Trawling

the towns she knew had she witnessed such frenzy, not even on the busiest market day. Nobody seemed to know anyone, and almost everyone looked blank or sad: no one spoke.

Madeleine had thought carefully about the expedition. The first day was to be devoted to walking around central London, mainly just looking at places that she already knew homeless people frequented, and on the second they would try to speak with and invite a few people. If necessary they would prolong the visit. As to the eternal feminine problem of what to wear Tom had said, 'It's no use dressing for the West End or the City. And don't look tweedy either, that'll put people off right away. Dress as if you were Molly's mother. No need to look scruffy, that'd be dishonest, but keep it simple. Don't bring back obvious alcoholics either, because you're not equipped to deal with them now. That may come later if your plans are successful, but to start with keep things simple, start at the shallow end.'

She decided to heed his advice.

On their first evening, in the Underground, they came upon a group of young people squatting against the wall at the base of an escalator. Slightly apart from them a young woman, perhaps a little older than Molly, lay propped up, wrapped in a blanket with a begging cup beside her. Her expression was one of placid boredom. She was somewhat emaciated, and both of them felt drawn to her. Madeleine moved slightly towards her and smiled. The girl managed a flicker of acknowledgement and turned away.

Madeleine felt very much alone, helpless, separated by age, money, circumstance, everything – and even by physical distance for there she was literally looking down at the girl; what on earth was there to do or say? Her business experience failed her utterly. They might as well be living on separate continents.

Molly solved the problem very simply. She plumped herself down beside the girl and said,

'My name's Molly, what's yours?'

'Rosie.'

'Mind if I sit here?'

'Not particularly.'

'My friend's over there. Mind if she comes too?'

'It's a free country, so they say.'

Madeleine and Molly Go Trawling

Molly beckoned Madeleine to join them. The moment of decision felt like an eternity. Suppose anyone she knew should see her now? How could she pretend not to be a fraud? Was she imitating those Victorian ladies in elegant dresses visiting the workhouse to see how the lower orders lived? Just voyeurism? But she must not let Molly down, and especially not Jim to whom their project meant so much. She sat down gingerly next to Rosie on the other side from Molly, first surreptitiously checking whether the floor was clean and feeling an utter fool and exhibitionist. She imitated Molly and instead of starting with a question said, 'I'm Madeleine. We're from Gloucestershire. Ever been there?'

'No, I lived near Birmingham.'

They all remained silent for a while. Molly continued, 'Will you be staying here long?'

'Can't stay long anywhere. They move you on.'

'But what about tonight? Have you got a hostel?'

'Don't know. Maybe; depends if they're full!'

'What happens if they are?'

'I find a corner somewhere. Under a bridge if I can, or a doorway. What's it to you, anyway?'

'I used to live rough, but that was in the country and we could usually find an old shed or somewhere warm.'

'We! I can't imagine your friend sleeping rough.'

'No, that was before I met her. I meant me and the boy I was with.'

'What happened to him?'

'He made me pregnant, and then he pushed off.'

Silence ensued. Molly produced a bar of chocolate.

'Like some?'

Rosie accepted a piece suspiciously, and then devoured it.

'Thanks. Why are you doing this?'

'Well, when I was doing what you're doing I was quite glad if somebody came to speak.'

'I suppose it's nice,' murmured Rosie distantly.

Madeleine asked, 'If we come back tomorrow will you be here again?'

'S'pose so, unless someone's already pinched my pitch.'

Madeleine and Molly Go Trawling

'See you tomorrow, then.'

Madeleine felt emotionally drained, and needed to unravel the confused prospect that was forming in her mind. She took Molly to a tea shop. They said little on the way, each wrapped in her own thoughts. Although the sight of destitute people sleeping rough was familiar enough, Madeleine had never imagined herself speaking with one. It had been strangely unsettling, not alarming, and she was glad to have done it. Molly was mentally reliving her own time as a drifter, savouring her present luck and wondering what tea in the great city would be like. It was in fact the first time she had had tea away from home, and was intrigued to see that the waitress brought it on a tray with the various items set out in much the same way as Madeleine had taught her at Briar Cottage. They were both undergoing a rapid educational experience, all the better for being shared.

Over tea they got down to the business in hand.

'How do you think it went?' asked Madeleine.

'I didn't know what to say.'

'But you did nearly all the talking. You were wonderful; all you said seemed to come so naturally. I thought I was the one who was stuck for words.'

'Do you think Rosie's likely to come? Is she the right sort of person?'

'I certainly hope she'll come, and I think she might be all right, though we don't really know a lot about her, do we? Anyway, Mary Jenkins did warn us against being judgmental.'

'And she did warm up after a while.'

In the evening they walked around the streets and saw several men sleeping rough, but although they tried to break the ice their search was fruitless and they retired to James's and Madeleine's flat for the night.

Next day they were pleasantly surprised to find Rosie as agreed. She was nonplussed at the suggestion of going to live in a cottage in Gloucestershire.

'I don't see what's in it for you.'

'Let's say that my husband and I are very happy and would like to see other people happy too. And this is a way of doing it.'

'I don't get it – but I haven't much to lose, have I? I still don't see how I can be any use farming. I've never even been round a farm.'

'You can learn, and there'll be plenty of help. At least it will give you a chance to sort yourself out and anything is better than this, surely.'

That was how Assunta began. Although Madeleine's first 'trawl' had produced only one resident occupant, a second cottage was filled almost immediately afterwards when James found a married couple through Rudge, the Vicar of Brocklechurch, whom he met on a visit to Honeyman's bookshop.

Walter and Dorothy Smith were in their forties, in a desperate situation. He had been in and out of prison for petty offences and was finding it hard to get employment. They had drifted around the country and ended up appealing to Rudge for help. He was able to do a little for them financially, but when he told a potential employer about Walter's record a wall went up.

'Do you think it would be fair and prudent to place them next to a young woman?' asked James.

'I can't guarantee anything, but I don't think he's really an evil man, and his wife's in a dreadful state of health. There's at least a chance they'll not mess up this opportunity.'

'A case of seventy times seven?'

'Something like that.'

With Madeleine, James broached the question of whether Molly should be invited to move into the third cottage. They discussed it with her.

'It's better accommodation than your present cottage.'

'I'm happy where I am, but I don't mind moving if you think I should,' she replied thoughtfully. 'There's only one thing that bothers me... Aren't you afraid the others might think I've been put there as the boss's spy?'

The thought had never occurred to them.

'I never thought of myself as the boss, rather as a friend,' James ventured.

'Oh, I know that, but you are the boss, even if you're a very kind one.'

James and Madeleine realised they looked at life one-sidedly, their background blinding them to the way they might seem to the underdog.

Madeleine and Molly Go Trawling

In the event Molly did move in, Assunta became a small community, and Molly's good sense averted the potential danger that she feared. James and Madeleine provided her with an old Morris Minor, which enabled her to continue working at Briar Cottage and occasionally to take the girls to school.

22: Katarzyna Calls In a Debt

Fifteen hundred miles away, in a small town near Krakow, Katarzyna's mind was in turmoil. She and her husband Henryk were often able to receive the Polish Service on the BBC. Antoni used his stage name of 'Chopin', under which he was well known, since it gave authority to his pronouncements in the arts and cultural programmes. His defection put his sister in no danger because he had not been a political figure, but it had infuriated her father-in-law and even more his twin brother, for whom it was hugely embarrassing to be associated in any way with a defector.

Katarzyna and Henryk worked at the local hospital, she as a nurse, he as a doctor. They were still childless after several years of marriage, being unwilling to bring children into the bleak society which they inhabited, and used their spare time studying foreign languages, which they felt opened windows on a wider world and might be useful if conditions were to change. They also devoted themselves to helping the aged and housebound in the neighbourhood. By following that kind of lifestyle they tried to isolate themselves from the regime at the same time as not cutting themselves off from their fellow countrymen. Henryk's father despised them for it but regarded them as harmless, while Kazimierz made no secret of his contempt for anyone who did not actively support the regime.

In the course of his broadcasts Antoni alluded from time to time to the freedom that the arts enjoyed in the West but was careful not to say anything that might cause his sister trouble. He had no doubt that Kazimierz read the transcripts of his broadcasts assiduously in order to find material which could be used to sully the favourable image of him that still prevailed in intellectual circles despite, or in the eyes of many, on account of, his defection.

Kazimierz was friendless, not a loner by disposition but

through circumstances. As a secret policeman he had colleagues, but the very nature of his work bred suspicion and his 'friendships' were but skin-deep. He took interest in nothing but his work, had no time for relationships with women except when he could use them as tools of his trade, and his intellectual life was confined to studying Marxist–Leninist literature. He was a member of the comparatively rare breed of utterly dedicated Marxists, in which sense he could be described as an honest man. He was a political fanatic, lonely, suspicious, not greatly liked even by his colleagues, but given the respect which his incorruptible single-mindedness engendered. Within the limits imposed by his beliefs he was an honourable man.

There was but one chink in Kazimierz's armour – his sister. He was deeply conscious of his debt to her, for she had acted as a mother ever since the day in 1944 when his father and Janek had vanished and she had assumed responsibility for the family. Through that terrible autumn and their subsequent migration to the countryside, and after the end of the war, she had devoted herself heroically to her young brothers' welfare. He realised that she had never spared herself, had gone without food in order that they might have some, meagre though it was, had undertaken menial jobs to earn enough to clothe them and had deferred her own education in order to ensure theirs. Not even the contempt in which he held her adherence to the Catholic faith could blind him to the knowledge that he probably owed her his life. In spite of their irreconcilable religious and political outlook they were friends.

He never visited Katarzyna at home because of the antipathy between him and Henryk, but they would occasionally meet for lunch, when he took her to a restaurant. It was on one such occasion, just a year after Antoni's defection, that she told him cautiously about her desire to go the West.

'I don't suppose you can understand it,' she said, 'but now that Antek is in London I'd love to see him again!'

'Kasia, you realise that as far as I'm concerned he's a traitor.'

'You see him as a traitor, I see him as my little brother, just as I see you. Perhaps even as a sort of son. We can't wash out our shared history.'

'Yes, I do understand your feeling for him, of course I do, even if I can't share it.'

'I feel that a part of me is with him, just as part of it is with you.'

'I expect you could get a permit for a visit, though you wouldn't be able to take much money with you. Presumably that wouldn't matter since the famous broadcaster could look after you. Of course, in view of Chopin's defection –' he uttered the name with distaste –'the authorities might suspect that you also want to defect, in which case they might well refuse.'

Katarzyna looked him straight in the eyes.

'Kasik, I am not talking about a visit. I want to escape from Poland.'

'*What!* Why are you telling me this? It puts me in a terrible position!'

'Kasik, please hear me out. I've done a lot of thinking about this, believe me, and I'm sure it's what I want. Besides… if ever I were to have a child, which in view of my age is becoming unlikely, I wouldn't wish to bring it into a communist state. I'm sorry if that hurts you, but there aren't many secrets between us.'

Kazimierz looked pained. He replied gently, 'Yes, I realise that. But if you did manage to leave I should miss you very much. You know that.'

'Of course I do. The choice tears at my heart, but only you can help.'

'Think of the practicalities. You can't do it officially so it would involve a risky journey… and could you even be certain of a welcome wherever you went?'

'I've given it a lot of thought. The shortest way would be through Czechoslovakia and then to Vienna. From there we could get to England easily enough, and as Henryk and I are both qualified we'd be regarded as useful people and be able to support ourselves, even if we have to do some retraining first…'

Kazimierz's face clouded.

'Don't you feel you should use your qualifications in the service of your country, of Poland?'

'Let's try not to get into politics, Kasik, but as things are I find it hard to think of this as my country. Deep down I think you understand.'

Katarzyna Calls In a Debt

A long pause ensued. Kazimierz was torn between duty and the love and gratitude he felt towards his sister.

'Well, what exactly are you asking of me?'

The woman, who, as a teenager, had faced daunting odds, and survived, did not beat about the bush.

'I'm asking you for advice and practical help on how to beat the system – without putting yourself at risk, of course.'

He realised that the time for repaying the debt of twenty years ago had come, and he trembled.

'Let's meet here again in a week's time. I'll see what I can come up with. Oh, Kasia, what are you doing to me?'

23: Ruth's Seventieth

A lively party was gathered for pre-lunch drinks on William's and Rebecca's lawn. Family and a few good friends were celebrating Ruth Silvermann's seventieth birthday. Jacob had feared she might not have reached it because she had not enjoyed good health for some years, but she was a fighter and felt that life was eminently worth living. She was a model wife, mother and grandmother. It was scarcely surprising that her family wanted to fête her, not just because of the milestone of seventy but as an icon. She had been an inspiration to Madeleine who had been in London for a week, helping Rebecca with the arrangements. Jacob helped too, as he had done in the matter of domestic chores for some years, and on their visits James and John had been amused to see his huge bulk at the kitchen sink and even at the cooker, puffing away at his ubiquitous cigar, thereby effectively chasing his wife off to the drawing room to rest. John referred to his speciality as *boeuf bourguignon au cigare*.

Jacob, too, had slowed down of course. He was a few years his wife's senior, but since physical activity had never been one of his characteristics the slowing down was obvious only to those who knew him well. He never referred to it. Guy Rowlands was there, distinctly bowed but still handsome: he perched on his shooting stick, talking to Jacob – inevitably – about the old days, the Company and Constance Todd.

Isaac had come from his post in Rome with Irena, his recently wed Italian wife. James had brought Assunta; and John and Antoni, who had become a close friend of Jacob's, sharing long talks on the arts and philosophy, completed the party. Irena wore her Catholicism lightly and was intrigued at Assunta's name, and slightly abashed at the perfectly natural way in which the little girl explained why it had been chosen.

Guinevere, now quite a young lady, and Assunta went round with plates of nuts and olives, performing the function of daughters of the house, while William stood behind the improvised bar dispensing drinks.

Many of the party scarcely knew Irena, so they naturally clustered around her and Isaac. Her English was fluent and even colloquial, spoken with an execrable accent. Rebecca, who had, of course, been at their wedding, immediately engaged her in conversation, of which there was no shortage as she had been to Florence and Rome more than once with William. Isaac had overcome his initial slight suspicions about Antoni's intentions at the time of his defection, and they spoke easily and knowledgeably since news broadcasting was part of Antoni's duties. James and John, watching the ebullient group, reminisced about the early days when they used to meet at the Silvermanns'.

'Of course, school was great,' said John, 'but I think it was with Jacob that my education, in the broadest sense, really took off.'

'I couldn't agree more, and I know just what you mean by "in the broadest sense". Jacob was our guru.'

'You say that, even though he's to all intents and purposes an atheist?'

'There's a story about Disraeli being quizzed on religion. He said that all wise men should have a religion, and when he was asked what his was he replied, "Wise men never say"!'

'So that means you're not wise, since you make no secret of yours.'

'It all depends on what you mean by wisdom, oh patient enquirer.'

'True, oh sage.'

And so they continued, slipping back into the style of banter they used as boys and had tended to discard during their troubled years.

Rebecca and Madeleine called them to lunch.

No one in the party was a heavy drinker but the wine was good and conversation ranged wide.

Ruth, with her customary solicitude, said to James, 'These family occasions make one thoughtful, don't they? Is there any more news of the rest of your family?'

'Not since Antoni finally came back. Naturally he brought me a spoken message from my sister, just as I sent her one back with him, but I haven't written. Perhaps I'm being over-careful, but I don't want to put her in any sort of awkward position. It's impossible to know how much censorship there is.'

'She was all right a year or so ago, wasn't she?'

'Yes. As she's a nurse and her husband a doctor, they're better off than many by Iron Curtain standards, but that doesn't mean much.'

'And as for our brother, my twin, the less said the better,' said Antoni.

'I suppose,' said Jacob, 'that it is possible to have a code of ethics and preserve one's self-respect as the servant of a totalitarian regime. But it must be very difficult. So many pressures.'

'In a state with a secret police, and where members of a family and people who are supposed to be friends denounce one another, there can't be self-respect. Not if you want to survive,' said Antoni.

'But surely, Antoni,' said Guy, 'you demonstrated that self-respect can exist.'

'Yes, but only by getting away from the regime!'

'Supposing', said Madeleine, 'that you hadn't been able to get out – and let's face it, most people who want to can't – you'd probably have preserved your integrity by retreating from public life and withdrawing into a shell.'

'Probably, but that would be a sort of dying.'

'Self-respect may call for that,' said James solemnly and thoughtfully.

'Isn't it the case,' said Isaac, 'that in a great many walks of life decisions have to be made that affect one's self-respect, or sense of honour, to put it in an old-fashioned way? Don't we all live to a greater or lesser extent in a sort of prison – in the armed forces, the civilian professions, businesses, political parties, I dare say even in the Church or a family, where the people we work with may act in a way we feel is reprehensible, and we have to decide what to do about it?'

'And then,' said Guy, 'we decide whether we do more harm by insisting on what we're sure is ethically right, and thereby wrecking useful and precious relationships, than by turning a blind eye and hoping the situation won't repeat itself? Which is exactly what made the rise of Hitler possible.'

'Indeed,' said Jacob with feeling.

At that stage the glazed look on the girls' eyes reminded Rebecca to tell them to go and play in Guinevere's room or the garden. The discussion continued.

'I think it's very difficult to establish absolutes in the absence of an ethical system,' said John. 'For example, was it possible to be a truly honourable man and also a committed Nazi? I'm pretty sure that the Nazis who committed suicide at the end chose what they felt to be the least bad option, preferable to hanging. They had essentially been serving themselves in a fundamentally evil system; morality didn't come into their thinking at all. Basically a bunch of crooks. On the other hand the Captain of the *Graf Spee* was an honourable man trying to serve his country in the clutches of an evil system: he had what you might call the code of a patriot, and a military code. The fact that he was a decent man was demonstrated by the humane way he treated the Allied prisoners on board. Of course no one can be absolutely certain why he shot himself, but it certainly wasn't the best option in the physical sense, for he would simply have been interned in Uruguay, like his crew, until the war was over. Sorry, I've been delivering a lecture. I'll shut up!'

'It's difficult, isn't it,' said Guy, 'to tie self-respect to a label, but I think not letting people down has something to do with it.'

'Ah!' exclaimed Irena, joining in for the first time. 'At last a piece of good Anglo-Saxon common sense! How do you say it sometimes, Izzy, "doing the decent thing"?'

'Don't accuse me of being Anglo-Saxon, darling,' laughed Isaac.

'As one of the representatives of the Anglo-Saxon race here present,' interposed Guy, 'let me suggest that there are many important things that are hard to define but can be understood by their effects. An example of self-respect that means a lot to me is Captain Oates's action and words as he walked out of the tent so as to give his companions a chance to survive.'

A respectful silence fell across the group.

'Indeed,' said Jacob, 'just as there must have been instances of that sort of thing at the time of the Final Solution.'

A further pregnant silence.

Jacob continued. 'In the Latin languages there is an expression that goes part of the way to defining it, such as *amour propre*; and in German too – *Selbstachtung*. So the idea of love comes into it.'

'But,' said James, 'it is love that, although beginning with one's self, must stretch out to others unless it is to remain a sterile self-enjoyment.'

Nods of approval all round.

'From which', he continued, 'I deduce that self-respect now requires the gentlemen to chase the ladies into the drawing room, whilst we tackle the washing up.'

After the requisite protest the ladies agreed.

24: Honour

As the Silvermanns' party was gathering, a much smaller group stood beside a car in a remote corner of south-western Poland, not far from the Czechoslovak border. The car was discreetly concealed near the entrance to a forest track; the two men and a woman waited a while, engrossed in thought. From the boot of the car they brought out two well-filled rucksacks, which they placed on the ground, and resumed their silent waiting. The stillness of the forest, the omnipresent scent of resin and the sunlight filtering gently through the foliage of the broadleaved trees should have induced a sense of calm and well-being, but the magic did not work for the silent group trying to appear unconcerned despite their mental turmoil, each contemplating the uncertainty of the future.

Kazimierz broke the silence. 'You might as well set off now.'

They checked their position and the route marked on their maps.

'Do you want to go over the details once more?'

Katarzyna and Henryk declined. They had assiduously studied the instructions that Kazimierz had prepared and knew, as far as was possible without having covered the ground, what to expect. He had obtained Czechoslovak currency for them and their rucksacks were packed with nutritious rations. They were as ready as they would ever be. Henryk looked at Kazimierz and extended his hand.

'I don't know why you're doing this, but thank you. I hope things work out for you as well as for us.'

Kazimierz returned the handshake.

'Oh I don't know either; we all have our weaknesses.' And he managed a watery smile.

Katarzyna embraced him. Their emotion was too great for many words. She said, 'Have you got a message for your brothers?'

'I hardly remember Janek, but say nice things to him from me. As for Antoni...' he paused, wrestling with the words, forcing them out. 'Tell him I hope he's happy, and that I expect him to look after our big sister.'

Katarzyna and Henryk swung their rucksacks on to their backs.

'I'll watch you disappear over the hill, and then I'll go home,' said Kazimierz. 'I fancy having a cigarette first.'

They set off at a brisk pace, not looking back, up the gentle slope. Kazimierz went to the glove box where he retrieved a bottle of vodka and his revolver. He enjoyed the cigarette, then took a large draught of the vodka, not swallowing it but savouring it rather as a small boy might make a lump of chocolate last as long as possible. As the walkers were about to vanish over the top of the slope they looked back and waved, although they could not make out Kazimierz in the gloom of the trees.

A gentle breeze blew away from them down the slope.

They did not hear the shot.

25: Some Practical Philosophy

Ruth, Rebecca, Madeleine and Irena, comfortably settled in the drawing room, began with some inconsequential conversation about interior decoration and the flowers that were available in autumn, which tailed off as the excellent meal and the agreeable nature of the occasion took effect. If the ladies did not quite curl up and snooze, they came close to doing so. After a while Ruth brought the others back to reality.

'I really do think we're all very lucky in our husbands. I don't remember seeing any man help with household chores when I was a girl. Of course, I suppose Izzy's official duties don't give him much opportunity to do so, but he used to be quite handy as a boy.'

'Oh, but he does help sometimes. Of course we're lucky, we have a maid for some of the time, but when we're by ourselves he likes to help. I suppose his parents brought him up properly! You wouldn't find many Italian husbands doing the washing up.'

They all agreed that none of their husbands was a male chauvinist, although Rebecca had to admit that William's intentions were often better than his achievement.

Madeleine, who had spoken rather less than the others, looked thoughtful.

'You know, I've been thinking about what we were saying over lunch concerning self-respect... Jacob brought the idea of love into it but we didn't follow up that line of thought; it came to an end when the men shoved us away and got on with the washing up.'

'Well, that was a practical demonstration of it, thank goodness,' said Rebecca.

'It struck a chord in me, and helped me to understand what makes Jim tick. We don't speak much about religion at home because he knows a little of it goes a long way with me, but when he does it's nearly always about love. He says very little about what I'd call the "charity" side of religion, and I must admit that's what I used to think religion was mainly about.'

Some Practical Philosophy

'But aren't the Poles terribly Catholic?' asked Irena archly. 'I would have expected him to go in for all the ceremonies and holy occasions!'

'Oh, don't get me wrong. Jim is a hundred per cent Catholic, but he stands back and thinks for himself. He says religion is like gardening, you have to know what and when to prune!'

'He likes having religious objects around, doesn't he,' said Rebecca, 'the odd icon or crucifix and so on?'

'Yes, but not a great many. They're there, but not intrusive. They never were, not even before we married.'

'In Italy lots of people have their walls covered with holy pictures. They're just part of the furniture.'

'And do they mean much to people, or are they really just, as you say, part of the furniture.'

'To some people more than to others, I suppose. It's not something I've thought about.'

'Well,' continued Madeleine, 'there is a strong practical side to Jim's faith, and that's something I can share with him.'

She launched out into an enthusiastic account of how the Assunta project came into being, her eloquence growing as she described what they had achieved; the others, caught up in her momentum, said not a word. Whenever she paused they waited for her to continue. She was taking them into territory not only unexplored but also unimagined. When she ran out of steam Irena said, 'That's the sort of thing we'd leave to one of the religious orders in the Church.'

'Similar ideas have been tried out here in the past by philanthropically minded people, but not often.'

'As a social experiment I think it's wonderful. I do hope it works out. I rather envy you, and I'm sure we'd love to see it,' said Rebecca.

'Well,' replied Madeleine, 'it's not meant to be a tourist attraction but you'd be very welcome to come and see for yourselves.'

Ruth thought long and hard, and said thoughtfully, 'A sort of kibbutz in Gloucestershire. Well, well!'

A rattle of crockery announced the arrival of the men with the coffee trolley.

Ruth said, 'This has been a lovely birthday. Thank you all so much.'

26: Sanctuary

Katarzyna and Henryk kept up a steady pace through the late afternoon. Kazimierz's advice had been to get close to the border before dark, camp, and cross over before first light. They had calculated that with reasonable luck and at an average of twenty-four kilometres a day they should be able to cross the Slovak region and reach the Austrian border in a little over a week – or at most, a fortnight. Their intention was to keep away from centres of habitation as far as possible in order not to display their lack of fluency in the language; they hoped that in the countryside the money they carried would buy them food without questions being asked. They would, of course, have to be prepared not to take the most direct route.

Their first night passed uneventfully, even though they did not sleep well. They were accustomed to walking and camping as a recreation so that the absence of urban comforts presented no problems, but in the stillness of the night the boldness of their undertaking pressed in on them. They had left all their possessions apart from a few items of sentimental value, and on arrival in England, assuming they succeeded, would be dependent on Antoni and Janek for an unpredictable period of time. In the meantime it was best not to dwell on matters beyond their control, but that was more easily said than done. They were only too glad to dismantle their tiny shelter just before daybreak, take a quick breakfast of bread, cheese and coffee, and set off.

Kazimierz had indicated several points at which he felt confident the border would not be guarded, and his prediction proved right. They moved cautiously out of Poland and, in the gathering daylight, walking through country indistinguishable from the previous day's, the worries of the night slipped away. They discussed their overnight fears.

'We must concentrate on thinking positively,' Henryk said.

'Yes, we've done our planning as adults; burnt our boats, and

Sanctuary

now we must live in the present moment, like children on holiday.'

'Some holiday! Travel hopefully, eh?'

'Exactly. And do you know I'm actually enjoying this. It sounds absurd, but that's really how I feel.'

'Me too. Our first holiday abroad!'

They held hands for a while as they walked.

Katarzyna was right when she referred to the successful planning they had done. They had confided in no one but Henryk's unmarried sister, whom they trusted implicitly, and had left her a letter concerning the disposal of their property, which they bequeathed to her with a request that part of their money be given to their parish priest to be used for the poor. Now they were indeed travelling light.

The weather was kind to them; good walking weather.

For a few days their path lay through hilly country and they saw no one. As they moved away from the forested upland they began to see signs of cultivation; a few villages and isolated farms, which they avoided until they felt the need for fresh rations, and were able to buy eggs, milk and bread without arousing suspicion. They were making good time.

As they approached the Austrian border the ground became much more open, with little natural cover and more buildings. Their earlier euphoria began to evaporate. On one occasion they remained concealed in a small wood for half a day, about ten kilometres from the border, in order to rest before the final walk to the planned crossing point. They decided to appear unhurried as they approached it, and to their delight entered Austria without mishap, reaching the outskirts of Vienna on the twelfth day. They cleaned themselves up, Henryk shaved and, speaking more than adequate German, had no difficulty in making their way to the British Embassy.

27: Joy

James was happy, indulging in one of his favourite pastimes, reverie. A fire crackled in the grate, Madeleine sat opposite him reading a novel, wind and rain hammered at the windows: he could look back on a fruitful harvest in more senses than one. Assunta squatted on the floor with Kate, cutting out paper animals and buildings for an imaginary farm. He watched the smoke from his pipe curl upwards and occasionally he would blow some smoke rings: heaven on earth.

Madeleine winked at him. 'Wonderful, isn't it? Time for something to go wrong.'

Since pessimism was not one of her characteristics, the remark startled him. She continued, 'Things have gone very well for us but you can hardly say the same for a great many people in lots of places.'

Madeleine had indeed changed over the years. To his delight her awareness of the world outside the sphere of business had increased beyond measure. He looked back at the girl with whom he had fallen in love for her feminine charm rather than for her wit or interest in the things that were important to him, essentially a sensual attraction. Now they were truly partners.

'You're thinking about Czechoslovakia?'

The Prague Spring had come and gone, snuffed out by Soviet tanks.

'Yes, for example, but nearer home too. Assunta village looks like being a success, but what we're doing there is just a drop in the ocean.'

Eastern Europe was more immediately in his mind than was Assunta.

'The Soviet grip is as strong as ever. Thank goodness Kasia and Henryk are out of it.'

Katarzyna and Henryk, after a period of verification of their qualifications, were happily employed in their professions in

London, where Antoni had found them a flat not far from his.

'What did you mean by "time for something to go wrong"?'

'I wasn't thinking of anything in particular. It's just that it all seems too good to be true.'

'Let's hope it isn't.'

They talked over what had been achieved since their reunion. Assunta had been a resounding success. Its first occupant, Rosie, had stayed a couple of years and then found employment as a waitress, and also a boyfriend, in Brocklechurch; they saw her from time to time. Walter Smith had kept out of trouble and worked on the farm. Since those original members of the community, there had been many others, and the number of cottages had grown to twelve. Not all the 'settlers', as James and Madeleine referred to them between themselves, had been successful. One couple had vanished overnight, taking much of the furniture and fittings with them; but that disappointment was mitigated by the evident anger of their neighbours. It had never been the intention to tie occupancy to working on the estate and indeed many of the settlers did not take to it. After regaining their self-respect, they left to find more congenial urban employment. Enough did, however, decide to remain on the land to produce a more or less permanent community of about ten adults.

The farm and garden centres had prospered, as had James's great interest, the plantation of exotic trees. The Great Walling Arboretum, as it came to be called, had from the beginning received enthusiastic support from Kew, and one of James's delights was the frequent visits of experts who came to give advice and to praise. But, if Madeleine had changed over the years, so had he. Whereas before their reunion the concept of the arboretum had been his principal interest, his contribution to posterity, he now derived even greater fulfilment from the success of Assunta. People, he had realised, mattered more than concepts. Increasingly he understood the ideals that fuelled John's devotion to his work, and he realised that he had unconsciously drawn on his friend's practical dedication to the less fortunate members of society.

'Never forget Poland' had been his father's valediction. He had obeyed it on and off, though at one stage the flame had

Joy

burned low, but thanks to Madeleine's initiative and subsequently Antoni's, Poland had come to him. Everything seemed to have come together, strands of events that he had not planned but had gladly fostered. He had much to be happy about.

He and Madeleine chatted on in their deservedly self-congratulatory mood until she reminded the girls of the time, and he followed them up to tell them a bedtime story. Little Kate often spent nights with them and Molly did not object.

Later, over dinner, he said, 'We've patted ourselves thoroughly on the back, haven't we? Where do we go from here?'

'Do we have to go anywhere in particular...? I suppose Assunta could be enlarged but I think we've got enough on our plate, don't you? A time for consolidation rather than innovation perhaps?'

'I expect you're right, my dear, as usual.'

It was true. Whereas some years ago his mind was ever on the alert for some new project, he was now at ease with what he had and was. Things can only get better, he thought.

A few evenings later, when again they were sitting together, he answered the telephone to hear John speaking steadily but in a tone of confident excitement.

'My dear Jim, I want you to do me a favour. Would you please be my sponsor?'

'Doubtless, old chap. What is it to be? Climbing Kilimanjaro, a half marathon for the underprivileged...?'

'Nothing like that, though it is a sort of peak, metaphorically speaking.'

'You intrigue me.'

'I'd like you to be the sponsor at my Confirmation.'

'What!'

'Surely you're sensed it coming... I'm being received into the Church and it seems that as an adult I can make my First Communion and be confirmed at the same ceremony.'

'This is wonderful news – but seriously, I'd no idea. I must have been blind.'

'Yes, it was rather dim of you, particularly as apart from the Holy Spirit, who came into it, you provided the background.'

250

Joy

'Me? I've never tried to proselytise.'

'I expect that's got a lot to do with it. You were the channel. It was the result of a lot of remarks you've dropped over the years, and particularly just by being yourself. I think it started with an incident which you've probably forgotten. Do you remember how you stood up to that ass O'Neill when he tried to make fun of you for wearing your father's cross? I've watched the way you've dealt with adversity and turned it into something creative and good. Assunta village was certainly a factor too. More a matter of what you are, rather than what you've said.'

'Dealing with triumph and disaster, as Kipling put it? Well, thanks: I'm rather overwhelmed. As a matter of fact I've often admired the spirit in which you've undertaken your vocation – not that that's made me want to be an agnostic!'

Madeleine was staring hard at James, baffled as to the subject of the conversation and intrigued at the joy that radiated from him.

John continued, 'I'll give you details of when and where later on. My love to the ladies, and I recommend a dose of your favourite single malt to restore your composure.'

'I'll need it. God bless.'

'What on earth was all that about?' asked Madeleine.

He told her.

'Good Lord!' she said.

'Exactly.'

The following Easter they all went to John's parish church, where he was duly received and confirmed. As a gift James had commissioned a replica of his father's cross.

'I'll never be without it,' said John in a voice that trembled.

'Now, just a small word of advice,' said James. 'Beware of becoming too damn holy. That sometimes happens to converts, and they're impossible to live with for a few years. And don't set your critical faculties aside; don't believe everything you're told!'

'Ah, the sage surfaces through the saint.'

'What's the difference?'

28: Disasters

November 1970

It was Assunta's half-term holiday. She had retired to bed and her parents sat by the fireside discussing their financial affairs. Things were going very well; the garden centres, Assunta, the farm and estate.

No vestige of worry clouded their joy. James was still rejoicing at John's conversion and often alluded to it.

Madeleine said, 'You know, darling, there's nothing I'd like more than to do as John has. I realise how happy that would make you, but it wouldn't be honest to pretend just to please you. You do understand, don't you?'

'Of course. Just as it wouldn't be honest of me to deny that it's my dearest wish, but it must come from your own conviction.'

'You see, I simply don't have any feelings in that direction. I know it means a great deal to you, and that you live according to your religious principles. In fact I suppose I've benefited from them because they've made you the man you are; kind and honourable and considerate and all the other qualities I love and admire in you, but the way feels closed to me. I just can't connect.'

'I say, thanks for the glowing testimonial, I'll know where to go for a reference if ever I need one!'

'I'm not joking, you really are the way I've described, but to me it just seems sensible to behave as you do, and I try to imitate you, but I don't find it necessary to base it on God. I think I believe in a God, but as the source of everything and not because he has any direct meaning for the way I live.'

'Fair enough. There are lots of people like you. Do you know, darling, in twenty-five years this is the first time we've had this sort of conversation?'

'Probably because I've never felt comfortable talking about "God and all that". I've always enjoyed being on the sidelines when you've had philosophical conversations with our friends, and I've joined in a little once or twice, but the idea of God and what you'd call an Ultimate Purpose has always been beyond my grasp. I don't feel I need the idea in order to live a decent life. I wish I could, for your sake.'

'You're your mother's daughter. Mummy was among the kindest people I've known, but I never heard her refer to God or church. In fact the only occasions I remember her having anything to do with a service were the occasional wedding or funeral, or on Remembrance Day. But in the way she acted towards people I'd describe her as a truly Christian woman.'

'I suppose the only direct Christian experience she, or I, ever had was at school assemblies, where we picked up a few prayers and hymns, and that was that.'

'I'd say you both benefited from the collective Christian heritage. What'll happen in the next generation or two, Lord knows.'

They talked on happily about other things, content in the security of their union. Towards bedtime James made Madeleine a cup of hot chocolate as usual, poured his nightcap and brought both to the fireside.

'I've got to spend a couple of hours at the estate office in the morning. Didn't you mention you wanted to go shopping in Brocklechurch?'

'Yes, and I thought I'd take Assunta to Honeyman's and see what he's got in the way of children's books.'

'See what takes her fancy; it'll give you some clues for Christmas.'

'That's what I had in mind, darling. I'm not just a pretty face, you know.'

'Indeed.'

They sipped their drinks and retired to bed, holding hands until they slept as they had always done.

The next day James returned to the house after his session at the estate office, and was making himself a cup of coffee in the kitchen when he heard the sound of an approaching car followed by a ring at the front door.

Strange, he thought, Madeleine must have forgotten her key.

Disasters

It was not Madeleine at the door, but a policeman. James waited for what seemed an eternity, his heart throbbing.

Madeleine had crashed head-on into a lorry. She and Assunta had been killed instantly.

Later, having returned from Brocklechurch after identifying the bodies, James telephoned John, who said simply, 'Let me sort out a few things in the office this afternoon and I'll be with you.'

He arrived early the following morning.

'Jim, you've got to look after yourself; you look ghastly.'

'I know. But I simply can't think straight. It's good of you to come so soon!'

'No sooner than you were there for me when my parents died.'

'I suppose that's true, but what about your caseload? Your absence many not go down too well with your superiors.'

'Then to blazes with them: priorities, you know, old chap.'

'I've been trying to think about the funeral, and the burials. I suppose I could get permission for burial on the estate...'

John thought carefully before replying.

'Perhaps you could, but is it really a good idea? It's difficult to think clearly at a time like this, but would it be wise? You know it's quite important to let go at a certain point, and if they were buried here you'd find yourself visiting the graves every day. Why not the cemetery at Great Walling? It isn't far.'

'I dare say you're right. Even though Madeleine's not Catholic...' he paused, embarrassed at his use of the present tense... 'old Father Ryan wouldn't raise any objection.'

'Of course not.'

'You're right. All this is so strange. I feel as though I were living outside myself, as if none of this were happening, and yet it is so horribly, horribly, real. I can't tell you how much your being here helps me, you're my anchor to reality.'

'If you make the funeral arrangements I'll ring round our friends. I'm sure you don't want to repeat the facts to them all.'

'Thank God you're here!'

Molly came in with tea and sandwiches, quietly as a mouse, and vanished equally invisibly.

Disasters

'She's been wonderful. She's hardly said a word since I broke the news to her, and little Kate's heartbroken – not that she can really take it in, I suppose.'

'It's hard to tell how much children of her age can understand.'

'Yesterday I had a family, now I have only friends, but what good friends they are. But I mustn't wallow in self-pity, must I?'

He managed a watery smile.

'I think a little self-pity is permissible, and it's perfectly in order to cry oneself to sleep.'

'You know, I want to cry, but the tears just don't come. When I went to identify... them–' he could not bring himself to use the words 'bodies' –'I couldn't allow myself to believe they were Madeleine and Assunta. They seemed scarcely damaged but they were so dreadfully quiet.'

'Oh my dear Jim. I wish I knew what to say.'

'You needn't say anything, just be here.'

'Fr Ryan will be here soon.'

'Well, when he arrives I'll leave you with him and go to make the phone calls.'

Fr Ryan was a tired old man. He walked with a pronounced stoop and was only too glad to accept the chair that James offered him. His weary manner belied the kindly directness of his approach.

Although they had never become close friends they had grown to understand each other over the years. He clasped John's hand, and held it for a while.

'It is futile to try and understand this. All you can do, hard as it is, is to accept it.'

James nodded.

'And you can be sure that you will meet them both in heaven. Although your wife was not a Catholic she was a good woman and a faithful wife and mother. She is safe with Jesus.'

'My dear Father, you have mellowed over the years,' said James with a vestige of a smile.

'Indeed, if I can't be mellow at my age... I expect I must be nearly twice yours.'

'Age is what terrifies me. I am forty and the thought of all the

Disasters

years to come without them strikes a chill into my heart.'

'Consolation and acceptance will come, slowly. In the meantime you will have not only memories but also the very real presence of what you achieved together. The good work you both did in creating your rescue village will help to bear you up. I hope you will continue to support it as a living testimony.'

'Most certainly. You're right, it will be a real help.'

'I believe your friend Mr Stonor is staying with you?'

'Yes. He is a great comfort.'

They talked on for a while until Fr Ryan took his leave, and John returned to the study.

'I've spoken to them all. Was Father Ryan helpful? Did he give you a lengthy and holy discourse?'

'Not at all, in fact he scarcely touched on God. Yes, I'm glad of his visit. Do you remember, years ago, I told you he might be unexciting but was a suitable pastor for a country parish? Well, I didn't think I'd be at the receiving end... Now pour the whisky, John.'

They sat for a long time, largely in silence.

★

The funeral was a revelation to James. John had gathered all the remaining family: Katarzyna, Henryk and Antoni and the great friends, Jacob and Ruth, both visibly frail; Guy, a shadow of his former self; William, Rebecca and Guinevere; and even Isaac and Irena, who had travelled far and fast to be present; Tom and Mary, who looked broken at the loss of a friend and of a dearly loved goddaughter; Rudge, the Vicar of Folding; old Honeyman and many of James's friends from the British Legion; and the 'settlers' en masse. Old Mrs Brand propped herself up on Molly's arm. Many people from the locality and from Assunta's school were there. The size of the congregation reflected the esteem in which James and his family were held, and despite his grief he warmed to their affection.

When all had left John remained with him. They discussed the gathering at the funeral and sadly realised it was probably the last time that all the old friends would meet. Ruth had declined noticeably since they had dined together to celebrate her seventieth birthday, Jacob too, and Guy had had difficulty negotiating the uneven ground in the graveyard.

'The old people won't be with us much longer,' said James. 'If we wish to see them we'll have to go up to town: it's virtually the end of the old firm's generation.'

'It's all in the past, but,' John added gently, 'despite all that's happened we must look to the future…'

'Objectively I know you're right, but I'm going to need a lot of time. Now let's talk about you for a change. It's wonderful having you here but I'm really worried about the effect this long absence may have on your job.'

'Don't worry. I'm entitled to some leave, but to tell you the truth I've become rather disenchanted with my work and the thought of doing something else has passed through my mind more than once lately.'

'What's gone wrong?'

'Nothing specifically, but it has become increasingly bureaucratic and some of the thrill has faded. I might try my hand at some writing.'

'You won't do anything precipitate, will you? I always felt that for you the work was more in the nature of a vocation than a job.'

'Yes, that's bothered me a bit, but I've been doing it for nearly twenty years… We'll see. Things move on. And not only for me.'

Book III

29: Betrayal

Five Years Later – 1975

For James, life moved on slowly. Ostensibly he pulled himself together quickly; he kept up a courageous front, and in business he attended efficiently to all that was necessary. He employed a supervising manager for the garden centres to oversee the tasks formerly administered by Madeleine, he took care about his appearance when he had to attend public functions, and he did not let his self-respect slip. Without enthusiasm he accepted an invitation to become a magistrate on the Brocklechurch bench.

Inwardly he felt hollow, back where he had been sixteen years previously while he was still separated from Madeleine. His life lacked purpose and often he wished he could divest himself of his responsibilities. The past five years had seen a succession of funerals. Jacob and Ruth had died. So had Mrs Brand and Fr Ryan, who was replaced by a much younger man with whom James had difficulty in building a rapport. He knew that he was held in great respect and even, since he was appointed to the bench, in some awe. He often felt a fraud, just going through the motions: he sensed Madeleine at his elbow gently teasing him about his introspection as she had done in their early days. One night he dreamed that she had urged, 'Let go, Jim, let go.' But he could not. Even the work with Assunta now seemed dry and sterile: much of it devolved on Molly, who had grown in stature and confidence and occasionally went alone on a 'trawling' expedition when a vacancy occurred.

She continued to act as his housekeeper, discreetly attending to his needs and then disappearing into the background, never intruding. Little Kate, no longer little but seventeen, was rarely about the house: she attended secondary school in Brocklechurch, was doing well and occasionally came round to ask him for help with her studies. Assunta could have been at university by now…

Even his visits to old Honeyman's bookshop, and meeting Rudge for some broadening conversation, failed to raise his spirits as they used to.

John had retired from the probation service, as he had predicted, and bought a house in Great Walling. They met frequently. On one visit James had said, 'Well, the consolation is that things can't get much worse.'

He was mistaken. One morning, not long after the visit he retrieved the newspaper from the front door and settled down to read it in his study. He got no further than the front page:

SOVIET SPY RING UNMASKED

Apparently a spy network had been discovered as a result of two years' work by the security services, and several arrests made in university departments, defence establishments and, improbably, in a couple of famous publishing houses. Much of the activity had been in the West Country, and further disclosures were expected in the next few days. James did not have to wait until then, for the morning delivery of mail brought him a letter with a postmark that surprised him, since he had no correspondents there. The letter was as short as it was disturbing.

Dear Mr Todd,

By now you will know through the press and the radio the reason for the unseemly haste of my departure. We all have ideals, in which we place our faith, and although ours are so different I hope you can respect my convictions, even though you do not share them. I assure you that I respect your faith even though I believe it to be unfounded. There is such a thing as the community of honest men.

Over the years I have come to value the all too brief opportunities of exchanging some philosophical and literary conversation, and believe that a human spark was struck between us. It has grieved me not to have been able to speak more honestly with you about my political position. We shall never be able to meet again but I shall ever remember you as a civilised man for whom I felt a genuine affection, which I dare to believe, was reciprocated. The country from which this letter was posted bears no relevance to my present whereabouts, and I suggest that in our best interests you should now burn it.

With warmest regards,
Augustus Honeyman

James leaned back in his chair feeling utterly empty; his mind remained blank for a few minutes. Old Honeyman a Soviet spy. An improbable one, but presumably a spy does not go around wearing a trade label; disappointing none the less. He felt disenchanted, let down and yet heartened at Honeyman's evident embarrassment at having used him, as well as his other aficionados, as a smokescreen. When ideologies were involved, nothing else, not even friendship, was sacred. In the circumstances was the word 'sacred' out of place? Probably not, because Honeyman had his own godless religion – faith in humanity he had once called it – with its creed, saints and martyrs. That a man of his intelligence should embrace Marxism was understandable, if mistaken; for its creed, if not taken too far, made an appeal to both the head and the heart. But that he should see the current Soviet regime as an upholder of Marxist principles was astonishing: a blind faith if ever there was one. Whatever excuses James might wish to make for him out of affection, the fact remained that old Honeyman was a traitor to his country, to the country that had welcomed the homeless Polish boy and which, for all its faults and shortcomings, was a decent place in which to live. Had Honeyman paused to consider the possible consequences to freedom if the regime for which he worked were to succeed in its aims?

And yet, Honeyman's letter revealed a pang of conscience, an unease. Nothing was simple. He wished he knew Honeyman's background, the route by which he had arrived at the terrible act of treachery. What must stir in a man's mind to bring him to such a decision? Was it a gradual slide or a jump? James felt within himself a resurgence of patriotism, for his adopted country and for his native land, which had lain low during the years in which he had been making his way in the world. The words of nurse Edith Cavell, which he had learned at school, rang in his mind: 'Patriotism is not enough, I must have no hatred or bitterness towards anyone.' Of course, patriotism could be misguided, one must look critically at one's country as at one's church, but try to reform it from within, out of love, not from outside out of hatred. Britain was a free country where the Marxist was able to speak and publish without fear of a secret police. He was sure that his father's 'Never forget Poland' had not been said in a spirit of 'my country, right or wrong'.

And what of Antoni's defection, was that treachery? Were Antoni and Honeyman to be bracketed together? Surely not, for Antoni's ideals of artistic freedom were impossible to achieve from within his country. On the other hand it would presumably have been possible for him to have mocked the regime, clandestinely publishing lampoons and distributing them at great risk of imprisonment or worse. Perhaps that would have been the more manly course, and then to accept martyrdom if it fell to his lot. Perhaps other dedicated men and women chose that, and had not enjoyed his opportunity of escaping to the West. How difficult it was to be certain whether one was taking the easy way out; indeed, nothing was simple.

Fancy having Augustus for a first name! The sign over his shop stated merely 'The Brocklechurch Bookshop', and James had never known Honeyman's first name. There was something prim and proper about being Augustus, almost quaint and most unrevolutionary; a name that went with tea on the vicarage lawn in a Victorian novel; an excellent cover.

Ivor Rudge came to see him.

'I expect you'll be as irritated as I am. I had a strange visit yesterday. A couple of chaps called on me out of the blue. They weren't exactly wearing belted mackintoshes but they had a whiff of that about them – from some security service or other. They quizzed me about Honeyman, wanted to know whether he had ever expressed political views of an extreme nature. I couldn't help them, and quite honestly I took an instant dislike to the fellows. Honeyman was far more simpatico. I got a letter from him this morning and I dare say you'll be hearing from him too.'

James showed him Honeyman's letter and they exchanged the little information they possessed.

'I shouldn't be surprised if you were to be visited by the belted raincoats soon.'

'It has knocked me for six, I can assure you,' said James, 'I don't know how to react. Since Madeleine died old Honeyman's has been one of my lifelines. I don't expect another civilised bookshop will open in Brocklechurch. Probably the premises will be taken over by some multipurpose firm selling stationery and newspapers and trashy novels, without any love for books or for civilised conversation.'

'Probably. I looked there on my way to you. There's a policeman on duty outside and a forbidding sort of notice stuck to the door. What a disappointment!'

'That's putting it mildly. Not so much the loss of a little corner of civilisation as the knowledge of Honeyman's treachery. I wonder exactly what his present feelings are...'

'Nothing is as it seems. It is as though something good has been defiled. Do you think the friendliness he showed us was entirely sham, a part of the cover?'

'No, I believe a genuine bond of affection existed, as he expresses in his letters; we were not just customers and browsers. And yet...'

'Yes, there's always the "and yet"; part of the human condition, I suppose.'

Rudge's prediction was right. Not long after their conversation the belted raincoats called on James, who received them with a cold courtesy which became colder and blunter when they alluded to his Eastern European connections. Finally he said in his most icy manner, 'I suggest, gentlemen, that if you wish to make any further insinuations, however oblique, you put them in writing. I think this conversation has run its course, don't you?'

They left, and he heard no more.

His heart, however, remained heavy. Bereavement had been followed by the disillusion of treachery. In the face of loss he felt inadequate. It was only to be expected that the death of his wife and daughter should radically change his life, but while he struggled with the daily pain of loss his intellect told him he should not only keep attending to his various responsibilities but should move on. But in which direction?

After the first two years, which he endured in a state of quasi-monastic seclusion, attending only to essential business, and during which time his friends refrained from thrusting their care upon him, and after John had come to live in Great Walling, he made a positive effort to move on. He developed the custom of weekly or fortnightly dinners with John, Tom and Mary and occasionally with Rudge, usually at Briar Cottage but from time to time at their houses. With the passage of time these meetings, which they called the dining club, came to mean more and more to him. To begin with it tore at his heart to entertain using the table settings which Madeleine had handled, to see the chair she had occupied used by someone else, but he persevered and anguish was slowly replaced by acceptance. She had liked these people, and her memory was perpetuated in them. He ceased to feel guilty at coming very close to happiness without her: John assured him that with her practical nature she would not have wished him to be miserable.

On those occasions James attended to the cooking himself, sometimes with a little help from Molly. He hesitated to ask her to join them at table lest she should feel embarrassed, but he felt increasingly uncomfortable at treating her to some extent as a servant. Her situation was anomalous, not that she ever hinted at it. One day, when John had come for tea, James put the suggestion to him.

'Long overdue, since you ask me. I don't think you realise how close she and Madeleine had come through working on Assunta. She had become a sort of younger sister to Madeleine, or so it seems to me at any rate.'

'I must have been blind.'

'Indeed.'

'And while we're on the subject, has it ever occurred to you that the reason she goes about her household duties here so unobtrusively is that she doesn't want to appear to be thrusting herself on you when you are in what might be described as a vulnerable state? In addition to her devotion to Madeleine she feels indebted to you for so much that she doesn't want to take advantage.'

'Utterly blind.'

Molly brought the tea. James said gently, 'Won't you get yourself a cup and join us?'

She looked slightly puzzled but fetched the cup and sat down near them, somewhat gingerly.

'I hope there's nothing wrong.'

'Far from it, Molly. John and I' (it was the first time he had referred to him as John when speaking with her) 'were thinking how pleased we'd be if you'd join us at table when the dining club meets. After all, you're really part of the family now.'

She blushed. 'Oh I don't know, I'm not sure it'd feel right. I wouldn't know what to talk about.' She stared hard at the floor.

'Come on, Molly,' said John, 'you've worked closely with Jim and Madeleine; you really are a part of the firm. Assunta would never have got off the ground without your help.'

'That's very true,' said James.

'I may have made some contribution to it, but…' she hesitated… 'it'd feel as if I was stepping into Madeleine's place as the lady of the house, and I respected her so much that it would evoke a strange feeling in me. And what would your friends think?'

'Leave that to us,' said James.

'Well then,' John said, 'I do hope you'll decide to join us.'

After she had left the two friends looked at each other in amazement.

'That wasn't the old Molly speaking,' said James.

'No. Did you ever hear her use that kind of language? "My contribution", the word "evoked"? They're not Molly-type expressions.'

They realised that hitherto their knowledge of her vocabulary had been limited to hearing her speak of domestic matters and about the progress of Assunta.

John said, 'Of course it is reasonable to suppose that having been in contact, if only at a distance, with the sort of language that you and your circle use some of it would rub off on her, but even so…'

'She's clearly a more complex character than we took her for and, speaking for myself I suspect I've been guilty of some unconscious stereotyping.'

'Me too, and with rather less excuse than you in view of the sort of work I did. I didn't live in the privileged chambers of your ivory tower.'

Betrayal

'Do you think she'll decide to join us?'

'About fifty-fifty, I'd say.'

Only later did they come to discover that for several years Molly had systematically set out to, in her own words, 'better myself'. She had struck up a friendly relationship with some of the teachers at Kate's school, including Mary Jenkins, and through them received advice on what to read and how to obtain books. A travelling library based on the main one in Brocklechurch visited Great Walling fortnightly carrying largely trivial literature, romances and thrillers, but Molly arranged through the kindly old sub-postmaster to order and return the books that she had been recommended to read and were available in the main library. She bought herself a dictionary, and read every day, irrespective of how hard she had worked, with grim determination, like a miner at the coalface.

What began as an exercise 'to better myself' soon became a pleasure in itself. She started modestly by reading from the English classics and, since many of them dealt with country matters and social problems, their content connected to some extent with her experience, which helped to prevent her being deterred by some of the unfamiliar language. She begged Mary not to tell James or Madeleine about her venture. 'It's my secret,' she told her, as though she were a child not wishing to reveal the secret of her house in the trees. It had been hard not to tell Madeleine, for they had become so close in many respects; but as she explained to James and John years later, 'I wanted to surprise you all.'

'Well,' John had said, 'you certainly succeeded!'

In the event, she did decide to attend the dining club, and when it met at John's she went there in advance to help prepare the meal, John's culinary skill being very much of the bachelor type. All noticed a great improvement in the cuisine once she became involved.

John's house at Great Walling was handsome and spacious. It stood on the edge of the older part of the village with a view over fields and woodland on which it was unlikely that building would take place. He had made a clean break with his former career and devoted himself to writing and studies of which he had been starved during his dedicated life in the probation service. He also did a certain amount of sick visiting on an unofficial basis, and helped at the Citizens' Advice Bureau in Brocklechurch.

In the spring of 1977 the dining club met at John's house, the usual group being augmented by Antoni, who was down for a long weekend. James was immediately struck by the subtle changes in the appearance of the dining room. Flowers were arranged on the sideboard, a small floral centrepiece adorned the table, table napkins were neatly folded and tastefully set on the side plates, each grapefruit hors d'oeuvre was graced with a cherry, and instead of John's usual fruit salad made by opening various tins and emptying their contents into a large bowl it was served in individual little bowls and decorated with a sprig of fresh mint. A feminine touch indeed.

But what struck him most was that Molly sat at the other end of the table from John, which gave him furiously to think, for when they dined at Briar Cottage she made a point of never occupying Madeleine's place. He felt a little twinge of – what exactly – was it jealousy? He immediately reproached himself, but experienced a moment of pain at what was now denied to him. Then the sensation passed, as he rejoiced at his friend's changed circumstances and the obvious contentment in his expression. The first toast was, as usual, to absent friends, and ghosts drifted across his mind: so much happiness, such riches of friendship; it was always a solemn moment, but more than solemn, grief-laden. The moment seemed eternal, but conversation began at once.

'What is your daughter doing?' Antoni asked Molly.

'She is in her second year at university, only one more to go. I think she's doing well but I can't tell, it's all beyond me.'

'Bristol, isn't it?' asked Rudge. 'Frightfully good place. What is she reading?'

'Mathematics. Fancy that!'

Antoni was baffled at the term 'reading'. Surely mathematics was not something one read.

'She's going to be a really modern woman,' said Mary. 'It seems a long time since we were teaching her sewing and cooking here.'

'So you'll be attending her graduation next year,' said James, with an ache in his heart, trying not to betray the emotion that seized him.

'Yes, that'll be a strange experience for me.'

'You deserve it, Molly, you've been a wonderful mother,' said Tom.

'With a maths degree the world will be her oyster,' said Rudge.

'I do not know about oysters,' said Antoni, baffled yet again, 'but is there not still much difficulty for a woman to work in scientific places?'

'I know what you mean, Antek,' replied James, 'but things are getting better. Of course teaching is an obvious answer but that may not be what Kate wants. A lot will depend on how good a degree she gets.'

Conversation turned to how John was using his new-found freedom.

'I believe you're doing some writing,' said Rudge. 'Of what kind?'

'From experience. We've lived through an amazing period of history, so I thought I'd have a shot at something sociological. I'm working on short stories at the moment but my aim is to write a decent novel. I suppose that's many people's aim but it's not easy. Writer's block used to be just a term to me, now I know what it means and how it feels!'

'In my trade,' said Rudge, 'I need to do a little writing each week in preparing my sermon, but I have the advantage of having a clear aim before I start. My problem is how to express the ideas in terms which will convey the essentials to the simplest members of my congregation at the same time as not sounding trite to the more sophisticated.'

'I think there's a similarity between composing a sermon and being a serious journalist,' said Tom. 'In each case you have to put ideas across in a short space of time, and the chances are that however hard you work to express yourself well very few people will remember much of what you said or wrote after, say, a day or two.'

'In the case of my sermons,' laughed Rudge, 'I suspect you are being too generous. Most people will have forgotten what I said by the end of the service. I won't deny it can be discouraging, but it's worth doing one's best for the few who really listen.'

'I believe that some preachers,' said John, 'use books of collected sermons, or else keep their notes and re-use them later on.'

Rudge grinned. 'Yes, it's tempting, but in my opinion a great mistake. I scrap my notes and start from scratch the following year. I think it makes for a fresher approach, and even though the essence of the great Christian themes is unchangeable, the way they are presented must be adapted to the particular year.'

'I'd hesitate to push the analogy too far,' said James, 'but it's a bit like marketing. The idea, or the product, remains the same but the presentation must adjust to the time and the clientele.'

'Your example is good,' said Antoni. 'Also in the arts, especially in the arts, there is always development in the way a basic idea is presented, and sometimes if the new form is imaginative enough it is possible to see more clearly the original idea.'

They chatted on about art and writing, until Molly brought coffee. She wore an eager look, as if lying in wait for an opportunity. When everyone had been served and a copious meal had produced a temporary slackening of conversation she dropped her bombshell.

'I am thinking of taking a degree.'

An astonished silence followed.

'That's wonderful news,' said James, 'you are a dark horse. I'd no idea.'

'Neither did anyone else here. I haven't even told Kate yet, but I've been thinking about it ever since she got all excited when she was planning to go to university.'

'Why is she a black horse?' asked Antoni.

They explained.

Molly described how she had spoken to the careers department at Kate's school and been told about the Open University, and how she had nursed the idea, and had been saving up for the fees. As she took on more and more duties around the house and on the estate, James had gradually increased her salary, and she had wondered which subjects she should take. She spoke with a childlike enthusiasm, often slipping out of her more educated vocabulary as she revealed her hitherto secret aspirations.

'I've kept it all to myself. I didn't even tell Mary with whom I shared the secret of my early reading because it all seemed so unrealistic, a dream, but I'm telling you now because although it's going to take a long time I really do believe it'll happen one day. At the moment it's still a pipe dream. Not that I smoke a pipe,' she added, reverting to a childish simplicity.

'So you'll be leaving us eventually to go on to higher things,' said James.

'Oh no, this is where I'm happy, you're my family and I'll not leave until you tell me to go. You've all been so good to me and Kate. No, I want the degree to prove something to myself, not to get away from you.'

'What do you mean to study?' asked Mary.

'Well, don't laugh, but I have been thinking of a combined degree in theology and geography. Theology simply because it looks so interesting, and geography because, well, I've listened to you and Tom talking about your travels and it just fired my imagination.'

'Molly,' said James, 'you're amazing!'

30: New Growth

A few months after Molly's great revelation, James and John were sitting in the study at Briar Cottage taking a postprandial glass after enjoying a simple dinner together.

'You may have wondered, my dear fellow, why I sought this audience,' said John.

'Yes and no. I think I have some idea, but press on.'

'How are things with you now, really?'

'You mean, am I learning to let go? To some extent and in a certain sense. The searing pain of waking to find myself alone has not exactly gone away, I don't suppose it ever will, but I am coming to accept it as a fact of life. Their absence no longer penetrates every minute of my day; instead it has been replaced by – how can I put it? Their loving presence. I find myself talking to myself a lot, often aloud. I've heard it said that that's often a feature of people who have spent a long time in lonely places. Am I miserable? No. Often sad? Yes.'

'I did wonder whether Molly would have grown on you, and whether in the fullness of time something more than friendship might have developed...'

'A reasonable enough thought. I can't deny that I have been conscious that, as you once mentioned, she is a handsome woman – hardly a girl any longer, as we have recently discovered, and a much deeper person than we thought. Yes, it would be dishonest to deny that I have occasionally felt a stirring of the flesh. I am very fond of her, but not in a million years could I imagine her taking Madeleine's place. Now tell me what is in your mind, or should I say in your heart?'

'Is it really as obvious as all that?'

'Well, over the years we have come to know pretty much how the other feels.' He smiled. 'I think you are asking my permission to fall in love with Molly, which is absurd, though charming, because I have never owned her! I think she'd make a wonderful

New Growth

wife and you a great husband. You have my blessing.'

A look of relief radiated from John.

'I haven't asked her, of course, because I wanted to know how you felt; I couldn't possibly have done anything to hurt you. But I'm pretty confident that she shares my feelings.'

'Marriage might be just what you need. Your vocation for helping those in trouble sustained you for many years, and although you have found several useful and interesting things to do perhaps they don't satisfy you completely. Am I right?'

'Of course, oh wise one. You've hit the nail on the head.'

'And after many years of devotion to a caring profession you now miss having anyone in particular to look after?'

'Exactly. I think the time has come to embrace the vocation of marriage. And of course in addition to looking after', he grinned, 'there's the added bonus of being looked after.'

'She's a remarkable woman.'

'I know. I must admit that the recent revelation of her deeper interests is what finally helped to make me want to take the plunge. I mean that however much I was drawn by physical attraction, I don't think I could unite myself fully to someone who displayed no interest at all in things of the mind.'

'You're wise, John. I believe that physical attraction without shared interests was the cause of my early difficulties with Madeleine. Discovering that we would work as a pair was what brought us back together. Marriage must go deeper than mere mutual convenience.'

'It's a vocation, and having enjoyed one vocation for a long time I now find that, as you say, there is something lacking. Not the old one, which I shed deliberately for reasons that you know, but I believe I can find a new one in marriage.'

'If anyone can make a success of it, you can.'

*

John and Molly were married in the summer of 1979. Molly in her direct way had asked James to give her away saying, 'After all, you're the nearest thing to a real father I've ever had.'

Their honeymoon took the form of a continental tour, the first stage in satisfying Molly's ambition to travel. They bombarded their friends with postcards which they exchanged at meetings of the dining club.

James worked hard, having to deal with Molly's duties on the estate, but she had made it clear that on her return she had every intention of resuming her tasks.

'I'm a working woman,' she said, 'and I'm not going to be a kept wife.'

She was as good as her word, and got back to work with her customary energy until one day near Christmas she told James, 'I think you ought to be looking for someone to replace me, if only for a while after Easter...'

James did not immediately make the connection but was delighted when Molly invited him to be godfather. He asked what the baby was to be called.

'Why – James, of course! What else if it's a boy?'

When eighteen months later Molly gave birth again, this time to twin girls, James was moved to tears that they were to be Madeleine and Assunta. With three young children on her hands, Molly was obliged to devote herself to her family. Only reluctantly did she give up all active duties with James's business, but he welcomed her comment on his ideas. With the passage of time John, too, became increasingly interested, so that in 1982 James decided to link all aspects of the estate into a limited company, with the three of them as the initial directors. He had lost something of his earlier resilience and drive, had not really got over the loss of his wife and child, and came to depend increasingly on his friends. He concentrated on the exotic woodland, his metasequoias and the avenue of gingkos.

John Humphries, a 'settler' of several years standing who had come to Assunta with a history of drug dependence and had come through his ordeal, was a graduate in estate management and became responsible for the estate as a whole. John Stonor watched over Assunta, while the garden centres had for several years been the responsibility of Edward Surtees, the manager whom James had appointed after Madeleine died. They were a good team.

Katarzyna and Henryk had spent a short holiday at Briar Cottage. They had one child, Stephen, named in honour of his maternal grandfather; and because it was an easy adaptation of 'Stefan' it would not saddle the boy with a foreign sounding name which might embarrass him at school.

James sat in his study with John, who said, 'So the visit was a success and you were able to practise being an uncle? Does young Stephen take to the country life?'

'Very much so, though he shows signs of following in his father's footsteps by going in for medicine. But it's early days yet. Yes, being an uncle is fun. Of course your children call me uncle, which I love, but there's something special about being a real one.'

'Kosher, as Ruth might have said?'

'Indeed. The next best thing to being a grandfather, I suppose...'

A moment of gloom descended on him. He thrust it aside.

'Do you ever wonder how things might have been but for the war?'

'I don't brood about it, but in a sense the aftermath of the war lingers on, what with Kasia and Antek being here.'

'Don't you want to visit Poland? You could do so perfectly safely, couldn't you?'

'I could, of course, but I have no friends there, and odd though it may seem I'd feel rather a stranger, a tourist, in what should be my own country. This is my home now, and I prefer to leave it at that. Of course there is Kazimierz, but the thought of his serving the system is too painful to dwell on. In fact it serves as a deterrent to my going there.'

'It would be impertinent of me to comment on that. Those of us who never suffered occupation simply can't imagine what it does to one's outlook. But looking at the picture of Our Lady of Czestochowa, unless it is there just as an ornament, makes me wonder whether there aren't any roots left.'

'That's just it, the roots are there but the plant above the surface has withered. I often think of and pray for my parents and the friends I remember, but I can't claim that I want to go back to the country, because what I knew has gone for ever.'

'For ever? Rather sweeping, don't you think? Don't you see a glimmer of hope in the Solidarity movement?'

New Growth

'Perhaps, but in my lifetime? I don't know.'

They chatted on about John's growing family. He said,

'You know, Molly is a most extraordinary person.'

'Certainly, but what prompts that remark out of the blue?'

'She has such an enquiring mind, and yet is so crashingly sensible. If ever anyone had both feet on the ground it's her.'

'Any particular instance of that?'

'Yes. In her theology and philosophy she has a mind with a cutting edge and doesn't swallow everything her tutors say, but in her daily Catholicism she retains a childlike simplicity, sticking to the practices she picked up during her abysmal apology for an early education, and which she never quite abandoned in spite of her early troubles.'

'I suppose that applies to a lot of "routine" Catholics.'

'Yes, but most of those never jump across the fence, as it were, and use their minds in an intellectual sense, as she has.'

'Presumably if she is happy with that simple faith she's lucky, and it would be a pity to stir the waters.'

'Of course, but I can't help being puzzled at the dichotomy.'

'Are her studies going well?'

'Fantastically. I just don't know how she copes with three children and me, as well as continuing to think constructively about the firm.'

'You're a lucky man, John. Make the most of it. I must concentrate on my exotic trees…'

James's serious face said more than he had uttered.

31: Kismet

James, John and Molly had just returned from a brief visit to London where they had attended Guy Rowlands's funeral. Antoni had come to Briar Cottage with them to enjoy a short respite from his duties at the BBC. The four of them were taking a gentle stroll on a drab October afternoon among the trees of the exotic plantation which, although still small, were prospering.

'It's a pity Guy didn't quite make his century,' said James, 'but what a grand old man he was.'

'Indeed,' replied John, 'and a lucky and happy one too, being able to live on his own and look after himself to the very end. I suppose it's what we all wish for ourselves. Strange he never married; he was a damned good-looking old chap.'

'I bet he had a few girlfriends along the line, but in a sense he married the Firm and it became his family.'

'As we are now wedded to our firm.'

'I shall be grateful always for the help he gave me when I wanted to come to England,' said Antoni.

'He lived through an amazing period of history,' said James, 'as we all have. You and your colleagues must be tremendously excited at the way things are developing in Poland, Antek.'

'Yes, every day we get bits of news that give us hope. I don't think the movement for reform can be stopped, but there will be trouble before the long night is over.'

James smiled at the way Antoni's handling of English had evolved.

'And talking of trouble,' said the ever practical Molly, 'I don't like the way those clouds are piling up. I think we ought to be making for shelter.'

They agreed. John and Molly went home and the two brothers retired to Briar Cottage to prepare their dinner. They spoke, as usual when they were on their own, in Polish.

'We have talked about this, Janek, but tell me, have you never thought of marrying again. It is seventeen years since Madeleine died.'

'Of course it has passed through my mind, and I can't deny that there are times when I feel a great gaping emptiness, but I simply couldn't do it. I would feel I was being disloyal to Madeleine's memory. I know that after a happy marriage many widowers do remarry, but it just isn't a solution for me. In fairness to my new wife I'd have to accept that she would wish to change the way many things are done in the house, which would be entirely reasonable but would cause me pain. No, I'm better off as I am, enjoying the company of my good friends and keeping Madeleine's memory as my very own treasure. If Assunta had survived I might have felt differently... Have you never thought of marrying?'

'Only in passing. My life was fulfilling enough as an artist and so it is now. I shall die an old bachelor, like Guy.'

'Well, don't be in too great a hurry.'

They chatted on, disposing of a bottle of Polish vodka which Antoni had brought, and went to bed.

At about two in the morning James was woken by what seemed like an earthquake. The house shook, its fabric creaked and the noise was deafening. Glass rattled in the old window frames, tiles clattered off the roof. The phenomenon continued for several minutes. James pressed the light switch but no light came. He got up, grabbed his torch and hurriedly put on some clothes. He and Antoni met on the landing. The noise and tremor abated as suddenly as they had arisen.

'*What on earth was that?*' they asked simultaneously.

'An earthquake?' suggested Antoni.

'That wouldn't account for the wind! The power lines must be down.'

There was nothing to be done but wait for daylight.

At first light they went to the Land-Rover. Many of the outbuildings had been damaged and the yard was littered with debris.

'I must look at the plantation,' said James as they drove off, carefully avoiding scattered timbers and shattered glass.

On their way they saw several big trees broken, smaller ones uprooted. They reached the plantation. James's worst fears were realised. The gingkos had suffered most; about a third of them lay on their sides, others had branches torn off. The metasequoias, being shorter, had fared better but many had been blown over. The work and hopes of many years lay, if not totally in ruins, seriously damaged. John Humphries was already on the site. He knew what the loss meant to James and had the delicacy to refrain from uttering platitudes such as, 'It could have been far worse.' Antoni gently grasped James's shoulder.

'You're going to start again.'

'Yes,' he replied simply.

In reply to James's question, John Humphries assured him that Assunta had suffered little damage, and apart from terrifying some children and nervous people, the storm had not greatly affected the village. The houses were modern and had been well built; the chief damage had been caused by power lines being blown down over gardens.

Out of courtesy James and Antoni drove over to Assunta to speak with the 'settlers', and found John and Molly already there on the same errand.

'How's the plantation, Jim?' they asked.

'It'll take some straightening out,' he replied with masterly understatement.

He did not immediately tackle the problem at the plantation, but waited until he had seen Antoni off to London and electric power and the telephone lines had been restored, which took a few days. Then he started a fire in his study for company, settled comfortably in his armchair, lit his pipe and took stock. He had, quite deliberately, refrained from making plans or decisions for a few days because they were not essential. There had, after all, been no loss of life or damage to people on the estate, and the deep personal wound of the shattered trees was best solved after a period of calm reflection.

In the comfort of his study the James of former days reasserted himself. After the initial shock the devastation of his exotic woodland had dashed his spirits less than he would have expected. Instead he sensed a resurgence of his old resilience. Madeleine was at his side, gently urging him to be positive. 'You can put it right,' she was saying, 'it's only a setback, and time is still on your side. And Assunta is still intact. Think of what you've got and don't dwell on what you've lost.'

'Practical as ever, my dear,' he murmured, 'and you're quite right of course, as usual.'

The great storm had surely been the final great grief, after Warsaw, Madeleine's and Assunta's deaths and Honeyman's treachery. He felt a savage surge of energy race through his whole self; difficulties were there to be overcome, and overcome them he would. He reached for pen and paper and roughed out a plan of action.

With John Humphries's help the wrecked trees were removed. Those that could be saved were replanted and Kew, impressed at what he had already achieved, was generous with replacements. Within five years the plantation's scarring by the storm was no longer obvious, and if the trees were of unequal size it did not matter, for what difference would a few years' growth ultimately make in the life of big trees?

32: Peace

In the autumn of 1993 Katarzyna, who had retired from nursing, invited James to London for a few days. Assuming that he would be able to meet Antoni, he seized the opportunity of taking some photographs of the plantation to show him how far it had recovered since the night of the great storm.

His sister and, on his return from the hospital, Henryk both appeared to be in a state of nervous excitement but James did not comment on it. When Antoni arrived in time for dinner he, too, showed signs of happy anticipation, rather like a parent who was looking forward to giving a child a surprise. James remarked on their exceptional good humour, but all Katarzyna would say was 'wait until after dinner', and Antoni smiled conspiratorially. She took her time, served an excellent meal and asked him many questions about affairs in Gloucestershire. He showed his photographs. Henryk and Antoni were approaching retirement and there was much talk of plans for spending their forthcoming leisure. Travel was enthusiastically mooted, and also a greater indulgence in the finer things of life, the pursuit of the arts for which their busy professional lives had denied them time. Meanwhile James became increasingly intrigued at the secret which was to be revealed. At last, over coffee and vodka Katarzyna pushed back her chair and said, 'Now, little brother, your patience is about to be rewarded.'

She explained that Antoni had been back to Warsaw several times for conferences with Polish radio and had discovered that Kazimierz's file had been unearthed in the archives of the Police Department. It revealed that his body had been found near his car on the Czechoslovak border: he had apparently died by suicide.

The passage of time caused James not to grasp the significance of the location straight away.

'It seems', said Henryk, 'that Kazimierz waited until we had vanished over the hill and then took his own life.'

Peace

James was silent for a moment before responding slowly, 'So in helping you to get away he sacrificed himself…'

'We'll never know for certain what was in his mind. He could probably have returned to his duties without arousing suspicion. After all, he would have been away from Police Headquarters for only a day and a bit, and he was sufficiently senior in the service not to have aroused undue suspicion and in any case to have covered his tracks. But my reading of his mind is that he felt he had betrayed his principles and could not live with the knowledge.'

'So in the end he put family before loyalty to the regime?'

'That's how it seems,' said Katarzyna solemnly, 'and it was the action of an honourable man.'

'I dare say,' said Antoni, 'that he realised he owed his life, as indeed I do, to our sister's sacrifice for us after the Warsaw Rising. Without her selflessness we would have starved.'

'Yes,' agreed James, 'suicide is suicide, but Kasik did not see things through our eyes and we are not to judge.'

'In a sense I am happy that he did what he did because until now I could not respect him,' said Antoni. 'Sad though it is, it's a sort of cleansing. He has rejoined the family.'

'May he rest in peace,' replied James, and they all drank a toast to his memory.

Printed in the United Kingdom
by Lightning Source UK Ltd.
102444UKS00001B/25-27